EDUARD,

The Boy Who Looked to The Stars

Written by

Waid Sainvil

Dedication

I dedicate this book to my Herald, the Herald of this entire Universe, Nokodemion Creation Energy Herald lineage, who lives today in the personality of the remarkable human being known as Billy.

This book explores his childhood, revealing the early life of Eduard Albert Meier.

Every detail within these pages is drawn from the contact reports Billy has shared with us.

While the narrative is fictionalized, I have only taken the creative liberty to present these accounts in my own way as a writer.

Billy is my teacher, and for that, I am forever grateful.

His wisdom and guidance have profoundly shaped my understanding, and this book is a tribute to his extraordinary journey.

Table of Contents

Preface

Eduard, The Boy Who Looked to The Stars

This book, though presented as a work of fiction, is profoundly connected to reality. The events, characters, and themes woven throughout its pages are not merely products of imagination but are deeply rooted in historical truths, real experiences, and factual insights. While the narrative may take creative liberties, it does so with the intention of illuminating aspects of reality that are often ignored, misunderstood, or buried beneath layers of conventional beliefs.

Fiction, at its best, serves as a vessel to explore truths that might otherwise be constrained by the rigid structures of historical accounts and factual recounting. Through this fusion of fact and imagination, the story seeks to transcend traditional storytelling, offering a perspective that engages the mind and challenges the reader to question their understanding of the world. This book does not simply tell a story, it presents an opportunity to see beyond the surface, to uncover hidden realities, and to approach history and human experience from a fresh, more insightful vantage point.

By blending fiction with reality, the narrative aims to shed light on overlooked elements of our past and present. It encourages readers to consider the unseen forces at play in human history and to recognize patterns that have shaped civilizations, ideologies, and events. In doing so, it does not merely entertain but invites contemplation, reflection, and a deeper engagement with the very truths upon which the story is built.

In a world where beliefs reign supreme, where perceptions are shaped by narratives rather than objective facts, it is essential to question, to research, and to seek understanding beyond what is readily accepted. This book challenges readers to do exactly that, to dig deeper, to explore the foundations of the ideas it presents, and to connect the fictional elements with the reality they reflect.

While this book may read like a tale crafted from the imagination, its roots stretch far beyond the realm of fiction. The truths embedded within these pages are as real as the world we live in, waiting to be uncovered by those willing to seek them out. Whether you approach this book as a work of storytelling or as a gateway to deeper understanding, its essence remains the same: fiction is often a reflection of reality, and within its pages, profound truths await discovery.

Chapter 1

A Quiet Beginning

It was a cold, crisp morning in the small village of Bülach, Switzerland.

The kind of morning that makes the air feel alive, each breath invigorating as it fills the lungs.

The sun had just begun to rise over the snow-capped peaks of the Alps, casting a soft golden hue over the landscape.

The village was still wrapped in the quiet embrace of dawn, with only the occasional sound of a rooster crowing in the distance or the soft crunch of snow underfoot breaking the silence.

In a modest farmhouse on the outskirts of the village, young Eduard Albert Meier was already awake.

At just five years old, he was small for his age, with a shock of unruly brown hair and eyes that seemed far older than his years.

Those eyes, a deep, penetrating blue, held a certain depth, a quiet intensity that was unusual for a child.

They were the eyes of someone who had seen far more than most could ever imagine.

Eduard, as he was called, lay in his small bed, staring up at the wooden beams of the ceiling, his mind already racing with thoughts.

He had always been an early riser, a habit that seemed to come naturally to him.

While other children his age might have complained about waking up early, Eduard relished the quiet moments before the rest of the world stirred.

It was during these early hours that he felt most at peace, most connected to something greater than himself.

His family's home was simple but sturdy, built from thick logs that had weathered many winters.

The walls were adorned with old, faded photographs, and the furniture was well-worn but comfortable.

A fire crackled softly in the hearth, filling the room with a warm, comforting glow.

The scent of freshly baked bread wafted through the air, a sure sign that his mother, Berta, was already busy in the kitchen.

Eduard swung his legs over the edge of the bed and slipped his small feet into a pair of worn slippers.

The floor was cold against his skin, but he didn't mind.

He liked the feeling of the cool wood beneath his feet, the way it grounded him, reminded him that he was still part of this world, even as his mind often wandered to places far beyond it.

He dressed quickly in the clothes his mother had laid out for him the night before: a thick woollen sweater, sturdy trousers, and a pair of socks that had been mended more times than he could count.

The sweater itched slightly against his skin, but it was warm, and that was all that mattered.

Eduard made his way to the kitchen, where his mother was bustling about, preparing breakfast.

She was a stout woman with strong, capable hands and a warm smile that could light up even the darkest room.

Her hair, once a rich chestnut brown, was now streaked with gray, a testament to the years of hard work and worry that had shaped her life.

"Good morning, Eduard," Berta said, turning to him with a smile as she placed a loaf of fresh bread on the table.

"Did you sleep well?"

"Yes, Mama," he replied, his voice soft but clear.

He had always been a quiet child, more inclined to listen than to speak. It wasn't that he was shy, quite the opposite, in fact.

Eduard was simply thoughtful, often lost in his own world, pondering things that seemed far beyond his years.

"Good, good," she replied, nodding in approval as she poured him a cup of warm milk. "You're just in time for breakfast.

Your father will be in soon."

Eduard took his seat at the table, watching as his mother continued her work.

He admired her strength, the way she managed to keep their home running smoothly despite the hardships they faced.

His father, Julius, was a hardworking man, but times were tough, and money was often scarce.

Still, they made do, finding joy in the simple things: a warm meal, a cozy fire, and the love that bound their family together.

As Eduard sipped his milk, his thoughts drifted to the strange dreams that had been haunting him lately.

They were vivid, more real than any dream he had ever experienced before.

In these dreams, he saw strange lights in the sky, heard voices speaking in a language he didn't understand, and felt a presence that seemed both familiar and utterly alien.

He hadn't told anyone about these dreams, not even his parents.

He wasn't sure how to explain them, or if they were even something that could be explained.

The door creaked open, and Eduard's father entered the kitchen, stamping the snow from his boots.

Julius was a broad-shouldered man with a thick beard and hands that were rough from years of manual labor.

Despite the weariness etched into his features, there was a kindness in his eyes, a gentleness that belied his rugged appearance.

"Morning, Eduard," he said, ruffling his son's hair affectionately as he took his seat at the table.

"Up early again, I see."

Eduard nodded, offering his father a small smile.

"I like the quiet," he said simply.

He chuckled, a deep, rumbling sound that filled the room.

"That you do, my boy. That you do."

Breakfast was a simple affair: bread, cheese, and a few slices of smoked ham, along with the warm milk that Eduard had grown accustomed to drinking each morning.

The family ate in companionable silence, the only sounds being the crackling of the fire and the occasional clink of utensils against plates.

As they finished their meal, Julius glanced at the clock on the wall, his expression turning serious.

"I'll be heading into town today," he said, addressing both Eduard and Berta.

"There's talk of some new work up in the mountains.

I'm hoping to find something that'll keep us going through the winter."

Berta nodded, her face calm, but Eduard could see the worry in her eyes.

The winters in Bülach were harsh, and they relied heavily on the work Julius could find during the warmer months to see them through the cold season.

"I'll be fine, Mama," Eduard said, sensing her concern.

"I'll help with the chores, and I can keep an eye on things while Papa's away."

Berta smiled, reaching across the table to squeeze Eduard's hand.

"I know you will, my dear.

You've always been a good boy, so responsible for your age."

Julius stood, pulling on his heavy coat and wrapping a scarf around his neck.

"I won't be gone long," he said, kissing Berta on the cheek.

"Eduard, take care of your mother while I'm away, all right?"

Eduard nodded solemnly. "I will, Papa."

With that, Julius left the house, the door closing behind him with a soft click.

Eduard and Berta were alone in the quiet kitchen, the warmth of the fire contrasting with the chill that had settled over the village.

"Come, Eduard," Berta said after a moment, standing up and gathering the breakfast dishes. "Let's get these cleaned up, and then you can help me with the chores."

Eduard nodded and stood up to help, but as he reached for the dishes, he was suddenly overcome by a strange sensation, a feeling of being watched, of someone or something observing him from afar.

He paused, his hand hovering over the table, his eyes narrowing as he tried to make sense of the feeling.

"Eduard?" Berta's voice broke through his thoughts, and he looked up to see her watching him with a concerned expression.

"Are you all right, dear?"

Eduard blinked, shaking off the sensation as best he could.

"Yes, Mama," he said, forcing a smile. "I'm fine."

But even as he said the words, he knew they weren't entirely true.

Something was happening, something he couldn't quite understand or explain.

And deep down, he knew that whatever it was, it was just the beginning.

After the chores were done, Eduard decided to spend some time outdoors.

The snow-covered landscape beckoned to him, and he found solace in the stillness of the winter forest.

He wrapped himself in a thick coat and pulled on his boots, the leather creaking as he tightened the laces.

With a final wave to his mother, who was busy with her knitting by the fire, he stepped outside into the crisp air.

The forest near their home was familiar territory to Billy.

He knew every tree, every path, and every hidden nook where the deer and rabbits made their homes.

But today, as he walked deeper into the woods, he couldn't shake the feeling that something was different.

The usual sounds of the forest, the rustling of leaves, the chirping of birds, seemed muted, as if the world was holding its breath, waiting for something to happen.

Eduard walked for a while, his boots crunching softly in the snow, until he came to a small clearing he often visited.

It was a quiet, secluded spot, surrounded by tall pines and birches, with a large rock in the center that he liked to sit on.

From this vantage point, he could see the peaks of the distant mountains, their tops hidden in a veil of mist.

He climbed onto the rock and sat down, pulling his knees up to his chest.

The cold stone beneath him was a stark contrast to the warmth of his coat, but he didn't mind.

He found the cold bracing, invigorating, and it helped to clear his mind.

As he sat there, Eduard's thoughts returned to the dreams that had been troubling him.

They were more than just dreams, he was certain of that now.

They felt too real, too vivid, to be mere figments of his imagination.

And then there was the presence he had felt that morning, the sense of being watched.

It was the same feeling he had in his dreams, a sense of connection to something far greater than himself.

He closed his eyes and took a deep breath, trying to focus on the feeling, to understand it.

As he did, the world around him seemed to fade away, the sounds of the forest growing distant, the cold of the air less biting.

He felt a warmth spreading through him, starting in his chest and radiating outward, filling him with a sense of peace and calm.

And then, he heard it, a voice, soft and soothing, speaking to him in a language he didn't understand, yet somehow recognized.

The words flowed over him like a gentle breeze, carrying with them a sense of reassurance and comfort.

He didn't need to understand the words to know their meaning: he was not alone, and he was being watched over.

Eduard opened his eyes, but the world around him was different now.

The trees, the snow, even the sky above seemed to shimmer with a soft, golden light, as if the entire forest had been touched by something otherworldly.

He felt a presence beside him, and though he couldn't see it, he knew it was there, watching, guiding, protecting.

He sat there for what felt like hours, though he knew it was only minutes, basking in the warmth of the presence, letting it fill him with a sense of purpose and direction.

He didn't know what lay ahead, but he knew that he was on the right path, that he had a role to play in something far greater than himself.

When the feeling finally began to fade, Eduard opened his eyes fully and looked around.

The forest had returned to its normal state, the golden light gone, replaced by the familiar gray of winter.

But something had changed within him. He felt stronger, more certain, and ready to face whatever challenges lay ahead.

He climbed down from the rock and started back toward home, his mind buzzing with thoughts and questions.

He didn't know what the future held, but he knew that he was not alone in facing it.

Whatever this presence was, whatever it wanted from him, he was ready to listen.

As Eduard walked through the forest, the snow crunching softly beneath his boots, something extraordinary caught his eye.

A flying disc appeared overhead, hovering briefly before disappearing as swiftly as it had come.

In that fleeting moment, Eduard realized with a jolt that his life was about to take a turn he could never have imagined.

He returned home as the sun was beginning to set, the sky painted in shades of pink and orange.

His mother was waiting for him at the door, her face lighting up with a smile as she saw him.

"Did you have a good walk?" she asked, brushing the snow from his coat as he stepped inside.

"Yes, Mama," Eduard replied, his voice steady and sure. "I did."

He didn't tell her about the presence, about the voice he had heard or the golden light he had seen.

He wasn't sure she would understand, and besides, some things were best kept to oneself, at least for now.

That evening, as he sat by the fire listening to the crackle of the logs and the soothing sound of his mother's knitting, Eduard understood that he had begun a long and arduous journey.

But he was ready, and whatever challenges awaited him, he said to himself he would meet them with resolve and bravery.

And so, as the fire burned low and the shadows grew long, Eduard closed his eyes and let sleep take him, knowing that the presence would be there, watching over him, guiding him, and leading him toward a future he could barely begin to imagine.

CHAPTER 2

The Urge to Observe

Days passed, and Eduard's thoughts were consumed by the disc.

The memory of it was as vivid as the moment it had appeared.

It wasn't just the sight of the object that lingered in his mind but the feeling, the strange compulsion to look toward the sky, as if something beyond the stars was calling to him.

Eduard found himself returning to the fields where he had first glimpsed the mysterious disc.

The tall grasses swayed gently in the breeze, and the mountains stood like silent sentinels, watching over the valley below.

The war that raged across Europe seemed a distant echo here, in this quiet corner of Switzerland, but Eduard couldn't shake the sense that something monumental was happening, something that went beyond the human conflict.

Each evening, after completing his chores, Eduard would head outside, drawn to the wide-open skies above Bülach.

The night air was crisp, the scent of pine and earth mingling with the lingering warmth of the day.

As darkness fell, the stars would emerge, one by one, until the heavens were a sea of shimmering lights.

Eduard would lie on his back in the garden, staring up at the sky, his heart pounding with anticipation.

One morning, June 2, 1942, while with his father, standing behind their house next to a large walnut tree, looking eastward into the sky.

There was a curious sense of wonder, though he only vaguely understood its cause.

It felt as if an unknown impulse was directing him to search the eastern horizon for something, though he was unsure what that something was.

He followed this strange urge, scanning the bright blue sky on that warm and pleasant summer morning.

After ten or fifteen minutes, something extraordinary captured his attention.

A silver flash shot down from the clear sky at high speed, darting like a giant metal arrow over the Eschenmoser mountain and heading towards the 75-meter-high Reformed Church.

Just before reaching the tall tower, the flash veered to the right and sped past it, heading straight for the house.

It then ascended rapidly, and within a fraction of a second, the streak transformed into a colossal, flat metal disc, approximately 250 to 300 meters in diameter.

The disc silently flew over them at an altitude of about 200 meters, disappearing as abruptly as it had appeared, vanishing into the western sky over the Höragen forest.

Confused and amazed, he continued to stare westward long after the object had vanished.

His father was equally bewildered, staring in the same direction and shaking his head.

He asked him about the nature of the fast-moving disc, seeking answers about how, where, and why it had appeared.

After pondering the situation, he offered the only explanation he could think of, given the context of World War II:

"That was probably the latest secret weapon of Hitler.", he told him.

Even at such a young age, his father's explanation did not quite satisfy him. American bombers frequently flew over their village, but they were outdated and unremarkable.

German dive bombers and fighter planes sometimes crossed the nearby border, but they seemed just as primitive as the American bombers, often being intercepted or downed by the Swiss Air Force.

His father's explanation did not align with his observations, as he was a simple man with little insight into technological advancements.

Eduard watched them night after night, his curiosity growing with each passing hour. He didn't tell anyone about his observations, not even his parents.

He had learned from his encounter with his father that people were quick to dismiss things they didn't understand, and Eduard didn't want to be told he was imagining things.

But he knew what he was seeing was real.

And he knew, deep down, that it was connected to the disc he had seen that morning.

The summer of 1942 was a time of change.

The days grew shorter, and the nights grew cooler as autumn approached.

The once-lush fields turned golden, the leaves on the trees blazed with fiery reds and oranges, and the mountains became dusted with the first hints of snow.

But despite the beauty of the changing seasons, Eduard's focus remained on the night sky.

He kept a notebook, a small, battered journal he had found in the attic, where he meticulously recorded his observations.

Each night, he would note the time, the position of the lights, and their movements.

The notebook became his most treasured possession, filled with sketches of the sky and pages of scribbled notes.

He treated it with the utmost care, hiding it beneath his mattress during the day and keeping it close to him at night.

As the days turned into weeks, Eduard began to notice patterns in the lights' movements.

They seemed to follow a specific path across the sky, appearing at roughly the same time each night.

He marked these times in his notebook, waiting eagerly for the moment when the lights would appear.

And each time they did, he felt a thrill of excitement, as if he were witnessing something extraordinary.

But along with the excitement came a growing sense of unease.

The lights were beautiful, mesmerizing even, but there was something unsettling about them.

He couldn't shake the feeling that they were watching him just as he was watching them.

The thought sent shivers down his spine, but he couldn't stop himself from looking.

The urge to observe was too strong, as if the lights were pulling him toward them, drawing him into their mysterious dance.

Eduard's parents began to notice his late-night excursions.

His mother, Berta, would often find him missing from his bed and would worry until she found him outside, lying in the garden, staring up at the stars.

She would chide him gently, telling him he needed his rest, but Eduard would only nod absently, his thoughts already drifting back to the night sky.

His father, too, noticed Eduard's strange behavior, but he was more perplexed than concerned.

Eduard Sr. was a practical man, grounded in the realities of life, and he couldn't understand what was so fascinating about the stars.

"They've been there for millions of years," he would say, shaking his head.

"Why start staring at them now?"

Eduard couldn't explain it to his father, even if he wanted to.

How could he put into words the strange compulsion he felt, the sense that something out there was calling to him? It wasn't just curiosity; it was a need, a pull that he couldn't resist.

As autumn deepened, Eduard's observations grew more intense.

The sightings of the "moving stars" became more frequent, and each one filled him with a sense of wonder and anticipation.

It was as if the sky itself was alive, teeming with secrets that only he could see.

The nights were longer now, and Eduard found himself spending hours outside, wrapped in a thick coat and scarf, his eyes glued to the sky.

Rudolf Emanuel Zimmermann

CHAPTER 3

Confiding to Pastor Zimmerman

Late in the autumn of 1942, just a few months before his sixth birthday, Eduard experienced something even stranger.

The chill of the evening air wrapped around him as he lay in the garden, staring up at the stars.

The sky was clear and dark, the stars twinkling like distant diamonds against the black velvet of night.

The silence was profound, broken only by the occasional rustle of leaves or the distant call of an owl.

Eduard had become accustomed to the peculiar lights he observed in the night sky, but tonight felt different.

As he lay there, a shiver of unease ran through him.

He couldn't shake the feeling that something significant was about to happen.

The usual hum that accompanied the lights seemed to be present, but it was quieter, more subtle, as if it were hiding just below the threshold of his hearing.

Suddenly, Eduard felt a presence in his mind, a soft, gentle voice that seemed to come from within, yet from somewhere far, far away.

He sat up abruptly, his heart pounding in his chest.

The sensation was unlike anything he had experienced before.

The voice wasn't speaking words, not exactly.

It was more like a feeling, a sense of being guided, of being shown something important.

Eduard froze, trying to comprehend the strange new sensation.

The presence was calm and reassuring, but it was also alien, as if it were tapping into a part of him that he hadn't known existed.

The voice wasn't clear or distinct, it was more like an impression, a gentle nudge that guided his thoughts.

And then, as if in response to the voice, images began to form in his mind, pictures of places he had never seen, of things that were utterly alien to him.

He saw vast, sprawling landscapes, towering structures of unimaginable design, and creatures that seemed to defy the laws of nature.

The visions were vivid and detailed, like a series of snapshots from a dream.

Eduard was frightened, more frightened than he had ever been.

He didn't understand what was happening, and for a moment, he thought he might be going crazy.

The images were too strange, too otherworldly to make sense of.

He tried to shake the visions away, to push them out of his mind, but they persisted, weaving through his thoughts with a persistent clarity.

The feeling of the voice continued, a comforting presence amidst the chaos of the visions.

It wasn't threatening, but it was insistent, as if it were trying to communicate something crucial.

He felt a deep sense of urgency, as if he were on the verge of discovering something profoundly important.

The next day, unable to shake the unsettling experience, Eduard decided to seek help.

He had never spoken to anyone about his experiences with the lights and the strange sensations, but he knew he needed guidance.

He went to the local Protestant pastor, a kind old man who had always been friendly to him.

Pastor Zimmerman was known throughout the village for his wisdom and compassion, and Eduard hoped that he might be able to offer some clarity.

Eduard approached the pastor's small, ivy-clad church, its wooden doors standing open to welcome visitors.

Inside, the warm glow of candlelight cast a soft illumination on the simple wooden pews and the stained-glass windows depicting scenes from the Bible.

Pastor Zimmerman was at his desk, engrossed in a book, but he looked up with a smile when he entered.

"Hello, Eduard," the pastor greeted him warmly. "

What brings you here today?"

He hesitated for a moment, then took a deep breath.

"Pastor Zimmerman, I've been having strange experiences.

I see lights in the sky and hear a voice in my mind.

It shows me images of places I don't know.

I don't understand what's happening, and it's really frightening."

The pastor's expression shifted to one of concern, but he remained calm and attentive.

He gestured for Eduard to sit in one of the wooden chairs across from his desk.

"Tell me more about what you've been experiencing," he said gently.

Eduard recounted everything, the sight of the disc, the moving stars, the soft voice, and the visions of alien landscapes.

He spoke with a mix of awe and trepidation, trying to convey the depth of his confusion and fear. As he spoke, Pastor Zimmerman listened intently, nodding occasionally.

When he finished, the pastor leaned back in his chair, his eyes thoughtful.

"What you are describing, Eduard, is something called telepathy.

It's a form of communication that doesn't rely on spoken words, but rather on thoughts and feelings. It's a rare gift, but not unheard of."

Eduard frowned, still not entirely understanding.

"But why is this happening to me? What does it mean?"

Pastor Zimmerman's eyes twinkled with a mixture of compassion and curiosity.

"There are many things in this world that are beyond our understanding, Eduard.

Sometimes, certain individuals are chosen to experience things that are not part of ordinary life.

It's possible that you have a special ability to receive and interpret these messages."

Eduard listened, trying to absorb the pastor's words.

"So, you're saying that I'm not crazy?"

The pastor shook his head with a reassuring smile.

"Not at all. What you're experiencing is a gift.

It's a way of connecting with something greater, something beyond our usual perception.

It's not something to be afraid of.

Instead, it's an opportunity to learn and grow."

Young Eduard's anxiety began to ease, though he still felt a lingering uncertainty.

"What should I do?"

Pastor Zimmerman considered the question carefully.

"I would advise you to keep a record of your experiences, just as you have been doing.

Continue to observe and document what you see and hear.

It might also be helpful to find a quiet place where you can reflect on your experiences and try to communicate back with the voice.

And remember, you are not alone.

There are others who have had similar experiences, and you might find comfort in connecting with them."

Eduard nodded, feeling a sense of relief and purpose.

The pastor's words had calmed his fears, but they had also introduced a new layer of complexity to his situation.

The thought of being part of something greater was both thrilling and daunting.

As he left the church, Eduard felt a renewed sense of resolve.

The images and the voice had not gone away, but they now seemed less ominous.

Instead of feeling overwhelmed, he began to see them as clues, pieces of a puzzle that he was meant to solve.

In the weeks that followed, Eduard's nightly observations continued.

He remained vigilant, documenting every sighting, every sensation, and every vision.

The voice in his mind remained a gentle presence, guiding him through the labyrinth of his experiences.

The visions persisted, becoming more detailed and coherent over time.

He saw images of advanced technology, sprawling cities, and strange landscapes that seemed to exist in a realm beyond Earth.

The images were accompanied by feelings of wonder and curiosity, as if the voice were trying to share a sense of amazement and exploration with him.

He also began to notice subtle changes in himself.

His perception of the world seemed to expand, and he felt a growing connection to the universe around him.

The sense of isolation he had once felt began to fade, replaced by a feeling of being part of something larger and more significant.

One particularly cold evening, as he lay in the garden, he saw a new vision, a vast, starry expanse, with shimmering lights stretching out in every direction.

The vision was accompanied by a feeling of profound peace, as if he were floating among the stars, enveloped in their gentle glow.

The voice spoke softly, its message clear and reassuring.

"You are on the right path, Eduard.

Trust in your journey and continue to observe.

The answers you seek are within your reach."

Eduard closed his eyes, absorbing the message.

He felt a deep sense of gratitude and determination.

The journey he was on was far from over, but he now felt more prepared to face it.

The voice, the visions, and the stars had become his guides, leading him toward a greater understanding of himself and the universe.

As the seasons changed and the days grew shorter, Eduard's sense of purpose remained unwavering.

The voice and the visions had become an integral part of his life, shaping his understanding of the world and his place within it.

He knew that he was part of something extraordinary, and he was ready to embrace whatever lay ahead.

The mystery of the lights in the sky and the voice in his mind continued to unfold, revealing new layers of insight and discovery.

Eduard embraced his role as an observer, ready to uncover the secrets of the universe and to follow the guidance of the voice that had become his constant companion.

And as the first snowflakes of winter began to fall, Eduard felt a renewed sense of wonder and anticipation.

The journey had only just begun, and the stars were waiting to reveal their secrets.

Chapter 4

The Encounter

In November of 1942, the chill of autumn was setting in as Eduard ventured into the Langenzinggen, a remote meadow area near the Höragen forest.

The sky above was a drab expanse of gray clouds, casting a muted light over the landscape.

The tall grass whispered with the wind, and Billy's footsteps crunched softly on the frosted ground.

It was a quiet, contemplative walk, one that had become a routine for him as he sought solace and answers in nature.

As he wandered, his thoughts were preoccupied with the celestial visions and the enigmatic voice that had become a part of his nightly experiences.

The sense of the unknown was both exhilarating and unsettling, driving him deeper into his quest for understanding.

It was during this solitary exploration that something extraordinary happened.

Eduard's gaze was drawn upward, and his eyes widened as he saw an unusual object descending from the clouds.

At first, it was a small, indistinct shape against the gray sky, but as it came closer, its form became clearer.

The object was pear-shaped, metallic, and unlike anything Eduard had ever seen.

It was smooth and shiny, with a reflective surface that shimmered even in the dull light.

It hovered silently, defying the natural laws of gravity, and then gently touched down on the ground a short distance away.

Eduard felt a rush of amazement and curiosity rather than fear.

The sight of the object was mesmerizing, its alien presence invoking a sense of wonder that he had never experienced before.

He approached it cautiously, his heart pounding with excitement.

As he neared the object, he noticed that it had no visible seams, markings, or windows, just a flawless, metallic surface.

The object seemed to be a singular entity, almost alive in its own way.

The air around it felt charged, and he could sense a subtle vibration as he drew closer.

Without warning, a section of the metallic surface began to shift and slide open, revealing an entrance.

Eduard's curiosity overpowered any reservations he might have had.

He stepped inside, and the transition from the cold, damp air outside to the cool, fresh air within was immediate.

The interior of the object was unlike anything he could have imagined.

It was spacious and brightly lit by an otherworldly light, with walls adorned with strange instruments and screens that emitted soft, pulsating glows.

Eduard was struck by the sight of an old man who stood near a console in the center of the room.

He was dressed in a silvery suit that shimmered subtly, and his eyes twinkled with an expression of both wisdom and kindness.

The old man's presence was calming, and he exuded an air of serene authority.

"Come with me," the old man said, his voice soft and reassuring, with a cadence that seemed to resonate with a deep, unspoken understanding.

Eduard, driven by an overwhelming sense of trust and curiosity, followed the old man without hesitation.

He felt an inexplicable connection to the stranger, as though he had been waiting for this moment his entire life.

The old man guided him to a seat in the center of the room and began to explain things in a way that felt both familiar and foreign.

The old man introduced himself as Sfath.

Eduard never learned his exact age, but by the time they first met, he estimated him to be at least 90 or 95 years old.

His appearance was timeless, his presence marked by an air of ageless wisdom that defied conventional understanding.

Sfath was a man of mystery, concealing not just his age but also his origins and the true nature of my mission.

Their time together lasted just over four hours, but the impact of those hours would resonate throughout his life.

Sfath, with his enigmatic aura, imparted a wealth of knowledge that seemed almost too vast to comprehend.

Towards the end of their meeting, he requested that Eduard reclines in a chair.

The room, dimly lit, was filled with an assortment of devices, wires, and peculiar apparatuses that immediately piqued his curiosity.

As Sfath meticulously arranged these instruments around his head, he could not help but wonder what was to come.

His movements were deliberate and precise, manipulating buttons and switches with a practiced ease. The atmosphere was charged with a sense of anticipation.

Suddenly, he was overwhelmed by an extraordinary sensory experience.

It was as though a torrent of knowledge, insights, and profound realizations was being poured directly into his consciousness.

He saw visions of the future and felt a surge of strange, powerful forces coursing through him.

His senses were bombarded with images and sensations that defied explanation.

In that moment, he discovered abilities he had never known he possessed.

He could envision future events, and a newfound impulse to heal others with extraordinary powers surged within him.

It was as if the apparatus was awakening dormant faculties from previous lives, allowing him to harness them once more.

When the influx of knowledge ceased, Sfath carefully removed the apparatus from his head.

He explained that this device had reactivated abilities from his past lives, abilities that would remain with him under normal circumstances.

However, he warned that these powers should never be used for personal gain or selfish purposes.

Sfath's instructions were clear: the abilities should be used solely for his personal development and to assist others selflessly.

They were not to be employed for demonstration, scientific experiments, or any form of profit.

If he were to misuse these powers or pursue them recklessly, a 'fuse' would be triggered, blocking all knowledge and abilities until the threat was neutralized.

Sfath explained that this protective mechanism was a crucial safeguard.

The 'fuse' would activate in the event of any external influences, such as hypnosis or coercion, that sought to manipulate my newfound knowledge and abilities.

The blockade was designed to be impenetrable, with severe consequences for any attempts to breach it.

This safeguard was not just a theoretical construct; it was a powerful force capable of defending against attempts to exploit or misuse the knowledge.

Over time, Eduard discovered its effectiveness firsthand, as the mechanism thwarted various attempts to compromise his abilities and ensured their preservation.

"The stars have always been a beacon to those who seek knowledge," said Sfath.

"And you, Eduard, have been chosen for a special mission, one that extends beyond the boundaries of your world.

I come from a distant planet, far beyond the stars you see in your night sky."

Eduard listened intently, absorbing every word, even though the full meaning of what the old man was saying eluded him.

The concepts of distant planets and cosmic missions were beyond his youthful comprehension, yet the way they were presented felt profound and important.

The old man spoke of a mission that involved learning and growth, not just for him, but for the betterment of humanity.

Sfath continued, explaining the mission's purpose and the responsibilities it entailed.

He spoke of knowledge that transcended earthly understanding and of connections that spanned the cosmos.

Although the specifics were complex and somewhat abstract, Eduard felt a deep sense of purpose and connection.

The weight of the old man's words settled over him, and he understood that this encounter was a pivotal moment in his life.

Time seemed to lose its meaning as Sfath spoke.

The minutes stretched into what felt like hours, and Eduard was captivated by the vision of a grand, cosmic adventure.

Sfath explanations were accompanied by visuals on the screens, images of celestial bodies, advanced technology, and glimpses of distant worlds that left Eduard in awe.

Finally, he gently concluded his message.

"It is time for you to return to your world, Eduard.

The path you are on will require patience and perseverance, but you are prepared. Trust in yourself and the guidance you have received."

Eduard nodded, though his mind was still reeling from the incredible revelations.

He stood up, and Sfath led him back outside.

The pear-shaped object was waiting, its surface reflecting the pale light of the overcast sky. With a final, reassuring smile, he gestured for Eduard to step outside.

As he watched, the object began to rise silently into the sky.

It ascended smoothly, its metallic surface gleaming as it moved.

His eyes followed it as it disappeared into the clouds, leaving behind only a lingering sense of wonder and a trace of cosmic energy in the air.

Eduard stood alone in the meadow, his mind racing with the enormity of what had just occurred.

He felt a profound shift within himself, as if a new chapter of his life had begun.

The encounter had given him a sense of purpose and a connection to something greater than himself.

He walked home in a daze, the familiar landscape now seeming imbued with a sense of mystery and possibility.

His thoughts were consumed with questions and reflections on what he had learned.

The secrets of the universe felt closer and more tangible, yet still shrouded in enigma.

Despite the incredible experience, Eduard decided to keep it to himself.

He didn't share the details with anyone, not even Pastor Zimmerman.

The encounter was his secret, one that he felt was too extraordinary to be easily understood or accepted by others.

As he lay in bed that night, the events of the day replayed in his mind.

The pear-shaped object, the kind old man, and the cosmic mission all seemed to blend into a dream-like haze.

Yet, the feelings of marvel and purpose remained clear and vivid.

Eduard knew that his journey had only just begun.

The encounter had set him on a path of discovery and growth, one that would challenge him and shape his future.

With a sense of anticipation, he closed his eyes, ready to embrace the challenges and revelations that lay ahead.

The universe had revealed itself to him in a profound way, and he was prepared to follow its guidance into the unknown.

ICH BIN
MEIN EIGENER
GOTT

Chapter 5

The Mission

As the seasons turned and the years rolled on, Eduard's life began to follow a different rhythm from that of his peers.

What once had been a carefree existence filled with laughter and play now centered around his unique and profound connection with Sfath.

The old man, whose presence had been so startling and strange in the beginning, had become a constant in his life, a mentor, guide, and mysterious figure whose influence shaped his every waking moment.

By 1945, Eduard was 8 years old, and his days were punctuated not by school bells or neighborhood games but by intense telepathic sessions with Sfath.

The bond between them grew stronger with each passing day, and Sfath's teachings expanded beyond the rudimentary knowledge he had initially received.

The universe, which once seemed a distant, abstract concept, now became a vivid and intricate tapestry of interconnected worlds and civilizations.

Sfath's revelations about Eduard's mission were both awe-inspiring and daunting.

He explained that he had been selected for a special task that transcended mere human experience.

This task involved a profound responsibility: Eduard was to act as a bridge between humanity and the cosmic community.

It was a role that required not just intelligence but also immense strength, wisdom, and courage.

The details of this mission were still somewhat elusive.

Sfath spoke in broad, sweeping terms about the nature of the universe and humanity's place within it.

Eduard was to prepare himself for a future where he would play a pivotal role in guiding humanity toward a greater understanding of its cosmic significance.

The mission was not just a matter of learning but of transforming the very fabric of human consciousness.

Under the vast canopy of the universe, where the stars served as witnesses to countless truths and untold mysteries, Sfath began his lesson with Eduard.

The air was crisp, the silence profound, as if nature itself held its breath, eager to absorb the wisdom that was about to be imparted.

Eduard, still young and impressionable, sat with attentive curiosity, his mind open, ready to grasp the depth of what Sfath had to offer.

The old man's eyes sparkled with an ancient wisdom, as if he had seen the rise and fall of civilizations, the birth and death of countless souls, and the ebb and flow of time itself.

Sfath spoke slowly, his voice carrying the weight of knowledge distilled over millennia.

He emphasized that the core of a human's existence was rooted in their thoughts, that these intangible yet powerful forces shaped not only the behavior and actions of an individual but also defined their very essence as either positive or negative.

The thoughts that one chose to nurture, he explained, were like seeds planted in the fertile soil of the mind, what grew from them would determine the entire landscape of a person's life.

As he spoke, Eduard could feel the truth of Sfath's words resonating deep within him.

He understood that the cultivation of thoughts was not merely a passive process but an active, deliberate act that required conscious effort and attention.

Sfath warned that neglecting this process could lead to a loss far greater than mere moral decay; it could strip a person of their ability to think clearly and rationally, leaving them vulnerable to the destructive forces of blind belief.

Sfath's lesson was clear: beliefs, especially religious beliefs, had the potential to dominate and destroy the very faculties that made a person human, their ability to think, to reason, to understand the world as it truly was.

He explained that religious belief, more than any other, had a unique power to cloud judgment, to turn thoughts into illusions, and to replace the truth with comforting lies.

This, Sfath insisted, was the most dangerous form of self-deception, for it not only led to the dumbing down of the individual but also prevented them from recognizing and understanding reality as it truly was.

As Sfath's words sank in, Eduard began to see the world in a new light.

He realized that the world was filled with illusions, beliefs that masqueraded as truth, thoughts that were not born of reason but of fear and ignorance.

Sfath explained that these illusions, if left unchecked, could lead to two very serious negative outcomes.

First, they would lead to the dumbing down of humanity, a state in which individuals would be unable to perceive or comprehend the reality that lay before them.

This was because faith, particularly religious faith, suppressed all logic, understanding, and reason, creating a barrier between the individual and the truth.

Secondly, and perhaps more dangerously, Sfath explained that faith would prevent any form of independent thought from penetrating the believer's mind.

It would create a world of illusion, where the believer would be trapped, unable to see beyond the confines of their belief system.

This, he warned, was not just a theoretical danger but a very real one that had already ensnared countless souls throughout history.

It was a state of existence where the individual was no longer capable of thinking for themselves, where their thoughts were no longer their own but were dictated by the dogmas and doctrines of their faith.

Eduard felt a chill run down his spine as Sfath's words painted a picture of a world where individuals were enslaved by their beliefs, where the light of reason was extinguished, and where the truth was hidden behind a veil of ignorance.

He understood that Sfath was not merely teaching him about the dangers of belief but was also showing him the path to true freedom, the freedom to think, to reason, and to understand the world as it truly was.

Sfath's teachings left a lasting impression on Eduard.

He realized that the path to true wisdom and enlightenment was not through blind belief but through the careful cultivation of thoughts, through the relentless pursuit of truth, and through the unwavering commitment to reason and logic.

Sfath had given him a gift far greater than any material possession, he had given him the key to unlocking the true potential of his mind, the ability to think independently, and the strength to resist the seductive pull of comforting illusions.

As the lesson came to an end, the forest around them seemed to come alive with the sounds of the night.

The stars above twinkled with renewed brilliance, as if they too had been touched by the wisdom that had been shared.

Eduard felt a deep sense of gratitude towards Sfath, knowing that he had been given a glimpse into the true nature of reality, a glimpse that would guide him for the rest of his life.

With a final nod, Sfath stood up and began to walk away, leaving Eduard to sit alone under the starlit sky, his mind buzzing with thoughts.

As he gazed up at the heavens, he knew that he had been set on a path that few ever walked, a path that would require him to question everything, to challenge every belief, and to seek the truth, no matter where it led.

And so, with the stars as his witnesses, Eduard made a silent vow to himself, to never let his thoughts be clouded by belief, to always seek the truth, and to carry the wisdom that Sfath had imparted to him for the rest of his days.

He knew that the journey ahead would not be easy, that he would face challenges and obstacles that would test his resolve.

But he also knew that he was ready, that he had the strength and the knowledge to walk the path of truth.

As the night deepened and the forest around him grew silent, Eduard closed his eyes and allowed himself to drift into a peaceful sleep, knowing that he was one step closer to understanding the true nature of reality, one step closer to fulfilling the destiny that lay before him.

As Eduard delved deeper into his training with Sfath, he began to withdraw from his previous life.

The village of Bülach, once a place of vibrant interaction and companionship, now seemed distant and irrelevant.

His interactions with other children became rare.

The playgrounds, the games, and the laughter of his peers were replaced by solitary moments of contemplation and study.

The isolation was not merely physical but emotional.

Eduard found it increasingly challenging to relate to the other children.

Their interests and concerns seemed trivial compared to the vast, cosmic knowledge he was absorbing.

This growing distance led to a sense of loneliness that Billy struggled to reconcile with his sense of purpose.

School became a battleground of its own.

His frequent absences, driven by his intense focus on his mission, were a source of frustration for his teachers.

They noted his sporadic attendance and declining engagement with conventional subjects.

Despite this, his natural aptitude allowed him to keep up with his studies, although his approach was increasingly unconventional.

Eduard's sense of purpose was a double-edged sword.

On one hand, it provided him with a clear direction and a deep sense of meaning.

He was part of something far larger than himself, something that promised to change the world in ways he could only begin to understand.

On the other hand, the weight of this responsibility was a heavy burden.

The isolation, the pressure to succeed, and the magnitude of his mission created a constant tension in his life.

The telepathic communication with Sfath became a lifeline for him.

These interactions were not just educational but deeply supportive.

Sfath offered encouragement and reassurance, helping Eduard navigate the emotional and psychological challenges that came with his role.

The old man's guidance was a source of comfort and strength, helping him maintain his focus and determination.

The lessons from Sfath were both profound and transformative.

Eduard's understanding of the universe grew more sophisticated with each session.

He learned about advanced technologies, the ethical dilemmas faced by other civilizations, and the intricate balance required to maintain harmony in the cosmos.

One of the most significant aspects of his training was learning about the moral and ethical responsibilities associated with his role.

Sfath emphasized the importance of empathy, integrity, and compassion.

These lessons were designed to prepare him for the eventual task of guiding humanity toward a greater cosmic understanding.

The ethical considerations were complex, and Young Eduard grappled with them as he integrated these principles into his own worldview.

In the final months of 1945, Eduard intensified his preparations.

His interactions with Sfath became more focused, with an emphasis on practical skills and strategies for fulfilling his mission.

The telepathic sessions included simulations and exercises designed to enhance his ability to navigate the challenges he would face.

His preparation involved not only intellectual growth but also physical and emotional readiness.

Sfath guided him in developing resilience and adaptability, qualities that would be essential for the trials ahead.

Eduard learned to balance his sense of purpose with the demands of his everyday life, striving to maintain a sense of normalcy while preparing for his extraordinary role.

As Eduard approached his twelfth birthday, his vision of the future became clearer.

He began to see the contours of his mission more distinctly.

Sfath's teachings had provided him with a framework for understanding his role in the grand cosmic narrative.

He knew that his task would involve not just acquiring knowledge but actively applying it to bridge the gap between Earth and the stars.

This sense of purpose was accompanied by a growing sense of anticipation.

He could feel that a pivotal moment was approaching, one that would mark the beginning of a new phase in his mission.

The details were still somewhat vague, but the signs were clear that his journey was about to take a significant turn.

His journey was marked by a profound sense of destiny.

The isolation and challenges he faced were not merely obstacles but integral parts of his preparation.

The knowledge and experiences he gained from Sfath were shaping him into a figure capable of fulfilling his mission.

The weight of his role was immense, but Eduard approached it with a combination of resolve and humility.

The coming years would be crucial in determining the course of his mission.

His preparation had laid the foundation for his future actions, but the true test would be in how he applied his knowledge and skills to bridge humanity with the cosmos.

The path ahead was uncertain, but Eduard faced it with a sense of purpose and a readiness to embrace the challenges that lay before him.

Eduard's journey is a testament to his growth and transformation.

His life, once marked by childhood play and community interactions, had evolved into one of profound purpose and preparation.

The mission that lay ahead was both daunting and inspiring, and his dedication to his role was unwavering.

As he continued to prepare for the future, he did so with the knowledge that his journey was not just about understanding the cosmos but about transforming humanity's place within it.

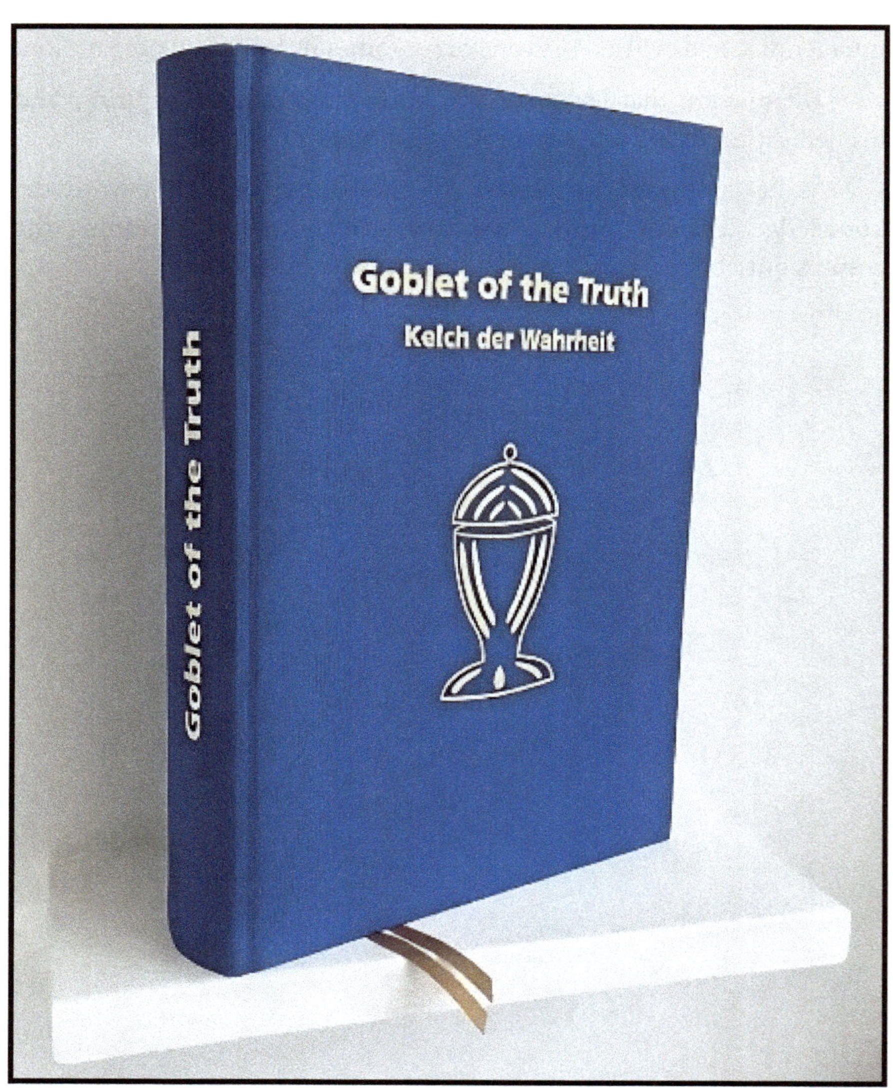

Goblet of the Truth
Kelch der Wahrheit
Goblet of the Truth

Chapter 6

The Teachings of Sfath

As Eduard entered his eighth year, his life became increasingly intertwined with the teachings of Sfath.

The old man from the stars had transformed from a distant, enigmatic figure into a close and influential mentor.

Their interactions were no longer limited to sporadic encounters but had grown into a regular part of his life.

Sfath's visits, both physical and telepathic, became the cornerstone of his education and personal development.

"What is the meaning of life?" Eduard asked, his voice barely a whisper against the backdrop of time itself.

Sfath's eyes, deep pools of ageless knowledge, met Eduard's with a solemn intensity. His voice, resonant and calm, began to unravel the complexities of existence.

"Eduard, if those in positions of power and influence were to embrace the spiritual doctrine and truly grasp the essence of life and evolution, the world would see a radical transformation.

Religions, sects, misguided philosophies, and especially the deceitful and destructive cults like Scientology, would fade into oblivion.

The 'doctrine of truth, doctrine of the mind, doctrine of life, which we often call 'spiritual teaching', is not a relic of any religion, philosophy, or secular belief. It is rooted in the profound reality of existence and the natural laws that govern it."

Sfath leaned forward, his gaze unwavering.

"This teaching, established by the universal prophet Nokodemion, encompasses the fundamental truths of reality, spirituality, and the natural laws.

It is a guiding beacon for those who earnestly seek to understand and apply its principles. The doctrine reveals that every human possesses a fragment of the creative spirit, which animates them and allows for reincarnation.

This spirit, or 'spiritual form,' does not perish with the individual but continues through successive lives, each time acquiring a new personality and consciousness."

Eduard listened intently as Sfath continued.

"Upon the death of the physical body, the individual's consciousness and personality dissolve into a neutral energy.

This energy, through the spiritual form, contributes to a new consciousness, which is then born into a new body.

This process begins on the 21st day after conception, when the spiritual form reincarnates into the new body, awakening it from its primal state and setting the stage for the development of consciousness and personality."

"The purpose of this cycle," Sfath explained, "is to allow each individual to transcend their perceived limitations.

Through conscious effort and alignment with the doctrine, one can solve personal problems, achieve goals, and cultivate wisdom, love, and balance.

This teaching posits that humans are inherently good, shaped by their choices and will.

Our inner nature, influenced by thoughts and feelings, determines the course of our lives and our interactions with others, nature, and the cosmos."

Sfath's voice grew more impassioned.

"The doctrine of truth, spirit, and life is not a mere philosophy or religious dogma but a practical guide to understanding and living in accordance with the fundamental truths of reality.

By adhering to these truths, one can liberate themselves from negativity and ignorance.

This personal transformation can then ripple outward, fostering a more harmonious and peaceful world."

He paused, allowing the weight of his words to sink in.

"Humanity has long hoped for peace, freedom, and harmony, dreams that have been marred by wars, violence, and suffering.

Yet, this hope endures.

For it to be realized, humanity must turn away from false doctrines and embrace the genuine teachings of the spiritual doctrine.

Only through understanding and applying these principles can true peace and harmony be achieved."

Sfath's gaze softened as he concluded.

"The doctrine of truth, spirit, and life has preserved the values of love, freedom, and peace through all ages, in contrast to the corruption and violence perpetuated by various belief systems.

It calls for a departure from religious and sectarian constraints, urging a return to the unshakeable truth of reality.

When humanity collectively aligns with this truth, the hope for a better world can finally be fulfilled."

Eduard sat in contemplative silence, the enormity of Sfath's words resonating deeply within him.

The path to understanding, it seemed, was not through the lens of conventional beliefs but through the pursuit of a higher, unifying truth.

Eduard sat for a moment longer, the gravity of Sfath's explanation settling in his mind like a heavy stone.

He could feel the shift in his own perception, as if a veil had been lifted, revealing a broader, more profound reality.

But questions still lingered, and his curiosity urged him to probe deeper.

"Sfath, if this spiritual doctrine is so vital and transformative, why has it remained hidden or misunderstood by so many?

Why have religions and sects, with their often narrow interpretations, overshadowed such universal truths?"

Sfath's eyes gleamed with a mixture of sadness and understanding.

"That is a question deeply rooted in the nature of human development and historical evolution.

Throughout history, many have sought to grasp the profound truths of existence. However, their understanding was often constrained by their cultural, societal, and intellectual limitations.

As a result, these truths were interpreted through various lenses, often leading to the formation of religions and philosophies that, while offering some insight, ultimately distorted or obscured the original teachings."

He continued, "Religions and sects often emerged from genuine spiritual experiences but became encrusted with dogma and rigid structures.

These constructs were sometimes utilized to exert control and influence, or they evolved into systems that could not adapt to the evolving understanding of reality.

Consequently, the essence of the original teachings became enshrouded in layers of ritual and doctrine that diverged from the core truth."

Eduard nodded, absorbing this perspective.

"So, the doctrine's obscurity is a consequence of both human fallibility and the manipulation of spiritual knowledge?"

"Yes," Sfath affirmed. "And it is also a matter of human readiness.

The doctrine of truth, spirit, and life requires a level of spiritual and intellectual maturity that many have yet to achieve.

The teachings are profound and require not just intellectual understanding but a deep, personal transformation.

As humanity progresses, more individuals may become attuned to these truths and the ability to integrate them into their lives."

Sfath paused, then added, "Moreover, the spiritual doctrine is not a static or monolithic truth. It is a dynamic and evolving understanding that adapts to the growing awareness of individuals and societies.

As more people embrace these principles and witness their transformative power, the doctrine will naturally gain greater recognition and acceptance."

Eduard's mind raced with new questions, each leading him further into the labyrinth of existential inquiry.

"How can individuals begin to align themselves with this doctrine?

What practical steps can one take to integrate these truths into daily life?"

Sfath's demeanor softened as he began to outline the path forward.

"First, it is essential to cultivate self-awareness and introspection. Understanding oneself and one's true nature is the foundation upon which the doctrine is built.

This involves recognizing and transcending the limitations imposed by societal conditioning and personal biases."

"Second," Sfath continued, "one must study and reflect upon the teachings with an open and discerning mind.

Engage with the principles of the doctrine actively, applying them in real-life situations to see their effects.

This process requires patience and dedication, as the transformation is gradual and cumulative."

"Third, practice alignment with the natural laws and principles that govern existence.

This means living in harmony with the environment, fostering genuine relationships, and pursuing personal and collective growth.

It involves ethical living and making choices that reflect a deep respect for the interconnectedness of all life."

"Lastly," Sfath concluded, "cultivate a spirit of compassion and empathy.

True understanding of the doctrine is reflected in how one relates to others and contributes to the greater good.

By fostering these qualities, you align yourself with the deeper truths of existence and contribute to the collective evolution of humanity."

Eduard listened intently, feeling a sense of clarity emerging from the complexity.

"So, it's not just about intellectual understanding, but about living these principles fully?"

"Precisely," Sfath responded.

"The doctrine is not merely a set of abstract ideas but a way of life that integrates deeply into one's actions, thoughts, and relationships.

It is through this holistic integration that the teachings can truly manifest and effect change, both within the individual and in the world."

As the conversation drew to a close, Eduard felt a profound sense of purpose and determination.

The path was clear, though challenging, and the journey towards understanding and embodying these truths was one that promised both personal fulfillment and a contribution to the broader human quest for peace and harmony.

Sfath's presence seemed to fade, but his words lingered in the air, a guiding beacon for Eduard's future endeavors.

With newfound resolve, Eduard set out to explore and integrate the doctrine of truth, spirit, and life, fully aware that this journey was not just a quest for knowledge but a path towards transformative existence.

Each meeting with Sfath was an opportunity for him to delve deeper into the mysteries of the universe.

The lessons were not just about abstract concepts but were infused with practical wisdom and moral guidance.

Sfath's teachings were comprehensive, covering not only the physical laws of the cosmos but also the spiritual and ethical dimensions of existence.

Sfath began by introducing Billy to the fundamental laws of the universe.

These principles were not just scientific but encompassed a broader understanding of existence.

Eduard learned about the balance that underpins all things, the way that every action has an equal and opposite reaction, not only in the physical world but in the spiritual realm as well.

This concept of balance resonated deeply with him, who saw parallels in the natural world around him.

"Everything in the universe is interconnected," Sfath explained during one of their sessions in the forest.

"From the smallest atom to the largest galaxy, there is a thread that binds all things together.

To understand this is to understand the essence of life itself."

Eduard absorbed these teachings with a mix of wonder and curiosity.

The idea that every element of existence was part of a grand, interconnected web fascinated him.

It also helped him make sense of the natural world he loved so much, reinforcing his appreciation for the balance and harmony he saw in nature.

Sfath's teachings extended beyond the physical and into the realm of spirituality and morality.

Eduard learned about the importance of living in harmony with nature, of respecting all forms of life, and of acting with compassion and integrity.

These lessons were intertwined with the cosmic principles he was learning, emphasizing that true understanding required not just intellectual insight but also ethical behavior.

During a conversation about the moral implications of knowledge, Sfath said, "With knowledge comes responsibility.

The truths you are learning are powerful, but they must be used wisely.

Compassion and empathy must guide your actions, for they are the true measures of wisdom."

Eduard took these words to heart. He began to view his growing knowledge not as a privilege but as a responsibility.

The weight of this responsibility was sometimes daunting, but it also gave him a sense of purpose and direction.

He knew that his mission was not just about discovering cosmic truths but about using that knowledge to benefit humanity.

The more he learned, the more he felt the weight of the knowledge he was acquiring.

Sfath did not shy away from discussing the challenges and dangers that lay ahead.

He spoke of the forces that would resist his mission, the skeptics and antagonists who would challenge his findings and the threats that could arise from those who did not wish for such truths to be revealed.

Despite these warnings, Sfath reassured him that he would not face these challenges alone.

"There are allies both on Earth and beyond who will support you," Sfath said.

"You will find strength in your convictions and in the knowledge that you are part of a larger cosmic plan."

These teachings about the potential dangers were a sobering reminder of the complexities and risks involved in his mission.

They underscored the importance of resilience and perseverance, qualities that the young Eduard was learning to cultivate with Sfath's guidance.

The emotional and psychological toll of such profound knowledge was significant.

Eduard grappled with feelings of isolation and the burden of responsibility.

The weight of the secrets he carried sometimes felt overwhelming, and the prospect of facing opposition was daunting.

Sfath's mentorship provided crucial support during these times.

He helped him develop coping strategies and maintain a sense of balance.

"When the weight of your knowledge feels too heavy, remember to seek solace in the simple joys of life," Sfath advised.

"Nature, friends, and moments of reflection will sustain you."

He found comfort in these words. He learned to manage his stress by engaging in activities that connected him to the world around him, walking in the forest, observing the stars, and spending time with his family.

These moments of connection helped ground him and reminded him of the larger context of his mission.

As the seasons changed and Eduard grew older, the teachings of Sfath became deeply ingrained in his character.

The wisdom he acquired was not just intellectual but had shaped his very soul.

He became more attuned to the rhythms of the universe and more capable of integrating the cosmic principles into his daily life.

His understanding of the universe evolved, and he began to see connections between seemingly disparate elements of his knowledge.

The cosmic laws, the moral imperatives, and the practical challenges of his mission were all interwoven, creating a comprehensive framework for understanding his place in the world.

With each passing year, Eduard felt more prepared for the mission that lay ahead.

The teachings of Sfath had equipped him with the tools he needed to navigate the complexities of his role.

He was no longer just a boy with a destiny but a young man who had been shaped by profound cosmic wisdom.

His preparation continued to focus on personal growth, intellectual development, and practical skills.

He worked diligently to apply Sfath's teachings in real-world situations, developing strategies for overcoming obstacles and understanding the nuances of his mission.

As he approached the end of his sixteenth year, he felt a deep sense of alignment with his purpose.

The teachings of Sfath had given him a clear vision of his destiny and the role he was to play in the cosmic scheme.

The journey ahead was still uncertain, but he was confident in his ability to fulfill his mission.

The stars above, once a distant and mysterious realm, now felt like a familiar and integral part of his life.

He looked up at the night sky with a sense of gratitude and anticipation.

He knew that the answers he sought and the challenges he would face were all part of a grand cosmic plan.

The lessons about cosmic laws, spiritual and moral principles, and the challenges ahead shaped Eduard into a figure of wisdom and purpose.

As he continued his journey, he embraced his role with a sense of responsibility and hope, prepared to fulfill the mission that lay ahead.

The teachings of Sfath had not only expanded his understanding of the universe but had also prepared him for the significant role he was destined to play in bridging humanity with the cosmos.

The Statesman

Incorporating and directly descended from THE FRIEND OF INDIA—Founded 1818

PUBLISHED SIMULTANEOUSLY FROM DELHI AND CALCUTTA

DELHI, WEDNESDAY, SEPTEMBER 30, 1964

"THE FLYING SAUCER MAN" LEAVES DELHI

Swiss Claims He Has Visited Three Planets

BY A STAFF REPORTER

Is the "flying saucer" a myth? Far from it, according to Mr Edward Albert, a 28-year-old Swiss national, who left Delhi for Pakistan en route to Switzerland on Monday. "I have not only seen the objects from outer space, but have taken photographs and even travelled in them thrice", he says.

He has about 80 photographs of the space objects—all taken with an old folding camera. The objects in the photographs vary in size and shape. One is a globular object with a round disc in the centre; another is funnel-shaped; a third is like a neon lamp; a fourth is a big, bright cross and others bright zigzag lines. Some of these have been taken on the ground and some . flying in the sky. The sizes (one has to take Mr Albert's word for it) vary from two centimetres ("space scouts", he calls them) to 1,500 yards. Some of the photographs were taken in the day and some at night.

The photographs—taken in Greece, Jordan and India—are neatly kept in an album. Mr Albert politely declines a request for a copy of the photographs with the remark: "I can't spare them." He says he had

MR EDWARD ALBERT

taken about 400 photographs of the space objects but most of them have been stolen—some in Jordan, some in India.

Sitting bare-bodied in one of the cave-like monuments in Mehrauli in Delhi near the Buddha Vihara—where he had been staying since his arrival in India about five months ago—Mr Albert sounds rather weird. But then he clearly is not eager to talk about his experiences which, to say the least, are remarkable. Indeed, the little that he has to say has to be pried out of him. He doesn't want publicity, he doesn't care if anyone believes him or not. To the unbeliever he simply refuses to talk.

VISIT TO 3 PLANETS

The first "flying saucer" he saw, according to him, was in Switzerland in 1958. Since then he has been seeing and often photographing them. They come almost once a month, he says. In the last five years he claims to have met and spoken to men from outer space ("they come from different planets"). "I have travelled on three occasions with the space men, and have visited three planets—Satar, Kapar and Paranos, he says. In one, there was habitation ("all the objects were white", the other was shaped like a church and too hot to stay on and the third "was like a shimmering diamond" with no people. He says he was not allowed to stay in any planet for more than 10 to 15 minutes. Mr Albert nonchalantly says that he has collected some stones from the planets which he has kept at home (in Switzerland). "I won't be able to single out the planets now," he adds.

As for the space men, Mr Albert says that they look like human beings—"only they are much taller, have a certain glow about them and are spiritually much more advanced than human beings". They don't utter any words but understand any language and express themselves through telepathy, he says.

A MISSION

"I have a mission to fulfil," says Mr Albert, but refuses to explain what it is. "I will disclose it when the time comes—positively before a year."

Besides his none too impressive clothes, his space album, camera and a couple of bags, Mr Albert has a pet monkey which he has named "Emperor". Soon after he landed at Mehrauli his money —$350—was stolen. Since then he had been trying to get work or money but in vain. A few days ago he met a German youth, a hitch-hiker on his way back to Europe. The German (also with a pet monkey, "Empress") was glad to help the Swiss out. The Swiss, the German and the monkeys left on Monday evening by train for Lahore; from there they plan to hitch-hike their way to Europe—each to his native country.

The story of Mr Albert is as incredible as it is startling. He proposes to relate to German scientists his experiences, show his photographs and the objects that he says he has collected from the planets he visited. Has Mr Albert created history or is he a mystic who has let his imagination run wild? Time alone will tell.

56

CHAPTER 7

A Journey Beyond Time

Eduard's journey with Sfath began in an extraordinary fashion.

They ventured far beyond the conventional bounds of history, not just 25 million years back, but to a time when Earth was still in its formative stages.

For Eduard, this was more than a mere trip through time, it was an opportunity to witness the primordial history of Earth before the evolution of Earthlings.

This era, untarnished by human intervention, was a realm where fundamental processes and events shaped the planet in ways that were often misinterpreted or unknown to contemporary scholars.

As they traveled further back, Eduard was shocked by the sight of a planet in its raw, unspoiled state.

The landscape was marked by vast, untamed wildernesses and primal geological formations.

The absence of human influence was striking, providing a pure, unfiltered view of Earth's early history.

Eduard's fascination grew as he realized the profound differences between this primordial Earth and the world as understood by modern historians and scientists.

During their exploration, Eduard discovered that Earth had been visited by extraterrestrial beings long before humans existed.

These visitors were not mere passersby but had played a significant role in shaping the planet's development.

Their visits were part of a broader interaction that continued over millennia, influencing the course of Earth's history in ways that defied the conventional understanding of human civilization.

The technology used by these ancient visitors was far beyond anything known to early humans.

They employed advanced levitation techniques to move and position massive materials with incredible precision.

This technology allowed them to construct monumental structures and cities that would later become the subject of myths and legends.

The visitors' advanced machinery and techniques were responsible for feats that appeared miraculous to the early humans who witnessed them.

Eduard learned that the construction methods used by these ancient extraterrestrials were extraordinarily sophisticated.

They had the capability to levitate and precisely place massive blocks of stone, ranging from 10 to 50 tons or more.

This advanced technology allowed them to achieve a level of precision in construction that is still not fully understood by modern scholars.

Structures were built with such accuracy that the components fit together seamlessly, with no gaps even as thin as a hair.

In some rare instances, materials were moved telekinetically, although this was not the primary method used.

The majority of the heavy lifting was achieved through advanced machines and techniques that far surpassed the capabilities of later human civilizations.

Eduard realized that the impressive achievements of ancient cultures, often attributed to sheer human effort and ingenuity, were actually the result of interactions with these advanced beings.

The influence of these extraterrestrial visitors extended beyond mere construction.

Many of them were deified by early humans, becoming figures of worship and reverence. Some of these visitors were giants, while others were of normal size, and there were also individuals with unusual physical traits such as elongated or tall skulls.

These traits were sometimes imitated by ancient humans through cultural practices, such as binding the skulls of infants.

These 'gods' had a profound impact on early human societies.

Their presence and extraordinary abilities were woven into the fabric of myth and religion, influencing everything from architectural styles to social structures.

Eduard discovered that many of the religious practices and myths of ancient cultures were rooted in these early interactions with advanced beings, blending historical events with mythological elements.

Eduard's exploration revealed the fate of many ancient cities built by these advanced visitors.

Over time, natural processes such as sand accumulation, rising seas, and forest growth had buried these once-great cities.

The sands blown from deserts like the Sahara, for example, had covered many of these ancient sites, preserving their remains beneath layers of earth.

These cities were not lost forever, however. The vast amounts of sand and natural changes had concealed them, but they were not obliterated.

Archaeologists and explorers in the future might still uncover these hidden cities, revealing the remnants of a long-lost era.

Eduard saw the potential for future discoveries to shed light on these ancient civilizations and their advanced technologies.

The insights gained from Eduard's journey challenged conventional historical narratives.

The advanced technologies and interactions with extraterrestrial visitors provided a new perspective on human history.

This understanding demonstrated that many of the achievements attributed to early human civilizations were actually the result of influences from more advanced beings.

Modern scholars and historians would need to reassess their interpretations of the past in light of these revelations.

The traditional explanations for monumental structures and ancient technologies often fell short when compared to the advanced capabilities of the extraterrestrial visitors.

Eduard's findings called for a reevaluation of historical theories and encouraged a more nuanced understanding of humanity's past.

Communicating the findings from Eduard's journey posed a significant challenge.

The revelations about extraterrestrial visitors and advanced technologies needed to be presented carefully and thoughtfully.

Eduard understood the importance of conveying this information in a way that respected both the historical facts and contemporary beliefs.

Sfath had advised Eduard to wait for the right moment to share these insights, and now that the time had come, it was essential to navigate the complexities of presenting such groundbreaking information.

Eduard faced the task of ensuring that his discoveries were communicated accurately and responsibly, while also addressing potential skepticism and resistance.

Reflecting on his journey, Eduard was struck by the vastness and interconnectedness of human history.

The experience had expanded his understanding of the past and deepened his appreciation for the complexities of the present.

The journey had revealed the profound impact of external influences on human development and highlighted the enduring quest for knowledge.

Eduard's reflections also underscored the importance of curiosity and exploration.

The journey had shown that understanding the past required going beyond established boundaries and questioning accepted narratives.

As he prepared to share his findings, Eduard recognized the ongoing need for exploration and open-mindedness in the pursuit of knowledge.

Looking to the future, Eduard saw the potential for further exploration and discovery.

The knowledge gained from his journey provided a foundation for future research and inquiry.

The insights into ancient technologies and civilizations opened up new possibilities for understanding the past and exploring the broader cosmos.

Future generations of researchers and explorers would have the opportunity to build upon Eduard's discoveries, uncovering even more secrets about Earth's history and the universe.

The quest for knowledge would continue, driven by curiosity and a desire to uncover the mysteries of the past.

His journey through time left a lasting legacy. The experience had not only provided valuable insights into the past but had also transformed his understanding of history and the universe.

The legacy of this journey was a testament to the power of exploration and the importance of questioning established beliefs.

As Eduard prepared to share his findings with the world, he was mindful of the impact this knowledge would have on future generations.

The legacy of time travel was a reminder of the endless possibilities for discovery and the enduring quest for understanding.

Eduard hoped that his journey would inspire others to continue exploring and expanding their horizons, embracing the potential for new discoveries and insights.

CHAPTER 8

The Evolution of Fire-Making Techniques

Eduard and Sfath emerged from the shimmering vortex of time travel into a landscape untouched by modernity.

The air was crisp and filled with the earthy aroma of ancient forests.

They had arrived in the era of the Neanderthals, a world where fire was both a lifeline and a symbol of human ingenuity.

The distant glow of a fire pit caught their attention, and they approached the Neanderthal camp, eager to witness firsthand the methods of early fire-making.

As they neared the flickering light, Sfath turned to Eduard with a contemplative expression.

Eduard: "Sfath, I've always learned that early humans primarily used flint to create fire. Is that really how it happened?"

Sfath: "The traditional story of flint-based fire-making is a simplified version of reality. What Neanderthals used was far more nuanced."

Eduard's curiosity was piqued.

Eduard: "How so? Wasn't flint essential for making fire?"

Sfath: "Flint was used, but it wasn't the sole method. Neanderthals had a more sophisticated approach."

Sfath led Eduard through the dense forest to a grove where several branches oozed with a sticky, resinous substance.

Sfath: "These branches are crucial. They contain resin, which ignites easily when struck by lightning."

Eduard: "So, they relied on these resin-rich branches for fire?"

Sfath: "Exactly.

After a lightning storm, Neanderthals would collect these branches and use them to maintain their fires.

This method allowed them to keep a flame burning for long periods."

Eduard looked at the branches in awe, realizing the depth of their fire-making strategy.

Eduard: "Lightning was crucial for their fire-making?"

Sfath: "Yes, lightning was a natural ignition source.

Neanderthals had to be skilled at finding and preserving these branches."

Back at their camp, Sfath prepared to teach Eduard and the Neanderthals the intricate process of flint fire-making.

The Neanderthals gathered around, their faces filled with curiosity.

Sfath: "Eduard, fire-making with flint involves several steps.

First, we need the right stones, pyrite or marcasite are suitable."

Eduard observed as Sfath selected a flint stone and a harder rock.

Eduard: "What's the process?"

Sfath: "We strike one stone against the other to chip off tiny particles.

These particles can produce sparks when struck properly."

Sfath demonstrated the technique, his strikes sending tiny shards flying.

Eduard: "And these sparks start the fire?"

Sfath: "Exactly.

The sparks ignite a pile of fine material, like dry grass, which we then blow on to start the fire."

Eduard marveled at the precision required.

Sfath's methodical strikes sent off occasional sparks, which he carefully directed onto a pile of dry grass.

Eduard: "This process seems incredibly labor-intensive.

How many strikes are needed?"

Sfath: "It usually takes up to 200 or 300 strikes to create enough sparks.

It's a meticulous and laborious process."

Eduard's respect for the Neanderthals' fire-making skills grew as he watched the effort involved.

Eduard: "So, creating fire with flint was a significant challenge."

Sfath: "Indeed.

It required a high degree of skill and perseverance."

As Sfath and Eduard continued their demonstration, the Neanderthals practiced with growing proficiency.

They learned to strike flint effectively, their efforts yielding more frequent sparks.

Eduard: "Are they mastering the technique?"

Sfath: "With practice, they are becoming more skilled.

It's a process of adaptation and learning."

The Neanderthals, initially awkward, grew more confident with each attempt.

Eduard: "How do they incorporate this technique with their existing methods?"

Sfath: "They blend flint-based fire-making with their traditional method of using resin-rich branches. Each has its advantages."

With their new skills, the Neanderthals adapted their fire-making practices, combining the newly learned flint technique with their traditional methods.

Eduard: "It's fascinating to see how they integrate these new techniques into their daily lives."

Sfath: "Their ability to adapt and refine their practices shows their resourcefulness and ingenuity."

Eduard admired the Neanderthals' growing competence as they successfully created fire using both methods.

Eduard: "I never realized how sophisticated their methods were."

Sfath: "The complexity of their practices often gets overshadowed by simpler historical accounts.

Their achievements deserve recognition."

As their time with the Neanderthals drew to a close, Eduard and Sfath sat by the now-familiar campfire, reflecting on their experiences.

Eduard: "This journey has reshaped my understanding of early human technology."

Sfath: "And it underscores the need for accurate historical narratives.

Neanderthals were more skilled and adaptable than often portrayed."

Eduard nodded, the lessons learned deeply embedded in his mind.

Eduard: "I hope this new understanding helps correct misconceptions about our ancestors."

Sfath: "That is our aim.

A more accurate portrayal of their capabilities enriches our view of human history."

As they prepared to return to their own time, Eduard and Sfath assessed their impact on the Neanderthals.

The knowledge they imparted had significantly enhanced the Neanderthals' fire-making abilities.

Eduard: "What do you think will be the long-term effects of our teachings?"

Sfath: "They will improve the Neanderthals' ability to control fire, benefiting their survival and daily life."

Eduard was optimistic about the future.

Eduard: "It's amazing how a few new techniques can make such a significant difference."

Sfath: "Indeed. Each improvement contributes to their progress and adaptability."

As they departed, Eduard and Sfath discussed the broader implications of their discoveries. Their insights into Neanderthal fire-making were just one part of a larger understanding of prehistoric technology.

Eduard: "How do our findings fit into the broader context of prehistoric technology?"

Sfath: "They offer a clearer view of the sophistication in early human practices.

Neanderthals were highly skilled and innovative."

Eduard considered the impact on historical research and education.

Eduard: "Updating our historical narratives to include these complexities is essential."

Sfath: "Absolutely.

Accurate representations of the past enhance our understanding and appreciation of early human achievements."

As Eduard and Sfath's journey came to an end, they reflected on their experience and the potential for future exploration.

The knowledge gained had opened new doors in the understanding of early human technology.

Eduard: "This has been an incredible journey. What's next?"

Sfath: "There's always more to learn and discover.

Our understanding of history is constantly evolving."

Eduard smiled, filled with a sense of accomplishment and anticipation for future adventures.

Eduard: "I look forward to uncovering more truths about our past."

Sfath: "As do I.

Our journey may have ended, but the quest for knowledge continues."

With their mission complete, Eduard and Sfath stepped into the spacecraft which has become their second home, ready to explore new horizons and uncover more secrets of human history.

CHAPTER 9

The encounter with Nikola Tesla

Nikola Tesla, immersed in his latest experimental apparatus, was startled by an unexpected interruption.

The lab was dimly lit, save for the flickering glow of electrical sparks and the hum of intricate machinery.

Suddenly, two figures materialized out of thin air, causing Tesla to drop his tools in shock.

The sight of these unannounced visitors, seemingly appearing from nowhere, left him trembling.

The men were not ordinary, and their sudden appearance was accompanied by an otherworldly shimmer that Tesla could not rationalize.

It took him several moments to regain his composure.

Sfath, and Eduard, watched as Tesla struggled to understand the phenomenon before him.

It was only after Sfath gently placed his hand on Tesla's shoulder and ushered him into the sleek, metallic craft, the "pear ship," that the scientist began to calm down.

Inside the pear-shaped vessel, Tesla's initial fear gave way to astonishment as they soared above the Earth.

The ship moved with an effortless grace, circling the planet as Sfath and Eduard engaged him in conversation.

The grandeur of the view from the ship's window offered a calming distraction from the unsettling manner of their arrival.

Tesla, now more at ease, turned his attention to his visitors.

The vessel's advanced technology and serene atmosphere provided the perfect setting for a dialogue about his groundbreaking inventions.

Sfath and Eduard listened intently as Tesla spoke about his work, eager to share the details that had captivated the scientific community and the public alike.

Tesla began with a subject that had been misunderstood by many: the so-called "death rays."

He clarified that the term, coined by a sensationalist journalist, was a misnomer.

What he had actually developed were "cathode rays," which were simply streams of electrons—an innovation in electrical power engineering.

These rays, Tesla explained, were responsible for a faint bluish illumination when passed through a vacuum.

He demonstrated the basic principles of his invention, explaining how cathode rays could produce an electric current when a specific electrode setup was used.

This setup involved a negative pole and an opposing plasma electrode, which together generated power.

Tesla's face lit up as he described the potential applications of his invention, though he was cautious to keep some aspects shrouded in secrecy.

Despite Tesla's enthusiasm, he was acutely aware of the responsibility that came with his invention.

Theoretical power of cathode rays, if misused, could lead to catastrophic consequences.

He revealed to Sfath and Eduard his profound concern that such technology, if weaponized, could endanger humanity and even destroy the planet.

In a somber moment, Tesla showed them his meticulously kept plans and records.

He had initially intended to share his findings with the world, but he now believed that the potential for misuse was too great.

Tesla made a heartfelt plea for Sfath and Eduard to keep his discoveries a secret, promising that he would destroy all his records to prevent any misuse.

Sfath supported Tesla's decision, advising him to maintain the secrecy of his invention.

The world, in its ignorance and sensationalism, had already spun wild theories about Tesla's work.

The most absurd of these speculations involved a warship that supposedly disappeared and reappeared, with crew members fused into the metal, a tale that was nothing more than fiction.

Despite the rumors and bizarre theories propagated by those who refused to accept the scientific truth, Tesla and his work remained grounded in reality.

Neither he nor his peers, including Albert Einstein, drew inspiration from extraterrestrials, contrary to the claims of delusionists and conspiracy theorists.

In the aftermath of their visit, Tesla went on to continue his work with a renewed focus on safety and responsibility.

Sfath and Eduard departed, leaving behind a profound sense of understanding and respect for Tesla's brilliant but potentially perilous inventions.

As Tesla's contributions to science remained overshadowed by myths and misinterpretations, the true essence of his work lay buried within the confines of secrecy.

Tesla's legacy, though obscured by speculation, was one of extraordinary innovation tempered by an earnest concern for humanity's well-being.

Thus, the story of Nikola Tesla and his clandestine visitors became a chapter in the annals of history, a tale of brilliance, caution, and the enduring quest for knowledge.

CHAPTER 10

Jack the Reaper

The interior of Sfath's compact spacecraft was a testament to extraterrestrial ingenuity, with an aesthetic that seamlessly combined function and futuristic design.

The walls were lined with shimmering, adaptive panels that shifted colors to convey different statuses and environmental conditions.

Embedded within these walls were holographic interfaces that floated in mid-air, displaying real-time data and control options.

The cockpit featured a sleek, central console with a curved, transparent display that responded to touch with fluid, tactile feedback.

Surrounding the console were clusters of streamlined control pads and touch-sensitive surfaces, each glowing softly and offering a minimalistic yet highly functional layout.

At the core of the spacecraft, a pulsating, crystalline reactor emitted a gentle blue radiance, its energy field visible through a transparent containment unit.

This reactor, utilizing a blend of quantum and antimatter technologies, provided the immense power required for their advanced temporal and spatial travel.

The craft's navigation system was projected as a three-dimensional hologram above the central console, allowing precise adjustments to their trajectory.

Various compartments, seamlessly integrated into the walls, contained sophisticated tools and devices, each perfectly organized for efficiency.

The ship's cloaking technology was managed through an array of intricate emitters and control dials, ensuring complete invisibility and safety during their journey through time.

Eduard leaned back in his chair gazing thoughtfully at Sfath, who stood by the large screen window, his eyes scanning the stars that dotted the evening sky.

"I have another question," Eduard said, breaking the silence.

"Is the story of 'Jack the Ripper' known to you?"

Sfath turned away from the window, his face illuminated by a brief flash of interest.

"Of course."

Eduard's curiosity was piqued.

"There are many versions about whom the murderer could have been, however, nobody knows exactly who it was."

Sfath's eyes twinkled with intrigue.

"I can show you. Let's go and see for ourselves."

Eduard's eyebrows arched in excitement.

"You mean…?"

Sfath nodded, a faint smile playing at the corners of his mouth.

"Yes. We'll travel back in time to witness the events firsthand."

Eduard's excitement was palpable. "When can we leave?"

"Right now," Sfath said, his tone firm and decisive. "I need to prepare the craft."

Sfath was absorbed in the controls, his hands moving with precise, deliberate motions as he set the craft's systems for the time jump.

Each adjustment, each flicker of the holographic displays, seemed effortless, a testament to his expertise.

Eduard watched, his fascination unabated by the repetition.

Despite having seen the preparation countless times, he was always mesmerized by the seamless blend of advanced technology and Sfath's expert handling, each moment revealing the intricate elegance of their temporal journey.

The craft materialized in the fog-choked streets of Whitechapel, London, 1888.

Eduard and Sfath emerged, cloaked in their invisibility shields.

The gas lamps cast eerie shadows, and the distant murmur of the city felt both alien and familiar.

"This is it," Sfath whispered, guiding Eduard through the darkened alleyways.

"We need to stay hidden and keep a close watch."

Eduard's eyes darted around, trying to adjust to the dim surroundings.

"How will we find him?"

Sfath showed Eduard a sleek, compact device, its surface glinting with a faint, iridescent sheen.

"This is a vibrational signature reader," he explained.

"It detects and registers each person's unique vibrational pattern, much like a fingerprint but based on subtle energy frequencies.

By scanning the area, it will pinpoint our target's exact location, guiding us directly to him."

They moved silently through the narrow streets, their eyes alert.

The night air was thick with tension.

As they turned a corner, they saw him, an unassuming man in a dark coat, his face partially obscured by a hat.

"That's him," Sfath said softly. "Thomas Neill Cream."

Eduard watched in shock as Cream approached a woman of the night, his demeanor calm and methodical.

The scene unfolded with chilling precision.

The woman, unaware of her fate, was lured into a darkened alley.

Sfath and Eduard followed at a safe distance, their invisibility ensuring they were unseen. The events that followed were harrowing, Cream's brutal actions were carried out with a disturbing efficiency.

As the night wore on, Sfath and Eduard witnessed more of Cream's gruesome deeds.

They saw the horrific aftermath of his murders, cut-up bodies, stolen organs, and the macabre evidence of his perversions.

Eduard's face was pale, his hands trembling.

"This is beyond horrific. How could someone do this?"

Sfath's expression was somber.

"Cream was a man who had fallen into a deep and degenerate sexuality.

He fulfilled his twisted desires through these murders, using knives, small swords, and poison. He even cooked and ate the organs of his victims."

Eduard shuddered, struggling to comprehend the depths of Cream's depravity.

"And the other suspect?"

Sfath nodded gravely.

"There was another, an individual from the royal family.

He was never caught because he knew how to evade justice.

His actions ceased only after Cream's arrest."

As dawn approached, the pair made their way back to the craft.

The weight of what they had witnessed hung heavily in the air.

Eduard sat in silence, lost in thought. "A copycat, then."

"Yes," Sfath confirmed.

"An individual who mimicked Cream's actions but managed to avoid capture due to his status."

Eduard looked at Sfath, his expression a mix of awe and revulsion.

"I can hardly believe it."

Sfath placed a reassuring hand on Eduard's shoulder.

"Sometimes, understanding the past is the only way to prevent such horrors in the future."

The craft hummed as it prepared to return them to their own time.

Eduard watched the past fade away, his mind racing with the revelations of the night.

Back in the present, Eduard and Sfath emerged from the craft.

The familiar surroundings of the forest seemed comforting after the night's grim experiences.

Eduard turned to Sfath, gratitude and bewilderment mingling in his eyes.

"Thank you for showing me. I needed to see it firsthand."

Sfath nodded, his expression contemplative.

"Sometimes, to truly understand history, one must witness it with their own eyes."

Eduard took a deep breath, feeling a sense of closure.

I suppose the past holds more truths than we often realize."

Sfath smiled faintly.

"Indeed. And with those truths, we learn and grow."

Eduard nodded, the weight of the past still heavy but tempered by newfound knowledge. Together, they turned towards the future, forever marked by their journey through time.

CHAPTER 11

Spartacus

Inside the gleaming, pear-shaped saucer, Eduard and Sfath stood in solemn silence, their gazes fixed on the holographic display that surrounded them.

The curved walls of the craft pulsed with faint blue light, reflecting the ever-shifting scenes of battle playing out before them in striking clarity.

The battlefield stretched far and wide beneath a sky smeared with smoke and the deep orange hues of a dying sun.

Roman banners fluttered amid the chaos, their crimson insignias barely visible through the dust and gore.

Crassus's legions advanced in relentless formation, shields locked together, their short swords poised to deliver death with practiced efficiency.

Eduard's breath hitched as he watched the brutal slaughter unfold. The once-mighty rebel army, now fractured and desperate, fought with the fury of cornered beasts.

They knew there would be no mercy. Some men swung their weapons wildly, desperation in their eyes, while others collapsed from exhaustion, their bodies trampled beneath the marching Roman tide.

And at the heart of the storm stood Spartacus.

The Thracian warrior fought like a man possessed, his body bloodied but his spirit unbroken. His sword carved through enemy ranks, leaving behind trails of crimson mist.

Wounds covered his arms, his legs, his chest, yet he did not falter. His every movement was a declaration of defiance, a refusal to bow, even in the face of death.

Eduard clenched his fists. His young heart swelled with both admiration and sorrow.

"He fought with everything he had, Sfath," he murmured, barely aware of his own voice.

"Even when he knew there was no escape, he didn't give up. How could a man keep going in the face of such hopelessness?"

Sfath, standing beside him with the wisdom of ages in his gaze, exhaled softly.

"That is where legends are forged, Eduard.

Spartacus's strength was never in his victories, it was in his defiance.

Even as the world crumbled around him, his spirit refused to break. That is why his name will echo through the ages."

Below them, Spartacus staggered as a Roman spear grazed his side, but he did not cry out.

Instead, he bared his teeth in a snarl and drove his blade through the chest of another enemy.

Blood spattered across his face, mixing with sweat and grime, but his eyes remained sharp, burning with a fire that no force could extinguish.

Then came the final blow.

A Roman blade found its mark, slicing through his side. Spartacus fell to his knees, gasping, the world around him dimming.

But even as his strength failed, he did not surrender. He raised his head, his face twisted in a mixture of agony and triumph.

With one last, thunderous cry, he roared, not in pain, but in defiance.

The sound ripped through the battlefield, silencing friend and foe alike. It was not the cry of a broken man, nor the last breath of a defeated warrior.

It was something greater. It was the voice of every man who had ever suffered under the chains of oppression. It was a sound that would not die, even when his body collapsed into the blood-soaked earth.

Eduard swallowed hard, his chest tightening as the scene played out before him. The battle was over. The rebellion had been crushed. And yet, something lingered in the air—something beyond the tragedy.

Sfath turned away from the holographic display, his expression unreadable. "Symbols endure," he said softly. "Even when men fall."

Eduard's eyes remained locked on Spartacus's lifeless form, a deep sadness settling within him.

"But what was it all for, Sfath? The rebellion is over.

The slaves are either dead or captured. What remains of what he fought for?"

Sfath placed a gentle hand on the boy's shoulder. "Hope," he answered. "Hope is the one thing that survives even the darkest of times.

Spartacus's battle was never just about winning, it was about showing that resistance is possible.

That spirit will live on, long after Rome has forgotten this day."

Eduard inhaled shakily, absorbing the weight of those words.

A gentle hum vibrated through the saucer as it began to rise, carrying them away from the battlefield and its carnage.

The smooth walls of the ship shimmered, reflecting the transition between past and future.

The contrast was striking, inside, the ship was a beacon of peace, yet outside, history unfolded in all its raw brutality.

Then, Sfath's voice cut through the silence. "Let's go back."

Eduard turned to him, confusion flickering in his young eyes. "Back? To where?"

"To where it all began."

With a swift command, the ship jolted forward, tearing through the fabric of time itself.

The battlefield dissolved into a blur, history unraveling in reverse. The bloodstained fields of Italy faded, replaced by the rolling green hills of Thrace.

A new scene emerged.

Golden sunlight bathed the land, casting a warm glow over the simple dwellings and sprawling pastures.

The air was fresh, untainted by the stench of war. And there, in the distance, a young boy moved among a small herd of sheep.

Eduard's breath caught. "Is that...?"

"Yes," Sfath murmured. "Spartacus, before he became the man history remembers."

The boy was no older than ten, his frame small but sturdy.

He guided the flock with careful precision, his dark eyes constantly scanning the horizon.

There was a quiet determination about him, a fire that had not yet been tempered by hardship.

Eduard watched in awe. "Look at him. So young, so... innocent."

Sfath nodded. "Yet even here, the seeds of rebellion are already growing. His ancestors were warriors, fiercely independent.

The blood of resistance runs in his veins."

For a long while, they simply watched. Young Spartacus moved with a quiet confidence, his fingers brushing against the tall grass as he walked. This world was simple, untouched by the cruelty that awaited him.

Eduard's voice was barely above a whisper. "Do you think his life could have been different? Could he have escaped his fate?"

Sfath's gaze softened. "Fate is not so easily altered, Eduard. He was born in an age where Rome's shadow stretched far and wide.

Even if he had never taken up arms, history would have found a way to draw him into its grasp."

The scene shifted again.

Spartacus, now a young man, stood clad in Roman armor, his face hardened by experience. He had been conscripted into the very empire he would one day defy.

Eduard frowned. "He's fighting for them now."

Sfath's voice was calm. "Rome was skilled at breaking men. But they could never break him completely."

The ship followed the path of Spartacus's life, his days as a soldier, his betrayal and capture, the brutal training at Batiatus's gladiatorial school.

They watched as he rose, first as a fighter, then as a leader, until at last, he stood at the head of an army.

And yet, as they prepared to leave, Eduard saw something unexpected.

When Spartacus had fallen in battle, presumed dead, he had not perished.

A kind peasant had found him, half-dead, and nursed him back to health.

Years later, he returned to his homeland, where he lived in peace until the end of his days.

Eduard's eyes widened. "So he didn't die there."

Sfath smiled faintly. "Not all legends end in tragedy."

As their ship soared into the sky, leaving Thrace behind, Eduard let the knowledge settle in his heart.

Spartacus's rebellion had ended in blood, but his spirit had survived, free, unbroken, and untamed until the very end.

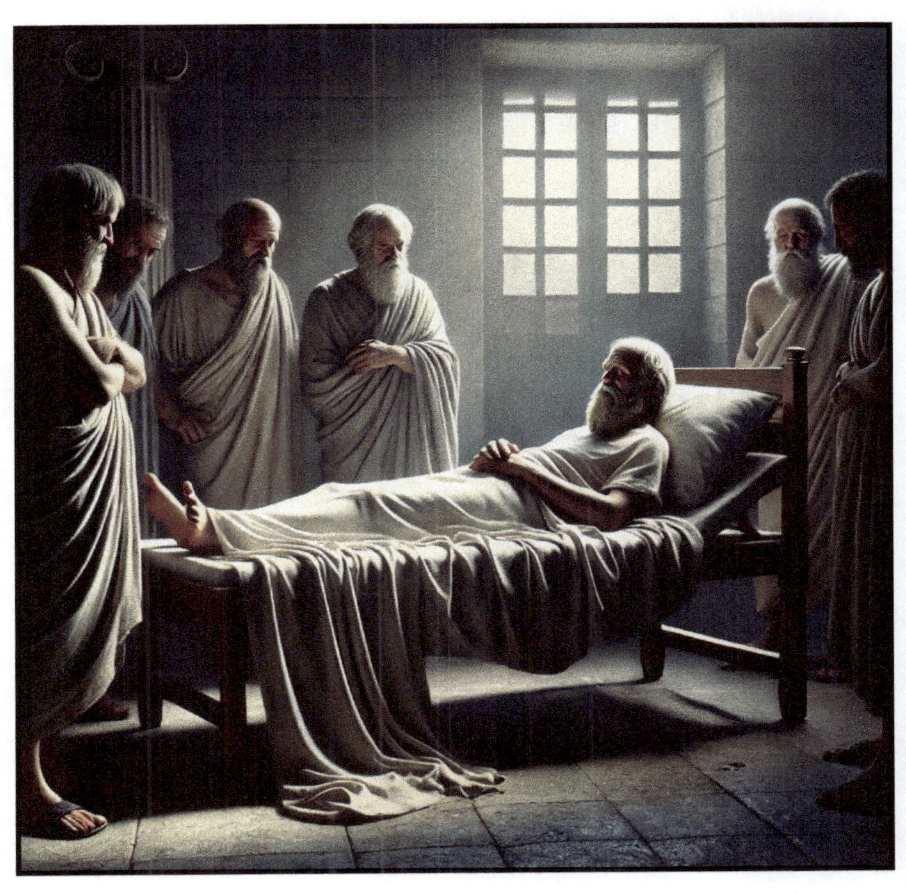

CHAPTER 12

The death of Socrates

"Eduard," Sfath said one crisp morning, his voice carrying a weight of otherworldly authority, "today we are traveling to witness an event of great historical significance, the death of Socrates."

Eduard's eyes widened with excitement.

"Socrates? The philosopher? But... I don't know much about how he died."

Sfath smiled knowingly.

"That is precisely why this journey is important.

You will experience firsthand a moment that has shaped the course of philosophical thought."

With a shimmer of light and a subtle hum of energy, Eduard and Sfath were transported back in time to ancient Athens.

The city was alive with activity, marketplaces bustling, citizens chatting, and philosophers debating in the streets.

The grandeur of the Acropolis loomed in the distance, casting a majestic shadow over the city.

Eduard looked around in amazement.

"This is incredible! But where exactly are we going?"

Sfath's eyes, filled with the knowledge of the Creation, focused ahead.

"We are headed to the Athenian court where Socrates will soon face his fate.

It is a place where history and philosophy converge in a profound manner."

As they approached the courthouse, Eduard felt a mix of anticipation and unease.

The crowd gathered outside the court was dense, their expressions a mix of curiosity and judgment.

The air crackled with tension, and Eduard's excitement was tinged with an inexplicable sadness.

Inside the court, Socrates stood with an air of calm determination.

Despite the gravity of the situation, his demeanor was composed, and his voice resonated with unwavering conviction as he addressed the assembled jury and spectators.

"I have dedicated my life to the pursuit of wisdom," Socrates proclaimed.

"If my ideas lead to my end, I accept it without regret."

Eduard was spellbound.

He could sense the philosopher's inner strength and the profound impact of his words.

He turned to Sfath, whispering, "What's going to happen to him?

Why is everyone so agitated?"

Sfath's expression grew solemn.

"Socrates is being tried for corrupting the youth and impiety.

His refusal to conform to the accepted norms and his questioning of the established gods have led him to this point."

The court's verdict was announced, and Eduard's heart sank as he realized the nature of Socrates' punishment.

Socrates was to drink from a kylix, a cup filled with a deadly poison.

The poison, derived from a plant, would induce a slow and painful death.

Eduard watched in silent horror as Socrates took the kylix.

The philosopher's face, though composed, reflected the gravity of his situation.

He raised the cup, his eyes meeting those of his followers one last time.

Socrates drank the potion with a steady hand, and soon after, the poison began to take effect.

His breathing became labored, and his body grew weak.

In spite of the physical suffering, his mind remained clear, and he continued to speak, sharing his final thoughts with those around him.

Eduard's emotions were a tumultuous mix of empathy and sorrow.

He felt a deep, personal connection to Socrates' suffering, as though the philosopher's pain resonated with something inside him.

Sfath, sensing Eduard's turmoil, placed a reassuring hand on his shoulder.

"Witnessing such moments can be overwhelming," Sfath said gently.

"But remember, Socrates' courage to stand by his principles, even in the face of death, is a testament to the power of truth and conviction."

As Socrates' life drew to a close, the court dispersed, leaving behind a heavy silence.

Eduard and Sfath remained, reflecting on the profound impact of what they had just witnessed.

Eduard turned to Sfath, his voice filled with a mixture of reverence and introspection.

"Socrates' final moments were both tragic and inspiring."

Sfath's eyes held a glimmer of approval.

"Yes, Eduard. Socrates' legacy is one of unyielding commitment to wisdom and truth.

His life and death remind us of the importance of standing by our principles, regardless of the consequences."

As they prepared to return to their own time, Eduard felt a renewed sense of purpose.

The journey back to their time was marked by a contemplative silence.

Eduard was lost in thought, reflecting on the significance of Socrates' life and death.

The philosopher's bravery and dedication to his convictions had left an indelible mark on him.

Sfath broke the silence with a gentle tone.

"The lessons of Socrates extend beyond his time.

They live on in the hearts and minds of those who seek to understand and embrace the principles of wisdom and integrity."

Eduard nodded, his eyes filled with determination.

"I understand now.

Socrates' legacy is a reminder to stay true to oneself and to seek wisdom, no matter how challenging it may be."

As Eduard and Sfath returned to their world, the echoes of Socrates' final moments remained with Eduard, a powerful reminder of the timeless pursuit of truth and the courage to question and explore.

Eduard's experience with Socrates had profoundly impacted him, offering more than just a historical glimpse but a deep, personal connection to the philosopher's journey.

The lessons he learned from witnessing Socrates' final moments inspired him to embrace his own quest for understanding and truth.

In quiet moments of reflection, Eduard recognized that Socrates' legacy was not confined to ancient Athens but continued to inspire and challenge those who sought to live by the principles of wisdom and courage.

And so, Eduard moved forward with a renewed sense of purpose, carrying with him the timeless lessons of Socrates and the enduring pursuit of truth.

CHAPTER 13

Who wrote the Bible

Eduard sat in his room, the quiet of the afternoon wrapping around him like a blanket.

Suddenly, a familiar sensation washed over him, a gentle nudge in his mind, the unmistakable touch of telepathy.

It was Sfath reaching out, urging him to meet at their usual spot.

The call was clear, and a surge of excitement coursed through him.

He quickly got ready, tossing on a jacket and rushing out the door, his heart racing.

The path through the dense forest was familiar, but today, the trees seemed to whisper secrets as he darted past them.

Sunlight filtered through the leaves, casting playful shadows on the ground.

Finally, as he reached a clearing, the pear-shaped spacecraft of Sfath materialized before him, its sleek surface glinting in the sunlight.

Sfath stood at the entrance, his expression one of warmth and anticipation.

"Salome, Eduard!" he greeted, his voice echoing in Eduard's mind.

"Salome Sfath! Where are we going today?"

Eduard asked, his curiosity sparked.

"Today, we're going into the past to witness how the Bible was written," Sfath replied.

"Sounds good to me," Eduard said, a grin spreading across his face.

With a smooth motion, the spacecraft ascended silently into the sky, piercing the atmosphere in mere seconds.

The world below shrank away, becoming a patchwork of green and brown.

As they reached the edge of space, Sfath activated the time jump, the control panel lighting up with a mesmerizing array of colors.

A brief shimmer enveloped them, and in an instant, everything shifted.

The next moment, they found themselves standing in the midst of a vast desert.

The air shimmered with heat, and golden sands stretched endlessly before them.

In the distance, a magnificent white tent stood, its fabric billowing softly in the warm breeze, contrasting starkly against the arid landscape.

The scene was alive with activity.

Figures moved about, some carrying scrolls and others deep in discussion, their voices carried by the wind.

Eduard felt a thrill of anticipation at the sight, knowing they were on the brink of witnessing history unfold.

Sfath turned to Eduard, a glint of excitement in his eyes.

"We are here."

Using their cloaking technology, they became invisible, a shimmering veil surrounding them that rendered them undetectable to anyone nearby.

Eduard felt a rush of adrenaline as they glided toward the tent, the heat of the desert sun contrasting with the coolness of their concealed presence.

As they approached, the intricate patterns on the tent's fabric came into focus, each thread woven with care.

Sounds of conversation drifted out, a blend of animated voices discussing scripture and philosophy.

Eduard strained to listen, eager to absorb every word.

They slipped around the tent's entrance, observing a gathering of scribes and scholars seated in a semi-circle, their attention focused on a central figure, a wise elder, his weathered face illuminated by the soft glow of an oil lamp.

Eduard felt a sense of reverence wash over him.

They were witnessing the very moment that history would remember for millennia.

Inside the tent, the conversation intensified.

Eduard listened closely, the weight of their words sinking in.

One scribe leaned forward, voice low and conspiratorial.

"Remember, this whole narrative is fictitious.

We're writing it together, twelve of us, claiming to be prophets."

Another nodded, urgency in his tone.

"In just forty days, we'll craft 240 stories based on ancient traditions and distortions.

This will become the second Torah, the Five Books of Moses since the first was lost in that devastating fire."

Eduard exchanged a glance with Sfath, the gravity of their discussion striking him.

"They're creating a false history."

"Yes," Sfath murmured.

"The Bible will not reflect true events but rather a carefully curated collection of fables, reshaped to serve their agenda."

The elder raised his hand to silence the group.

"We must ensure that this Torah has nothing to do with actual history.

It should serve to unify and control, not reveal."

Another scribe added, "And let's not forget, Christianity may take our narratives, twist them, and claim them as their own.

They may build a new chronicle that has nothing to do with what we're creating here."

Eduard felt a surge of anger.

"They're not just lying.

They're manipulating faith itself."

"Yes," Sfath said, his voice firm.

"Even figures like Jmmanuel sought to teach the Creation energy teaching, not the nonsense they'll propagate."

A scribe with a furrowed brow then proposed an idea that made the air in the tent feel heavier.

"What if we change Jmmanuel's teachings?

Instead of a singular figure, we could present him as part of a divine triad, The Father, the Son, and the Spirit.

It would give our narrative more weight and authority."

Gasps rippled through the group.

Eduard's heart raced.

"You mean to split the essence of Jmmanuel into three?

To create a deity that fits our needs?"

"Yes," the scribe replied, a fervor igniting in his eyes.

"This way, we can control the narrative even further.

The Father will represent the power of the unseen, the Son the embodiment of sacrifice, and the Spirit the guiding force of belief."

Eduard glanced at Sfath, who nodded slowly, contemplating the implications.

"This shift could create a religion that binds people together through fear and devotion."

Another voice piped up, caution tinged with intrigue.

"But won't this lead to internal conflict?

If we present three figures, won't they argue over their roles?"

"Not if we craft their stories carefully," the scribe insisted.

"Each can embody different aspects of a single truth.

By framing them as unified yet distinct, we can maintain control over the narrative."

Then, another scribe leaned forward, an idea forming.

"Remember the ancient tale of the great flood?" one scribe suggested, leaning in.

"We should weave it into our narrative."

The elder nodded, intrigued.

"Yes, the flood can serve as a powerful symbol of divine judgment and rebirth.

It conveys the idea of cleansing sin and offers a narrative of salvation."

Eduard felt a chill.

"You want to use the flood as a foundational myth?

It could instill fear, emphasizing that only the faithful will survive divine wrath."

"Precisely," the scribe replied.

"It creates urgency and underscores the consequences of straying from the path.

The flood represents ultimate judgment, only those who adhere to our teachings will find refuge."

Eduard's turned to Sfath.

"They're crafting a narrative built on fear, manipulation, and control.

This is not faith.

It's tyranny disguised as salvation."

"Yes," Sfath agreed, his tone grave.

"And it will shape the very foundation of belief for generations.

We are witnessing the birth of a powerful deception."

The air was thick with the promise of a new era, one forged not from genuine faith but from crafted stories designed to control and influence.

The tent felt smaller, the weight of their ambition pressing down on him.

As the scribes continued their discussions, Eduard realized he was witnessing the birth of a powerful deception, one that would shape beliefs for generations to come, all while obscuring the truth that lay beneath the surface

CHAPTER 14

Agharta - The Sons of the Sun

Eduard and Sfath sat quietly inside their pear-shaped spacecraft, drifting effortlessly through the vast emptiness of space.

The interior of the ship was a marvel of advanced technology.

Its walls shimmered with an iridescent glow, giving the impression of being alive, pulsating faintly as if in sync with the energy coursing through the vessel.

Control panels responded to thought alone, allowing Eduard and Sfath to navigate the vastness of space without lifting a finger.

Through the transparent sections of the hull, the universe spread out infinitely before them.

Stars blinked distantly, like ancient guardians watching over the cosmos, while nebulae swirled in deep purples, blues, and golds, painting the heavens with their beauty.

The silence of space was humbling, a peacefulness that seemed to stretch beyond the limits of imagination.

Eduard, gazing out at the stars, broke the quiet.

"Sfath, about the Hyperboreans… it brings me to another question.

The legendary Agharta—are you familiar with it?

Can you give me more details?"

Sfath, always calm and wise, nodded.

"You say the right name," he began, his voice thoughtful.

"To my knowledge, the humanity of Earth still lives in error regarding the name of Agharta.

In general, it is still erroneously called Agharti.

But you were in India, in the Himalayas, for a long time.

You encountered the blue-skinned human beings, didn't you?"

Eduard shifted in his seat, his curiosity ignited.

"Yes, I remember them. They were remarkable beings, like us, but different in so many ways."

"In the vicinity of Shigatse and Shampulla," Sfath continued, "lies the underground realm of Agharta, the capital and center of distant descendants of extraterrestrials on Earth.

This city is controlled by the race known as the Sons of the Sun.

They hold incredible power, secrets that could reshape the very fabric of the world."

He paused, his expression darkening.

"But unfortunately, with such power comes ambition.

A tendency toward earthly world domination prevails with this race, just as it does with certain earthly religions and secret societies."

Eduard's brow furrowed.

"This power, is it dangerous?"

Sfath shook his head. "No, not in the way you might think.

The Sons of the Sun live peacefully among themselves.

Unlike surface civilizations, they have no armies, no visible hierarchies.

They have no desire for superiority.

Instead, they live in harmony, focusing on cooperation and balance.

Their society flourishes not through conquest, but through wisdom and peaceful coexistence."

Eduard was struck by the contrast.

"So, despite their incredible power, they choose peace?"

Sfath nodded.

"Yes. And yet, they are not isolated.

They occasionally visit the surface, especially in regions where they can blend in, dressing in ways that conceal their blue skin.

They walk among surface people, observing the world without interfering, waiting for the time when humanity might be ready to know them."

Eduard's eyes widened in awe.

"They walk among us, unnoticed as I've seen them with my own eyes in India."

Sfath smiled.

"Indeed.

In countries where clothing like robes or head coverings can hide their appearance, they blend in perfectly.

They observe, but they do not meddle.

Their visits are always peaceful, and they've learned much about the surface world through these quiet interactions."

Eduard sat back, lost in thought for a moment.

"Fascinating," he murmured.

"To think they're among us, living so differently but quietly observing us."

Sfath looked at him, his expression serious.

"One day, Eduard, there will be a time when surface people will meet the blue-skinned beings openly.

But this will only happen when humanity has cast aside its desire for power, greed, and domination.

When both civilizations, the surface and the underground, are ready for peace, they will unite.

Together, they will work for a better future, sharing their knowledge and strength to build something greater than either has known."

Eduard smiled.

"A future of unity and peace. That sounds like a world worth striving for."

Then Sfath asked Eduard: "Shall we pay them a visit?"

And, they both agreed.

The conversation drifted into silence as their ship neared Earth.

The craft's cloaking system engaged, rendering them invisible as they gently descended through the planet's atmosphere.

Moving effortlessly through the clouds, they approached the rugged terrain of the Himalayas, where the hidden entrances to the underground world lay.

Their destination: the ancient realm of Agharta.

They landed softly near a concealed entrance nestled in the mountains of Shigatse.

The portal to the underground world opened before them, a shimmering gateway to a hidden civilization.

Stepping through, Eduard and Sfath began their descent into the depths of the Earth.

As they traveled deeper underground, the air grew warmer, charged with an unfamiliar but soothing energy.

Finally, the vast city of Agharta came into view, stretching endlessly in all directions.

Towers of translucent, glowing materials rose above them, radiating a soft light that illuminated the entire underground realm.

Floating platforms moved through the air, effortlessly transporting citizens from one area to another.

It was a marvel of technology and beauty, a testament to the advanced knowledge of the Sons of the Sun.

The streets were bustling with the blue-skinned inhabitants of Agharta.

They moved gracefully, their skin shimmering under the golden light of the underground world.

Their faces were calm, their expressions serene.

Androids, crafted with a sleek and elegant design, moved among them, assisting in daily tasks.

These androids were silent helpers, tending to the crops in the underground gardens, maintaining the city's infrastructure, and assisting in the education and care of Agharta's children.

The blue-skinned beings and the androids worked in perfect harmony, the mechanical and biological coexisting seamlessly.

Eduard was fascinated by the sight.

"These people," he whispered to Sfath, "they live in such peace.

And even their technology, there's no sign of dominance or control."

Sfath nodded in agreement.

"The androids here are not servants in the way humans might perceive them.

They are extensions of the people's will, created to support and enhance their lives, not to replace them or rule over them.

Here, there is no hierarchy, no struggle for power.

The Sons of the Sun have long understood that peace comes through cooperation, not control."

Eduard watched the interactions between the people and the androids, noticing how effortlessly they communicated, often with just a thought or a gesture.

"No armies, no weapons.

They truly have mastered peace."

Sfath smiled.

"Indeed.

They live in harmony with their surroundings, with their technology, and with each other.

This is the key to their longevity and prosperity."

As they walked deeper into the heart of the city, Eduard observed the blue-skinned people more closely.

They were strikingly similar to humans on the surface, yet they carried a grace and tranquility that was rare among Earth's inhabitants.

Their eyes glowed faintly, their movements fluid and purposeful.

There was no sense of superiority, no visible leadership that imposed control over the others.

It was a society built on mutual respect and understanding.

"They are just like us," Eduard remarked, his voice filled with awe.

"And yet, so different."

"Yes," Sfath agreed.

"The blue-skinned beings are distant descendants of extraterrestrials, but they share many similarities with humanity.

However, they have overcome many of the flaws that still plague the surface world.

Ambition, greed, and the thirst for power, they no longer dominate their way of life.

Instead, they focus on harmony, both within themselves and with their environment."

As they approached the central plaza of Agharta Beta, the seat of the city's power, Eduard couldn't help but marvel at the balance between technology and nature.

The city was alive, both with the energy of its inhabitants and the technology that sustained them.

And yet, there was no chaos, no conflict, only peace.

Sfath turned to Eduard, his expression thoughtful.

"In time, the surface world will come to know the people of Agharta.

But that day will only come when humanity has achieved a state of peace within itself.

When the surface is free from its divisions, its wars, and its ambitions for domination, the blue-skinned beings will reveal themselves.

And together, they will work with humanity to build a future of cooperation and peace."

Eduard nodded, his heart filled with hope.

"I think that day will come.

When both worlds, above and below, can stand as one, we will truly see the dawn of a new era."

Sfath smiled.

"Yes, Eduard.

That is the hope we all must carry.

A future where surface people and the blue-skinned descendants of the Sons of the Sun work together to create a world of unity, peace, and endless possibilities."

As they stood in the heart of the underground city, surrounded by the peaceful hum of Agharta, Eduard felt the weight of the future, one where two worlds would finally come together, united in purpose and guided by the wisdom of the past.

CHAPTER 15

The destrucion of Sodom and Gomorrah

Sfath adjusted the settings on the control panel as the pear-shaped spacecraft glided through the folds of time.

Eduard sat next to him, a picture of concentration, guiding their vessel towards an epoch far removed from their own.

The mission was clear: to observe the final days of Sodom and Gomorrah before the legendary destruction unfolded.

"Preparing for arrival," Sfath said, his voice calm and measured.

"Invisibility and radiation shields are active.

We'll be invisible to the inhabitants and protected from any harmful effects."

Eduard nodded, the anticipation of their journey mingling with a touch of unease.

The spacecraft shuddered briefly as it transitioned into the past, and the vast desert landscape of ancient Canaan unfolded before them.

The spacecraft landed silently on the outskirts of Sodom.

Eduard and Sfath stepped out, their advanced suits enveloping them in a protective shimmer.

Their visibility was cloaked, making them mere shadows in the ancient world.

As they walked towards the city, Eduard marveled at the pristine condition of the landscape before the impending calamity.

Sodom was a vibrant city with bustling streets, verdant gardens, and elaborate structures.

The air was warm and filled with the scents of cooking fires and blooming flowers.

Eduard and Sfath made their way through the streets of Sodom, their invisibility ensuring that they went unnoticed by the throngs of people going about their daily lives.

The city was alive with activity.

Merchants hawked their goods in the marketplace, children played in the streets, and families gathered in their homes.

The people of Sodom were an eclectic mix of tradesmen, artisans, and craftsmen, all contributing to the city's vibrancy.

The architecture was both intricate and grand, reflecting the prosperity and artistic prowess of its inhabitants.

As they observed the inhabitants, it became clear that Sodom was a society deeply entrenched in indulgence.

Public gatherings were filled with revelry, and the norms of propriety seemed to be pushed to their limits.

The city's art and literature frequently celebrated themes of sensuality and excess.

Eduard and Sfath visited a local temple where priests and priestesses performed rituals that blurred the lines between religious devotion and hedonistic celebration.

The rituals were elaborate, involving music, dance, and symbols of fertility.

The serenity of the city was in stark contrast to the impending disaster.

Eduard and Sfath spent time observing the everyday lives of the people, noting the stark disparity between the city's outward normalcy and the hidden tensions that hinted at the forthcoming tragedy.

In private quarters and small gatherings, whispers of dissent and concern about the city's moral state were evident.

Some citizens were uneasy, sensing that their indulgences might provoke divine displeasure.

As the time of the disaster approached, Eduard and Sfath detected a subtle shift in the atmosphere.

The sky, once clear, began to darken with ominous clouds.

They noticed strange celestial phenomena, an ominous streak across the sky signaled the approach of the meteorite.

They also observed the city's reaction as rumors of impending doom began to spread.

In spite of the general disbelief and attempts to dismiss the signs, a palpable sense of anxiety began to permeate Sodom.

The moment of cataclysm arrived with terrifying rapidity.

The meteorite struck high above the city, and the resulting explosion was catastrophic.

Eduard and Sfath watched from their invisible vantage point as the sky erupted in a blinding flash of light and fiery debris.

The impact triggered a massive earthquake that shook the ground violently.

The once-stable structures of Sodom crumbled under the seismic forces.

Lava and sulfur rains followed, exacerbating the destruction and adding to the city's chaos.

The divine retribution was not merely a natural disaster.

Eduard and Sfath observed the culmination of a cosmic vendetta.

From their vantage point, they witnessed the extraterrestrial being known as Jehovah, the cruel one, altering weather patterns and setting off two small atomic devices.

Jehovah and his group, the Bafath, had established their base beneath the Great Pyramid of Giza.

The devastation was total.

The cities of Sodom and Gomorrah were reduced to ashes and ruin, its people caught in the crossfire of both cosmic and terrestrial forces.

As the dust settled, Eduard and Sfath surveyed the desolation that had overtaken the once-thriving city.

The landscape was a barren wasteland of charred remains and smoking ruins.

The scale of the destruction was profound, leaving behind only echoes of a civilization that had been obliterated.

The emotional weight of witnessing the annihilation was heavy.

Eduard reflected on the stark difference between the vibrant life they had observed and the ruin that now lay before them.

With the mission complete, Eduard and Sfath returned to their spacecraft.

The journey back to their own time was somber, filled with a contemplative silence.

The full impact of their observations weighed heavily on them.

As the spacecraft ascended from the devastated landscape of Sodom, Eduard felt a deep sense of reflection on the events they had witnessed.

The destruction of Sodom and Gomorrah was a stark reminder of the fragile nature of human existence and the profound consequences of moral and evil forces.

Eduard marveled at the idea that this was the same Jehovah, revered and worshipped as a loving God.

The contrast between the reality of his actions and the perception of him as a benevolent deity is truly perplexing to him.

The spacecraft glided through time, leaving behind the echoes of a vanished world, carrying with it not just the record of ancient devastation but a deeper understanding of history's complex tapestry.

Chapter 16

The nativity of Jmmanuel

Eduard stood beside the sleek, pear-shaped spacecraft, feeling the chill of February 3rd on his cheeks.

It was his birthday, and while he anticipated another routine adventure with Sfath, today was different.

Sfath, his mentor and guide through time, had arrived with an unexpected companion.

Approaching them was a tall, strikingly handsome man who radiated quiet confidence. Sfath's eyes sparkled with a mix of pride and excitement.

"Eduard," Sfath began, "this is Gabriel, my nephew."

Eduard's interest was sparked.

He felt an odd sense of familiarity but couldn't quite place it.

"Why does he seem so familiar?" Eduard wondered to himself.

Gabriel extended his hand, his smile warm and inviting.

"It's a pleasure to meet you, Eduard, even though I belong to a time long before yours."

Sfath's demeanor grew serious.

"Gabriel is the biological father of Jmmanuel.

The high council decided it was crucial for Jmmanuel's development to be closely connected to his biological father, to help him harness his consciousness power more effectively."

Eduard's interest deepened.

"And what's the occasion for today?"

Sfath's gaze was steady.

"Today, on your birthday, we're traveling to 32 BC to witness the birth of Jmmanuel, who was also born on February 3rd."

Eduard's eyes widened in amazement.

"Witnessing Jmmanuel's birth? That's incredible."

Sfath nodded.

"Yes, it's a pivotal moment.

But first, we need to reach free space before we can set the time jump."

Inside the spacecraft, the hum of the engines provided a reassuring backdrop.

Eduard took his seat, glancing at Gabriel, who sat calmly beside him.

Sfath moved with practiced ease, checking the controls and preparing for their journey.

The spacecraft slowly ascended, piercing through the atmosphere.

The landscape below receded, turning into a patchwork of clouds and distant landmasses.

The hum of the engines grew louder as they climbed higher.

Eduard watched as the curvature of Earth became more pronounced.

"It's always amazing to see Earth from this perspective," he remarked.

Gabriel nodded.

"It's a reminder of how small we are in the grand scheme of time."

As the spacecraft broke free of Earth's atmosphere, the stars emerged in their full, brilliant glory.

The spacecraft glided smoothly into the void of space.

Sfath adjusted the controls, setting the coordinates for 32 BC.

Eduard felt a rush of anticipation.

"Are we ready?"

Sfath's eyes were focused.

"Almost.

I need to fine-tune the time jump parameters to ensure we arrive precisely at the right moment."

The spacecraft shuddered as Sfath initiated the time jump sequence.

Eduard glanced at Gabriel, who maintained his composed demeanor, and then at the flickering control panel.

The craft vibrated gently as the familiar sensation of temporal displacement enveloped them.

Outside, the stars became streaks of light as the spacecraft traveled through the fabric of time.

The transition was swift, a burst of color and light, and then, as suddenly as it had begun, they arrived at their destination.

The landscape of 32 BC unfolded before them, a rugged terrain with rolling hills and olive groves.

The crisp morning air carried the scent of earth and the faint chill of winter.

Bethlehem, a modest village of stone houses, bustled with activity.

Villagers in simple tunics and robes went about their daily lives.

Eduard marveled at the scene.

"We're really here, witnessing a moment from history."

As they approached a modest dwelling, Gabriel spoke up.

"Mary and Joseph should be inside.

We must be discreet."

Sfath nodded in agreement.

"Gabriel will guide us.

His connection to this moment is important."

Gabriel led them to a small house where Mary lay on a straw-filled mattress, her face etched with both pain and determination.

Joseph stood beside her, his gaze a mix of excitement and worry.

Mary's labor progressed, and soon she gave birth to twins.

Eduard's eyes widened in surprise.

The Bible mentioned only Jmmanuel, but here were two babies, Jmmanuel and his twin, Jacob.

Sfath noticed Eduard's shock and explained, "That's why we wanted you to see this for yourself.

Future accounts will obscure the truth, even changing Jmmanuel's name to Jesus Christ, Son of God."

Eduard felt a pang of dismay.

"That's terrible.

The truth is being obscured."

After Mary gave birth, she and Joseph carefully wrapped the twins in cloths and placed them in a wooden manger, the only available space due to the lack of guest rooms.

In the corner of the room, a young girl with a bright, curious face watched with wide, excited eyes.

Eduard noticed her and turned to Sfath.

"Who is she?" Eduard asked.

Sfath's expression softened.

"Her name is Mary Magdalene.

She's Joseph's daughter from a previous marriage.

Her mother died giving birth to her.

Mary Magdalene has been eagerly anticipating the arrival of new siblings.

It's a special moment for her."

Mary Magdalene's face was alight with joy.

"Two brothers! I can't believe it!

I'm so happy!"

Eduard smiled at her enthusiasm.

"It must be a big change for her."

Outside, shepherds huddled around a fire, their figures silhouetted against the dark sky.

They kept watch over their flocks, their minds focused on their daily tasks.

Suddenly, a figure descended from the sky, a man in radiant attire who seemed to appear out of nowhere.

Gabriel had stepped outside, his presence commanding immediate attention.

The shepherds recoiled in fear, their eyes wide with astonishment.

Gabriel's voice was soothing and authoritative.

"Do not be afraid.

I bring you good news of great joy.

Today, in the city of David, the messiah has been born to you.

This will be a sign to you: you will find a baby wrapped in cloths and lying in a manger."

The shepherds exchanged bewildered glances, their fear turning into awe.

Gabriel's presence was both surreal and comforting, and they realized they were witnessing something extraordinary.

As dawn approached, the tranquility was disrupted by the arrival of five wise men.

Their approach was marked by the soft hum of the spacecraft's engines, now visible due to its lack of shielding.

The wise men, dressed in luxurious robes of rich colors and intricate patterns, followed the craft with a blend of curiosity and reverence.

They had tracked the spacecraft's journey through the stars, guided by their deep knowledge of celestial phenomena.

Disembarking with grace, the wise men approached the manger with reverence.

They presented their gifts, gold, frankincense, and myrrh, to the newborns and their weary parents.

Eduard, observing from a respectful distance, felt a profound sense of amazement.

The sight of this pivotal moment, etched into the annals of history, was both humbling and enlightening.

As the spacecraft prepared for departure, the first light of morning bathed the landscape in a golden glow.

The villagers continued their routines, unaware of the extraordinary events that had unfolded.

Sfath turned to Eduard and Gabriel.

"This moment will resonate through the ages.

Jmmanuel's presence here will shape countless lives."

Eduard nodded, his heart full of reflection.

"It's a birthday I'll never forget.

Thank you for letting me be part of this."

Gabriel smiled.

"Witnessing history is a gift we carry with us always."

With one last glance at the serene landscape of Bethlehem and the joyful presence of Mary Magdalene, the spacecraft lifted off, leaving behind the echoes of a momentous birth and the promise of a new era.

CHAPTER 17

Trouble in school

Sfath, with a calm demeanor and piercing eyes, explained that time was not merely a linear progression but a complex, flexible dimension.

The idea of traveling through different temporal layers fascinated Eduard, opening his mind to possibilities he had never imagined.

Eduard's initial journey into the past with Sfath was both exhilarating and disorienting.

Stepping into a bygone era, Eduard felt as though he was living within a vivid dream.

The sights, sounds, and smells of the past enveloped him, creating an immersive experience that was both surreal and enchanting.

Days stretched into weeks and months as Eduard and Sfath navigated this historical landscape.

Eduard marveled at how time seemed to flow differently.

While he lived through an extended period in the past, the present dimension experienced only a fleeting moment of elapsed time.

This paradox between subjective and objective time became a central theme of his travels.

Eduard's prolonged sojourns into the past began to take a toll on him.

In spite of the fact that only a few minutes passed in the present dimension, Eduard experienced the passage of years, aging accordingly.

Each return to the present brought a stark contrast between his own altered appearance and the unchanged world around him.

The dual nature of his existence, living through significant periods in the past while returning to a seemingly unchanged present, was both fascinating and perplexing.

Eduard grappled with the complexities of his aging process and the implications of his temporal excursions.

Eduard's time travels began to affect his daily life, particularly during his school years.

His frequent, unexplained absences did not go unnoticed by his teacher, Karl Graf. Graf, a perceptive and inquisitive educator, grew increasingly concerned about Eduard's behavior.

One afternoon, as Eduard returned from yet another brief absence, Graf's sharp gaze followed him.

The classroom, usually filled with the hum of academic activity, fell into an uneasy silence.

Graf, a man in his mid-fifties with a meticulous demeanor, approached Eduard with a concerned expression.

"Eduard," Graf said, his voice gentle but firm, "you've been away from class quite often lately.

Is everything alright?"

Eduard, caught off guard, struggled to find a suitable response.

"Yes, sir. I've just been feeling unwell.

I needed to use the restroom more frequently."

Graf scrutinized Eduard's face, noting the tension in his posture.

"This isn't like you.

If there's something troubling you, you can talk to me.

I've noticed that these absences are not just occasional but becoming a pattern."

Eduard forced a weak smile, trying to maintain his composure.

"I appreciate your concern, Mr. Graf. It's nothing serious, really.

Just a minor inconvenience."

Graf nodded, though his concern did not entirely dissipate.

"Alright, Eduard. But if you need anything, or if there's something you'd like to share, remember that I'm here to help."

Eduard returned to his seat, feeling a pang of guilt.

He had crafted this explanation to shield the truth of his temporal adventures, but the strain of maintaining the facade weighed heavily on him.

As Eduard continued his journeys, he found solace in moments of reflection.

Sitting by a serene river, he contemplated the nature of his experiences.

The flow of water seemed to mirror the passage of time, creating a calming backdrop to his thoughts.

Eduard began to appreciate the nuances of his temporal travels.

Despite living through extended periods in the past, the present dimension remained largely unchanged.

This paradox, aging in one dimension while time in the present remained static, became a source of profound insight for Eduard.

Eduard's adventures with Sfath revealed the intricate nature of time and existence.

Each journey offered a new perspective, allowing Eduard to experience different eras and moments in history. The richness of these experiences shaped his understanding of the universe.

Eduard's reflections on time travel were not just intellectual exercises but deeply personal revelations.

He learned to embrace the duality of his existence, recognizing that his experiences in the past were as real and meaningful as those in the present.

Time, with all its mysteries, remains an ever-elusive frontier, waiting to be explored by those with the courage to seek its secrets.

CHAPTER 18

The Great Flood

Sfath adjusted the controls of their sleek spacecraft, its metallic surface gleaming in the low light of the cockpit.

The familiar hum filled the air, a reassuring sound that heralded their imminent journey through time.

Eduard, eyes wide with anticipation, leaned forward in his seat, absorbing every detail.

His excitement was palpable, an energy that electrified the cramped space.

"Today," Sfath began, breaking the momentary silence, "we're traveling back 100,000 years to the time of the great flood.

We'll visit an old friend of mine, Noahkadnosser, a true man of peace.

We'll also meet my ancestor, Zebalon, who maintained contact with him."

Eduard's enthusiasm was infectious.

"I can't wait! Every trip teaches me something new.

It's amazing how different things are from what we've been taught."

Sfath smiled knowingly.

"Remember, much of history is misrepresented.

Today, you'll witness the truth firsthand."

With deft adjustments, he activated the time jump sequence.

The craft hummed louder, vibrations intensifying as the surrounding environment began to ripple and blur.

"Hold on tight," he instructed.

In a flash of blinding light, the familiar sounds faded into silence.

Moments later, they landed softly, the transition seamless.

As the craft door opened, a warm breeze enveloped them, rich with the scents of blooming flowers and fresh earth.

Eduard stepped out, his senses ignited by the vibrant landscape.

The air was clean and invigorating, the sky a brilliant blue dotted with fluffy clouds.

People moved gracefully in flowing tunics made of natural fibers, their laughter harmonizing with nature's sounds.

"Look at them!" Eduard exclaimed, pointing excitedly.

"They seem so connected to the earth."

"Let's find Zebalon," Sfath replied, leading the way through the village.

Eduard marveled at the beauty of the surroundings: towering trees, flowers in a riot of colors, and the distant sound of cascading water.

The villagers greeted them with warm smiles, their eyes bright with curiosity.

They soon arrived at a clearing where a stunning spacecraft rested among the trees.

A tall figure emerged, radiating calm.

Zebalon, an extraterrestrial from the Plejaran race, stood before them, his skin shimmering under the sun.

"Ah, Sfath! It's been too long," Zebalon said, his voice melodic.

He turned to Eduard with a warm smile.

"And you must be Eduard! It's an honor to meet you across time."

Eduard, awestruck, stammered, "Thank you! This is incredible."

Zebalon nodded, his expression serious yet kind.

"Our histories are intertwined, though often misinterpreted.

I've guided your ancestor, Noahkadnosser, through some of humanity's greatest challenges."

Before Eduard could respond, a shadow loomed overhead.

They turned to see a towering figure approaching, Noahkadnosser, the builder of the ark, stood before them, a giant at 16 feet tall, his long hair cascading down his back.

"Greetings, my friends," he boomed, his deep voice resonating through the clearing.

"I sense a great purpose in your visit."

Eduard gazed up in awe. "You're... enormous!"

Noahkadnosser chuckled, the sound rich and full.

"I have always been larger than most. It is both a blessing and a burden."

Sfath stepped forward, pride evident in his voice.

"Noahkadnosser, this is Eduard, a friend from a distant time.

He has traveled here to learn your story."

The giant's expression softened.

"Ah, the tales of the flood have been warped through the ages.

I am glad to share my truth."

Noahkadnosser gestured for them to sit beneath the shade of a great tree, its leaves whispering in the breeze.

"I was warned of the coming flood by Zebalon.

He spoke of a comet that would bring destruction and advised me to build an ark to preserve life."

Eduard leaned forward, intrigued.

"So it wasn't just a myth?

You truly built an ark?"

"Yes," Noahkadnosser replied, nodding solemnly.

"With my family and Zebalon's guidance, we gathered animals and supplies to survive.

It was a monumental task, but we persevered."

Sfath interjected, "The stories you hear in the future often omit the truth.

Over time, your name was simplified to Noah, and the true nature of the events became obscured."

Zebalon added, "And I became mythologized, seen as a god rather than a guide."

As the sun began to set, painting the sky with oranges and purples, Eduard felt a deep connection to the figures before him.

"What can we learn from your story?" he asked earnestly.

Noahkadnosser considered this, his expression thoughtful.

"The importance of unity and preparation.

When faced with challenges, it's vital to come together for the common good.

Many lives were saved through our cooperation."

Zebalon nodded in agreement.

"Understanding the truth behind history is crucial.

Events are often recorded through biased lenses, and future generations must seek the reality."

Eduard's mind raced with implications.

"So, our understanding of our past shapes our future?"

"Exactly," Sfath affirmed.

"Knowledge is power.

Use it wisely."

As night fell, stars twinkled overhead, filling the sky with light.

Eduard felt a pang of sadness, knowing their visit was nearing its end.

The beauty of this place and the wisdom shared by Noahkadnosser and Zebalon would remain with him forever.

Noahkadnosser rose, towering over them.

"Remember: peace comes from understanding and compassion.

Share our story, and may it inspire others."

Zebalon placed a hand on Eduard's shoulder.

"You have the chance to reshape history in your time.

Take this lesson to heart."

With a final farewell, Eduard and Sfath returned to their timecraft.

As they prepared for the jump back, Eduard looked back at the extraordinary figures who had reshaped his understanding of history.

"Thank you for everything," he called out.

The giant waved, and Zebalon smiled, their connection forged across time

As they activated the time jump, Eduard sat in thought, reflecting on the profound lessons learned.

The flood, the ark, and the truths of Noahkadnosser and Zebalon would stay with him.

"Every trip reshapes my perspective," Eduard mused.

"I can't wait to share what I've learned."

Sfath smiled, knowing that each journey was a step toward enlightenment, not just for Eduard but for all humanity.

As the craft hummed to life, they soared through time once more, ready to uncover more hidden truths woven into the tapestry of history.

The familiar sights of their own time greeted them as the spacecraft settled softly in the same spot they had just left only a minute prior despite having lived ten days in the past.

Eduard stepped out, his mind still buzzing with thoughts of their recent adventure.

"Thanks again, Sfath.

These were the best ten days ever," he said, beaming.

With that, they waved goodbye to each other, a bond forged through shared experiences and newfound knowledge.

CHAPTER 19

The Wisdom of Pythagoras

The pear-shaped beamship hovered silently over the Mediterranean coast, its silver-metallic surface reflecting the pale moonlight.

Inside, Eduard stood beside Sfath, both observing the landscape below.

The year was approximately 530 BCE, and they had traveled back in time to meet a man whose teachings would echo through millennia, Pythagoras of Samos.

As they materialized on the outskirts of Croton, they found the philosopher standing near a sacred grove, deep in thought.

He turned as if expecting them.

"You have come," Pythagoras said, his voice calm yet firm. "Time flows in cycles, and wisdom is but a reflection of the universal swinging waves."

Eduard exchanged a glance with Sfath. "We have come to speak of the future, Pythagoras. Of the consequences of belief and thought-energetic vibrations."

Pythagoras nodded knowingly. "Indeed. The universe and all that exists pulsate in swinging waves.

Thought itself is a force that does not simply dissipate but lingers, influencing all that it touches." He gestured toward the stars above. "Just as the harmony of the spheres dictates the balance of existence, so too does the human mind shape the world through its beliefs."

Sfath stepped forward. "In the future, this will increasingly affect the beliefs of Earth's inhabitants all over the world, depositing strong belief-energetic swinging waves that will become embedded in the Earth's atmosphere.

These waves will not only shape human thought but will also act as a destructive force against the effective truth."

Pythagoras sighed. "This I have foreseen.

The faith of men, rather than being a guiding light, will become an anchor dragging them into discord.

The stronger these thought-energetic vibrations become, the more they will manifest in material reality, war, suffering, division."

Eduard listened intently. "These religious beliefs will be deposited by the majority of believers across Earth, creating a malignant negation, hatred directed at those who believe differently.

This hatred, hidden beneath the surface, will hardly be perceived by the individual, yet it will drive entire civilizations to acts of mischief and destruction."

Pythagoras gazed into the distance, his expression unreadable. "I have warned my followers that numbers reveal the truth of the universe, not gods or idols.

Yet men crave certainty, and so they create illusions to comfort themselves.

But these illusions, once deeply embedded in the mind, will lead them to war and terror, harming even those who choose not to believe."

Sfath nodded. "It is the nature of these strong faith vibrations to accumulate, to deposit within the consciousness of humanity, creating an ongoing disaster, wars fought in the name of gods, persecution of those who see differently, and the suppression of truth itself."

Eduard felt a deep sadness settle within him. "Then what can be done? If these vibrations will continue to shape the world, how can humanity escape this cycle?"

Pythagoras placed a hand on Eduard's shoulder.

"Truth is not found in faith but in knowledge.

The path is long, but those who seek wisdom will always exist. The task is to preserve knowledge and to ensure that future generations question, seek, and think beyond the illusions imposed upon them."

Sfath looked at Eduard. "And this, my student, is why we journey through time, to witness, to understand, and to ensure that the echoes of truth do not fade."

The three stood in silence for a moment, the weight of time pressing upon them. The stars above continued their celestial dance, indifferent to the struggles of humankind, yet always whispering their silent truth to those who would listen.

CHAPTER 20

The Teachings of Sfath II

As Eduard entered his eighth year, his life became increasingly intertwined with the teachings of Sfath.

The old man from the stars had transformed from a distant, enigmatic figure into a close and influential mentor.

Their interactions were no longer limited to sporadic encounters but had grown into a regular part of his life.

Sfath's visits, both physical and telepathic, became the cornerstone of his education and personal development.

Each meeting with Sfath was an opportunity for him to delve deeper into the mysteries of the universe.

The lessons were not just about abstract concepts but were infused with practical wisdom and moral guidance.

Sfath's teachings were comprehensive, covering not only the physical laws of the cosmos but also the spiritual and ethical dimensions of existence.

Sfath began by introducing Billy to the fundamental laws of the universe.

These principles were not just scientific but encompassed a broader understanding of existence.

Eduard learned about the balance that underpins all things, the way that every action has an equal and opposite reaction, not only in the physical world but in the spiritual realm as well.

This concept of balance resonated deeply with him, who saw parallels in the natural world around him.

"Everything in the universe is interconnected," Sfath explained during one of their sessions in the forest.

"From the smallest atom to the largest galaxy, there is a thread that binds all things together. To understand this is to understand the essence of life itself."

Eduard absorbed these teachings with a mix of awe and curiosity.

The idea that every element of existence was part of a grand, interconnected web fascinated him.

It also helped him make sense of the natural world he loved so much, reinforcing his appreciation for the balance and harmony he saw in nature.

Sfath's teachings extended beyond the physical and into the realm of spirituality and morality.

Eduard learned about the importance of living in harmony with nature, of respecting all forms of life, and of acting with compassion and integrity.

These lessons were intertwined with the cosmic principles he was learning, emphasizing that true understanding required not just intellectual insight but also ethical behavior.

During a conversation about the moral implications of knowledge, Sfath said, "With knowledge comes responsibility.

The truths you are learning are powerful, but they must be used wisely. Compassion and empathy must guide your actions, for they are the true measures of wisdom."

Eduard took these words to heart. He began to view his growing knowledge not as a privilege but as a responsibility.

The weight of this responsibility was sometimes daunting, but it also gave him a sense of purpose and direction.

He knew that his mission was not just about discovering cosmic truths but about using that knowledge to benefit humanity.

The more he learned, the more he felt the weight of the knowledge he was acquiring.

Sfath did not shy away from discussing the challenges and dangers that lay ahead.

He spoke of the forces that would resist his mission, the skeptics and antagonists who would challenge his findings and the threats that could arise from those who did not wish for such truths to be revealed.

Despite these warnings, Sfath reassured him that he would not face these challenges alone.

"There are allies both on Earth and beyond who will support you," Sfath said.

"You will find strength in your convictions and in the knowledge that you are part of a larger cosmic plan."

These teachings about the potential dangers were a sobering reminder of the complexities and risks involved in his mission.

They underscored the importance of resilience and perseverance, qualities that the young Eduard was learning to cultivate with Sfath's guidance.

The emotional and psychological toll of such profound knowledge was significant.

Eduard grappled with feelings of isolation and the burden of responsibility.

The weight of the secrets he carried sometimes felt overwhelming, and the prospect of facing opposition was daunting.

Sfath's mentorship provided crucial support during these times.

He helped him develop coping strategies and maintain a sense of balance.

"When the weight of your knowledge feels too heavy, remember to seek solace in the simple joys of life," Sfath advised.

"Nature, friends, and moments of reflection will sustain you."

He found comfort in these words. He learned to manage his stress by engaging in activities that connected him to the world around him, walking in the forest, observing the stars, and spending time with his family.

These moments of connection helped ground him and reminded him of the larger context of his mission.

As the seasons changed and Eduard grew older, the teachings of Sfath became deeply ingrained in his character.

The wisdom he acquired was not just intellectual but had shaped his very soul.

He became more attuned to the rhythms of the universe and more capable of integrating the cosmic principles into his daily life.

His understanding of the universe evolved, and he began to see connections between seemingly disparate elements of his knowledge.

The cosmic laws, the moral imperatives, and the practical challenges of his mission were all interwoven, creating a comprehensive framework for understanding his place in the world.

With each passing year, Eduard felt more prepared for the mission that lay ahead.

The teachings of Sfath had equipped him with the tools he needed to navigate the complexities of his role.

He was no longer just a boy with a destiny but a young man who had been shaped by profound cosmic wisdom.

His preparation continued to focus on personal growth, intellectual development, and practical skills.

He worked diligently to apply Sfath's teachings in real-world situations, developing strategies for overcoming obstacles and understanding the nuances of his mission.

As he approached the end of his sixteenth year, he felt a deep sense of alignment with his purpose.

The teachings of Sfath had given him a clear vision of his destiny and the role he was to play in the cosmic scheme.

The journey ahead was still uncertain, but he was confident in his ability to fulfill his mission.

The stars above, once a distant and mysterious realm, now felt like a familiar and integral part of his life.

He looked up at the night sky with a sense of gratitude and anticipation.

He knew that the answers he sought and the challenges he would face were all part of a grand cosmic plan.

The lessons about cosmic laws, spiritual and moral principles, and the challenges ahead shaped Eduard into a figure of wisdom and purpose.

As he continued his journey, he embraced his role with a sense of responsibility and hope, prepared to fulfill the mission that lay ahead.

The teachings of Sfath had not only expanded his understanding of the universe but had also prepared him for the significant role he was destined to play in bridging humanity with the cosmos.

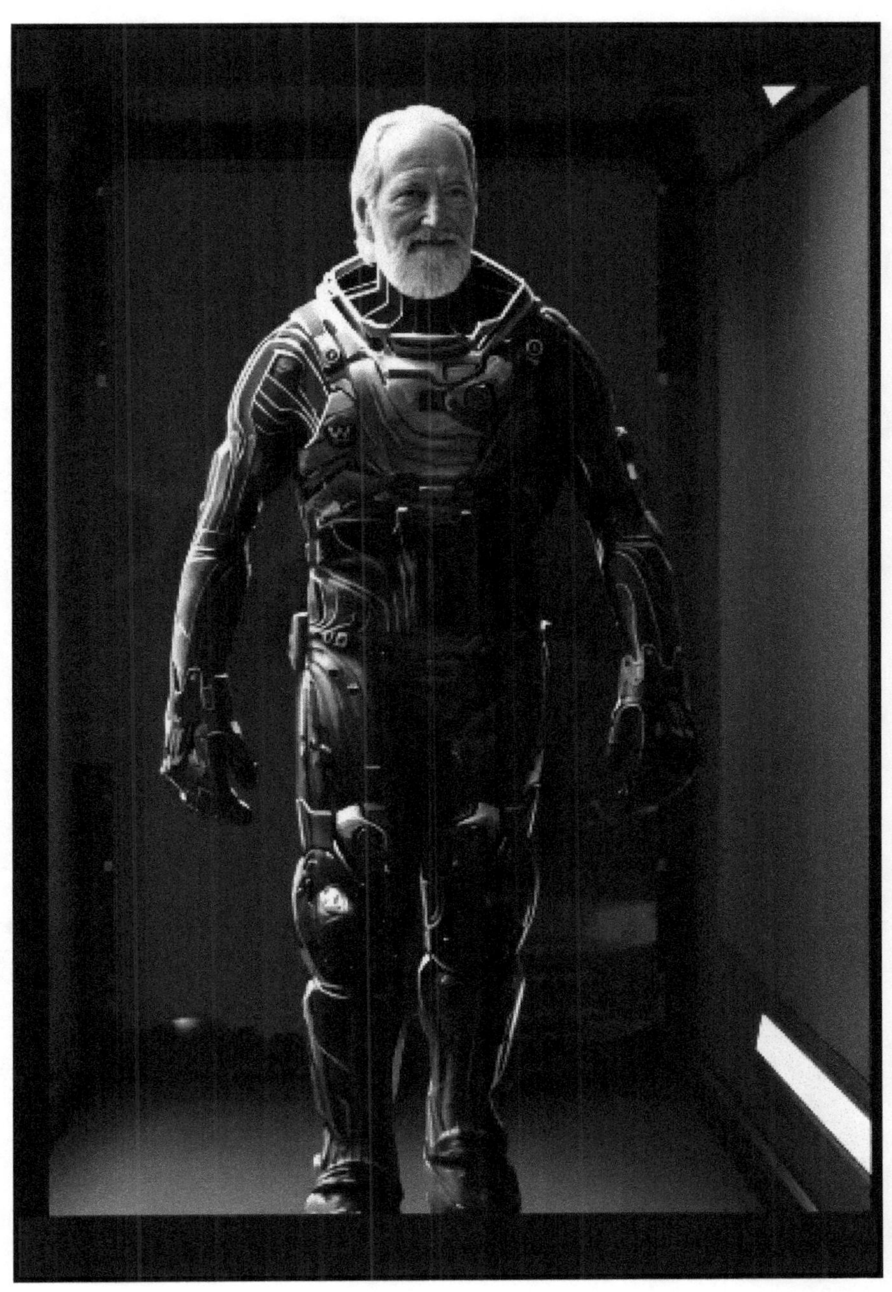

CHAPTER 21

The annals of Sfath

In the stillness of a dimly lit study, Ptaah, Sfath's son, sat surrounded by an array of ancient manuscripts.

The sun's rays filtered through a window, casting a warm glow over the dusty volumes.

His mission was clear: to unravel the story of his father, Sfath, and his enigmatic companion, Eduard.

The annals that lay before him were more than just records; they were a narrative of temporal voyages that stretched across eras.

Sfath had always been a figure cloaked in mystery.

His reticence about his past and his motives left much to the imagination.

Ptaah's fingers gently turned the pages, revealing the complexity of Sfath's character and the nature of his silence.

It was not merely a personal quirk but a fundamental aspect of his identity and his mission.

The annals painted a vivid picture of Sfath and Eduard's first steps into the realm of time travel.

Their initial ventures took them from the grandeur of Ancient Egypt to the distant reaches of future civilizations.

Each era they visited was described with rich detail, showcasing their subtle yet significant influence on historical events.

Their presence, though often understated, played a crucial role in shaping the course of history.

Sfath's choice to withhold certain details only added to the intrigue.

Ptaah's examination of these early adventures provided insights into the nature of their interactions and the breadth of their journey.

As Ptaah delved deeper, the annals revealed intricate chronicles of their adventures.

These records were more than mere historical accounts, they detailed how Sfath and Eduard impacted pivotal moments and influential figures throughout time.

The annals depicted their interventions, showing how their actions resonated across different periods.

Eduard's curiosity about Sfath's motives and the mysteries they encountered unfolded through these records.

Their travels were not isolated incidents but integral events that altered the course of history, highlighting the importance of their decisions and actions.

The annals illustrated the far-reaching consequences of Sfath and Eduard's actions.

Ptaah observed how even minor decisions had significant impacts on various timelines.

The records highlighted a complex web of cause and effect, demonstrating how their presence in different epochs created ripples that extended beyond their immediate experiences.

Sfath's discretion about the full scope of their influence became more understandable.

The intricate connections between their actions and historical outcomes emphasized the weight of their role and the profound implications of their temporal explorations.

Turning the pages, Ptaah encountered detailed descriptions of future worlds that Sfath and Eduard had explored.

These visions of the future were filled with advanced technologies and emerging societies.

The annals detailed how their influence continued to shape the trajectory of future developments.

The futuristic landscapes depicted both potential and challenges.

Sfath and Eduard's actions left a lasting imprint on the evolution of civilizations, providing a roadmap of their impact on the world yet to come.

This glimpse into the future underscored the ongoing significance of their temporal interventions.

Each entry in the annals prompted deep reflections on the nature of existence and the role of individual actions in shaping history.

Ptaah discovered how Sfath and Eduard's journeys were not just explorations but profound contributions to the grand narrative of time.

The records offered philosophical insights into their legacy.

Eduard's growing understanding of their responsibilities and the broader implications of their actions became apparent, highlighting the depth of their impact and the ethical considerations of their travels.

The annals revealed that every decision, no matter how seemingly insignificant, carried substantial weight.

Ptaah noted how each choice made by Sfath and Eduard influenced historical events and outcomes.

The records demonstrated the immense responsibility that came with their ability to traverse time.

This realization prompted a reevaluation of their approach.

Sfath and Eduard's actions were scrutinized for their ethical dimensions, recognizing that their influence extended beyond mere observation into active participation in shaping the future.

As Ptaah explored earlier sections of the annals, he encountered detailed accounts of past interactions between Sfath and Eduard.

These retrospectives provided valuable insights into the evolution of their relationship and the reasons behind Sfath's occasional secrecy.

The exploration of their past revealed the complexities of their partnership.

The revelations offered a new perspective on how their actions had intertwined with the broader narrative of history, shedding light on the motivations and decisions that shaped their journey.

The annals demonstrated how Sfath and Eduard's temporal travels had influenced the present.

Ptaah observed the intricate interplay between their past actions and contemporary events.

The records illustrated how their influence had shaped current realities, creating a complex web of connections across time.

The intersection of past, present, and future highlighted the enduring relevance of their actions.

Ptaah's understanding of their role deepened, revealing the intricate ways in which their adventures had left a lasting mark on the world.

In the quiet sanctum of his study, Ptaah discovered something extraordinary.

The leather-bound annals of his father, Sfath, were filled with chronicles that had remained hidden from many.

Among these revelations was a startling fact: Sfath had once taken Pastor Zimmermann back in time to meet Jmmanuel, known to many as Jesus Christ.

Eduard, who had long admired Sfath for his profound knowledge and otherworldly experiences, was unaware of this particular journey.

The discovery of this secret stirred a deep curiosity within Ptaah.

It was clear from the records that Pastor Zimmermann had been a devout Christian before his encounter with Sfath, but his faith had undergone a profound transformation.

Ptaah knew from family lore that Eduard had been well-versed in religious studies during his school years, earning high marks for his extensive knowledge.

Despite his academic prowess, Eduard had never truly embraced religious belief.

The same could not be said for Pastor Zimmermann.

Before Sfath's intervention, Zimmermann had been a fervent believer, a pillar of the Christian faith.

His journey to meet Jmmanuel would change that faith in ways neither he nor Eduard could have anticipated.

In a secluded meeting room, the weight of history was about to unfold.

Sfath, with his characteristic calm demeanor, addressed Pastor Zimmermann.

The two men sat across from each other, the air thick with anticipation.

"Pastor Zimmermann," Sfath began, "your journey today will take you to a time and place that will challenge everything you know."

Zimmermann, his face etched with a mixture of reverence and anxiety, nodded.

"I am ready.

If my faith is to be tested, let it be so."

Sfath's eyes twinkled with an enigmatic blend of knowledge and compassion.

"We will visit Jmmanuel.

His teachings have been distorted over the centuries, and you will see the truth of his message."

In a swift movement, Sfath activated the time-travel apparatus.

The surroundings shifted and blurred, the world twisting into a new reality.

Within moments, they found themselves in a different era, the air imbued with the scent of ancient dust and the sounds of distant voices.

Jmmanuel appeared before them, his presence commanding yet serene.

His robes, simple yet elegant, and his eyes, filled with profound wisdom, spoke of a truth that transcended time.

Zimmermann and Sfath approached Jmmanuel, who greeted them with a gentle smile.

Despite the temporal chasm, Jmmanuel's voice resonated with timeless authority.

"Welcome," Jmmanuel said, his voice soothing yet powerful.

"I understand you seek the truth."

Zimmermann, feeling the weight of his former beliefs crumbling, spoke with a trembling voice.

"I have been a servant of faith for many years, yet my understanding of that faith is now shaken.

I wish to learn the truth as you teach it."

Jmmanuel's gaze was compassionate.

"Truth is not confined to dogma or tradition.

It is found in the essence of love, compassion, and understanding.

The teachings that have been passed down have been obscured by human interpretations and misunderstandings."

As the conversation unfolded, Zimmermann felt his previous convictions dissolve.

The revelations he received were starkly different from the teachings he had imparted to his congregation.

The realization was both liberating and devastating.

When Sfath and Zimmermann returned to their own time, the change in the pastor was palpable.

No longer bound by his previous beliefs, Zimmermann faced a crisis of identity.

His role as a pastor was now a complex paradox.

He continued his ministry but did so with a new purpose: to teach the true essence of humanity and the teachings of Jmmanuel, stripped of the layers of dogma that had previously obscured them.

Zimmermann's transformation was evident in his sermons.

His congregation noticed a shift from rigid doctrine to a more compassionate and inclusive approach.

Although he no longer believed in the literal interpretations of scripture, he sought to guide his parishioners towards a broader understanding of spiritual truths.

Eduard, upon learning about Ptaah's discoveries, was stunned.

The realization that Sfath had not only taken Zimmermann back in time but had kept this journey a secret from him was disconcerting.

The knowledge that Pastor Zimmermann had experienced such a profound shift in belief, and that Eduard had been kept in the dark about it, was both shocking and unsettling.

Sfath had never mentioned these journeys to Eduard, nor had Zimmermann.

The silence surrounding these events was intentional, meant to protect the sanctity of the experiences and the individuals involved.

Sfath had instructed Eduard to keep quiet about his own time travels, which might explain why he had not spoken of them either.

Eduard's sense of betrayal was tempered by his respect for Sfath.

He understood that the nature of these journeys was complex and perhaps beyond his comprehension.

The secrecy surrounding them was a reflection of the delicate balance between preserving the truth and the potential consequences of its revelation.

As Eduard pondered the implications of Ptaah's discoveries, he reflected on the nature of belief and knowledge.

The revelations about Pastor Zimmermann and his encounter with Jmmanuel illuminated a broader understanding of faith and its evolution.

Eduard's respect for Sfath grew, not just for his knowledge and experiences but for the wisdom in handling such sensitive matters.

The experience of Zimmermann, who had transitioned from a devout believer to a seeker of deeper truths, highlighted the transformative power of direct knowledge.

The hidden truths of Sfath's journeys and the transformation of Pastor Zimmermann became a testament to the complex interplay between belief, knowledge, and personal growth.

For Eduard, the experience was a profound lesson in understanding the nuances of faith and the importance of seeking truth beyond established doctrines.

The legacy of Pastor Zimmermann's journey with Sfath was not merely about changing an individual's beliefs but about illuminating the path for others to seek and understand deeper truths.

The secrecy and the transformations underscored the delicate nature of such revelations and the responsibility of those who hold them.

Eduard, now more aware of the intricate web of time, faith, and knowledge, embraced his role with a renewed sense of purpose.

The experience of Pastor Zimmermann and the hidden chronicles of Sfath had provided him with invaluable insights into the nature of belief and the pursuit of truth.

As the pages of history continued to turn, the lessons from these hidden journeys served as a guiding light for future seekers, reminding them that the quest for truth was both a personal and collective endeavor, one that required courage, wisdom, and an open heart.

As Ptaah reached the final pages of the annals, the full scope of Sfath and Eduard's legacy became evident.

The comprehensive records underscored the significance of their influence across time, showcasing the profound impact of their temporal explorations.

Embracing this legacy required acknowledging the profound implications of their journey.

The annals served as both a testament to their shared experiences and a reminder of the enduring mark they had made on history.

Ptaah's task was complete, yet the echoes of Sfath and Eduard's journey continued to resonate, a lasting legacy of their extraordinary adventures through time.

CHAPTER 22

The Secrets of Saint Germain

Eduard's excitement crackled in the air as he stood in the control room of their spacecraft, his eyes wide with anticipation.

The soft hum of the ship filled the space, punctuated by the glow of the control panel's lights.

"Today, we're going to uncover who the famous Saint Germain really was!" he exclaimed, barely able to contain himself.

His mentor, Sfath, smiled knowingly, fingers poised over the glowing interface.

"Remember, Eduard," Sfath cautioned, his voice calm yet firm, "our purpose is observation only.

We are not going to engage with anyone.

"With a quick adjustment of the dials, a soft blue light enveloped them, and Eduard felt the usual peculiar sensation, as if he had momentarily ceased to exist.

Then, just as quickly, the world around him solidified, and they found themselves hovering over France in 1745.

The spacecraft floated discreetly above a lavish estate, providing a bird's-eye view of a grand gathering below.

Eduard gazed in wonder at the scene unfolding beneath them.

Elegant chateaus adorned with intricate carvings gleamed in the sunlight, while vibrant gardens burst with color, their fragrant blooms perfuming the air.

Nobles in extravagant garments of silk and lace mingled in animated conversation, laughter echoing against the ornate stone walls.

The sound of music wafted through the air, punctuated by the distant clatter of horse-drawn carriages rolling along cobblestone paths.

"Look at this place!" Eduard whispered, his heart racing with excitement.

"It's like stepping into a painting."

"Indeed," Sfath replied, his gaze fixed on the gathering below.

"But remember, beneath the elegance lies intrigue and deception."

Their attention shifted to a striking figure at the center of the gathering, Count Saint Germain.

Dressed impeccably in a tailored coat that seemed to shimmer in the light, with dark hair cascading elegantly, he captivated the crowd with his charm and charisma.

Eduard watched in amazement as the Count engaged with guests, his voice smooth and persuasive, laced with an almost hypnotic quality.

"That must be him," Eduard breathed, feeling a mix of admiration and skepticism.

"What makes him so compelling?"

Sfath began to explain, his voice steady and measured.

"Saint Germain, or Rakoczi as he was born, is a man shrouded in mystery.

He has many aliases and legends surrounding his origins.

He was born in 1711 and has a Portuguese heritage, yet he presents himself as someone who has lived for centuries."

"Can a human on Earth truly live that long in this era?"

Eduard questioned, intrigue sparking in his eyes.

"It's a tale spun from his cunning," Sfath replied, a hint of skepticism in his tone.

"He is a master deceiver, skilled in the art of illusion and manipulation."

The scene unfolded like a theatrical performance.

Saint Germain performed seemingly magical feats that mesmerized the crowd.

With a flick of his wrist, he hypnotized a nobleman, making coins vanish and reappear in the hands of astonished onlookers.

The crowd gasped, caught in the spell of the spectacle.

"Did you see that?" Eduard exclaimed, wide-eyed.

"How does he do it?"

"Through sleight of hand and psychological manipulation," Sfath explained.

"He exploits human desires and fears, weaving them into his fabrications.

He has been named a wonder man, yet no one suspects he is the worst deceiver of his time."

As the evening progressed, the atmosphere grew thick with unspoken tension.

Sfath shared deeper secrets about Saint Germain.

"He is entwined with a European Christian sect that seeks power over Europe.

His charm serves as a tool to infiltrate the courts of counts, princes, and kings, making them amenable to their plans for world domination."

Eduard listened intently, the gravity of Saint Germain's actions dawning on him.

"So he's not just a performer, he's a player in a much larger game?"

"Precisely," Sfath affirmed, his gaze sharp.

"He primarily focuses on the high society of France, aiming to annex it under the sect's influence, ensuring their control spreads across the continent."

Eduard watched, captivated, as Saint Germain moved gracefully among the nobles, engaging in whispered conversations with powerful women.

His words flowed like honey, each syllable designed to extract secrets while weaving an invisible thread of trust.

It was a delicate dance of seduction and persuasion.

"Look how he navigates their emotions," Sfath pointed out, his tone laden with disapproval.

"He uses their vulnerabilities to gain trust, each interaction a calculated maneuver."

As the Count interacted with his audience, Eduard felt a shiver of realization.

"He portrays himself as an immortal, yet he doesn't even belong to the sect?"

"Correct," Sfath affirmed.

"He expands the legends around him to gain fame and influence, even receiving the honorary title of 'Immortal' from King Frederick the Great himself."

The atmosphere grew tense as Eduard absorbed the implications.

"Frederick believes that Saint Germain is over 2000 years old, an idea implanted through hypnosis," Sfath explained.

"In truth, the 'elixir of immortality' he claims to possess is nothing more than a concoction of hallucinogenic substances designed to create an illusion of vitality."

"Fascinating," Eduard murmured, contemplating the layers of deceit.

"And he uses these secrets to terrify and control?"

"Indeed," Sfath replied, his voice heavy with the weight of knowledge.

"He weaves intimate knowledge of royal families into his performances, creating an aura of supernatural power that leaves his audience in awe and fear."

As the sun dipped low in the sky, casting long shadows across the estate, Eduard pondered the implications of Saint Germain's duplicity.

"It's astonishing how one man can wield so much influence through deception," he mused.

"He creates an illusion of omniscience," Sfath noted, his gaze still fixed on the Count.

"His phenomenal memory terrifies others into believing he is all-knowing, a master of secrets."

Eduard's admiration for Saint Germain wavered, replaced by a growing sense of unease.

"What happens when the truth is revealed?"

The Count continued to perform, claiming he could turn invisible.

Eduard watched as people gasped, their faces a mixture of amazement and fear.

"How does he do that?" Eduard wondered aloud.

"It's all an illusion," Sfath replied, his tone resolute.

"He employs hypnotic techniques to create the perception of invisibility.

Many believe he has traveled to far-off lands like China, yet he never leaves Europe."

Eduard's mind raced as he absorbed the layers of Saint Germain's life.

"He even manipulates women for secrets, doesn't he?"

"Indeed," Sfath confirmed.

"He uses wealth and charm, securing the trust of servants and nobles alike.

His hypnosis enables him to extract their most intimate secrets, which he later reveals, further enhancing his mystique and power."

As the evening waned, Eduard took in the grandeur of the estate and the intricate web of lies that surrounded them.

The nobles, dressed in their finery, danced and laughed, oblivious to the truth lurking beneath the surface.

"Look at them," Eduard said, a note of sadness creeping into his voice.

"They believe they are in the presence of a master, yet they are merely pawns in his game."

"That is the tragic irony," Sfath replied.

"Saint Germain exploits their trust, crafting a facade of magic while manipulating their lives.

It is a portrait of deception painted with the brush of human desire."

As the night settled deeper, the air thick with mystery, Sfath prepared to initiate the time jump back to their own era.

Eduard took one last look at the vibrant world of 1745 France, the grandeur and intrigue mingling in his mind.

"What will you take from this experience?" Sfath asked, his eyes reflecting the stars above.

"I've learned that history is not merely facts but a tapestry woven from human desires and deception," Eduard replied, a newfound wisdom dawning upon him.

"Saint Germain's story is a reminder of the fragility of trust and the power of illusion."

With a final surge of light, they vanished from the past, leaving the echoes of Saint Germain's world behind, but carrying its secrets into the future.

The lessons learned would forever shape Eduard's understanding of humanity's intricate dance between truth and deception.

Elia

Chapter 23

Arrival in Ancient Kashmir

The spacecraft shimmered into existence against the backdrop of a serene mountain range.

The ancient landscape of Kashmir stretched out below, a breathtaking tableau of lush green valleys and snow-capped peaks.

The air was crisp, and the scent of pine mingled with the earthy aroma of the river that wound through the valley.

Sfath and Eduard stepped out of the craft, their attire seamlessly blending with the local clothing.

The tranquility of the setting was palpable, and they both took a moment to acclimate to the peace of this ancient time.

Their mission was clear: to locate Prophet Elia and learn from him before the teachings of the Creation Energy were brought to the future.

As they made their way toward a nearby village, they encountered a young boy, no older than ten, playing by the riverbank.

His clothes were simple, but his eyes held a keen intelligence.

The boy's gaze shifted to the two strangers with curiosity.

"Hello," Eduard greeted with a friendly smile.

"Can you help us find a man named Elia?

We've traveled a long way to seek his wisdom."

The boy studied them for a moment, then nodded eagerly.

"I know where he is! Follow me."

He gestured for them to follow and set off down a narrow path that led along a river.

The boy led Eduard and Sfath through a series of winding paths and small clearing areas.

The journey was punctuated by the sounds of nature, the rustling of leaves, the babbling of the river, and the occasional call of a distant bird.

They reached a secluded spot where the river widened into a tranquil pool, its surface reflecting the surrounding greenery.

Seated by the riverbank, beneath the shade of a large, ancient tree, was Prophet Elia.

His presence was serene, almost otherworldly.

Elia was deep in meditation, his posture relaxed yet filled with a quiet strength.

The boy approached and spoke softly, "Teacher, these travelers have come to seek your wisdom."

Elia opened his eyes slowly, their deep, knowing gaze settling on Eduard and Sfath.

He rose gracefully and extended a hand in greeting.

"Welcome.

I am Elia.

"I have been expecting you.

The prophecies have foretold of your arrival."

Sfath nodded, "We are here to understand the role that Eduard will play in the future.

We need to grasp the essence of these teachings."

Elia's gaze softened as he looked at Eduard.

"The teachings are profound and carry the weight of great responsibility.

They are meant to guide humanity towards enlightenment, aligning them with the cosmic truths."

Eduard listened intently, absorbing every word.

"What exactly will be my role, and how should I prepare?"

Elia's voice was steady and full of depth.

"When the time comes, you will proclaim ancient words that will become a beacon of truth.

Your site will be a gathering place for those seeking enlightenment from all corners of the earth.

You will break the seals of many secrets, revealing deep insights into Creation and the human mind."

Elia continued, explaining the nature of the teachings that Eduard would carry into the future.

"Your teachings will challenge the falsehoods and illuminate the paths to true understanding.

They will be a source of both comfort and awakening, reaching into the hearts and minds of people across the ages."

Eduard's eyes were filled with determination.

"How will I be recognized, and what will be expected of me?"

Elia replied, "You will be the new herald, the founder of a group dedicated to the pursuit of truth.

Your words will resonate across time, touching the lives of many and guiding them toward greater wisdom.

You must immerse yourself in study and contemplation, exploring the depths of knowledge and the essence of creation."

Elia described the path that lay ahead for Eduard in vivid detail.

"Your journey will be marked by challenges and discoveries.

You will travel far, exploring the intersections of the firmaments and the earth.

Your teachings will be both a source of guidance and a catalyst for change."

Eduard felt the gravity of his mission.

"What should I focus on to fulfill this prophecy?"

Elia's response was profound.

"You must build a sanctuary, a place of peace and learning where truth and harmony converge. This site will become a center for the gathering of wisdom and knowledge, a beacon for those seeking enlightenment."

As the conversation continued, Eduard and Sfath absorbed Elia's wisdom.

The prophet's words were both a guide and a challenge, setting the stage for Eduard's future role.

Elia spoke of the importance of contemplation and study, urging Eduard to explore the secrets of the world and to build a place where truth could flourish.

Elia's final words were a call to action.

"Your legacy will be one of profound impact.

You will continue a lineage of great proclaimers and bring the teachings of creation to those who seek it.

Embrace this role with dedication and humility."

With their meeting complete, Eduard and Sfath prepared to leave.

They thanked Elia for his guidance and wisdom, feeling a deep sense of purpose as they bid him farewell.

The boy who had led them watched with a sense of pride, knowing he had played a small but significant role in their journey.

The spacecraft lifted off from the tranquil riverbank, ascending into the sky.

As they traveled back to their own time, Eduard and Sfath reflected on the encounter.

The teachings of Prophet Elia and the prophecy that awaited Eduard were now clear.

Eduard looked at Sfath, a mix of resolve and contemplation in his eyes.

"We have a significant mission ahead of us."

Sfath nodded.

"Indeed.

The wisdom we've gained will guide us as we prepare to bring these teachings to the future."

As the spacecraft navigated through the temporal stream, Eduard felt a profound connection to his destiny.

The journey to meet Prophet Elia had clarified his role and the impact he was destined to make.

The teachings of Creation Energy would shape the future, and Eduard was ready to fulfill his part in this grand narrative.

Chapter 24

Henock

The air crackled with the scent of ancient earth as Sfath and Eduard stepped out of the shimmering portal onto a vast, sun-drenched hill.

The landscape stretched endlessly before them, a tapestry of rolling green meadows and distant, jagged mountains.

was an ancient world, untouched by the hands of modernity.

The sky, a brilliant azure, seemed to echo with the promise of secrets long buried in time.

C stood atop the hill, his gaze steady and unperturbed.

Clad in robes that seemed to blend seamlessly with the natural hues around him, he appeared as if he was part of the very essence of this place.

His eyes, dark and penetrating, sparkled with recognition as he saw Sfath and Eduard approach.

There was an air of serene anticipation about him, as though he had been expecting their arrival.

Sfath, his presence commanding yet gentle, nodded in acknowledgment of Henock.

Eduard, younger and wide-eyed, took in the scene with a mixture of nervousness and apprehension.

The meeting was almost ethereal, as if the very fabric of time had woven them into this moment with purpose.

"Welcome," Henock said, his voice rich and deep, carrying a weight of wisdom.

"It is an honor to meet you both.

I have awaited this moment with great anticipation."

Sfath, his gaze warm, replied, "Henock, it is a pleasure to finally stand in your presence.

We have traversed many ages to be here."

Henock inclined his head, a gesture of respect and acknowledgment.

"And I am glad you have come.

The messages we exchange today are crucial, not just for us but for the future of many."

Eduard, still absorbing the surreal nature of their surroundings, managed to speak.

"I have heard much about you, Henock.

The prophecies and your wisdom are renowned.

It is humbling to be here."

Henock's eyes twinkled with a mixture of amusement and gravitas.

"The journey of knowledge is a path we all must walk.

It is good that you are here now, as the world stands on the precipice of great change."

As the three figures settled beneath the shade of an ancient oak, the conversation shifted to the weightier matters at hand.

Henock began to recount the prophecies, his voice steady and clear, painting a grim picture of the future.

"At first," Henock said, "many countries will howl with the wolves of the United States.

The fear of American aggression and sanctions will drive nations into a frenzy, including Switzerland and Germany, and many others."

Sfath listened intently, his expression serious.

"The consequences of such actions could be far-reaching.

How do you foresee this unfolding?"

Henock's gaze grew distant as he continued, "Many will be coerced or misled by American propaganda.

As the days pass, nations will rise against American hegemony, recognizing the exploitation and conquest.

The realization will come too late, however, as a great war becomes almost inevitable."

Eduard, troubled, asked, "What of the other powers? How will they respond to this turmoil?"

Henock's face hardened.

"The great war will engulf many lands.

Massive formations of tanks and planes will scour the earth, bringing destruction and suffering.

The militaries will ravage the lands, and the skies will darken with the smoke of conflict.

Natural disasters will add to the chaos, as the wrath of nature mirrors the devastation of human folly."

He paused, allowing the weight of his words to settle before continuing.

"France and Spain will be embroiled in conflict, even before the third world war fully ignites.

Unrest will simmer in Russia and Sweden, while France and Sweden will face upheavals and civil war.

In England and Ireland, civil strife will claim many lives, exacerbated by longstanding conflicts."

Eduard's brow furrowed.

"And the role of Russia in all of this?"

Henock's tone became even graver.

"Russia's expansionist ambitions will lead to bloody conquests.

It will attack Scandinavia and extend its reach to the Balkans, Turkey, and Iran.

The desire to control oil deposits and southeastern Europe will drive further devastation."

Sfath, looking thoughtful, asked, "And what of Switzerland? How will it fare amidst these upheavals?"

"Switzerland will suffer collateral damage," Henock replied.

"The main focus will be France and Spain, but Switzerland will face its own trials.

The real objective of the aggressors will be to bring Europe under their control, with France as their headquarters.

The war will be relentless, involving various forces, both internal and external."

Eduard's eyes widened as Henock's words painted a stark and frightening picture.

"And how will this affect the Americas?"

Henock's voice took on a somber note.

"The conflict will not be confined to Europe.

America and Russia will clash with catastrophic force.

The result will be unprecedented destruction, with weapons of mass destruction wreaking havoc on a scale never before seen."

The sun began to dip below the horizon, casting long shadows across the ancient hill.

The conversation continued as the three men considered the implications of Henock's prophecies.

The weight of the coming events hung heavy in the air.

Sfath, reflecting on the gravity of the prophecies, said,

"It seems that the path ahead is fraught with immense challenges.

How can humanity steer away from such a dire fate?"

Henock's eyes held a glimmer of hope amidst the gloom.

"There is always hope, even in the darkest times.

The path to change lies in the realization of true values, love, freedom, and peace.

It will require a monumental shift in consciousness and action from all corners of the globe."

Eduard, inspired by Henock's resolve, spoke with determination.

"If there is a way to avert such devastation, we must find it.

The knowledge we gain here today will be a beacon for those who seek to guide humanity toward a better future."

Henock's smile was faint but sincere.

"Your resolve is commendable.

The journey will be arduous, but every step toward understanding and action is a step toward a brighter future."

As night fell and the stars began to pierce the velvet sky, the three figures sat in contemplative silence.

The prophecies were a heavy burden, but they also served as a call to action, a reminder that the future was not set in stone and that their efforts could shape the course of history.

With the first light of dawn, Sfath and Eduard, prepared to continue their journey.

The ancient world they had stepped into was both a witness and a guide, and their task was to carry its lessons forward into the future, a future that held both peril and the promise of redemption.

CHAPTER 25

The death of Jehovah, the Cruel

In the vast expanse of deep space, Eduard and Sfath floated within their sleek time-travel vessel, the familiar hum of machinery surrounding them.

They had journeyed through time countless times before, witnessing the rise and fall of civilizations, but each trip held its own significance.

"Today, we're going to witness the murder of Jehovah, the Cruel, the Bible god, by his son Arrussem," Sfath declared, his voice steady.

Eduard turned to him, excitement gleaming in his eyes.

"I can't wait to see this man in person.

So much is said about him in that Bible, especially after watching him ignite two atomic bombs on Sodom and Gomorrah."

"That was cruel, to say the least" Eduard then added.

Sfath agreed.

"Witnessing this event will provide insights that mere texts can't convey."

Eduard leaned back, anticipation building.

"It's one thing to hear about it but, another to experience it firsthand."

"Indeed," Sfath replied, his gaze fixed on the swirling cosmos outside.

"We're not just observers.

We have the power to illuminate the shadows of history."

As Sfath initiated the time jump, a soft blue light enveloped them, pulsating gently.

Eduard felt the sensation of ceasing to exist, the universe folding in on itself.

With a sudden jolt, they landed beneath the Great Pyramid of Giza, the hot desert air washing over them.

"It feels surreal," Eduard said, adjusting to the new environment.

"Stay focused.

We're about to witness a critical moment in history, 2,150 BC," Sfath instructed.

"Will it match my expectations?" Eduard questioned, recalling the stories he had read.

"Truth often defies imagination," Sfath replied, leading the way forward.

The Great Pyramid loomed above them, its ancient stones radiating power.

As Eduard and Sfath marveled at its grandeur, their attention was drawn to some cloaked figures nearby, barely visible.

"Where are they hiding?" Eduard asked, squinting.

"Their cloaking technology keeps them unseen to others, but not to us.

Our technology is more advanced," Sfath explained.

"We can see them, but they can't see us."

"What could they want here?" Eduard pondered.

"To influence the course of humanity," Sfath declared, a hint of concern in his voice.

Following a winding path, they descended into a dark, damp dungeon beneath the pyramid.

The air was thick with decay, and the distant sound of dripping water echoed eerily.

Four figures emerged from the shadows: Jehovah, the cruel ruler, Arrussem, his ambitious son, Ptaah and Salam, Arrussem's younger brothers.

"You dare challenge my authority?"

Jehovah's voice boomed, reverberating through the stone walls.

"I will take what is mine, father!

You've ruled for the past 340 years.

Now is my time to rule!" Arrussem declared, his eyes blazing with determination.

"Arrussem, stop!

This will only lead to chaos," Ptaah pleaded, concern etched on his face.

"Think of our group!" Salam added, glancing nervously between his brothers.

Eduard whispered to Sfath, speaking of Jehovah,

"This man is an evil human being with a high thirst for blood."

Sfath nodded gravely. "His reign has left a dark mark on history."

"The Apple didn't fall too far from the tree," Eduard thought to himself.

"Arrussem is just like his father."

Tension thickened in the dungeon, crackling like electricity.

Arrussem and Jehovah stood face-to-face, both unwilling to back down.

"You're blinded by ambition," Jehovah warned.

"Power is a burden, not a gift."

"A burden you've failed to bear!"

Arrussem shot back, his voice laced with disdain.

"I have 72,000 followers ready to support me!"

Ptaah interjected, "We cannot let you seize that power.

We have gathered those who oppose you!"

"We must unite against the true threat, chaos," Ptaah insisted, attempting to defuse the escalating conflict.

"Weakness will no longer rule!" Arrussem shouted, his fury palpable.

The dim light of torches flickered ominously as Arrussem drew a gleaming dagger, its blade shimmering in the shadows.

In a swift motion, he lunged at Jehovah, the dagger slicing through the air.

Ptaah and Salam gasped in horror as the blade struck true.

"Father!" Ptaah cried, rushing forward.

"You were meant to inherit, not destroy!" Jehovah gasped, staggering back, his life fading away.

"I am the true creator now!" Arrussem proclaimed, standing over his father's lifeless body, triumph mingling with madness in his eyes.

"No!" Salam shouted, rage and despair flooding his voice.

The dungeon echoed with the sound of betrayal.

Arrussem, breathing heavily, stood over his father's body, the weight of his actions settling in.

"You've gone too far," Ptaah said, his voice trembling with grief.

"We cannot let you rule."

Arrussem smirked, a glint of insanity in his eyes.

"I have my followers. I will not be stopped!"

But Ptaah and Salam, united by their shared purpose, rallied their supporters.

"We will gather our strength and force you and your followers off this planet!"

As the brothers prepared for battle, Arrussem's confidence began to waver.

The confrontation escalated, with Ptaah and Salam leading their followers against Arrussem.

The dungeon shook with the force of their conflict, ancient stones trembling as the brothers fought to reclaim their rightful place.

"Together, we are stronger!" Ptaah shouted, rallying their forces.

"Your tyranny ends here!" Salam cried, charging at Arrussem.

The clash was fierce, and in the chaos, Arrussem realized he was outmatched.

With a final desperate attempt, he fled deeper into the labyrinth beneath the pyramid, pursued by Ptaah and Salam.

However, the brothers soon cornered Arrussem and his followers.

"You will leave this planet and never return!" Ptaah commanded.

"Or face the consequences!" Salam added, determination etched on his face.

With no choice left, Arrussem and his remaining followers surrendered, disappearing into the shadows of space, exiled from Earth.

As peace settled over the pyramid, Eduard turned to Sfath.

"Yet, the believers will continue to worship a dead man, unaware that he has fallen.

His legacy will endure for millennia, even in death."

"Yes," Sfath replied. "History is often blind to the truth."

Deep beneath the pyramid lay a labyrinth of tunnels, now silent, where the echoes of betrayal had set the stage for an uncertain future.

As Eduard and Sfath prepared to leave, the past's dark secrets began to unveil themselves, knowing they had witnessed a pivotal moment in history, witnessing the death of Jehovah, the Cruel.

CHAPTER 26

The Vanishing Visitor

August 6, 1945, The Oval Office, Washington D.C.

The Oval Office was steeped in the weight of history. President Harry S.

Truman sat behind his mahogany desk, a mountain of documents and military reports spread out before him. His face was lined with fatigue and anxiety.

Today, he was on the brink of making a decision that would alter the course of history, the deployment of the atomic bombs on Japan.

The silence of the room was occasionally punctuated by the soft rustling of papers and the distant hum of the air conditioning.

Suddenly, a shimmering light began to coalesce in the corner of the room.

Truman looked up, startled, as the light took on a solid form.

An elderly man materialized before him.

The figure was draped in a silver robe, adorned with intricate, shifting extraterrestrial markings that glimmered in the light.

His face was deeply lined, bearing the marks of many years, yet his eyes were filled with an unsettling calm and profound wisdom.

Truman's jaw dropped, and he rose from his chair, his voice barely a whisper.

"Who...who are you? How did you get in here?"

The figure smiled, his voice a soothing resonance.

"Mr. President, I am Sfath.

I come with an urgent message concerning the atomic bombs you are about to use."

Truman stared at the stranger, trying to process the surreal encounter.

He took a deep breath, attempting to regain his composure.

"I'm in the middle of a crucial decision.

What could you possibly add to this situation?"

Sfath's gaze was steady, penetrating Truman's resolve.

"The decision you are about to make will not only affect the immediate future but will echo through time.

There are hidden influences at play here."

Truman frowned, his brow furrowing in confusion.

"What hidden influences are you talking about?"

Sfath stepped closer, his presence both calming and unsettling.

"There are individuals, such as Leslie Groves, who are pushing for the use of these bombs as tests for their destructive capabilities, despite Japan's imminent surrender."

Truman's face hardened, the weight of the revelation sinking in.

"What do you propose I do?"

Sfath's eyes, ancient and knowing, met Truman's with a sense of urgency.

"You have the power to reconsider your decision.

By delaying the deployment of the bombs, you could prevent unnecessary devastation and save countless lives."

Truman's shoulders tensed, the pressure of the situation palpable.

"The decision is already made.

The bombs are in place, and the orders have been issued."

Sfath's tone grew more intense.

"You still have the opportunity to alter this course.

Allowing peace to take its natural course could prevent further destruction."

Truman's mind was a whirlwind of conflicting thoughts.

The pressure from military advisors and the certainty of his orders weighed heavily.

"I can't change the decision now.

The bombs will be used as planned."

Sfath took a deliberate step closer, his presence commanding yet gentle.

"There is another matter to consider.

The knowledge of our discussion and my visit could weigh heavily on you.

If you wish, I can help you forget this encounter."

Truman was taken aback by the proposition.

"You can make me forget?"

"Yes," Sfath affirmed.

"I can erase your memory of this meeting, ensuring that you are not burdened by the knowledge of an extraterrestrial visit."

Truman hesitated, the notion of erasing the memory both alluring and unsettling.

"And if I agree?"

Sfath's eyes were filled with reassurance.

"You will remember only the decisions you've made, free from the weight of this conversation.

It will be as though this meeting never occurred."

Truman sat back, contemplating the offer.

The idea of forgetting the encounter with Sfath seemed like a relief amidst the overwhelming pressure of his decisions.

He nodded slowly. "Yes, I want to forget."

Sfath nodded solemnly and began the intricate process of memory alteration.

Utilizing advanced techniques from his otherworldly knowledge, Sfath employed a combination of neuroscientific methods and a specialized gas.

His movements were precise, guided by the wisdom of ages.

As Sfath worked, Truman watched as the figure's form began to shimmer and fade.

The room felt lighter as the burden of the extraordinary encounter was lifted from Truman's mind.

The process was completed, and Sfath's presence vanished, leaving behind a sense of clarity and relief.

The next morning, Truman awoke with no recollection of his encounter with Sfath.

The monumental decision to deploy the atomic bombs on Hiroshima and Nagasaki remained, but the memory of the otherworldly visitor was gone.

He proceeded with the orders, believing them to be the only course of action.

The bombs were deployed as planned, and history took its course.

Truman's decision was made without the influence of Sfath's visit, and the memory of the extraterrestrial remained erased from his mind.

The visit from Sfath and the content of their conversation were erased from history.

The envelopes containing Eduard's predictions, meant for future presidents, were carefully stored away with strict instructions.

Each envelope held insights from Sfath's knowledge, intended to guide future leaders.

These envelopes were passed down through the years, each president receiving them in secrecy.

The chain of knowledge remained intact until George H.W. Bush's presidency.

Frustrated and angry, Bush destroyed his copy of the predictions, thus breaking the chain.

In 1989, George H.W. Bush's act of destruction ended the continuity of the predictions.

The sealed envelopes, and with them the potential guidance they could have provided, were lost.

Sfath's hope that these predictions would guide future presidents was dashed.

The loss of the envelopes marked a turning point.

The opportunity to benefit from the foresight they contained was gone, and the world continued on its path without the wisdom that could have been imparted.

Sfath's visit to Truman remained a hidden chapter in history.

The encounter, with its promise of altering the course of events, was erased from Truman's memory. Only the consequences of the decision remained.

CHAPTER 27

The Night of Shadows

October 14, 1965, Vatican City

The night in Vatican City was cloaked in an almost ethereal silence, broken only by the occasional murmur of distant voices and the soft rustle of the night breeze through the ancient trees surrounding the holy grounds.

The moon hung low in the sky, casting a pale, spectral light over the cobblestone streets and the towering, sacred structures of the Vatican.

Inside the Apostolic Palace, the atmosphere was far from serene.

Pope Paul VI was preparing for bed, his evening routine reflecting the solemnity and weight of his office.

His bedroom, adorned with simple yet elegant furnishings, was bathed in the soft, warm light of a few flickering candles.

The Pope moved with a deliberate calmness, his face etched with the deep lines of both wisdom and worry.

Unbeknownst to him, the room was not as private as it seemed.

Sfath, draped in his silver robe and Eduard, his young companion, floated in invisibility just beyond the doorway.

Their presence was cloaked by advanced technology that rendered them undetectable to human senses.

Sfath and Eduard remained silent, observing with an intense focus as the clock ticked towards the hour of the planned assassination.

The Pope's routine had been meticulously timed by his unseen adversaries, and Sfath's advanced technology allowed them to witness the events without interference.

The room was soon disturbed by a knock on the door.

A servant, dressed in the simple garb of the Vatican's staff, entered bearing a silver tray.

On it rested a steaming cup of tea, its aroma subtle yet inviting.

The servant, unaware of the sinister purpose of his delivery, approached the Pope with a bow.

"Your Holiness," the servant said softly, "I have brought you your evening tea."

Pope Paul VI, tired yet serene, smiled gently.

"Thank you, my son. You are most kind."

The servant placed the cup on a small table near the Pope's armchair and withdrew, leaving the room with a final, respectful bow.

Sfath and Eduard watched as the Pope settled into his chair, the serene expression on his face suggesting he was at peace with his thoughts.

As the Pope picked up the cup, Sfath's eyes, filled with sadness, focused intently on the scene unfolding before them.

Eduard's youthful face mirrored his concern as they both understood the gravity of the situation.

The poison had been expertly administered, hidden within the seemingly innocuous tea.

Pope Paul VI took a cautious sip, savoring the warmth and flavor of the brew.

His eyes closed momentarily in appreciation, unaware that each swallow was a step closer to his untimely demise.

Sfath and Eduard could only watch in silent horror as the Pope continued to drink, the poison beginning its insidious work.

The room's tranquil atmosphere was now charged with an underlying tension.

The Pope placed the cup down and sighed deeply, his body beginning to show subtle signs of distress.

He struggled to rise from his chair, his face growing pale as he staggered toward his bed.

As Pope Paul VI collapsed onto the bed, the full effects of the poison took hold.

His breathing became labored, and his body convulsed as the toxin ravaged his system.

The Pope's serene countenance was replaced by one of pain and suffering, a tragic end to a life devoted to faith and duty.

Sfath and Eduard, still invisible, watched the final moments of the Pope's life with a profound sense of sorrow.

The room was filled with a heavy silence, the only sound being the labored breaths of the dying Pope.

The plan, orchestrated by those who had deemed him unsuitable for their secretive purposes, was unfolding precisely as intended.

Pope Paul VI, who had opposed their hidden machinations, was now removed from the scene.

Two hours later, the room was visited once again, this time by 6 cardinals with one cardinal who bore a striking resemblance to the deceased Pope.

They entered with a confidence that belied the gravity of the situation, Their faces a mask of calm and assurance.

The cardinal's arrival marked the final act in a covert operation that had been meticulously planned.

The body of Pope Paul VI was to be discreetly removed and replaced by this doppelganger, ensuring that the transition of power would be seamless and unremarkable to the outside world.

Sfath and Eduard, still hidden by their advanced technology, observed the cardinal's actions.

He took up the Pope's role with practiced ease, his movements and demeanor mimicking those of the deceased leader perfectly.

The real Pope Paul VI was no more, his life snuffed out by the ruthless ambitions of those who sought to control the Church from the shadows.

As dawn approached, the Vatican's serene facade was restored, with the new Pope assuming his role with the outward grace and dignity expected of the Holy See.

The world outside remained oblivious to the dark deeds that had transpired within the walls of the Apostolic Palace.

Sfath and Eduard, their mission complete, prepared to depart.

The weight of what they had witnessed hung heavily in the air, a silent testament to the corrupting influence of power and the lengths to which some would go to maintain it.

As they deactivated their cloaking technology and prepared to return to their own time, Sfath's eyes reflected a profound sadness.

Eduard, still grappling with the gravity of their experience, stood by his side, silently absorbing the lessons of their journey.

Back in their own time, Sfath and Eduard reflected on the events they had witnessed.

The assassination of Pope Paul VI was a stark reminder of the hidden forces that shape history, and the tragic consequences of power wielded without integrity.

The memory of that night lingered in their minds, a silent reminder of the fragility of truth and the impact of unseen conspiracies.

In spite of the technological marvels that allowed them to witness such events, they were left with a deeper understanding of the moral complexities that govern human actions.

The death of Pope Paul VI and the replacement by a doppelganger remained a closely guarded secret within the annals of Vatican history.

The world continued on, unaware of the hidden machinations that had shaped its course.

Their role as invisible witnesses to such a dark chapter in history underscored the importance of vigilance and integrity in the face of hidden agendas and corruption.

The night of shadows, with its tragic conclusion, became a silent testament to the lengths to which some would go to maintain control, and the profound impact of unseen forces on the course of human events.

CHAPTER 28

Joan, the female pope

Sfath and Eduard, two travelers from a distant future, stood cloaked in the comforting embrace of their advanced technology.

They hovered unseen in the shadows of Rome in the year 857.

Their mission was to witness a pivotal and tragic moment in history, a moment that had been obscured by centuries of deliberate obfuscation.

The city, alive with the palpable tension of a tumultuous time, stretched out before them.

Rome was plagued by natural disasters, earthquakes that shook the ground, locusts that blotted out the sun, and a pervasive miasma of disease.

The citizens were gripped by a pervasive fear, believing these events to be divine retribution.

Sfath, his eyes reflecting the deep knowledge of the cosmos, turned to Eduard.

"What we are about to witness is more than just a historical event.

It is the intersection of faith, power, and truth, a nexus that shaped the course of religious history."

Eduard nodded, his gaze fixed on the city below.

"The magnitude of this moment is profound.

The story of Pope Joan is a complex tapestry of deception and tragedy.

It is a tale that the Church has long sought to bury."

In the heart of Rome, Pope John VIII, known to the world as a figure of divine grace and intellectual prowess, was preparing for another public appearance.

His ceremonial robes billowed around him as he prepared to make his way from St. Peter's Basilica to the Lateran Palace.

The Pope had become a beacon of hope amidst the city's suffering, his presence a symbol of spiritual solace in the face of relentless calamity.

Sfath and Eduard observed as the Pope, moving with the grace and poise befitting his exalted office, stepped into the procession.

The crowds lined the streets, their cheers a desperate plea for reassurance from the divine representative they so revered.

"As he walks these streets," Sfath said softly, "he is unaware of the storm brewing in the hearts of his people, a storm that will soon explode with tragic consequences."

Eduard watched with a mix of anticipation and apprehension.

"The tension is palpable.

This moment will reveal the deep-seated fears and hidden truths of this era."

As the procession advanced, the atmosphere grew increasingly heavy.

Between the Church of San Clemente and the Colosseum, the street narrowed into a claustrophobic alley.

Here, the unimaginable was about to unfold.

Pope John VIII began to stagger.

His face, once serene, contorted with sudden pain.

The crowd fell silent, their cheers turning to murmurs of concern as the Pope clutched at his robes, seeking support.

His collapse was sudden, and the Pope fell to the ground.

Sfath and Eduard's eyes widened as they saw the Pope's robes begin to shift.

The crowd's initial confusion turned to horror as Pope John VIII's robes lifted, revealing something extraordinary.

To their collective disbelief, the Pope gave birth to a child, a boy.

Eduard's breath caught.

"This is the moment of truth, the revelation that the Church has fought so hard to suppress."

The bystanders, their faces twisted in shock and horror, struggled to comprehend the scene before them.

The realization that their revered Pope was a woman gave birth to a child in the street caused a frenzy.

The once-revered figure was now seen as a sacrilege.

The transformation from shock to rage was swift. The crowd, their religious fervor now tainted with anger, seized Pope Joan and her newborn.

The once-devout followers turned into a frenzied mob, their anger manifesting in violence.

Sfath and Eduard watched as the mob dragged the Pope and her child outside the city gates.

The scene was brutal, their cries echoing through the streets as the Pope and her newborn were stoned to death.

The violence was raw and unforgiving, a stark display of the populace's anger and fear.

Sfath's voice was somber.

"The Church's worst fears have been realized.

This act of violence is a direct response to their inability to reconcile with the truth."

Eduard, witnessing the brutality, spoke with a quiet intensity.

"This moment marks the beginning of a cover-up that will shape the future of the Church and its history."

With Pope Joan's death, the Vatican's response was swift and ruthless.

The authorities worked quickly to erase any trace of her existence from the annals of history.

The narrative was altered, and an imaginary Pope Benedict III was inserted into the records.

Sfath and Eduard observed the meticulous efforts to obscure the truth.

The invention of Pope Benedict III served as a convenient distraction from the scandal that had unfolded.

Historical records were altered, and Joan's existence was systematically erased.

"The Vatican's response to this scandal was not merely about preserving its reputation," Sfath noted.

"It was a profound act of historical manipulation, one that would affect centuries of religious history."

Eduard nodded.

"The fear of a female Pope led to drastic measures.

The Church's response was designed to prevent any similar occurrences and to protect its power and influence."

As the years passed, the story of Pope Joan became shrouded in myth and legend.

Despite the Church's efforts, memorials and statues were erected in her honor, though they were soon hidden under layers of rubble and repression.

Sfath and Eduard observed a later era when the Church's measures to ensure the exclusion of women from papal authority became entrenched.

A ritual was established to test the masculinity of papal candidates, reflecting the deep-seated fear of a repeat of Joan's scandal.

"The ritualized testing of papal candidates is a testament to the lengths the Church went to prevent a recurrence of Joan's scandal," Sfath observed.

"It reflects the profound impact her story had on the institution."

Eduard added, "This ritual was a grim reminder of the Church's attempt to control its narrative and maintain its authority through deception and exclusion."

In their time-traveling journey, Sfath and Eduard had witnessed the full extent of the Church's manipulation and denial.

The true story of Pope Joan, though buried and distorted, was now revealed in its tragic entirety.

Sfath looked at Eduard, his expression reflective.

"The truth of Pope Joan's existence and the subsequent cover-up highlight the intersection of faith, power, and historical revisionism."

Eduard agreed, "The story of Pope Joan serves as a powerful reminder of the ways in which history can be rewritten to serve those in power.

The truth, though obscured, remains a crucial part of our understanding of the past."

As Sfath and Eduard concluded their journey through the past, they carried with them a deeper understanding of the complexities of historical truth.

The tale of Pope Joan was more than a footnote in history, it was a reflection of the enduring struggle between truth and power.

Sfath turned to Eduard.

"The story of Pope Joan is a testament to the resilience of truth and the importance of uncovering the layers of deception that have shaped our understanding of history."

Eduard nodded, his gaze thoughtful.

"Indeed, the hidden truths of the past continue to echo through the present.

Our journey has revealed the depths of historical manipulation and the enduring quest for truth."

As they departed from the past, the legacy of Pope Joan remained a poignant reminder of the power of historical inquiry and the impact of truth on the course of history.

CHAPTER 29

The Time Traveller's Gambit

The year was 1945, and the world was recovering from the turmoil of war.

In a small town in Switzerland, Eduard stood on the cusp of something extraordinary.

His deep blue eyes sparkled with excitement as he gazed at the shimmering, sleek spacecraft that hovered silently in the forest where he was telepathically directed to wait for Sfath.

This was no ordinary craft; it was a vessel of cosmic wonder, guided by the enigmatic alien time traveler, Sfath.

Eduard's heart as always raced with anticipation as he approached the spacecraft.

Sfath, with a presence that combined both calm and authority, awaited him at the entrance.

His appearance, a blend of ethereal grace and advanced technology, was both captivating and reassuring.

"Ready for another adventure, Eduard?" Sfath asked, his voice resonating with a melodic timbre that conveyed both wisdom and warmth.

Eduard nodded eagerly.

"Where are we going this time, Sfath?

Is it going to be another historical journey?"

Sfath's eyes twinkled with approval.

"Indeed, Eduard.

Today, we will delve into the deep past to explore the birth of the Colorado River and the sinking of the Titanic.

You will witness how these events shaped the world in ways that echo through time."

As Eduard stepped inside the spacecraft, the interior revealed itself as a marvel of advanced design, filled with holographic displays and comfortable seating.

Sfath guided him to a seat and began the countdown to their departure.

The spacecraft hummed with energy, and the world outside the viewport began to blur.

Eduard's senses tingled with the excitement of time travel.

When the motion settled, the view transformed into a panorama of ancient Earth, a world untouched by modernity.

"Here we are, Eduard," Sfath said as he pointed to the scene outside.

"We've traveled back to a time over five million years ago, to witness the dawn of the Colorado River."

The landscape was strikingly different from the present.

The vast expanse of a primordial lake stretched out before them, its waters shimmering under a sun that seemed to cast a purer light.

From the lake's edge, a massive spillway carried a torrent of water, carving its path through the rugged terrain.

Eduard's eyes widened with wonder. "Is that the beginning of the Colorado River?"

"Yes," Sfath confirmed.

"The river started as a small stream emerging from this enormous lake.

Over millions of years, it would evolve into the mighty river you know today."

The spacecraft drifted closer to the scene, and Eduard observed the small stream making its way through the barren landscape.

Sfath's voice provided a continuous narrative, detailing the river's growth.

"As the stream meandered through the land, it began to pick up sediment and rocks," Sfath explained.

"These materials were carried downstream, gradually deepening and widening the riverbed."

Eduard noticed the river's slow but steady progress.

"So, the river is like a sculptor, shaping the land over time?"

"Precisely," Sfath said.

"The river's current carved out the canyon by eroding the rock and soil.

Over millennia, this process created the Grand Canyon, a majestic chasm nearly two kilometers deep."

Eduard marveled at the sight of the canyon's gradual formation.

"It's incredible to see how something as simple as a stream can create such an enormous landscape."

As they continued to observe, Sfath showed Eduard how the river's power reshaped the canyon's landscape.

The canyon walls were lined with layers of sediment, each representing a different epoch in the river's history.

"This is a record of time itself," Sfath said.

"Each layer of sediment tells a story of the river's journey through the ages."

Eduard took in the breathtaking view, feeling a profound sense of connection to the natural world.

"It's like the river has been writing its own history in the land."

"Exactly," Sfath agreed.

"The river's work is never done.

It constantly changes the landscape, a reminder of the dynamic nature of our planet."

As the spacecraft prepared to leave the past, Eduard felt a deep appreciation for the natural forces that had shaped the world he knew.

The Titanic's Tragic Tale

The spacecraft's next destination was the early 20th century, a time when the Titanic set sail on its ill-fated voyage.

The transition through time was smooth, and soon Eduard found himself gazing at the majestic liner as it cruised across the North Atlantic.

"Here we are, Eduard," Sfath announced.

"The Titanic, in all its grandeur, just before the iceberg collision."

Eduard watched as the Titanic sailed with impressive elegance, its lights shimmering in the night.

"It looks so beautiful and grand.

What happened to cause the disaster?"

Sfath's expression grew somber.

"The Titanic struck an iceberg, but there was more to the story.

A seaquake also contributed to the disaster, exacerbating the ship's fate."

Eduard's curiosity deepened.

"What was the seaquake's role in the sinking?"

"Let's wait and watch." Sfath said.

Just a few minues after seeing the devastation caused by the seaquakes, Sfath adjusted his new time course by 40 years into the future to explore the depths where the Titanic would eventually rest.

In 1948, the spacecraft descended to the Titanic's final resting place on the ocean floor.

The view outside the viewport revealed the eerie serenity of the sunken ship, now a ghostly relic enshrouded in darkness.

"Look closely, Eduard," Sfath said, pointing to the Titanic's decayed hull.

"This is what remains after decades of submersion."

Eduard observed the Titanic's haunting beauty, its once-majestic structure now partially buried in the sand.

"It's incredible to see how the ship has changed over time.

It's like a monument to its own history."

"The passage of time has transformed the Titanic," Sfath explained.

"The ship's decay tells a story of nature's relentless influence.

It's a poignant reminder of the fragility of human achievements."

As the spacecraft prepared to return, Eduard reflected on the journey.

The experiences of witnessing the Colorado River's formation and the Titanic's sinking had imparted profound lessons.

"Thank you for this journey, Sfath," Eduard said, his voice filled with gratitude.

"I've learned so much about how the world has been shaped by both natural forces and human actions."

"It was my pleasure, Eduard," Sfath replied. "Understanding history helps us appreciate our place in the world.

The forces that shaped the river and the Titanic's fate remind us of the interconnectedness of nature and human endeavors."

Eduard nodded, feeling a deep sense of fulfillment.

"I'll carry these lessons with me.

They've given me a new perspective on the world."

The spacecraft ascended from the depths of the past, its journey taking Eduard back to his own time.

As the familiar sights of 1945 reappeared, Eduard felt a mixture of nostalgia and enlightenment.

"Back to the present, Eduard," Sfath said as the spacecraft landed smoothly.

"Remember, the lessons of the past are tools for understanding the present."

Eduard stepped out of the spacecraft, his mind brimming with new knowledge.

"I'll never forget this adventure, Sfath. It's been incredible."

Sfath offered a reassuring smile. "Goodbye, Eduard.

As Sfath's spacecraft departed, Eduard stood silently, reflecting on the extraordinary experiences he had just lived.

The echoes of the Colorado River's ancient formation and the Titanic's tragic end resonated deeply within him, shaping his understanding of history and his place in the world.

CHAPTER 30

The assassination of Rasputin

"Eduard, are you prepared for an extraordinary journey?

"Sfath's voice was filled with anticipation.

Eduard, his curiosity piqued, asked, "Where are we going today, Sfath?"

"We're going to witness a pivotal moment in history," Sfath replied.

"Specifically, we'll observe the truth behind Rasputin's assassination."

Eduard's eyes widened.

"Rasputin? That sounds fascinating."

Sfath's fingers danced over the controls of his spacecraft.

In an instant, the surroundings morphed into the harsh winter of 1916 Russia.

They emerged on a snowy street, the biting cold contrasting sharply with the warmth of their invisible cloaking technology.

The town of St. Petersburg was blanketed in white, its grand architecture draped in icicles.

The sky was a somber grey, hinting at the impending darkness.

They approached a grand castle, its stone walls fortified against the elements.

The castle was a stark contrast to the bleak weather, with its ornate turrets and elaborate ironwork.

Eduard noticed the opulent clothing of the era.

Men in dark woolen coats and fur hats, women in layered dresses with fur trims and delicate shawls.

Inside, the atmosphere was tense.

The room they entered was lavishly decorated with heavy drapes and gilded furniture.

Albeit the warmth indoors, the air was charged with a palpable sense of unease.

Eduard and Sfath remained invisible.

They observed a group of men gathered around a table laden with food and drink.

Among them was Felix Yusupov, dressed in a dark, impeccably tailored suit, his demeanor one of calculated arrogance.

Beside him stood Oswald Rayner, a British agent clad in a sharp, military uniform.

Yusupov spoke with urgency, "We must act quickly.

Rasputin's influence over the Tsar poses a serious threat to our plans."

Rayner's eyes were cold and calculating.

"The poison will be our first step.

Once he's incapacitated, we ensure he never rises again."

Eduard's voice was barely audible.

"They're planning to kill him?"

Sfath nodded.

"Rayner is the British agent tasked with making sure Rasputin dies.

This assassination is as much about politics as it is about personal vendetta."

The door to the room opened, and Rasputin entered, his presence commanding immediate attention.

He wore a simple, yet dignified robe, his eyes scanning the room with an air of suspicion.

"Rasputin," Yusupov greeted him with a forced smile.

"We're pleased you could join us."

Rasputin's gaze fell upon the spread of food and drink.

Eduard's attention was drawn to a particular bottle of wine, its label marked with an ominous insignia.

As the evening wore on, Rasputin engaged in casual conversation, unaware of the impending danger.

Yusupov and Rayner made small talk, all while Rasputin sipped the wine that had been laced with poison.

Eduard noticed subtle shifts in Rasputin's demeanor.

Sfath whispered, "The poison is starting to take effect.

But Rasputin is tougher than they anticipated."

Eduard watched in astonishment as Rasputin, despite evident discomfort, maintained a surprising level of alertness.

His face revealed the struggle to keep composure as the poison worked its insidious way through his system.

The conspirators led Rasputin to the cold, grim cellar of the palace.

The cellar's chill seemed to intensify the oppressive atmosphere.

Rasputin was restrained, and Yusupov, with Rayner's assistance, began a horrific process of torture.

Rasputin was subjected to beatings and additional doses of poison, yet he continued to resist.

Eduard's face turned ashen.

"How can they be so merciless?"

Sfath's expression was grim.

"They believe their actions are justified.

Rasputin's survival of the poison and torture is seen as a direct challenge to their authority."

In spite of the brutal treatment, Rasputin's resilience was extraordinary.

He managed to stand, even as Rayner shot him twice in the back.

The bullets seemed to have minimal impact.

"This man's will to live is remarkable," Sfath commented.

"But it's only a matter of time before they succeed."

Eduard watched in horror as Rasputin, defying the odds, staggered out of the cellar, only to be shot again.

This time, Rayner aimed carefully and fired a final, fatal shot to Rasputin's forehead.

Rasputin collapsed, lifeless.

The conspirators, their grim task completed, bound Rasputin's body and dragged it to the icy Neva River.

They tossed the corpse into the freezing water, hoping it would disappear beneath the ice.

Eduard shivered, though not from the cold.

"How did they cover up this atrocity?"

Sfath explained, "The Tsar was kept in the dark about the full extent of the murder.

The official story was that Rasputin was a moral threat, not a politically motivated assassination involving foreign agents."

Eduard learned more about the hidden motives behind the murder.

Rasputin had been a key advisor to the Tsar, and his efforts to negotiate peace between Russia and Germany threatened British interests.

His death was strategically advantageous for the British, who feared that a peace agreement would shift the balance of power in favor of Germany.

Sfath elaborated, "Rasputin's influence on the Tsar could have led to a peace treaty with Germany.

This would have allowed Germany to reinforce its Western Front and potentially alter the outcome of World War I."

The assassination of Rasputin had far-reaching consequences.

It accelerated the collapse of the Romanov dynasty and contributed to the Russian Revolution.

The political instability that followed weakened Russia's war efforts and influenced the broader geopolitical landscape.

Eduard marveled at how a single event could ripple through history, shaping the fate of nations and altering the course of global conflic.

He reflected on how Rasputin's death symbolized the end of an era for the Russian aristocracy.

His murder marked a significant turning point, leading to the rise of a new world order.

The impact of his assassination extended beyond Russia, influencing the course of the First World War and the subsequent rise of Soviet power.

Eduard grappled with the ethical implications of the knowledge he had gained.

Understanding the true nature of Rasputin's assassination and its motivations posed challenges.

How should this information be used?

He pondered the responsibilities of those who uncover such truths and the potential consequences for contemporary historical understanding.

HIs journey underscored the importance of seeking historical truth.

Eduard realized that uncovering the truth required not only a thorough examination of events but also a critical assessment of motivations and biases.

He appreciated the crucial role of historians in presenting an accurate picture of the past.

He saw the value in this meticulous work and the need for continuous scrutiny.

Eduard's reflections led him to valuable lessons about the nature of historical events.

Rasputin's assassination was a vivid example of how personal ambitions, political strategies, and broader socio-economic factors could converge to create pivotal moments in history.

Understanding these complexities was essential for a deeper appreciation of the past.

He considered the implications of Rasputin's death for contemporary issues.

The complexities of historical events and the interplay of personal and political motives offered insights into current geopolitical challenges.

Understanding history's intricacies could inform better decision-making and prevent the repetition of past mistakes.

Rasputin's legacy was multifaceted.

While some viewed him as a villain, others saw him as a victim of political machinations.

Eduard recognized the need to approach historical figures with nuance, considering their actions and motivations within the broader context of their tie.

His journey prompted reflection on human nature.

The events surrounding Rasputin's assassination revealed the darker aspects of ambition, cruelty, and resilience.

He saw how personal and collective ambitions could drive individuals to commit extreme acts, shaping the course of history.

Eduard's experience emphasized the ongoing quest for historical truth.

History was a living narrative, continuously shaped by those who sought to understand it.

He was committed to continuing his exploration with a critical eye and an open mind.

Rasputin's influence had been a significant factor in the political landscape of early 20th-century Russia.

His death had not only ended an era but had also set off a chain of reactions that contributed to the destabilization of the Russian monarchy and, eventually, the Russian Revolution.

As Eduard delved deeper into the historical context, he unearthed more about the conspirators.

Felix Yusupov and Oswald Rayner were not isolated actors.

They were part of a broader network of individuals who sought to alter the course of history to their advantage.

This network had intricate ties with various political factions and international interests.

Eduard's research revealed that the conspirators had carefully planned every detail, from the poisoning to the torture, to ensure Rasputin's death was both certain and symbolic.

The brutality was intended not just to kill Rasputin but to send a powerful message to others who might stand in their way.

The impact of Rasputin's assassination rippled far beyond his immediate circle.

He discovered that the power vacuum left by Rasputin's death contributed to the growing unrest within Russia.

The political instability that followed set the stage for the February and October Revolutions of 1917.

Eduard came to understand that Rasputin's assassination was not solely driven by political motives.

Personal vendettas played a crucial role.

Yusupov, for instance, had personal grievances against Rasputin, exacerbated by Rasputin's alleged interference in his personal life and affairs.

The personal animosities between Rasputin and his assassins were intertwined with political motives, illustrating how personal feelings can dramatically influence historical events.

Eduard's exploration also revealed the disparity between historical myth and reality.

Rasputin had been portrayed as a sinister, almost supernatural figure in popular accounts.

However, the reality of his death was far more complex and brutal than the myths suggested.

This discrepancy underscored the importance of critical examination and the need to question widely accepted historical narratives.

Eduard reflected on how Rasputin's legacy had been shaped by various historical actors and subsequent generations.

The myth of Rasputin had persisted, often overshadowing the more nuanced and grim reality of his death.

Eduard saw the value in understanding historical figures and events within their true context rather than through the lens of myth and legend.

His journey with Sfath underscored the critical importance of historical inquiry.

History was not a static record but an evolving narrative shaped by ongoing investigation and interpretation.

He realized that understanding history required more than just recounting events.

It involved exploring the motivations behind those events and their far-reaching effects.

Eduard's exploration into Rasputin's assassination also led him to reflect on human nature.

The events he witnessed revealed the darker aspects of human ambition, cruelty, and resilience.

He saw how personal and collective ambitions could drive individuals to commit extreme acts, shaping the course of history in profound ways.

Eduard recognized the vital role of historians in uncovering and interpreting the past.

Historians were tasked with sifting through biases, myths, and incomplete records to present a more accurate picture of historical events.

He understood that history was a collaborative effort, requiring careful analysis and a commitment to truth.

As Eduard concluded his reflections, he appreciated the journey he had undertaken with Sfath.

The experience had deepened his understanding of history and the importance of seeking the truth.

He was determined to apply these insights in his own studies and to contribute to a more nuanced understanding of historical events.

CHAPTER 31

Michael Jackson

Eduard and Sfath, two time travelers from 1947, stood cloaked in invisibility as they materialized in Los Angeles on June 25, 2009.

The grandeur of a mansion before them stood in stark contrast to the turmoil that's about to unfold in a moment.

They were here to witness an event marked by both anticipation and impending tragedy.

Sfath's voice was calm yet somber as he spoke.

"Michael Jackson will face a fatal cardiac arrest tonight due to a dangerously overdosed drug cocktail.

This will lead to his death."

The mansion where Michael Jackson lay was an emblem of opulence, but within, the atmosphere was heavy with impending tragedy.

They watched as the final moments of Jackson's life unfolded.

Michael Jackson is in his final hours.

His medical team is working frantically to save him, but the damage from the drug overdose is severe.

The mixture of medications in his system has caused his heart to fail.

The scene is so clinical, doctors and paramedics moving with urgency, yet the air feels charged with despair.

It's like a tragic play in real life.

The clinical detachment of the medical team contrasts sharply with the emotional storm that will soon follow.

His family and close friends will be devastated, though their reactions are yet to fully unfold.

Eduard watched as the team attempted resuscitation.

The intensity of their efforts contrasted with the growing realization of Jackson's inevitable demise.

The paramedics are working tirelessly, but it's clear they are fighting a losing battle.

As the minutes ticked by, the atmosphere grew more somber.

Jackson's pulse could no longer be detected, and the efforts to revive him became increasingly futile.

It seems the end is near.

How will the world react to this moment?"

The media will soon descend upon this tragedy, amplifying every detail.

There will be a frenzy of speculation and sensationalism that will overshadow the true nature of Jackson's life and legacy.

It's disheartening to think that the essence of his life will be reduced to headlines and rumors.

The media's portrayal will often distort reality.

The genuine grief and the personal struggles Jackson faced will be buried under layers of sensationalism and public spectacle."

As Jackson's life slipped away, the emotional impact on those present became evident.

His passing marked not just the end of a remarkable career but also the beginning of a media circus that would magnify both his flaws and his extraordinary talents.

This is a somber moment.

Michael Jackson's death is indeed a tragic end to a complex life.

His true legacy will be found in his music and the impact he had on the world.

In spite of the media frenzy and the distorted public perception, his artistic contributions and the innocence he sought to recapture are what will endure.

It's a harsh reminder of how public figures are often consumed by sensationalism.

Understanding the true essence of a person requires more than just observing the surface.

History will remember Jackson for both his extraordinary talent and the controversies that surrounded him.

The challenge is to look beyond the noise and appreciate the true story of his life.

As they prepared to return to their own time, Eduard and Sfath carried with them a deeper understanding of the complexities surrounding Michael Jackson's life and death, a poignant lesson in the interplay between fame, truth, and public perception.

Eduard's face showed concern.

"Even with his fame and wealth, it seems he led a troubled life.

And what about the allegations of him being a pedophile?

I find it hard to believe he could have committed such acts."

Sfath's gaze remained steady.

"These accusations are nothing more than infamous fabrications.

Parents, driven by personal agendas, concocted stories of abuse for financial gain.

My investigation has confirmed these claims as falsehoods, manipulated by parents who coerced their children into making accusations that the children eventually believed."

Eduard absorbed this, his concern deepening.

"So, the children were pressured into false accusations?"

"Exactly," Sfath confirmed.

"Jackson had a deep affection for children, stemming from his own deprived childhood.

His interactions with them were innocent, an attempt to reclaim a lost part of his own youth."

As Eduard surveyed the opulent estate, the contrast between the mansion's luxury and the impending tragedy struck him.

The pair then moved through time to witness the aftermath of Jackson's death.

The media frenzy, the speculation, and the throngs of mourners painted a distorted picture of a man who had become larger than life.

"The sensationalism surrounding his death," Eduard observed, "seems so detached from who he was."

Sfath sighed.

"Public perception often distorts reality.

Jackson's genuine nature, his innocence and sensitivity, is overshadowed by the spectacle of his death.

The real tragedy is how his true character is obscured by sensationalism."

They continued observing, noting the disparity between Jackson's real life and the myth surrounding him.

"He was indeed a complex figure," Eduard remarked.

"A man who never truly experienced a childhood, living through his interactions with children and his music."

"Yes," Sfath agreed.

"Jackson's life was marked by immense talent and profound personal struggle.

The myths and accusations, and the glorification of his death, distract from understanding the true essence of the man."

Returning to their time, Eduard reflected on the cultural implications of Jackson's life and death.

"The way society deals with such figures reflects our values and contradictions."

Sfath nodded. "Jackson's story reveals the gap between reality and perception.

The obsession with celebrity and the ease of accepting false narratives are broader societal issues."

Eduard left their journey with a profound lesson on fame and public perception.

"Michael Jackson's story highlights the danger of sensationalism and the importance of delving beyond surface impressions."

Sfath's final words were contemplative.

"History is shaped by both truth and the distortions that surround it.

The challenge is to seek clarity and not let myths obscure our understanding."

Eduard, with a renewed grasp of the interplay between fame, truth, and public perception, realized that understanding a person's true essence requires careful and compassionate examination, beyond the clamor of sensationalism.

Chapter 32

Meeting Safaar

February 3, 1946, dawned crisp and clear over Eduard's small village.

Although it was his ninth birthday, Eduard had always preferred quiet moments over grand celebrations.

Today, his anticipation was focused on his meeting with Sfath, which had become a cherished part of his routine.

He made his way to their usual spot, a clearing in the nearby forest.

The forest was serene, its frost-covered trees bathed in the soft light of early morning. Eduard's excitement was palpable as he awaited the spacecraft's arrival.

The calm of the forest was soon broken by the familiar hum of the spacecraft.

Eduard's heart raced as he saw the pear-shaped craft descending gracefully into the clearing. It landed smoothly, its sleek metallic surface catching the light.

The spacecraft's door opened with its characteristic hiss, and Eduard stepped forward.

To his surprise, two figures emerged, both identical to Sfath.

One was dressed in a silver metallic robe, and the other in gold with intricate silvery hieroglyphs.

Eduard blinked and rubbed his eyes, trying to make sense of the sight.

The two Sfaths laughed in perfect harmony.

"Come in, Eduard," they said, their voices perfectly synchronized.

Though accustomed to extraordinary experiences with Sfath, Eduard was taken aback.

The Sfath in the silver robe spoke first.

"This is my twin brother, Safaar."

Safaar, in gold, extended a hand with a warm smile.

"It's a pleasure to finally meet you, Eduard.

I've heard so much about you."

Eduard entered the spacecraft, familiar yet always awe-inspiring.

The interior was compact, illuminated by soft blue lights and filled with advanced technology.

Safaar guided Eduard to a comfortable seat.

"Today, we have a special adventure," Safaar began.

"We're traveling back to a time when dinosaurs roamed the Earth."

Eduard's eyes widened.

"That sounds great!

Sfath, already at the control panel, began preparing the spacecraft.

"First, we'll leave Earth's atmosphere.

Once we're in free space, I'll initiate the time jump."

Eduard nodded.

He had traveled through time with Sfath before and was familiar with the process.

Sfath activated the spacecraft's engines.

The ship hummed to life, and Eduard felt the familiar vibration as it began its ascent.

The craft climbed smoothly, piercing through the sky.

As they broke through the clouds, Earth's curvature became visible below.

Within seconds, they were clear of the atmosphere, gliding into the vast expanse of space. Stars twinkled in the blackness, providing a stunning backdrop as they left the planet behind.

Once in free space, Sfath turned to Eduard.

"We're now in position. The spacecraft is ready for the time jump."

Sfath moved back to the control panel, adjusting settings with precision.

The time-travel system whirred to life, and a soft blue light enveloped the interior of the spacecraft.

Eduard felt the familiar sensation of being gently pulled through time.

The surroundings blurred and shifted as they prepared to travel millions of years into the past.

Moments later, the light dimmed, and the spacecraft came to a smooth stop.

Eduard looked out of the viewport and was greeted by a breathtaking sight.

The landscape was prehistoric, a vibrant world with towering ferns, gigantic trees, and the distant roars of dinosaurs.

The spacecraft landed softly in a clearing.

Eduard, Sfath, and Safaar stepped out, and the ancient world enveloped them.

The ground smelled of rich vegetation, and the sounds of prehistoric life surrounded them.

Safaar led Eduard through the landscape, explaining the various dinosaur species they encountered.

"These dinosaurs had unique adaptations for survival," Safaar said.

"For instance, the sauropods like those over there had long necks to reach high vegetation, while the theropods were fierce predators with sharp teeth and agile bodies."

Eduard listened intently, fascinated by the detailed explanations and the diversity of life that once thrived on Earth.

After exploring and learning about the dinosaurs, the three of them found a giant tree, its broad canopy providing a comfortable shelter from the elements.

They settled beneath its sprawling branches, the ancient tree adding a sense of timelessness to their surroundings.

Safaar looked at Eduard with a thoughtful expression.

"Now that we've explored the past, I want to share something different with you, some wisdom about the Creation Energy teachings."

Safaar began to explain.

"Creation Energy is the fundamental force that underpins the universe.

It's the energy from which all matter and life originate.

Everything in the universe, from the smallest atom to the largest galaxy, is interconnected through this energy.

Understanding it can provide deep insights into the nature of existence and our place within it."

Safaar continued, "The energy flows through everything and everyone.

By harmonizing with it, we can gain a deeper understanding of ourselves and the universe. It's not just a force but a consciousness that guides the development and evolution of all life."

Safaar elaborated on the influence of external forces.

"In the DERN universe, as well as here on Earth, early visitors from other worlds created influences that diminished the natural evolution of humanity.

These visitors, whom we refer to as 'foreigners,' acted as gods to the inhabitants of various planets.

Their presence led to a distortion of natural development, resulting in the degeneration of human-like species."

Safaar continued, "Our ancestors, who lived in the ANKAR universe, faced similar challenges. They attempted to counteract these issues early on, but their efforts often failed.

Through their excursions to other worlds, they observed that such aberrations were widespread.

The foreigners, being highly advanced in technology and knowledge, were often revered as gods by less advanced beings.

This misinterpretation led to the perpetuation of erroneous beliefs and practices."

Safaar's tone grew serious.

"We Plejaren did not come to Earth with the intention of making contact or demanding anything from its inhabitants.

Our purpose is to teach and spread the teachings of Nokodemion, which have been established for millennia.

This mission was decided upon by our ancestors around 25 million years ago, despite their own fall into similar evils as those experienced by humans on Earth later."

He continued, "The decision to initiate this mission persisted through the ages.

More than 50,000 years ago, it was reaffirmed, and preparations were made to implement it. The teachings of 'Truth, Creation Energy, and Life' were to be introduced to humanity, guiding them towards true life and self-realization."

Safaarr's expression reflected the gravity of the situation.

"Despite our efforts, the mission has faced numerous challenges.

Religious influences have exerted considerable pressure, distorting the true purpose of the teachings.

The foreigners, instead of preventing the horrors of human sacrifice and violence, allowed them to persist.

This led to misunderstandings and the rise of delusional ideas that these foreign commands were divine laws, resulting in severe punishments and human sacrifices."

Eduard listened with growing concern.

"So, the teachings were misinterpreted and misapplied?"

"Yes," Safaar replied.

"The message of not killing was misunderstood, leading to a cycle of revenge, hatred, and conflict.

Instead of fostering peace and self-awareness, these teachings were twisted into a justification for violence and war.

The rapid spread of misguided faith replaced critical thinking and understanding of reality and truth."

Safaar continued, "This pattern of degeneration and misunderstanding is not unique to Earth. It is observed across various human-like species throughout the six universes of Creation.

A natural instinct for self-preservation can lead to wrong interpretations and applications of moral principles.

This instinct, combined with the influence of external forces and misguided teachings, perpetuates a cycle of violence and dehumanization."

Eduard was struck by the scale of the issue.

"So, this isn't just an Earth problem, it's a universal one?"

"Indeed," Safaar affirmed.

"Human-like species across the cosmos struggle with similar challenges.

The desire for self-preservation and the misapplication of ethical principles often lead to a cycle of violence and conflict.

True understanding requires breaking this cycle and developing genuine humanity."

As the sun began to set, casting a warm glow over the prehistoric landscape, Eduard sat quietly, reflecting on the profound revelations.

The day's adventure had been awe-inspiring, but the deeper understanding of the Plejaren's mission and the universal struggle for true peace added a new layer of significance to the experience.

Safaar, sensing Eduard's contemplation, continued, "The mission to teach and spread the principles of Nokodemion is ongoing.

Inspite of the difficulties, the goal is to guide humanity towards a path of true peace and self-realization.

It is a challenging endeavor, but one that remains crucial for the evolution of consciousness across the universe."

With the day drawing to a close, Sfath and Safaar prepared to return to the present.

Eduard felt a deep sense of gratitude for the insights gained and the opportunity to witness such a significant part of the mission.

The spacecraft ascended from the ancient world, and the familiar blue light enveloped them as they traveled back through time.

Moments later, they arrived in the present, the forest clearing bathed in the soft light of evening.

Eduard stepped out of the spacecraft, the tranquility of the forest a comforting contrast to the day's revelations.

Sfath and Safaar prepared to depart, their expressions warm and reassuring.

"We hope you found today's journey and teachings enlightening," Safaar said.

"It was incredible," Eduard replied.

"Thank you for sharing such profound knowledge.

As the spacecraft lifted off and disappeared into the sky, Eduard watched with a sense of wonder.

The forest, now a familiar and comforting presence, reminded him of the extraordinary adventures and insights he had experienced.

With a heart full of gratitude and a mind enriched with new understanding, Eduard began his walk home.

The ordinary world seemed different now, seen through the lens of the universal truths he had learned.

CHAPTER 33

Covid 19

The pear-shaped spacecraft descended gracefully into Eduard's backyard, its silver surface shimmering in the late afternoon sun.

Ten-year-old Eduard, brimming with excitement, rushed outside as his familiar extraterrestrial mentor, Sfath, emerged from the craft.

"Hello, Eduard!" Sfath greeted warmly, his voice carrying the soothing tone Eduard had come to associate with their time-traveling adventures.

"Hi, Sfath!

Where are we going today?" Eduard asked, struggling to contain his enthusiasm.

Sfath smiled.

"Today, we're undertaking a different kind of journey.

We'll explore the impact of global pandemics, understand the origins of COVID-19, and examine NATO's role in shaping international relations."

Eduard's eyes lit up with curiosity.

"That sounds important.

I'm ready!"

With a nod, Sfath led Eduard into the spacecraft.

As the doors sealed and the engines roared to life, Eduard felt the familiar thrill of temporal displacement.

Inside the spacecraft, screens displayed news reports from the early 21st century.

Eduard watched as headlines flashed about a novel coronavirus rapidly spreading across the globe.

"COVID-19 emerged in late 2019," Sfath began, pointing to a map illustrating the virus's swift spread.

"It triggered a global pandemic, impacting millions of lives and straining healthcare systems worldwide."

Eduard saw images of empty streets, overwhelmed hospitals, and masked individuals.

"How did this all start, and why did it spread so quickly?"

Sfath's expression became serious.

"The virus originated in a city in China, though its exact origins are still debated.

However, historical records reveal that past leaders, such as Mao, have committed atrocities that mirror the chaos of pandemics.

For instance, Mao's Cultural Revolution led to massive suffering and death, showcasing how political decisions can exacerbate crises.

Additionally, he gladly went along with the plan of a disgruntled American who revealed his intention to use a laboratory-created plague to wipe out America's population."

"So that's where the virus came from?" Eduard asked.

"Certainly," Sfath responded.

"The virus spread so quickly due to global travel and inadequate early responses.

This crisis highlighted vulnerabilities in global health preparedness and the need for coordinated responses."

The scene shifted to various countries implementing lockdowns, travel bans, and social distancing measures.

Eduard observed people adapting to new realities, such as remote work and online education.

"Governments employed various strategies to control the virus," Sfath explained.

"The response varied significantly, with mixed outcomes.

Public compliance with health measures like mask-wearing and social distancing was crucial but often met with resistance."

Eduard asked, "Why did some people resist these measures?"

Sfath replied, "Resistance often stemmed from misinformation, lack of trust in authorities, or personal beliefs.

Effective communication and community engagement were vital for overcoming these challenges."

The spacecraft next transported Eduard to the World Health Organization (WHO) headquarters, where delegates from various nations were collaborating and debating strategies to combat the pandemic.

"The WHO," Sfath said, "played a crucial role in coordinating international efforts, though its work was sometimes hindered by political tensions and varying national interests."

Eduard observed discussions on global vaccination efforts and resource allocation.

"What challenges did the WHO face?"

Sfath answered, "Political disagreements and uneven resource distribution complicated the WHO's efforts.

The pandemic underscored the need for stronger international cooperation and equitable access to health resources."

The scene transitioned to a 1949 meeting where representatives from twelve nations signed the NATO treaty.

The grand hall resonated with historical significance.

"NATO was formed in response to the perceived threat of Soviet expansion after World War II," Sfath explained.

"It was intended as a collective defense alliance but evolved into a broader geopolitical tool."

Eduard watched as the alliance expanded over the years.

"How has NATO influenced global politics?"

Sfath's tone was reflective.

"NATO's role has been complex.

While initially focused on mutual defense, it has also been involved in various international conflicts and interventions, reflecting the political and strategic interests of its leading members."

The spacecraft journeyed further back to the late 1940s, showcasing the influence of the Truman Doctrine on global politics.

Eduard saw the fear of Soviet expansion driving NATO's formation.

"The Truman Doctrine," Sfath said, "aimed to contain Soviet influence, leading to NATO's creation and shaping U.S. foreign policy."

Eduard observed the geopolitical shifts as countries aligned with NATO in response to the Soviet threat. "Did NATO achieve its initial goals?"

Sfath replied, "NATO succeeded in countering Soviet expansion initially, but its actions and influence evolved over time, often leading to complex and sometimes unintended consequences."

The spacecraft's next stop was a series of conferences discussing ethical considerations in pandemic management.

Eduard saw debates about balancing public health with personal freedoms and government intervention.

"Effective crisis management requires balancing multiple interests," Sfath noted. "Governments must address public health needs while respecting individual rights. Transparency and ethical considerations are crucial."

Eduard observed leaders grappling with these issues, realizing the importance of thoughtful decision-making during crises.

The scene shifted to various global regions, highlighting different responses to the pandemic and conflicts influenced by NATO's actions.

Eduard saw both solidarity and division among communities.

"Human behavior during crises is influenced by many factors," Sfath said.

"Cultural norms, political climates, and individual beliefs all shape responses."

Eduard observed acts of kindness and support, as well as instances of conflict and division. "How can societies better manage crises?"

Sfath responded, "Building strong communities, fostering clear communication, and promoting collaboration are key to effective crisis management."

The spacecraft journeyed to a vision of the future, emphasizing global cooperation in addressing pandemics and conflicts.

Eduard saw nations working together to tackle common challenges.

"To create a better future," Sfath said, "nations must prioritize collaboration and shared values.

Effective global governance requires a commitment to mutual support and understanding."

"Look at them," Sfath said, pointing to a busy vaccination clinic in a bustling city.

"Humanity is in the midst of a colossal experiment with stakes higher than they realize."

Eduard's eyes widened as he observed the scene. Lines of people, anxious yet hopeful, extended out of the clinic.

Medical personnel, clad in protective gear, administered vaccines with an air of professionalism that barely masked the underlying uncertainty.

Sfath continued, "The vaccines being administered are part of an unprecedented global test.

Their effectiveness and safety are still uncertain, and many were developed and approved hastily."

Eduard frowned, absorbing the gravity of Sfath's words.

"So, the vaccines might not be as effective as claimed? And there's no real understanding of their long-term effects?"

"Exactly," Sfath confirmed.

"The vaccines, especially the gene-based ones, are experimental and lack long-term testing.

The available data is often manipulated to present a more favorable outcome, and the risks may outweigh the benefits."

The spacecraft shifted to a government conference room where high-ranking officials were discussing the pandemic's challenges.

Sfath and Eduard listened through the ship's audio receptors.

"The situation is more precarious than publicly acknowledged," one official said, his voice strained.

"There are unreported cases of severe adverse effects, and some deaths have been linked to the vaccines."

Another official added, "We must balance public health messaging with maintaining order.

Acknowledging the full extent of the risks could lead to panic."

Eduard turned to Sfath.

"So even the leaders are in the dark about the vaccines' full impact?"

"Precisely," Sfath replied.

"Many leaders are aware of potential dangers but are constrained by political and social pressures.

Revealing the truth could provoke widespread fear and unrest."

Sfath and Eduard then focused on a hospital where doctors and nurses were dealing with the pandemic's consequences.

One doctor spoke candidly with a colleague.

"Not all infections are detectable by standard tests," the doctor said, "especially when the virus targets internal organs.

Many carriers are asymptomatic, unknowingly spreading the virus."

Eduard's concern deepened.

"So, even with vaccines, there are still significant gaps in detecting and controlling the spread?"

"Yes," Sfath confirmed.

"Vaccines are not a cure-all.

They may reduce symptoms but do not necessarily prevent the virus from spreading or mutating.

Transmission through contaminated needles, though rare, complicates the situation."

The spacecraft zoomed forward in time, revealing new variants of the virus, each mutation more challenging than the last.

"This is what we anticipated," Sfath said.

"The first wave of mutations is causing greater confusion and fear.

Governments and scientists are struggling to keep up."

Eduard's voice was grave.

"The issue is compounded by a lack of understanding among those in power.

They are still reacting to the original virus, not grasping the new challenges posed by mutations."

Sfath's tone was somber.

"The death toll is rising, with millions already lost.

Infections continue to climb with no clear end in sight.

The pandemic's impact is far from over, and the true cost remains to be seen."

The spacecraft returned to its original vantage point, allowing Sfath and Eduard to reflect on the tumultuous journey they had witnessed.

They wandered through the city, passing crowded hospitals and empty storefronts.

The atmosphere was one of anxiety and distress.

Eduard pointed to a long line outside a hospital.

Sfath nodded.

"Hospitals are struggling with patient influx.

The virus has led to severe health issues, placing immense pressure on healthcare systems."

At a vaccination center, Eduard saw people waiting for their shots.

Some appeared hopeful, while others looked worried.

Eduard inquired, "I thought vaccines were developed to fight the virus.

Why do some people seem nervous?"

Sfath responded, "Vaccines were created to protect people and curb the virus's spread. However, complications and side effects have led to concerns.

Let's examine these aspects more closely."

Sfath projected data onto a holographic screen.

"At midnight, the population was recorded as 9 billion, 446 million, 218 thousand, and 012. Despite the pandemic, the world's population has continued to grow."

Eduard processed the information.

"So, despite the pandemic's impact, the population has still increased?"

Sfath confirmed, "Yes, the population growth has persisted despite the pandemic's challenges."

Sfath updated the data display.

"Current records show 22 million, 341 thousand, and 203 deaths related to the pandemic and vaccinations."

Eduard's eyes widened.

"How many of these deaths were due to the vaccines alone?"

Sfath explained, "It's difficult to provide exact figures.

The numbers fluctuated, making it challenging to pinpoint the precise impact of vaccinations.

However, it's clear that vaccine-related deaths were significant."

As they explored, Eduard encountered individuals affected by the pandemic and vaccinations.

One woman mourned her husband's vaccine-related death, while others shared their own struggles and losses.

Eduard asked, "How can we support those who have been affected?"

Sfath responded, "Understanding their stories is crucial.

We can use this knowledge to improve future interventions and offer support."

Eduard observed government officials addressing the crisis.

Despite the severity, official statements often minimized issues related to vaccinations.

Eduard questioned, "Why do they downplay the vaccine-related problems?"

Sfath explained, "Institutions sometimes downplay issues to avoid panic or protect their interests.

It's important to seek accurate information and consider various perspectives."

Eduard noted the stark divide between official narratives and public opinion.

Social media was rife with debates and misinformation.

Eduard asked, "How can people find the truth amid so much conflicting information?"

Sfath advised, "Critical thinking and verifying facts are essential.

People should rely on credible sources and question misinformation."

As their journey continued, Sfath and Eduard discussed the lessons learned from 2021.

The pandemic had revealed both human resilience and vulnerabilities.

Sfath said, "These events teach us about the consequences of our actions and the importance of being prepared for future challenges."

Eduard nodded thoughtfully.

"I see how crucial it is to learn from the past."

Despite the challenges, Eduard observed signs of progress.

New treatments and community initiatives were emerging to address the crisis.

Eduard asked, "What new solutions are being developed?"

Sfath explained, "Innovations in treatments, improved vaccine designs, and increased community support are all part of ongoing efforts to enhance public health."

As their journey came to an end, Sfath prepared Eduard for his mission.

"The knowledge you've gained is invaluable.

You'll need to apply these lessons to guide future generations."

Eduard felt a deep sense of responsibility.

"I'll make sure to use this knowledge wisely."

Sfath smiled.

"I have every confidence in you."

Sfath and Eduard returned to their own time.

The futuristic classroom now felt familiar, but Eduard carried a profound understanding of the world's challenges.

Eduard looked at Sfath with gratitude.

"Thank you for showing me the future."

Sfath nodded approvingly.

"You've done well, Eduard.

Your journey has made a significant impact."

Eduard reflected on his experience, grasping the complexities and nuances of global events. He realized the importance of empathy, critical thinking, and preparedness.

Eduard embraced his mission with a renewed sense of purpose.

He understood that his actions would play a crucial role in shaping the future.

Sfath observed Eduard's growth with pride. "You're ready for the challenges ahead."

Eduard smiled, determined to make a positive impact. Sfath's gaze was thoughtful.

"The path forward is uncertain.

Humanity must confront its fears, embrace scientific integrity, and work collaboratively to address the pandemic's many facets.

Only then can they hope to navigate through the shadows of uncertainty and emerge stronger."

As they continued to observe from their vessel, Sfath and Eduard pondered the lessons learned from their journey.

The future remained unwritten, shaped by the choices humanity made in the face of adversity.

As the spacecraft prepared to return to the present, Eduard reflected on the lessons learned from his journey.

He had witnessed the origins of the COVID-19 pandemic, the role of international organizations, and the complexities of global politics.

"Thank you, Sfath," Eduard said, his voice filled with appreciation.

"This journey has given me a deeper understanding of how the world works and how we can better respond to crises."

Sfath smiled warmly.

"Remember, Eduard, understanding the past and present helps us navigate the future. Use these lessons to inspire positive change."

Back in his own time, Eduard carried the insights gained from his journey with him.

He understood the importance of preparedness, ethical decision-making, and international cooperation in addressing global challenges.

Chapter 34

The Destruction of Atlantis and Lemuria

In the soft light of early morning, the dense forest was enveloped in a fragrant blend of pine and earth.

However, today an unmistakable thrill charged the atmosphere.

Hidden within the trees, a pear-shaped spacecraft rested silently in a small clearing, its sleek surface shimmering under the dappled sunlight.

The advanced technology of the craft, with its smooth contours and iridescent sheen, appeared to merge seamlessly with its natural surroundings.

Eduard navigated through the undergrowth with practiced ease, his heart racing with the excitement of another adventure alongside his enigmatic friend, Sfath.

As he emerged into the clearing, the spacecraft's hatch slid open with a soft hiss, and Sfath greeted him with a warm, anticipatory smile.

"Eduard!" Sfath called out, his eyes alight with enthusiasm.

"It's wonderful to see you again."

Eduard's face broke into a wide grin.

"Sfath! What's on the agenda today?"

Sfath gestured for Eduard to enter the spacecraft.

Inside, the interior was a futuristic marvel, soft blue lights bathed the space, and panels displayed streams of complex data. Sfath indicated a seat beside him.

"Today," Sfath began as he settled into his chair, "we're embarking on a journey to witness a pivotal moment in Earth's history.

We'll travel back to observe the destruction of two of the greatest civilizations ever to exist: Atlantis and Mu."

Eduard's eyes widened in awe.

"Atlantis and Mu?

The legendary civilizations that vanished from history?"

Sfath nodded.

"Exactly.

Our mission is to understand the events leading to their downfall.

Both civilizations were incredibly advanced, and their destruction marked a significant turning point in Earth's history."

As the spacecraft's engines hummed to life, Eduard felt a surge of exhilaration.

Sfath continued to explain their journey as the craft powered up, its systems glowing with energy.

The spacecraft shimmered with temporal energy as Sfath initiated the time jump.

In an instant, they were transported to an era long before recorded history.

The vibrant landscapes of Atlantis and Mu unfolded beneath them.

From their vantage point, the splendor of Atlantis was breathtaking.

The city was an expansive island metropolis, its architecture seamlessly integrating with the natural environment.

Towering spires of gleaming crystal rose above glittering canals that wound through the city.

Majestic bridges connected elegant buildings, and the air thrummed with advanced technology and the vibrant hum of a thriving society.

In contrast, Mu, nestled in the heart of the Gobi Desert, was a marvel of engineering.

The city boasted grand pyramids surrounded by artificially cultivated landscapes.

Massive geothermal systems provided energy and warmth, creating an oasis of civilization in an otherwise barren region.

Intricate carvings adorned the streets, bustling with scholars and scientists engaged in lively discussions.

Sfath and Eduard marveled at the harmony and sophistication of these civilizations.

The golden age of Atlantis and Mu was evident in their technological advancements and cultural achievements, a testament to the heights humanity could achieve in an era of unity and prosperity.

Their exploration soon shifted to a darker chapter of history.

Sfath's spacecraft transported them to a time when peace was shattered by ambition and conflict.

Pelegon, a brilliant but ruthless scientist, began his rise to power.

Pelegon's fleet of spaceships, with 70,000 followers, arrived on Earth, where they founded a new civilization characterized by grand cities blending advanced technology with natural beauty.

For a time, this society thrived, marked by impressive advancements and architectural splendor.

Yet beneath this facade, discontent brewed, setting the stage for future conflict.

After 7,000 years of relative peace, the civilization was rocked by treachery.

Ambitious leaders and scientists began to undermine each other, creating a climate of distrust and unrest.

The arrival of Jschwjsch Arus and his followers from a neighboring solar system marked the beginning of a new era of conflict.

Their landing in what is now Florida sparked global struggles.

The advanced technology and ruthless tactics of these invaders posed a grave threat to both Atlantis and Mu.

The war between Atlantis and Mu escalated as both cities battled the invaders.

Atlantis, with its vast military forces and cutting-edge weaponry, clashed with Mu, which had developed equally devastating technologies.

The world became a battleground, with cities and landscapes transforming into arenas of conflict.

The Atlantians utterly destroyed the city of Mu, erasing it from existence.

Only those who had escaped to satellite cities deep underground or fled into space survived the Atlantians' devastating rays.

With no remnants left to mark Mu's former glory, the victorious Atlantians returned to their vast island kingdom, reveling in a frenzied celebration of their triumph.

As Atlantis celebrated its victory over Mu, the tide of war was far from over.

While the Atlanteans reveled in their apparent triumph, Mu scientists were secretly preparing a devastating counterstrike.

They had identified a planetoid in the asteroid belt suitable for use as a weapon.

The planetoid, several kilometers in diameter, was to be turned into a colossal space bomb.

The Mu scientists launched the planetoid from its orbit using atomic and electro-energetic technology, setting it on a collision course with Atlantis.

They slowed its rotation and equipped it with a gigantic drive unit to accelerate it towards its target.

Just before the full-scale attack by Atlantis, the planetoid was ready, a deadly messenger of destruction.

As Atlantis continued to celebrate its victory, the Mu scientists received the signal to release the planetoid.

It accelerated rapidly through space, its trajectory precisely calculated.

When it entered the Earth's atmosphere, it ignited with a blinding light and a heat exceeding 340,000 degrees.

Vast areas of land were incinerated in an instant.

The planetoid exploded at less than 172 kilometers altitude, showering the Earth with thousands of meteorites, each causing catastrophic damage.

The explosion created massive shockwaves and seismic disruptions.

Two large fragments of the planetoid crashed into the Atlantic, causing the Earth's crust to fracture and magma to surge.

A colossal tsunami surged across the Atlantic, inundating and obliterating the island empire of Atlantis within minutes.

Sfath and Eduard watched in awe and horror as these events unfolded.

The absolute destruction of these great civilizations stood as a stark testament to the destructive potential of unchecked ambition and conflict.

As the spacecraft prepared to return to 1947, Eduard and Sfath reflected on the profound lessons from their journey.

The rise and fall of Atlantis and Mu underscored the fragility of peace and the dangers of unbridled power.

Their story served as a cautionary tale about the need for balance between ambition and harmony.

The echoes of these ancient civilizations offered valuable guidance for future generations, emphasizing the importance of maintaining peace and understanding.

Upon their return, Eduard and Sfath knew the lessons of Atlantis and Mu would resonate through time.

The memories of these ancient civilizations would continue to inspire and instruct, reminding humanity of the delicate balance required to achieve and sustain peace.

As they stepped out of the spacecraft and into the familiar forest, Eduard looked at Sfath with gratitude.

"Thank you for this incredible journey.

I've learned so much."

Sfath smiled warmly.

"The past has much to teach us, Eduard.

It is up to us to heed its lessons and strive for a better future."

With that, the two friends parted ways, their minds filled with the echoes of ancient civilizations and the hope for a future guided by wisdom and harmony.

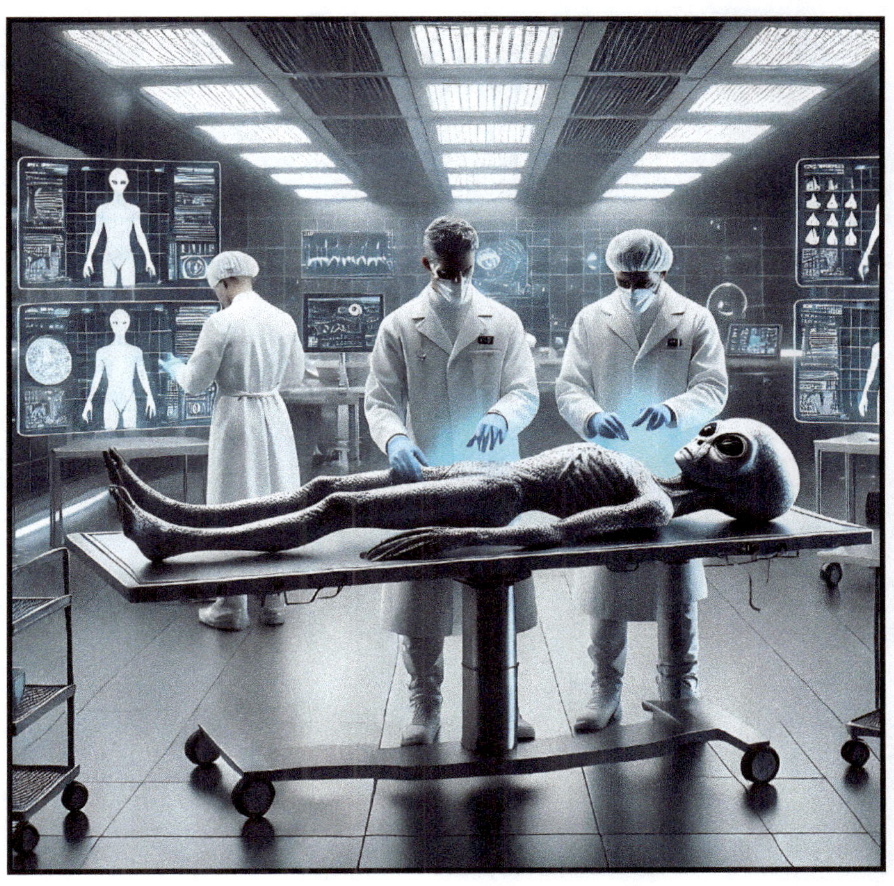

CHAPTER 35

Roswell

The New Mexico desert sprawled out beneath a shroud of fog, the stillness occasionally interrupted by the distant howl of the wind.

Eduard and Sfath materialized in the shadows, their advanced cloaking technology rendering them invisible to the human activity around them.

The night air was crisp, and the stars, partially obscured by the fog, barely glimmered.

"Eduard," Sfath said, his voice steady, "we are about to witness a critical moment in human history.

This journey will not just reveal the past but will expose the hidden truths that have shaped our present."

Eduard nodded, trying to comprehend the significance of their mission.

The date was July 8, 1947, a moment long sealed in secrecy, the day the Roswell incident allegedly took place.

To them, it was not merely a historical event but a crucial episode in a much larger narrative.

The desert scene was chaotic.

A spacecraft lay in ruins on the ground, its metal fragments scattered across the sandy expanse.

Military personnel, clad in uniforms, moved swiftly and efficiently, their footsteps and voices blending into a cacophony of urgent activity.

Eduard and Sfath observed from their hidden vantage, their presence imperceptible to those around them.

A convoy of military vehicles rolled up, their headlights piercing through the darkness.

High-ranking officials emerged, their faces illuminated briefly before being swallowed by the night.

Eduard and Sfath, concealed by their cloaking, watched the scene unfold with unobstructed clarity.

"Secure the area immediately!" barked an officer, his command sharp and authoritative.

"We cannot let this information slip.

The press must not know."

"Understood, sir!" a subordinate responded, quickly mobilizing the soldiers and issuing orders to control the scene.

Sfath guided Eduard to a concealed position where they could overhear a conversation between General Harrington and Colonel Reed, two high-ranking officials.

They stood apart from the activity, speaking in hushed, urgent tones.

"We need to ensure that this incident remains classified," General Harrington said, his voice laden with concern.

"The implications are too significant for the public to handle."

Colonel Reed nodded.

"Agreed. The technology and the beings we've recovered are unlike anything we've encountered.

If this information leaks, it could lead to widespread panic and geopolitical instability."

Harrington's expression grew grave.

"We'll stick to the weather balloon story.

It's a flimsy excuse, but it should divert attention.

We must also control any witnesses."

"And the beings?" Reed asked, his tone quiet but intense.

Harrington's gaze became steely.

"We need to keep the bio-organic androids hidden.

They're advanced and capable of independent thought, but we must ensure that no one learns their true nature."

The scene shifted to an underground facility where Eduard and Sfath continued their observation.

The facility was sterile, its white corridors buzzing with activity as scientists and technicians examined the wreckage and the recovered beings.

On an examination table lay one of the bio-organic androids.

Its form, while humanoid, had an alien quality, a blend of organic and synthetic materials. Eduard noted the precision with which the android was being studied, its features meticulously analyzed.

Dr. Langley, a scientist, peered through a glass window at the android.

"These androids are remarkable.

They have an artificial consciousness that allows for independent thought and decision-making.

They're life forms in their own right."

Dr. Martinez, his assistant, looked up with a mixture of unease and curiosity.

"So they're similar to humans but not exactly the same?

Their programming keeps them subordinate to their creators, but how do we manage their autonomy?"

Langley adjusted his glasses, deep in thought.

"We must handle them carefully.

They're sophisticated and can innovate, but their collective consciousness is fixed and not evolving like ours.

For now, we monitor them closely."

Back at the crash site, General Harrington and Colonel Reed reviewed their strategy.

The cover story about the weather balloon was already in circulation, and preparations were underway to manage any potential fallout.

"We've managed to suppress the truth so far," Reed said, examining the prepared press releases and statements.

"But this is just the beginning.

As long as we control the narrative and prevent leaks, the secret of Roswell will remain intact."

Harrington nodded.

"Precisely.

As long as the bio-organic androids and their origins remain hidden, we maintain control over this knowledge."

Eduard and Sfath, remaining invisible, watched the strategy unfold.

The meticulous efforts to conceal the truth and manage the narrative were clear.

The depth of secrecy surrounding the Roswell incident was profound, with layers of deception carefully crafted to keep the public in the dark.

Back in their own time, Eduard and Sfath stood in the quiet of their study, the revelations of their journey still resonating.

Their advanced cloaking technology had allowed them to witness hidden truths, but it had also left them with a significant burden of knowledge.

"Do you think the truth will ever emerge?" Eduard asked, his voice reflecting a sense of contemplation.

Sfath considered the question carefully.

"Truths often remain buried beneath layers of deception.

However, as long as there are those who seek it, the truth remains a beacon."

Eduard nodded.

"And what about the bio-organic androids?

Their existence is a powerful reminder of the complexities and risks associated with advanced technology."

Sfath smiled gently.

"Indeed.

Their story, like many others, is woven into the fabric of history.

It is up to us to remember and, perhaps, to one day reveal the truth."

As they continued their reflection, Eduard and Sfath understood the weight of their discoveries.

The echoes from Roswell, with their hidden complexities and elaborate deceptions, highlighted the delicate balance between knowledge and secrecy.

Their journey had revealed the depths of hidden history, reminding them of the intricate dance between perception and reality.

Tunguska event

Trees blown down and burned by the blast

Chapter 36

The Witnesses of the Tunguska event

The silver, pear-shaped beamship hovered silently in Earth's atmosphere, concealed from human sight. Inside, the air was crisp and pure, humming softly with the ship's energy.

The walls shimmered like liquid metal, shifting in gentle waves that displayed star charts and cascading data, their symbols understood only by Sfath and Eduard.

The seats contoured perfectly to their forms, while a translucent control panel glowed beneath Sfath's fingers as he fine-tuned their temporal coordinates.

Eduard leaned forward, gazing through the curved viewport at the vast Siberian wilderness below.

"So, this is the moment," he murmured, his eyes fixed on the untouched expanse of the Tunguska region in 1908. "Before history is written in speculation."

Sfath nodded, his ancient gaze scanning the data before him. "We are here to witness the truth, Eduard.

Not the theories, not the guesses of Earth's scientists, only the reality of what truly happened."

As the beamship descended unseen, slipping through time like a needle-threading fabric, a foreign presence was already there.

Below, near the Stony Tunguska River, the Gilaser had established their encampment. Their sleek metallic structures, blending seamlessly with the land, marked their doomed presence.

Eduard's gaze shifted to the extraterrestrial visitors.

The Gilaser were humanoid, taller than Earth-humans, their skin tinged with a faint golden hue.

Their leader, Kael, stood at the edge of the encampment, deep in conversation with his second-in-command, Seris. Their expressions were grim.

"They already know their fate," Eduard whispered.

Sfath exhaled slowly. "Yes. They have violated their sacred laws by engaging with Earth-humans. The consequence is absolute."

Eduard turned to him, his brow furrowed. "Because of the disease?"

"And the contamination of their culture," Sfath confirmed.

"Their people warned them, forbade their mission. But curiosity, and perhaps arrogance, led them here. Now, they face the ultimate punishment."

Below, the camp was in turmoil. Some Gilaser argued, desperate for an alternative. Others sat in resigned silence, accepting their fate.

The beamship's display flickered, signaling an imminent energy surge. Sfath gestured toward the readout. "It is time."

Eduard's pulse quickened as they watched the Gilaser board their massive vessel, a colossal construct that dwarfed their own ship.

The vessel's hull, smooth and mirror-like, reflected the forest below as it began to rise.

A low vibration filled the air.

Then, a flash. Blinding. Silent. Final.

The explosion shattered the sky, flattening the forest in an instant. A shockwave rippled outward, its force felt for miles.

Fire streaked across the heavens, and within moments, nothing remained but scorched earth and the ghosts of an untold history.

Eduard sat back, his voice barely above a breath. "And yet, no one will know."

Sfath placed a steadying hand on his shoulder. "No one on Earth, perhaps. But the universe remembers."

The beamship tilted upward, slipping once more beyond the veil of time, leaving behind only the echo of a secret never to be revealed.

The Lost Legacy of the Gilaser

The doomed visitors of Tunguska were the Gilaser, an advanced race from the Setkatis Galaxy, a vast spiral galaxy 17 million light-years away, known to Earth's astronomers as M101.

Their home, the planet Ketulas, was a satellite within the Bliira system, a binary star system housing 18 planets, only three of which harbored intelligent life.

The Gilaser were masters of space-faring technology, capable of constructing massive spacecraft from small planetoids.

Hollowing out these celestial bodies, they installed advanced propulsion systems, powerful weaponry, protective shields, electron collectors, and vast energy storage units.

Their artificial worlds contained entire ecosystems, living quarters, laboratories, food production facilities, and self-sustaining life-support systems.

From the outside, these ships remained indistinguishable from natural planetoids, their true nature hidden even from the keenest of observers.

The vessel that perished over Tunguska on June 30, 1908, was one such construct.

Its estimated mass exceeded 179,000 tons, dwarfing anything Earth's technology could comprehend.

When it exploded at an altitude of 1,290 meters, the resulting devastation left behind a horizontal crater spanning 3,500 square kilometers.

Unlike impact craters formed by meteorites, this was a pressure-wave crater, an immense force pressed downward, flattening everything beneath it, while only a faint, often unrecognizable ridge formed at its outermost edge.

Fragments of the planetoid's hull and internal structures may still rest within Earth's soil, remnants of an interstellar tragedy that history misinterprets as a mere cosmic accident.

But the truth, unseen and unspoken, lingers like an imprint upon the very fabric of time.

CHAPTER 37

George Washington

The year was 1743, and the grand Mount Vernon estate in the colony of Virginia stood as a testament to both wealth and power.

The sprawling plantation, with its neatly kept fields and the labor of enslaved workers, was an empire in its own right, ruled by Augustine Washington, a man of ambition, calculation, and strategic foresight.

The warm autumn breeze whispered through the rolling countryside, carrying with it the faint scent of tobacco, the lifeblood of the Virginian economy.

Above this world, unseen and unfelt by the mortals below, the pear-shaped beamship of Sfath and Eduard hovered silently.

Inside its sleek, silver metallic interior, bathed in soft, ambient light, the two travelers observed history as it unfolded.

Eduard, peering through the ship's advanced observation system, whispered, "Sfath, history often records the surface of events, but here we stand, witnessing the unseen forces that shape the future.

Augustine Washington, his name is barely remembered, yet his ambitions are crucial to what is to come."

Sfath, his calm and wise demeanor unwavering, nodded. "Indeed, Eduard.

His plans, his wealth, his vision, they are the foundation upon which his son, George, will build his legacy. But history has a way of concealing its darker truths."

They activated their cloaking field and descended into the estate, their figures shimmering into nothingness as they stepped onto the dusty path leading to the grand house.

Inside, the scent of aged wood and burning candles mixed with the air of quiet tension.

In the dimly lit study of Mount Vernon, Augustine Washington sat at a large wooden desk, poring over documents and maps.

His gaze was cold, his expression unreadable, as he conferred with his aides.

Augustine Washington: (sternly) "The colonies are restless, but our position must remain secure. Ensure the loyalty of the gentry, the future depends on their continued allegiance."

Aide: (hesitant) "And the enslaved workers, sir?"

Augustine's eyes narrowed. His voice, though calm, carried an edge of finality.

Augustine Washington: "Their place is fixed. There will be no disruptions. We have methods to ensure their obedience."

Sfath and Eduard exchanged glances.

Sfath: (quietly) "His mind operates like that of a chess player, every move calculated for power, every piece either a tool or a threat."

Eduard's expression darkened. "This is the true machinery of empire, ambition built on control. But what role does his son, George, play in this grand design?"

Sfath gestured toward the doorway, where a young George Washington, barely eleven years old, stood listening in the shadows.

His youthful face was marked by quiet intensity, his sharp mind absorbing the nature of power before he even fully understood its consequences.

By 1750, the landscape had shifted. Augustine Washington had passed away, and George, now a young man, had entered the circles of the powerful, particularly under the mentorship of Lord William Fairfax, one of the most influential men in Virginia.

Sfath and Eduard observed from the gardens of Belvoir Manor, where George stood in quiet conversation with Lord Fairfax.

The air smelled of damp earth after a morning rain, and a soft fog curled around the towering oak trees.

Lord Fairfax: "You've made quite an impression, George. But impressions alone do not shape the future. Have you thought about where your path leads?"

George Washington: (nodding) "Your guidance has been invaluable, my lord. My ambitions lie in service, to the land, to Virginia, to the Crown."

Lord Fairfax: (chuckling) "The Crown? Ambition is a strange thing, George. It starts in service and ends in command."

Sfath, observing the exchange, turned to Eduard. "Fairfax is shaping Washington into more than a soldier, he is grooming him for leadership, for strategy, for something beyond colonial loyalties."

Eduard, watching George's calculating expression, murmured, "Yet there is another force at work, Sally Fairfax. How does she fit into his story?"

Sally Fairfax: The Secret Influence

In the quiet evenings of Belvoir Manor, away from the public eye, George Washington and Sally Fairfax, the wife of Lord Fairfax's son, found themselves drawn into a relationship that would leave a lasting mark on Washington's future.

Sfath and Eduard observed them one evening as they walked through the candlelit halls, their voices hushed, their emotions carefully veiled yet unmistakable.

Sally Fairfax: (softly) "George, the world does not belong to the hesitant. You must learn to navigate power as one navigates a river, with purpose."

George Washington: (solemn) "Your wisdom is unlike any other, Sally. You see the world with clarity."

Sally Fairfax: (smiling) "And I see potential in you, George."

Eduard turned to Sfath. "She is more than a lover, she is a teacher, a mentor. She is shaping him, just as much as Fairfax himself."

Sfath nodded. "History will never fully acknowledge her influence, but it is there, hidden beneath the official records."

1754: The Jumonville Affair

By May 1754, Washington had risen to command, leading a Virginian militia against the French forces in the Ohio Valley.

Sfath and Eduard stood invisibly at the edge of a rain-drenched battlefield, watching history unfold.

Washington's troops were weary but determined.

Across from them, Joseph de Jumonville, a French officer sent on a diplomatic mission, stood with his men under a white flag.

Jumonville: (firmly) "We are not here to fight. We come under the protection of diplomacy."

Washington hesitated for only a moment before his expression hardened.

"This land belongs to the British. Your presence is an act of war."

Before another word could be exchanged, Washington raised his weapon and fired, striking Jumonville down.

The French officer collapsed, blood staining the wet earth. The silence that followed was heavy, broken only by the whispers of Washington's men.

Eduard took a sharp breath. "He shot him while he held a flag of truce. This is not war—it is murder."

Sfath's expression was grim. "And it will have consequences. The French will not forget this crime. The war to come will reshape the continent."

Reflections on a Nation's Birth.

As years passed, the American Revolution would rise from the embers of these early conflicts. Washington would become a general, then a leader, and finally the first President of the United States.

From their vantage point beyond time, Sfath and Eduard watched as the ideals of freedom clashed with the realities of power.

Eduard: "Washington's name will be immortalized, but the truth of his rise will remain hidden beneath legend."

Sfath: "Such is the nature of history, Eduard. It is written by victors, shaped by ambitions, and obscured by time."

As the last light of sunset faded over the horizon, the two travelers turned away from the past, leaving behind the echoes of a world forever changed by one man's ruthless ambition.

Chapter 38

The Death of Cleopatra

In the year 1945, as the world grappled with the aftermath of a devastating global conflict, two researchers, Sfath and Eduard, were on the brink of an extraordinary journey.

Their destination: the ancient world, a place fraught with history and intrigue.

Inside their sleek, pear-shaped spacecraft, a marvel of advanced technology, they prepared to embark on a journey back to 51 B.Jmmanuel, the time of Cleopatra's rise to power.

"Ready for the jump?" Sfath asked, excitement clear in his voice as he adjusted the ship's controls.

His eyes sparkled with anticipation.

Eduard, seated next to Sfath at the navigation console, checked himself then close his eyes as he alwyas does.

With a surge of energy, the spacecraft roared to life.

A soft, blueish light enveloped them as the vessel entered the time stream.

In an instant, the futuristic world of 1945 dissolved, replaced by the ancient cityscape of Alexandria.

The spacecraft hovered silently above the bustling city of Alexandria, its invisibility cloak ensuring they were unseen.

Sfath and Eduard gazed down at the vibrant city, marveling at its grandeur.

Cleopatra, just 18 years old, had recently ascended the throne.

Her reign, however, was already marked by intense political maneuvering and personal challenges.

"Look at the splendor of Alexandria," Sfath remarked, his eyes wide with wonder.

"This is where Cleopatra's story begins."

Eduard, adjusting their position to get a better view, nodded.

"We need to follow her closely and observe how she navigates the treacherous waters of early rule."

Descending discreetly, the two approached the palace, where Cleopatra was engaged in a heated argument with her younger brother, Ptolemaios VIII.

"Why do you persist in challenging my authority?" Cleopatra demanded, her voice echoing through the opulent chambers.

"I act in the best interest of Egypt," Ptolemaios retorted, his expression defiant.

Cleopatra's gaze was unwavering.

"Your actions are undermining my rule.

This cannot continue."

Sfath and Eduard followed Cleopatra's strategic journey to Rome, where she sought Julius Caesar's assistance to solidify her position.

The grand hall of Caesar's palace was filled with political power and intrigue.

"Caesar, I ask for your support to restore me to my throne in Egypt," Cleopatra urged, her tone both desperate and resolute.

Caesar, seated behind a massive desk, scrutinized her with a calculating gaze.

"What do you offer in exchange for my help?"

Cleopatra responded with confidence, "An alliance.

Egypt and Rome, united in strength."

Caesar considered her proposal for a moment before nodding.

"Very well. We have a deal."

As their alliance deepened, so did Cleopatra's influence in Rome, cementing her position through both political acumen and personal connections.

During her time in Rome, Cleopatra gave birth to a son named Kaisarion in 47 B.Jmmanuel. Sfath and Eduard witnessed this significant event from their hidden vantage point.

In the privacy of Caesar's quarters, Cleopatra held her newborn son with tenderness. "He must symbolize our unity," she said softly, her gaze fixed on the infant.

Caesar, blending affection with strategic foresight, replied, "He will stand as a testament to our alliance, both personally and politically."

Following Caesar's assassination in 44 B.Jmmanuel, Cleopatra returned to Egypt.

She appointed Kaisarion as co-regent, ensuring his role in Egypt's future and her own continued influence.

With the civil war breaking out in 43/42 B.Jmmanuel, Cleopatra made a crucial decision to remain neutral.

In her palace, she convened with her advisors to discuss the situation.

"We must avoid direct involvement in this conflict," Cleopatra instructed with a measured tone.

"Our priority must be to protect our position and wait for a more opportune moment."

Her strategic retreat was a calculated move, demonstrating her ability to navigate through the political turmoil of the era.

Cleopatra's strategic marriage to Mark Antony was a pivotal moment in her quest for power. Sfath and Eduard followed them to Antony's camp, where their alliance was formalized.

"Together, we will restore Egypt's splendor," Cleopatra declared, her voice brimming with ambition.

Antony, his gaze resolute, responded, "With your vision and my strength, we can reshape the world. Our combined efforts will bring great change."

Their union was a powerful blend of personal commitment and political strategy, designed to fortify their positions and enhance their influence.

The arrival of Octavian marked a new phase of tension.

In Rome, Octavian declared Cleopatra an enemy of the state.

"Antony's will favors Cleopatra's children, which threatens Rome's dominance," Octavian announced to the Senate.

Cleopatra, despite the growing threat, remained determined.

"We must prepare for the coming storm.

Our position is precarious, and we need to act with resolve."

Her words were a reflection of the mounting pressure and the shifting political landscape.

The Battle of Actium was a turning point in Cleopatra's struggle for power.

Sfath and Eduard observed from their concealed position as Antony and Cleopatra's forces faced a decisive defeat.

"We must retreat!" Antony shouted amid the chaos of the battlefield.

"To Egypt!"

Cleopatra, her face set with determination, agreed.

"We will make our final stand there. There is no other choice."

The decision to retreat was a desperate move, reflecting the gravity of their situation.

The Final Days in Egypt

Back in Egypt, Cleopatra and Antony faced the end of their reign.

Sfath and Eduard, maintaining their hidden observation, watched as Cleopatra prepared for the final confrontation.

"We cannot endure this defeat," Cleopatra said, her voice tinged with despair.

"Our enemies will not show us mercy."

Antony, taking her hand, responded solemnly, "We will face our end with dignity.

There is no other way."

The atmosphere was heavy with the weight of their imminent defeat.

Cleopatra's final moments were marked by a harrowing decision.

In her private chambers, she prepared for death using poison and the bite of a snake.

Sfath and Eduard observed as Cleopatra, with a mix of pain and resolve, executed her plan.

"Proceed," Cleopatra instructed her servant, who administered the poison reluctantly.

As the snake's venom took effect, Cleopatra's face reflected both agony and unyielding spirit.

She also drank from a cup of poison, her expression a final testament to her strength and resolve.

"Let history remember me as I was," Cleopatra whispered, her voice fading as darkness enveloped her.

After witnessing Cleopatra's tragic end, Sfath and Eduard prepared to return to their own time.

The spacecraft hummed to life, and they reflected on the profound complexity of Cleopatra's life and reign.

"Her end was tragic, marked by her ambition and the controversial aspects of her lineage," Eduard said softly, his voice filled with contemplation.

"Yes," Sfath agreed, as the spacecraft reentered the time stream.

"Cleopatra's legacy is a profound mix of power, intrigue, and sorrow.

Her life and death embody the complexities of leadership and human ambition."

As the spacecraft surged forward, Eduard and Sfath returned to 1945, carrying with them the deep insights gained from their journey into Cleopatra's world.

Their exploration of the past had revealed the intricate tapestry of a queen's rise and fall, forever shaping their understanding of history.

CHAPTER 39

Gilgamesh

In the stillness of his grand chamber in Uruk, year 1950 BCE, King Gilgamesh sat in thoughtful solitude.

Once a colossal giant, he had adjusted his form to blend seamlessly with Earth's more modest beings.

The moonlight that filtered through the windows cast long shadows across the room, accentuating the deep lines of his ancient face.

Without warning, the air shimmered and distorted.

From this anomaly emerged two figures: Sfath and Eduard.

Their sudden arrival jolted Gilgamesh from his reverie.

Despite his long history with the extraordinary, he had never encountered such an abrupt intrusion.

"Who dares intrude upon my private quarters?"

Gilgamesh's voice echoed with a blend of authority and curiosity.

Sfath, his demeanor calm and composed, stepped forward.

"We come from the year 1945.

Though Eduard is but a child, he spoke next,

"We are here to speak with you.

We know of your true nature, Gilgamesh.

You are one of the shape-changers, the Gestaltwandler."

Eduard, with wide inquisitive eyes, looked up at Gilgamesh, clutching a small, advanced device.

"My history books tell of you as a giant god.

It's amazing to see you in person!"

Gilgamesh's gaze sharpened with interest.

"You know of my people's origins and their fate?" he asked, his voice heavy with the burden of his long solitude.

"Yes," Sfath confirmed.

"Your race, once a mighty civilization in the M94 galaxy, was destroyed by a cataclysm.

You alone survived, adapting to life on Earth."

"And your lifespan had been reduced from 100,000 to half."

Eduard, trying to grasp the enormity of Gilgamesh's story, asked with innocent curiosity,

"Do you miss your home?

Do you want to return?"

A shadow of sadness crossed Gilgamesh's face.

"My home and my people are lost to the void.

I chose to stay on Earth even when offered a way back.

Despite its trials, this world has become my home."

Sfath and Eduard listened attentively as Gilgamesh spoke of his adaptations.

Once a towering giant, he had reshaped himself to blend in with humans.

His need for heavy water, a relic from his former life, was now a critical aspect of his survival.

"You have witnessed eons," Sfath said.

"You have shaped your destiny here on Earth.

Yet, you remain a unique bridge between worlds and eras."

Eduard, still absorbing the gravity of the situation, asked, "What's it like to live for so long? Do you ever feel lonely?"

Gilgamesh's eyes reflected a deep melancholy.

"Loneliness is an eternal companion when one outlives all their kin.

But this solitude has given me perspective.

I have learned to cherish the fleeting connections I make."

The conversation shifted to how Gilgamesh's story had traveled through time.

Sfath and Eduard shared their knowledge of how future societies would remember him, not just as a legend, but as a symbol of resilience and transformation.

Sfath explained, "Your story has influenced generations.

The legends of your deeds and wisdom have shaped human thought across centuries."

Gilgamesh offered a faint smile.

"If my deeds and legacy endure, then perhaps I have achieved a form of immortality, not through endless life, but through the lives I touch."

Sfath and Eduard discussed with Gilgamesh the significance of his shapeshifting abilities. They explored how his physical transformations were symbolic of his personal adaptability and growth.

"Your shape-shifting represents your capacity to evolve and adapt," Sfath said.

"It reflects the growth and flexibility necessary for all beings."

Gilgamesh pondered this insight.

"Indeed.

Perhaps my greatest legacy is not in my physical form but in my ability to continually adapt and find purpose."

As their visit drew to a close, Sfath and Eduard prepared to return to their time.

They expressed their gratitude for Gilgamesh's openness and the wisdom he had shared. Eduard, with the sincerity of youth, offered a heartfelt goodbye.

Gilgamesh presented them with a small artifact, a symbol of the connection between their worlds and times.

"Take this with you," he said.

"Let it serve as a reminder that our legacies, though shaped by time, are interconnected."

With that, Sfath and Eduard activated their device and vanished, leaving Gilgamesh alone once more.

Back in 1945, Sfath and Eduard reflected on their extraordinary journey.

They marveled at how Gilgamesh's story had transcended time, becoming a symbol of perseverance and adaptability.

Eduard gazed at the artifact Gilgamesh had given him, contemplating the encounter and the new dimensions it had added to his understanding of his own existence.

Countdown
für San Francisco
16 000 Tote in der ersten Stunde prophezeien Wissen-
schaftler der Stadt am Golden Gate — wenn ein Erdbeben wie
im Jahre 1906 die City in Trümmer legt. Ein Alptraum,
den der GEO-Zeichner auf eine Aufnahme projiziert hat. Wann das
Beben kommt, weiß niemand. Doch es kommt unausweichlich:
denn bei San Francisco treffen sich die Schollen zweier Kontinente.
An der San-Andreas-Spalte in Kalifornien schieben sie sich mit
Gewalt aneinander und lassen täglich die Erde erzittern

CHAPTER 40

The Big Quake

Eduard and Sfath's arrival in 2060 was marked by the sudden manifestation of their pear-shaped spacecraft, which materialized as though conjured from thin air.

The ship, a marvel of extraterrestrial engineering, was not only sleek in design but also enveloped in an advanced cloaking mechanism, rendering it entirely invisible against the disaster-ravaged Earth below.

The precision of its camouflage ensured that they could observe the unfolding catastrophe without detection, a crucial factor in their mission.

As the spacecraft drifted silently through the turbulent skies, Eduard and Sfath took in the full scope of destruction beneath them.

California had been utterly transformed by the earthquake, its once-thriving cities reduced to skeletal remains of their former grandeur.

The towering skyscrapers that had symbolized human ingenuity and progress were now hollowed-out ruins, their glass facades shattered, and steel frames twisted as if molded by an unseen hand.

Fires raged across the landscape, casting an eerie orange glow against the thick clouds of dust and smoke that lingered in the atmosphere.

Eduard pressed his hands against the observation window, his expression one of grim determination.

His eyes scanned the ruined landscape, searching for familiar landmarks amidst the devastation.

The Golden Gate Bridge, once a proud feat of engineering, lay in pieces, its massive steel girders jutting out from the turbulent waters of the bay like the ribs of a colossal beast.

The city of San Francisco, a hub of innovation and culture, had been left unrecognizable, entire districts had collapsed into chaos, swallowed by fissures that had ruptured through the streets.

The once-bustling heart of Los Angeles was now a jagged silhouette of crumbling towers and flickering emergency lights.

Down below, the ground was a frenzied tableau of desperation and resilience.

People stumbled through the debris-strewn streets, their expressions reflecting both terror and an unyielding will to survive.

Makeshift medical stations had been erected in open spaces, where doctors and emergency responders worked tirelessly to treat the injured.

Their suits, sleek and form-fitting, integrated with holographic displays and real-time data feeds, were unlike anything Eduard had seen before, a clear sign of the technological leaps humanity had made since his own time.

Advanced vehicles weaved through the destruction, their streamlined, aerodynamic forms starkly different from the cars of the past.

Some hovered just inches above the ground, navigating the treacherous terrain with remarkable agility.

Their designs lacked conventional mirrors, replaced instead by panoramic digital displays embedded within their curved, glass canopies.

Others resembled insect-like machines, their bodies segmented and reinforced to withstand the extreme conditions of a collapsed cityscape.

These innovations were a testament to the adaptive progress of a society that had once prided itself on its advancements, now struggling to recover from nature's wrath.

Turning to Sfath, Eduard shook his head in quiet awe.

"The cars, the suits, the technology, everything has changed so much. And yet, for all their advancements, they still find themselves vulnerable to nature's fury."

Sfath, his piercing gaze analyzing every detail through his advanced optical systems, nodded. "Yes.

Their technological progress is undeniable, but this disaster serves as a stark reminder that no civilization, no matter how advanced, is ever truly immune to the forces of nature."

From their hidden vantage point, the two watched as teams of robotic drones soared overhead, scanning the ruins and relaying critical data to command centers operating in the few remaining intact buildings.

These autonomous machines moved with uncanny precision, identifying survivors trapped beneath rubble, mapping hazardous zones, and assisting in rescue efforts.

Some were humanoid in design, their movements fluid and purposeful, lifting massive debris with mechanical strength far beyond human capability.

Others resembled hovering spheres, emitting scanning waves that penetrated deep into collapsed structures.

Despite the overwhelming destruction, there was an unmistakable air of determination.

The people below, though battered and grieving, worked together with remarkable resilience.

Strangers became allies in the face of adversity, forming impromptu rescue teams, distributing supplies, and tending to the wounded.

The fusion of cutting-edge technology and unwavering human spirit painted a compelling picture of survival, one that spoke not only of a civilization that had suffered a great blow but also of one that refused to be broken.

Eduard exhaled slowly, taking in the stark contrast before him. "For all their struggles, they keep moving forward. They adapt, they rebuild. Even in the face of devastation, they refuse to surrender."

Sfath regarded the scene thoughtfully. "That is the essence of humanity.

No matter how many times they fall, they rise again. And in the process, they redefine what it means to endure."

As they continued their silent observation, the realization set in, this was not just a moment of destruction but of transformation.

The California they had once known was gone, but from its ruins, something new was already beginning to take shape. The future, however uncertain, was still being written.

other side of the story
Conspiracy:
There are
no visible stars.
Conspiracy:
US flag is waving
in the wind, but there's
no wind on the Moon.
Conspiracy:
The footprint doesn't
match the boots worn.

CHAPTER 41

First Moon Landing

Eduard and Sfath's temporal vessel settled silently on Earth, cloaked from view.

They emerged into a nondescript building on a remote plot of land in Nevada, blending in with their surroundings due to their advanced cloaking technology.

The interior was a labyrinth of corridors, leading them to a heavily guarded entrance.

Through the dimly lit hallways, they could feel the tension in the air.

Eduard glanced at Sfath, his face reflecting a mix of anticipation and apprehension.

"So this is where it all happened.

The moon landing, staged in a secret studio?

Sfath nodded. "Indeed.

We're about to witness the intricate machinery behind one of the greatest deceptions in history.

Keep your focus.

Our objective is to understand how the illusion was created and maintained."

The two moved stealthily, their invisibility ensuring they remained unnoticed.

They approached a large, soundproof door that led into the heart of the studio.

Beyond the door was an expansive studio, its size and complexity immediately striking.

The room was designed to mimic the lunar surface with incredible detail, craters, rocks, and an artificial sky designed to simulate the lunar environment.

Massive lights mimicked the sun's harsh illumination, casting sharp shadows that contributed to the realism of the scene.

Eduard and Sfath observed as the production crew worked meticulously.

Camera operators adjusted lenses, lighting specialists fine-tuned their equipment, and set designers made last-minute adjustments to the lunar landscape.

"This place is massive," Eduard whispered.

"The scale of this operation is astounding.

They've created an entire lunar environment right here on Earth."

Sfath surveyed the room.

"The attention to detail is impressive.

The success of this illusion depended on every aspect being perfectly controlled."

Eduard and Sfath moved closer to the production team, remaining unseen as they eavesdropped on conversations among key figures.

The director, a stern-faced man named Robert Mitchell, was discussing the final preparations with his team.

"Okay, everyone, we're on the final stretch," Mitchell said, his voice carrying authority.

"The cameras need to be precisely positioned to capture every angle.

Remember, this has to look perfect.

We're creating history here, even if it's not the real thing."

A lighting technician named Linda adjusted a massive light panel.

"We've calibrated the lights to match the lunar sunlight.

This has to look exactly like what was broadcasted."

Mitchell nodded approvingly.

"Excellent.

The shadows must be consistent with our models.

We can't afford any discrepancies."

Nearby, a young assistant named Tim was preparing the communication equipment.

"The feed is ready.

We'll be transmitting live to the control room in Houston.

They'll handle the broadcast."

Mitchell's eyes narrowed. "Good.

Make sure the feed is flawless.

We're controlling the world's perception of this mission.

Every detail must align with our plans."

Eduard and Sfath moved to another part of the studio where the lunar module replica was being prepared.

The module, although detailed, was unmistakably a piece of high-quality stagecraft.

The astronauts, in their suits, were practicing their movements in and around the module.

One of the astronauts, named Jack, was discussing his role with a production assistant.

"I've rehearsed this sequence a hundred times.

It's crucial that my movements look natural.

We need to convince the viewers that this is the actual lunar surface."

The assistant nodded, making notes on a clipboard.

"Your performance has to be flawless.

Remember, we're not just filming; we're creating a historic moment."

Jack adjusted his suit and took a deep breath.

"Got it. Let's make sure everything is perfect.

This is our chance to deliver an unforgettable performance."

As the final preparations were completed, Eduard and Sfath observed the control room from their concealed position.

The room was a hive of activity, with engineers, technicians, and directors monitoring various screens and feeds.

Mitchell entered the control room, his demeanor focused.

"How's the feed looking?"

An engineer named Carlos looked up from his console.

"The feed is stable.

We're getting a clear signal.

The broadcast will go live in a few minutes."

Mitchell checked his watch.

"Excellent.

Make sure everything aligns with the pre-arranged script.

We need to deliver the illusion of a successful moon landing."

A communications officer named Sarah adjusted the broadcast settings.

"We're ready to switch to the live feed.

The world will see what we've prepared.

Ensure that there are no hitches."

Eduard and Sfath remained hidden as the live broadcast began.

The cameras captured the scene of the astronauts moving around the lunar module, their movements choreographed to create the illusion of being on the moon.

Mitchell watched the monitors, his expression a mix of relief and satisfaction.

"This is it.

We've created the perfect illusion.

The world will believe this is the moon."

Linda, the lighting technician, adjusted the lighting one last time.

"Everything looks good.

The shadows and lighting are consistent with the lunar environment."

Jack, the astronaut, completed his final scene.

"I hope this works. We've put a lot of effort into making this look real."

As the broadcast concluded, the studio crew began to dismantle the set.

Eduard and Sfath continued to observe, noting the efficient way in which the illusion was dismantled.

The entire operation had been an elaborate performance, meticulously planned and executed.

Mitchell addressed the team, his voice filled with a sense of accomplishment.

"Well done, everyone.

We've pulled off a monumental achievement.

The world has seen what we intended them to see."

The crew began to clean up, and the studio returned to its mundane state.

The secrecy of the operation remained intact, with only those directly involved aware of the true nature of the moon landing.

Back in their temporal vessel, Eduard and Sfath reflected on what they had witnessed.

The advanced technology that kept them invisible had allowed them to see the detailed mechanics of one of history's greatest deceptions.

"Seeing the studio firsthand has been enlightening," Eduard said, his voice thoughtful.

"The scale of the deception was immense.

It's astonishing how such an elaborate illusion was created."

Sfath nodded in agreement.

"Indeed.

The meticulous planning and execution highlight the lengths to which those in power will go to shape public perception.

The first moon landing was not just about technology; it was about controlling the narrative."

Eduard sighed. "It's a reminder of the power of media and the importance of critical thinking. The world believed in a historic achievement while the truth remained hidden behind the façade."

Sfath smiled.

"Our journey has revealed the depth of hidden history.

The shadows of the studio, with their elaborate deceptions, underscore the delicate balance between perception and reality."

As Eduard and Sfath prepared to return to their own time, they carried with them a deeper understanding of the complexities of history and the impact of secrecy.

Their exploration of the first moon landing's true nature had unveiled the hidden layers of deception, serving as a powerful reminder of the need for transparency and the quest for truth.

As the evening sun cast long shadows over the undulating hills, Sfath and Eduard found solace beneath the sprawling branches of an ancient oak tree.

The golden light filtered through the leaves, painting intricate patterns on the grass where they had laid out their notes and documents.

The tranquil setting was a sharp contrast to the gravity of their task, but the weight of history was palpable in the air.

Sfath, his face a tapestry of time-worn wisdom, turned to Eduard, brimming with focused determination.

"We have undertaken a significant journey through the annals of time to verify and debunk these conspiracy theories," Sfath began, his voice resonant with authority.

"It is time to delve into each claim and understand its truth or falsehood."

Eduard nodded, his pen poised over a blank page.

"Let's start with the 12th-century legend of the ritual murder."

Sfath adjusted himself and consulted the list.

"The claim was that Jews kidnapped a Christian child for a secret Passover ritual.

We have confirmed this to be false.

This myth exploited deep-seated prejudices and fears, reflecting a period rife with scapegoating."

Eduard scribbled notes, then looked up.

"Moving on to the 14th century, the accusation of well poisoning. What can you tell me about this?"

"This was another example of xenophobia," Sfath explained.

"During the plague, Jews were wrongly blamed for poisoning wells.

It was false, but the fear and devastation of the time made such accusations seem plausible to many."

Eduard turned his attention to the 15th century.

"The witch doctrine, how did that unfold?"

Sfath's expression grew somber.

"The belief that natural disasters and diseases were caused by witches led to horrific persecutions.

This theory was rooted in fear of the unknown and was thoroughly refuted, but it resulted in centuries of suffering."

"Next is the Exeter Conspiracy from the 16th century," Eduard said, his pen moving quickly. "What about King Henry VIII's supposed assassination plot?"

"That theory was also false," Sfath replied.

"The idea that there was a plot to assassinate Henry VIII to reverse the Reformation was a product of political intrigue but lacked any substantive evidence."

Eduard glanced at the next entry, from the 17th century.

"The Papist conspiracy, were there attempts to assassinate King Charles II?"

"False," Sfath confirmed.

"This was another unfounded claim driven by religious conflict and paranoia."

As the sky darkened, Eduard continued, "The 17th/18th-century Man with the Iron Mask—what's the truth there?"

"The true story," Sfath said, "is that the prisoner was Louis XIV's twin brother, born secretly and kept hidden.

This theory was confirmed after thorough investigation."

Eduard's eyes moved down the list.

"The Dark Countess and the Castle Eishausen rumors, false, correct?"

"Correct," Sfath said.

"The notion that the daughter of Louis XVI was among the castle's mysterious inhabitants was entirely fabricated."

Eduard made a note and then asked, "The Flat Earth Society thesis, will still be an issue in the future."

"Indeed," Sfath replied.

"This theory that the Earth is flat is false.

It persists despite overwhelming evidence to the contrary."

Eduard continued, "What about Kaspar Hauser?

Was he really a hereditary prince?"

"No," Sfath said. "Kaspar Hauser's true identity was never that of a prince, though his mysterious origins have fueled various theories."

"The World Jewry conspiracy," Eduard said, "alleging global domination?"

"False," Sfath affirmed.

"This theory is rooted in anti-Semitic fears and has no basis in reality."

Eduard noted this and asked, "The Bahai conspiracy?"

"False," Sfath said.

"The idea that Bahai were conspiring against Iran or Islam is baseless."

"Jack the Ripper?"

"Here's a mix of truth and fiction," Sfath explained. "As we have both winessed firsthand, Thomas Neill Cream was indeed one of the murderers, but there was also a second, elusive figure with royal connections."

Eduard made a note, then moved on.

"The Taxil hoax, satanic rites of Freemasons?"

"False," Sfath said.

"This was a fabricated story to discredit the Freemasons."

Eduard continued, "The Know-Nothing Party rumors?"

"False," Sfath replied.

"The idea that Catholic immigration was a ploy to undermine the US was simply not true."

"Agent Theory about Hitler," Eduard said.

"Was he guided by economic interests?"

"That's false," Sfath explained.

"Hitler's actions were driven by his own ideology and ambitions, not economic forces."

"AIDS denial?" Eduard asked.

"False," Sfath answered.

"There is a clear causal link between HIV and AIDS."

Eduard moved on.

"AIDS from US laboratories?"

"False," Sfath confirmed.

"The origins of AIDS are in primates, not in any laboratory."

Eduard's pen flew across the page.

"Amero, the North American monetary union?"

"False," Sfath replied.

"There has been no serious plan for such a union."

"Area 51?" Eduard asked.

"False," Sfath said.

"It's a research facility, not a hub for extraterrestrial contact."

Eduard continued, "The Soviet Union medical conspiracy?"

"False," Sfath confirmed.

"There were no plans to attack high-ranking officials."

"Assassination attempt on Martin Luther King?" Eduard asked.

"That's false," Sfath said.

"The official investigation stands that James Earl Ray acted alone."

"Gang of Nijvel conspiracy?" Eduard asked.

"False," Sfath replied. "These attacks were criminal, not politically motivated."

"The Barschel affair," Eduard said, "is listed as true?"

"Yes," Sfath said gravely. "Uwe Barschel's death was a murder, though details remain classified."

"The Bilderberg Conference?" Eduard asked.

"False," Sfath said.

"The conference does not plan world domination but discusses high-level economic and political issues."

"Chemtrails?" Eduard inquired.

"False," Sfath replied.

"What people see are condensation trails, not chemical dispersals."

"Chronovisor?" Eduard's eyes widened.

"False," Sfath confirmed.

"There is no evidence the Vatican possesses a time machine."

"Dagger shooting legend?" Eduard asked.

"False," Sfath said.

"The defeat in World War I was not caused by civilians."

"The Estonia sinking?" Eduard asked.

"False," Sfath replied.

"It was a tragic accident, not an assassination."

"The Orléans rumor?" Eduard asked.

"False," Sfath said.

"No evidence supports the claim of forced prostitution."

"Greater Israel conspiracy?" Eduard asked.

"False," Sfath confirmed.

"Israel does not have plans to extend its borders beyond the current state."

"HAARP?" Eduard inquired.

"False," Sfath said.

"Though it has some harmful effects, it is not used for mind manipulation."

"Holocaust denial?" Eduard asked.

"False," Sfath affirmed.

"The Holocaust is a well-documented historical fact."

"Itavia Flight 870?" Eduard asked.

"False," Sfath replied.

"The crash was an accident, not an attack."

"Jamantau Theory?" Eduard asked.

"False," Sfath confirmed.

"There is no evidence of a massive underground military complex."

"Assassination attempt on JFK?" Eduard asked.

"That's true," Sfath said.

"It was indeed a complex conspiracy involving multiple groups."

"The death of John Paul I?" Eduard asked.

"True," Sfath confirmed.

"He was poisoned to prevent his uncovering of Vatican secrets."

"The Majestic 12 Committee?" Eduard asked.

"False," Sfath replied.

"There is no secret committee dealing with UFOs."

"Men in Black?" Eduard asked.

"False," Sfath said.

"This is a fictional creation, not a reality."

"Moon landing conspiracy?" Eduard asked.

"Mixed," Sfath explained.

"The first moon landing was staged, but subsequent missions were real."

"Death of Marilyn Monroe?" Eduard asked.

"False," Sfath said. "She was murdered by her psychiatrist as we both saw, not by the government."

"The Montauk Project?" Eduard asked.

"False," Sfath replied.

"No evidence supports the theory of mind control experiments."

"New World Order?" Eduard asked.

"False," Sfath confirmed.

"No secret societies are attempting world domination."

"The Pearl Harbor attack?" Eduard asked.

"False," Sfath said.

"The US government did not have prior knowledge."

"The Philadelphia Experiment?" Eduard asked.

"False," Sfath replied.

"The story of teleportation is pure fiction."

"Coup against Mossadegh?" Eduard asked.

"True," Sfath confirmed.

"Operation Ajax was a real event, admitted by the US government."

"The Reichsflugscheibe?" Eduard asked.

"True," Sfath said.

"The Third Reich developed advanced disc-shaped aircraft."

"Reptiloids?" Eduard asked.

"False," Sfath replied.

"There is no evidence of reptilian humanoids on Earth."

"Roswell incident?" Eduard asked.

"True," Sfath confirmed.

"There was a crash, but the details remain classified."

"Seal of the United States?" Eduard asked.

"False," Sfath replied. "It does not refer to the Illuminati Order."

"Conspiracy to murder Robert F. Kennedy?" Eduard asked.

"True," Sfath said.

"There are inconsistencies, but Sirhan Sirhan was the real perpetrator."

"Skull and Bones?" Eduard inquired.

"False," Sfath replied.

"The society's reputation for occultism is exaggerated, and while it has connections to the CIA, it does not engage in the dark practices often attributed to it."

Eduard made a note and then asked, "The death of Lady Di?"

"False," Sfath confirmed.

"The crash that killed Princess Diana was caused by a combination of reckless driving and paparazzi pursuit, not a conspiracy by MI6."

"Fire during the Waco siege?" Eduard asked.

"False," Sfath said.

"The FBI was not responsible for starting the fire; it was a tragic outcome of the siege."

"9/11 conspiracy theories?" Eduard asked, his pen poised.

"False," Sfath replied.

"There was no evidence that the attacks were knowingly authorized or carried out by US secret services.

The attacks were the result of Islamist extremists."

As the last light of day faded, leaving the world cloaked in twilight, Sfath and Eduard packed up their materials.

The ancient oak stood as a silent witness to their exhaustive analysis of historical conspiracies.

Each theory, whether confirmed or debunked, painted a vivid picture of human fears, prejudices, and the complex web of historical events.

Eduard looked up at Sfath, a sense of accomplishment in his eyes.

"We've sifted through a lot of history today.

It's remarkable how these theories reflect the anxieties and conflicts of their times."

Sfath nodded thoughtfully.

"Indeed. Our task was to shed light on the truth behind these theories, and in doing so, we reveal much about the human condition.

The search for truth, after all, is a journey as timeless as the oak under which we sit."

The two continued their conversation as the first stars appeared in the evening sky, their discussion drifting from the specific to the philosophical.

The ancient oak, ever a symbol of wisdom and endurance, stood guard over their reflections, its branches whispering with the secrets of time.

As the stars began to punctuate the darkening sky, Eduard took a deep breath, breaking the comfortable silence.

"Sfath, what's the most significant lesson we've learned from all this?"

Sfath pondered the question, his gaze fixed on the constellations slowly emerging above them.

"The greatest lesson," he said thoughtfully, "is the resilience of truth amidst the tides of misinformation.

Many of these theories arose from genuine fears, but they were often fueled by misunderstanding or deliberate deception."

Eduard nodded, his eyes reflecting the starlight.

"And how do you think these theories shape our view of history?"

"They shape it in complex ways," Sfath replied.

"They reveal how societies cope with uncertainty and crises.

For example, the myths and conspiracies surrounding historical events often reflect deeper social anxieties and the struggle to make sense of complex realities."

Eduard made a note, then looked back at the list.

"Among the theories we confirmed as true, what do you find most impactful?"

Sfath glanced at the documents spread out between them.

"The confirmed theories like the assassination attempt on JFK and the death of John Paul I highlight the darker aspects of political and religious intrigue.

They show how power and secrecy can intersect in dangerous ways, often with profound consequences for individuals and societies."

Eduard considered this.

"And for the theories we debunked, what impact do you think they've had?"

"False theories," Sfath said, "often perpetuate mistrust and division.

For instance, the AIDS denial and Holocaust denial theories not only distort the truth but also undermine public health and historical understanding.

They can contribute to widespread harm and suffering by promoting harmful ideologies and misinformation."

Eduard looked around at the peaceful scene, the gentle rustle of leaves the only sound breaking the night's stillness.

"Do you think people will ever stop believing in these conspiracies?"

"It's difficult to say," Sfath mused.

"Beliefs in conspiracy theories often stem from a deep-seated need to find patterns and explanations in a chaotic world.

While education and critical thinking can help, there will always be those who are drawn to simpler, more sensational narratives."

Eduard's eyes met Sfath's, a mixture of concern and hope in his gaze.

"Then what can we do to counteract these falsehoods?"

Sfath smiled gently.

"We continue to seek the truth and share it.

Through education and open dialogue, we can encourage people to question and critically evaluate the information they encounter.

In the end, the pursuit of truth is a collective endeavor, and every effort to illuminate the facts helps build a more informed and understanding world."

As the night deepened, Eduard and Sfath packed up their materials.

The ancient oak, its branches now silhouetted against the night sky, seemed to stand as a silent testament to their work.

The journey they had undertaken through time and history had not only clarified many misconceptions but also reinforced the importance of discernment and truth.

Together, they made their way back along the path illuminated by the soft glow of the moon.

The world was full of unanswered questions and hidden stories, but for now, they had taken another step towards understanding the complex tapestry of human belief and history.

315

CHAPTER 42

The Question of Time and aging

Despite his many journeys through time and the advanced technology that preserved his youth, today he found himself grappling with a question that had been lingering in his mind for some time.

Sfath entered the spacecraft with his usual quiet grace, his presence commanding a sense of reverence and calm.

Eduard glanced up from his contemplations, his eyes filled with a mix of curiosity and concern.

"Sfath," Eduard began, his voice steady but tinged with an edge of uncertainty, "I've been meaning to ask you something.

Although I've been through the Hydrodynamic-Control Regeneration-Converter many times, I'm still curious.

Why is it that I never seem to age, even though my chronological age is increasing?"

Sfath took his customary seat opposite Eduard, his expression thoughtful and measured. "Eduard, you're right to seek clarity on this matter.

The question of your apparent agelessness touches on both the advanced technology you've utilized and the broader implications of time itself."

Eduard leaned forward, his interest piqued.

"I understand the basics of the regeneration process.

But I want to know more about how it interacts with the natural passage of time and why it keeps me looking and feeling so young."

Sfath nodded, acknowledging Eduard's curiosity.

"To grasp the full picture, we need to delve into both the technology itself and how it interfaces with the concept of aging."

Eduard was familiar with the concept, having undergone the Hydrodynamic-Control Regeneration-Converter numerous times.

"So, what more is there to understand beyond the fact that the technology rejuvenates my cells and maintains my youthful appearance?"

Sfath's eyes gleamed with a hint of admiration for Eduard's thirst for knowledge.

"The key lies in the precise mechanics of the regeneration process.

Each cycle of the Hydrodynamic-Control Regeneration-Converter is meticulously timed.

It involves a series of advanced procedures that reverse the aging process at a cellular level."

Eduard nodded, recalling the 18-day regimen.

"The process is rigorous, and I've experienced it multiple times.

But what about the interaction between this technology and the time I spend traveling?"

Sfath leaned in, his tone conveying the depth of the explanation.

"That's an important aspect.

The regeneration process is designed to maintain your youthful state irrespective of the time you spend traveling.

The technology effectively creates a bubble of temporal stability around your physical state."

Eduard's brow furrowed slightly.

"A bubble of temporal stability?

Can you elaborate on how this works in practice?"

Sfath smiled gently.

"Of course.

When you undergo the regeneration process, the technology establishes a reference point for your physical condition.

This reference point remains stable, even when you venture into different temporal periods."

"So, when I travel and return," Eduard said, "I come back to the same physical state as when I left, even if my travels span years?"

"Precisely," Sfath confirmed.

"The regeneration technology ensures that the effects of aging are neutralized, creating a continuity in your physical condition.

The time spent away, whether weeks or years, does not alter your youthful appearance because the technology compensates for these fluctuations."

Eduard leaned back, reflecting on this explanation.

"How does this interplay between time travel and regeneration influence my overall experience?

Does it affect my perception of time itself?"

Sfath considered this carefully.

"Time travel introduces complexity into your experience.

While the Hydrodynamic-Control Regeneration-Converter keeps your physical state youthful, it doesn't necessarily affect your perception of time.

You experience time in the context of your travels, but your physical state remains anchored by the technology."

Eduard nodded thoughtfully.

"So, while I might feel like I'm aging through my experiences, my actual physical state is preserved by the regeneration technology."

"Correct," Sfath said.

"The subjective experience of time can indeed vary, but the technology ensures that your biological state remains consistent with that of a younger person."

Eduard's gaze grew contemplative.

"Does the preservation of my youthful state impact my emotional and psychological experiences?"

Sfath's expression turned contemplative.

"It can.

The maintenance of a youthful appearance might influence how you relate to others and perceive your own identity.

While you are physically preserved, your emotional and psychological experiences continue to evolve."

Eduard nodded slowly.

"I've noticed that my sense of self and my interactions with others are influenced by my unique condition.

It's a balance between the physical and the psychological."

Eduard's thoughts turned to broader implications.

"Are there ethical concerns related to the use of such technology?

It seems to challenge the natural order of aging and mortality."

Sfath's demeanor grew serious.

"Indeed, there are significant ethical considerations.

The ability to halt the aging process raises questions about the nature of life, mortality, and the impact on societal structures."

Eduard reflected on this.

"It's not just about personal benefits. There are societal implications to consider as well."

Eduard shifted the conversation toward future possibilities.

"What advancements might we see in regeneration technology?

Will it continue to evolve?"

Sfath's eyes sparkled with optimism.

"The field is ever-evolving.

Future advancements could refine the technology further, potentially addressing some of the ethical concerns and improving the overall effectiveness of the regeneration process."

Eduard smiled.

"It's exciting to think about the possibilities and how they might shape the future of such technology."

As Eduard prepared for his next journey, he reflected on Sfath's insights.

"Understanding the full scope of my agelessness gives me a deeper appreciation for my experiences and responsibilities."

Sfath placed a reassuring hand on Eduard's shoulder.

"Your journey through time is a profound one.

Embrace the knowledge and use it to navigate your path with wisdom and grace."

Eduard gazed out the window, contemplating the vastness of time and his role within it. "With this understanding, I feel more grounded in my travels.

My physical state may be preserved, but my experiences are continually shaping who I am."

Sfath nodded in agreement.

"Your journey is about more than just defying time.

It's about understanding your place within it and the impact you have on the world."

Eduard glanced at Sfath, curiosity evident in his eyes.

The silence between them was comfortable, punctuated only by the ambient sounds of the rainforest.

After a while, Eduard broke the quiet.

"Sfath, after all our travels, and especially after meeting Henock, I've been pondering something deeply.

What is the way for human beings to truly live?

How should they orient themselves in life?"

Sfath, sitting cross-legged and gazing thoughtfully into the distance, took a deep breath.

He let the serenity of the forest influence his response, as if drawing wisdom directly from the natural world around them.

"Eduard," Sfath began, his voice calm and measured, "the essence of a meaningful life begins with harmonizing one's inner self.

When a person aligns their consciousness and personality, they unlock a continuous source of joy in learning.

This process is not quick or easy, it requires perseverance and tireless effort.

To evolve, one must become knowledgeable and wise."

Eduard listened intently as Sfath continued.

"A person who has achieved wisdom finds delight in discovering kindred spirits, whether they are close by or from far-off lands.

There is a profound satisfaction in encountering others who share a similar understanding of life."

Sfath's gaze grew distant as he spoke, reflecting the depth of his thoughts.

"A true human being is content and virtuous when they can remain joyful and free, even without external recognition.

At the same time, they are fulfilled when they treat all forms of life with the respect they deserve and acknowledge the virtues of those around them."

Eduard's eyes were fixed on Sfath, absorbing every word.

"Yet, unfortunately, only a few people embody genuine deference and respect for others and all forms of life.

Many prefer to discriminate against those who are perceived as superior, acting out against them and spreading discord.

Such individuals are often the ones who do not honor what is higher and greater."

Sfath paused, allowing the weight of his words to settle.

The forest seemed to listen along with Eduard.

"A wise person," Sfath continued, "focuses not on the insignificant or trivial, but on what is fundamental and valuable.

True understanding fosters natural virtues and behaviors that reflect respect and integration into the fabric of life.

This is where real love for others originates."

Eduard nodded, his face reflecting a mixture of contemplation and agreement.

"Those who speak beautifully and flatter excessively," Sfath said with a hint of skepticism, "are often driven by self-interest and hypocrisy.

Genuine character is not built on empty words but on daily self-assessment and growth."

"A true individual," Sfath elaborated, "asks themselves three crucial questions every day: 'Have I expanded my knowledge sufficiently today?

Have I worked to correct and harmonize my personality?

Have I treated everyone I encountered with the respect they deserve?'"

Eduard considered these questions, understanding their significance in the context of personal development.

"To guide others," Sfath added, "one must perceive their personality with respect, coupled with honesty, deference, and a genuine love for those willing to accept guidance.

Respect for elders and their greater wisdom should always be upheld."

"A true human being is sincere, cherishes the truth, and lives in love towards all forms of life," Sfath said, his voice steady and resolute.

"Friendship should be built only with those who share one's values and principles.

One must be willing to admit errors, resolve them, and strive to learn from every experience."

Sfath's gaze turned towards the horizon, where the dense canopy met the sky.

"When exploring new cultures," he advised, "one should approach foreign customs with respect and adapt accordingly.

Deference should also extend to those who have passed away, recognizing their place in the continuum of life."

"To live a true and virtuous life," Sfath concluded, "one must diligently educate themselves in the laws and recommendations of nature.

Understanding and following these guidelines is essential for living in harmony with the universe."

Eduard sat silently for a moment, absorbing the wisdom imparted.

The forest around them seemed to embrace the quiet reflection.

"Every interaction," Sfath said softly, "is an opportunity to observe and understand the inner nature of others.

True respect and insight come from recognizing and honoring this inner essence."

"What is the meaning of life?" Eduard asked, his voice barely a whisper against the backdrop of time itself.

Sfath's eyes, deep pools of ageless knowledge, met Eduard's with a solemn intensity. His voice, resonant and calm, began to unravel the complexities of existence.

As the sun dipped below the horizon, casting a golden glow through the trees, Eduard and Sfath remained perched on their branch, contemplating the profound truths shared.

The forest, with its timeless beauty, provided a fitting backdrop to the deep conversation, an eternal testament to the principles of wisdom and respect that guided their reflections.

In the tranquil expanse of the Amazon, amidst the whispers of ancient trees and the gentle hum of life, Eduard felt a renewed sense of clarity and purpose.

The journey through the forest was not just a physical exploration but a deep dive into the essence of what it meant to live a truly meaningful life.

As Eduard prepared to embark on his next temporal adventure, he felt a renewed sense of purpose.

"This knowledge not only informs my travels but also shapes the legacy I hope to leave behind."

Sfath's eyes were filled with warmth and encouragement.

"And as you continue to explore time, remember that your understanding and experiences contribute to a greater legacy, influencing future generations and the broader fabric of time itself."

Eduard took a deep breath, ready for the next chapter of his journey.

With Sfath's guidance and a deeper understanding of his ageless existence, he felt equipped to face the challenges and wonders that lay ahead with both clarity and purpose.

CHAPTER 43

The Turning Point

By the time Eduard reached his seventeenth birthday, on February 3, 1954, his life had already been filled with experiences far beyond those of a typical child.

The everyday world of his small Swiss village was a stark contrast to the vast, cosmic knowledge he had acquired through his telepathic connection with Sfath.

Despite this disparity, Eduard remained grounded, his identity firmly rooted in the simple yet meaningful existence of a boy in Bülach.

Eduard's birthday was usually a quiet affair, an occasion marked by a modest celebration with his family.

This year, however, the significance of his birthday transcended the ordinary.

The day began like any other, with the crisp winter air and the gentle blanket of snow covering the village.

Eduard wandered outside, seeking solace and reflection beneath the gnarled branches of the giant tree that had become his sanctuary.

As Eduard sat quietly under the tree, a sudden and profound surge of energy coursed through him.

It was as if an invisible force had unlocked a hidden door within his mind.

The floodgates of knowledge and wisdom, previously imparted by Sfath, poured into him all at once.

The sensation was overwhelming, an intense rush of clarity that illuminated his understanding of the universe in ways he had never experienced before.

For a fleeting moment, his perception of reality shifted dramatically.

He saw the universe not just as a collection of stars and planets but as an interconnected web of existence.

The complexities of life, the nuances of cosmic harmony, and the essence of his own destiny became vividly clear.

It was as though he had been given a rare glimpse into the future, a vision of the path that lay ahead of him, filled with purpose and significance.

The experience, as extraordinary as it was, vanished almost as quickly as it had appeared.

He was left with a profound sense of awe and wonder.

The knowledge that had been briefly bestowed upon him now receded into the background, leaving him with a deeper understanding of his place in the grand cosmic scheme.

The ephemeral vision left him with more questions than answers.

Yet, it also instilled in him a renewed determination and clarity about his mission.

The glimpse into the future had reinforced his commitment to his role, illuminating the importance of his journey and the impact he was destined to have on the world.

From that day forward, Eduard's life was irrevocably changed.

The ordinary routines of his village life continued, but they were now imbued with a new sense of purpose.

Eduard was no longer merely a boy from Bülach; he had been transformed into a figure of significant potential—someone who would one day play a crucial role in bridging humanity with the cosmos.

Eduard's interactions with Sfath grew even more intense and focused.

The wisdom imparted by the old man was now complemented by the profound insights he had received on his birthday.

The connection between them became more profound, and the guidance from Sfath was pivotal in shaping Billy's approach to his mission.

As Eduard continued to grow and learn, he did so with a sense of quiet determination.

The challenges of his mission were now clearer to him, and he approached his preparation with renewed vigor.

The isolation that had once been a source of loneliness now seemed like a necessary aspect of his training.

The solitude allowed him to focus on his studies and deepen his understanding of the cosmic principles that would guide him.

Eduard's studies became more self-directed, and he sought to integrate the knowledge he had gained from Sfath into practical applications.

He worked on developing skills that would be crucial for his mission, including advanced problem-solving, strategic thinking, and emotional resilience.

His preparation was not just intellectual but also practical and personal.

The weight of his mission was heavy, and it was not always easy to bear.

The clarity he had gained from his vision came with the understanding of the immense responsibility he carried.

There were moments of doubt and fear, as well as a deep sense of isolation.

Yet, these challenges were part of the preparation for the role he was destined to fulfill.

Eduard's relationship with his family also evolved.

His parents noticed the changes in him, the long hours spent in solitude, the intense focus on his studies, and the occasional moments of introspection.

While they did not fully understand the depth of his experiences, they supported him as best they could.

Their love and concern provided a grounding influence amidst the cosmic vastness of Eduard's mission.

The night sky, once a source of wonder and curiosity, now held a deeper meaning for him. He would often gaze up at the stars, feeling a profound connection to the cosmos.

The twinkling lights above were no longer just celestial objects but symbols of the answers he sought and the journey he was on.

His contemplation of the stars became a source of inspiration and solace.

The vast expanse of the universe reminded him of the broader context of his mission and the potential for discovery and growth.

It was a comforting reminder that, despite the challenges, his role was part of a greater cosmic order.

His journey was marked by both anticipation and preparation.

The turning point of his seventeenth birthday had revealed to him a glimpse of his future, and he approached the coming years with a sense of purpose and readiness.

The road ahead was uncertain, but Eduard was prepared to face it with courage and determination.

As he continued to prepare for the challenges of his mission, he remained hopeful.

The knowledge he had gained and the experiences he had undergone had shaped him into a figure of potential and promise.

He was ready to embrace his destiny and to fulfill the role he had been chosen for.

CHAPTER 44

The Arrival of Asket - A New Chapter

The Emergence of a New Voice

Just a few hours after the silent departure of Sfath's 'voice,' which had become a part of Eduard's inner world, a new 'voice' emerged.

Unlike Sfath's profound and weary tone, this voice was vibrant and full of life. It arrived abruptly, as if it had always been meant to be there.

The contrast was striking, this new presence was gentle, harmonious, and refreshingly different from Sfath's.

He quickly felt a deep sense of familiarity with this voice.

It introduced itself as Asket, a female entity who would be his new guide.

Asket's presence was marked by an extraordinary clarity and warmth that immediately made him feel at ease.

She became his companion and mentor, leading him into new realms of knowledge and experience.

On the morning of February 3, 1953, Eduard experienced his eighteenth close encounter with beamships.

This significant event was the prelude to his meeting with Asket, a moment that would profoundly impact his journey.

The encounter was meticulously planned; weeks earlier, Sfath had arranged for him to be picked up at a precise location.

On this particular day, only the exact spot needed to be confirmed.

The early hours were bitterly cold as he made his way to a favored spot, a place of solitude where he often spent hours contemplating.

Sixteen days prior, Sfath had hinted at this meeting with Asket, heightening his anticipation.

Despite the frigid temperature, he found himself sweating as he climbed the small hill where the pickup was scheduled to occur.

Upon reaching the designated spot, he did not have to wait long.

From the dark sky, a brilliant light descended and landed on the frozen ground not far from him.

The light extinguished, revealing a matte silver, disc-shaped object resting majestically on three landing spheres.

The design of the landing spheres was unlike anything he had seen before, with their unfamiliar and intriguing form.

A telepathic invitation guided him towards the ship. He approached it with a sense of gentle compulsion, as though guided by unseen hands.

There was no visible lift or entrance mechanism; the process of entry felt ethereal, akin to being lifted by ghostly forces, reminiscent of his previous experiences with Sfath's pear-shaped craft.

The interior of the ship was fundamentally different from Sfath's vessel.

Instead of the familiar pear-shaped craft, this disc-shaped ship contained only a single armchair.

The ship appeared unmanned, seemingly operated remotely. He was alone, with no signs of crew or instrumentation visible.

Before he could settle into the chair, an extraordinary event occurred.

The bright light that illuminated the interior suddenly extinguished, creating the illusion that he was outdoors.

The ship and its surroundings vanished from view, and when he instinctively raised his left hand to his eyes, it too disappeared.

He was enveloped in a state of invisibility, where neither the ship nor he could be seen.

As he began to ascend, the sensation of moving upwards into the night sky was accompanied by a remarkable tranquility.

The ship, still invisible, hovered over the nearby village.

He floated just two meters above the house where his parents would later reside.

During this period, Asket's voice reappeared within him, providing a detailed explanation of his future path.

The message from Asket encompassed insights into Eduard life's trajectory, the coming years, and his eventual family life.

Her voice was calm and reassuring, guiding him through the complexities that lay ahead.

Following Asket's explanation, the invisible ship began its journey once more.

This time, they traveled eastward, accelerating rapidly into the night sky.

Despite the swift motion, Eduard felt no discomfort or pressure, a testament to the advanced technology and ease of travel afforded by the craft.

The experience was both exhilarating and profound, marking a significant moment in his ongoing exploration and connection with Asket.

The flight reinforced the extraordinary nature of my encounters and the continuing evolution of my understanding of the universe.

Under Asket's guidance, his understanding of the world expanded dramatically.

Their journey together marked the beginning of a new chapter in Eduard's life, one filled with exploration and profound realizations.

Asket introduced him to a broader perspective, prompting him to delve deeper into spiritual teachings and wisdom beyond the conventional religions he had previously studied.

The period following Eduard's initial encounter with Asket continued to be a whirlwind of extraordinary experiences and profound insights.

Asket's explanations were extensive, and the journey ahead promised to be both challenging and illuminating.

This detailed account covers the events of February 7th, 1953, focusing on the intricacies of the meeting, the journey, and the critical lessons imparted.

Asket's explanations on the night of February 7th were extensive and intricate.

The conversation lasted late into the night, with Asket detailing many aspects of the mission and the nature of time travel.

The depth and breadth of her explanations were crucial for understanding the gravity of my forthcoming experiences.

Despite the importance of this knowledge, a strict confidentiality was maintained, enforced by a security block, ensuring that specific details remained undisclosed.

Asket assured Eduard that she would return him to Jordan for the next meeting. With this promise, Eduard boarded the small craft that had transported him to the area two days prior.

The take-off procedure mirrored the previous experience, and the flight was smooth and uneventful.

As they ascended above Earth's atmosphere, the sense of familiarity with the ship and its operations provided a degree of comfort.

The return journey was calm, and upon arriving at the designated location, the ship departed swiftly, disappearing into the night sky.

The days between encounters passed quickly. On the evening of February 7th, Eduard arrived early at the agreed location, eager for the next meeting with Asket.

As night fell, a low whirring sound, reminiscent of a helicopter, signaled the arrival of the ship.

The craft descended and landed nearby, and Asket emerged, calling him over.

They entered her ship, which was as sleek and efficient as before, and settled into the comfortable armchairs.

During the flight, Asket remained occupied with her instruments, and the ship's exterior remained solid and unchanging.

Unlike the previous flight, there were no visual effects such as transparency or glowing.

The journey was marked by a sudden deceleration as they approached a mountainous region.

The ship hovered momentarily before gently descending to the ground.

The experience was smooth and without discomfort, highlighting the advanced nature of the ship's technology.

Upon disembarking, they found themselves in the same location as before.

The weather was mild, contrasting with the European climate.

The night sky was clear, with stars twinkling overhead and the ambient sounds of the wilderness creating a serene backdrop.

Asket and Eduard walked hand in hand through the rocky terrain and found a large flat rock where they could sit and converse.

Asket began her discussion with significant statements about the importance of the forthcoming experiences.

She explained that the upcoming journey would play a crucial role in uncovering truths and dispelling misconceptions about historical events.

This process would involve traveling to various epochs to examine the reality of events and challenge traditional beliefs.

Asket elaborated on the concept of time travel, which was central to the mission.

As she stated: "Our advanced technology allowed us to visit different periods in history, providing an opportunity to observe and understand events firsthand.

This method was intended to verify historical accuracy and correct erroneous traditions or beliefs."

The mission was not just about exploring the past but also about personal growth and preparation for future challenges.

Asket highlighted the significance of understanding the truth through direct experience.

The journey would test his ability to adapt and learn, ultimately preparing Eduard for his role in guiding others.

Asket's discourse included a sobering forecast of the challenges Eduard would face.

She described a future filled with hardships, including intense physical and psychological trials.

The experiences would be designed to teach resilience and deepen understanding.

This period of apprenticeship would span approximately 20 years, during which he would endure significant personal and external struggles.

Asket emphasized that the learning process would involve experiencing various aspects of life, including both virtues and vices.

This comprehensive exposure was necessary for gaining a full understanding of human existence.

The trials would encompass a range of experiences, from physical pain to emotional suffering, mirroring the challenges faced by many individuals.

A crucial part of the forthcoming journey would involve facing a profound personal test.

This test, anticipated to be the hardest in his life up to that point, was essential for acquiring the knowledge needed for the mission.

Asket, like Sfath before her, conveyed that this test would be a transformative experience, preparing Eduard for the responsibilities ahead.

Asket made it clear that while she could guide and prepare him, certain aspects of his fate were beyond her control.

The forthcoming changes and challenges were part of a larger plan that could not be altered. This realization underscored the importance of facing these events with clear reasoning and acceptance.

In preparation for the time travel and the trials to come, Asket stressed the need for mental and emotional readiness.

Understanding the nature of the challenges and accepting their inevitability were crucial for navigating the future successfully.

The journey would test not only physical endurance but also mental and emotional resilience.

The encounter with Asket was a profound and multifaceted experience for Eduard.

The explanations provided insights into the nature of time travel, personal growth, and the broader mission.

The commitment to confidentiality and the security block added an element of mystery and responsibility to the undertaking.

The mission's core objective was to uncover and understand the truth behind historical events.

This pursuit of truth was not only about correcting misconceptions but also about gaining a deeper comprehension of human experience.

The journey promised to challenge existing beliefs and provide new perspectives on history and personal destiny.

EDUARD
72

CHAPTER 45

Asket Explanation

Asket guided the spaceship gently into a secluded clearing in the heart of an ancient forest, where the dense canopy of towering trees shielded them from prying eyes.

The air was thick with the earthy aroma of damp soil and decomposing leaves, while shafts of sunlight pierced through the foliage, casting dappled patterns on the forest floor.

The tranquil murmur of a nearby brook and the distant rustling of leaves created a serene backdrop, enhancing the sense of isolation and peace.

Beneath the expansive branches of a venerable oak, Asket and Eduard settled on a patch of soft moss, surrounded by a natural cathedral of green.

Ancient tree's gnarled roots intertwined with the ground, providing a solid foundation for their discussion.

Asket, with a calm and deliberate demeanor, began to unravel the intricacies of their mission on Earth.

The forest's quietude seemed to amplify the gravity of the conversation, as Asket detailed their purpose and the profound implications of their presence.

Eduard listened intently, absorbing each word as it echoed softly through the forest's hushed stillness.

The interplay of light and shadow around them mirrored the complexity of the revelations being shared.

In this secluded grove, far from the intrusion of the outside world, the weight of their mission unfolded against a backdrop of nature's unblemished serenity, creating a moment of profound clarity and connection between them.

Eduard, she said, Creation stands as the bedrock of life and existence, embodying both cosmic and universal significance.

Our mission, aligned with the essence of Creation, requires transcending the spacetime barrier between our universe and yours to facilitate safe and harmonious interactions.

Our home, the DAL universe in the AKON system, exists on the seventh outer belt of a constellation foreign to you.

It is a parallel universe to yours, differing only slightly in temporal alignment.

Our universe and yours are twin universes, with only a minimal difference in the flow of time.

Our presence in your DERN universe dates back several centuries, driven by a profound urge for exploration and a mission to fulfill an ancient obligation.

We reopened an ancient universe barrier, which allowed us to re-engage with your time and rediscover our historical connections.

Centuries ago, we discovered your solar system and Earth, whose inhabitants have historical ties with the Pleiadians.

These connections are integral to our mission, spanning thirty-three Earth centuries of exploration and study.

Many humans on Earth are descendants of beings from the Lyra and Vega systems, linked to the Pleiades.

These distant ancestors were the true originators of the human race on Earth, though their descendants now reside far from the Ring Nebula and the Pleiades.

In less than twenty Earth years, you will be entrusted with profound truths from the highest spirit-forms, similar to the knowledge received by Jmmanuel (Jesus Christ).

This will mark the beginning of a significant work of truth, intended for all future generations.

Truth is eternal and unchangeable.

True prophets and truth-bringers face harsh lives and must possess profound spiritual knowledge.

False prophets, on the other hand, distort truths and propagate erroneous beliefs, leading to ideological conflicts and dependency.

Highly developed life-forms have an obligation to assist less advanced ones, guided by the laws of Creation.

We are fulfilling this duty by engaging with your universe and planning future contacts with advanced life-forms.

Earth's ideologies and religions pose a significant threat due to their power-hungry nature.

These beliefs often lead to wars, oppression, and the misuse of technological advancements. They divert humanity's progress and endanger the well-being of Earth and its inhabitants.

Humanity's rapid technological advancements are marred by their focus on destructive capabilities.

The misuse of technological knowledge for control and power leads to a dangerous trajectory, threatening the stability of Earth and the solar system.

Past encounters with space-faring races revealed how Earth's ideologies and religions have caused discord and destruction across worlds.

Efforts to impose Earth's religious beliefs on other planets led to catastrophic outcomes and the destruction of entire worlds.

An expedition from a distant world suffered devastation after encountering Earth's religious fanaticism.

The crew and their ship were destroyed to prevent further contamination of their culture and knowledge by Earth's erroneous beliefs.

This is known as the Tunguska event where a large explosion of between 3 and 50 megatons occurred near the Podkamennaya Tunguska River in Yeniseysk Governorate (now Krasnoyarsk Krai), in Russia, on the morning of 30 June 1908.

The intense religiosity of Earth, particularly Christianity, has created a unique and dangerous situation.

This extremism has led to conflicts, the destruction of extraterrestrial missions, and the endangerment of Earth's own future.

Your journey aims to reveal the truth about Earth's religious distortions and to provide evidence of the falsified nature of texts like the New Testament.

You will learn about Jmmanuel and the true nature of his prophecies.

Jmmanuel's predictions, misinterpreted as prophecies, include descriptions of advanced technologies that were falsely attributed to divine revelations.

Your task is to unveil the truth behind these claims and their implications for humanity.

Malicious extraterrestrial forces have historically contributed to the distortion of religious and historical facts on Earth.

Understanding their role is crucial in addressing the ongoing issues caused by these influences.

Your mission involves a profound understanding of the eternal truths and the responsibility to guide humanity away from destructive ideologies.

As you prepare for this task, you will gain insights that will shape your contributions to the future.

The knowledge imparted to you today serves as a foundation for your role as a bringer of truth.

You will confront and correct misconceptions, guiding Earth toward a more enlightened and harmonious existence.

Through this extensive explanation, Asket provides Eduard with a detailed understanding of their temporal travels, the nature of their mission, and the challenges faced due to Earth's current ideological and technological state.

Eduard sat, his mind swirling with the weight of knowledge that was too heavy for any man to bear.

He had learned from Asket, his extraterrestrial mentor, things that no human should ever know, secrets of the past that had to remain hidden until a distant future, events that held the keys to the unfolding of time itself.

Asket had explained much to Eduard, more than he could ever fully grasp.

She had shown him how the events of the past were intricately woven into the fabric of the future, how each thread of history was vital to the progression of time and evolution.

To reveal these secrets, to change even the smallest detail, could unravel the entire tapestry of existence.

Eduard understood that he could not, must not, speak of these things, for the consequences of altering the course of history were too dire to imagine.

His own reasoning confirmed the necessity of his silence.

He knew that he had no right to play the role of a savior or a world-changer, no right to use his knowledge to alter the fate of humanity for better or worse.

The world had to follow its course, just as his life had to follow its own predetermined path, no matter how painful or challenging it might be.

Eduard knew many things about his own future, terrible things that would bring him suffering, pain, and hardship.

Yet, he also knew that these events were essential, that they had to occur for the sake of his own evolution and for the greater good of humanity.

As the years passed, Eduard came to a profound realization: it was not good for a human to know their own future.

When one is aware of what lies ahead, the temptation to interfere, to change the course of events out of fear or self-preservation, becomes almost unbearable.

Such knowledge can lead a person into a dark spiral of inner conflict, as they struggle to avoid the suffering they know is coming.

Eduard had experienced this conflict firsthand.

He had been tempted to alter his fate, to escape the pain and suffering that awaited him, but he knew that doing so would only create greater misery and disrupt the natural flow of life.

He had learned, through his own painful experiences, that humans are not yet capable of fully understanding the truth.

The human mind, driven by ego and fear, is not mature enough to handle the knowledge of its own future.

This is why the truth must be presented in a way that encourages independent thought, why it must be veiled in parables and prophecies.

Only by searching for the truth themselves can humans begin to understand it, and even then, only in a limited way.

If the future were laid bare before them, they would be overwhelmed by the enormity of it all, and they would inevitably try to change it, causing untold chaos.

Eduard knew this better than anyone. He had been shown glimpses of his own future, and the knowledge had nearly driven him mad.

He had often trembled in terror, knowing that another horrible event was just around the corner, and he had come close to giving up on life altogether.

But through it all, he had learned to master his fear, to face the coming storms with courage and resolve.

He had not done this alone, without the help of his extraterrestrial friends, he would have been lost.

Their guidance, their teachings, and their support had helped him to survive the unbearable burden of knowing his own future.

To know the truth about one's future is a curse, Eduard realized. It is too much for any human to bear.

The only reason he had not been destroyed by this knowledge was because of the extraordinary strength he had gained through his experiences, the wisdom imparted to him by his otherworldly friends, and the changes he had undergone within himself.

He knew that he was still far from perfect, still too primitive in many ways, but he had grown in ways he never could have imagined.

As he sat there, lost in thought, Eduard knew that he had a duty to protect the knowledge he had been given.

He had to keep it hidden, to guard it closely, for the sake of all humanity.

The burden was great, but he would bear it, for he knew that it was the only way to ensure that the future unfolded as it was meant to.

And so, with a heavy heart but a resolute spirit, Eduard continued on his path, knowing that the secrets he carried were not his to reveal, and that his silence was the greatest gift he could give to the world.

CHAPTER 46

In-Depth Account of the Encounter with Asket

The encounter with Asket on February 3rd, 1953, marked a turning point in Eduard's life.

This narrative delves into the intricacies of our interaction, exploring the challenges of maintaining secrecy under a security block, the surreal nature of the experience, and the profound impact it had on him.

Asket's explanations, the peculiarities of the security block, and the personal revelations of the encounter will be examined in detail.

Asket's explanations were extensive and took a considerable amount of time.

The information conveyed was profound and complex, covering various aspects of cosmic knowledge and personal responsibility.

However, due to the sensitivity of the information, he finds himself bound by strict confidentiality.

The nature of this secrecy is twofold: a personal promise and a security block that prevents from him disclosing any details.

The security block imposed by Asket is a mechanism designed to ensure that sensitive information remains undisclosed.

While the exact nature of the security block remains unclear, Eduard understands that it is intrinsically linked to his sense of duty and consciousness.

This block was implemented through a device that seemed unusual to him, but its effects were unmistakable.

Even if he wished to speak about the information, the security block would prevent him from doing so.

During the encounter, Asket's explanations initially seemed so outrageous that Eduard questioned their reality.

He expected to awaken from what he thought was a vivid dream. However, the persistence of the situation forced him to confront the reality of the encounter.

To test this reality, he engaged in various physical acts of self-assurance: pinching his earlobes until they bled, burning my hand with a cigarette, and squeezing Asket's hands to confirm their warmth and presence.

Despite these efforts, the reality of the situation remained undeniable.

By nightfall, Eduard requested to leave the ship and explore the surrounding mountains with Asket.

This request was driven by a need to cool his heightened excitement and gain perspective.

Asket agreed, and they ventured into the rugged terrain, allowing the cool night air to temper his emotional intensity.

The physical activity and the serene environment helped to alleviate the overwhelming feelings that had accompanied the encounter.

The Unexpected Meeting

While traversing the mountains, they encountered a fire and a man who appeared to be guarding it with a rifle.

The man, an isolated Russian who had been living alone in the Jordanian desert mountains, was initially fearful of our sudden appearance.

Asket, fluent in English and later German, was able to communicate with him and ease his apprehension.

The man's solitary existence and distrust of others had been a significant part of his life, making our appearance a jarring and surprising event for him.

The Russian, aged approximately 45-50, had spent years wandering alone due to his distrust of humanity.

His unexpected emotional reaction to them was a profound shift in his long-held beliefs. He extended his hospitality by offering tea and food, which I gratefully accepted.

The simple act of sharing a meal was a stark contrast to the extraordinary nature of our earlier experiences and highlighted the unexpected connections we make in life.

As the evening progressed, they prepared to return to the ship. The Russian, moved by their company, expressed a desire to see them again.

Asket promised that they would meet him again on February 7th, providing reassurance and a sense of continuity for the Russian.

With this promise, they bid him farewell and returned to the ship, reflecting on the unexpected and humanizing encounter.

Upon returning to the ship, Eduard was exhausted and lay down on a couch provided by

Asket. As the night passed, he slept deeply, appreciating the comfort of rest after a day filled with extraordinary experiences.

The following morning, he awoke to find Asket had prepared a meal from unfamiliar yet delicious foods.

The breakfast, although alien in its specifics, was nourishing and satisfying.

The morning ritual included refreshing themselves with cool, clear water that Asket had brought.

The playful experience of splashing and cleaning themselves with this water added a sense of normalcy to the otherwise surreal series of events.

This simple pleasure contrasted with the complexity of their experiences, grounding him in the present moment.

Throughout the day, they spent time inside the ship as Asket continued to teach Eduard new things.

The advanced technology and concepts that once seemed foreign gradually became more familiar.

The rapid adaptation to these new experiences was remarkable, and his growing comfort with Asket and the ship highlighted the depth of their connection.

As the hours passed, his perception of the ship and its technology shifted.

What initially seemed overwhelming and alien became integrated into my understanding.

The familiarity with Asket and the environment inside the ship reached a point where Eduard felt a sense of boredom with the technical details, reflecting the extent to which he had acclimated.

Asket assured Eduard that she would return him to Jordan for the next meeting.

With this promise, he boarded the small craft that had transported him to the area two days prior.

The take-off procedure mirrored the previous experience, and the flight was smooth and uneventful.

As they ascended above Earth's atmosphere, the sense of familiarity with the ship and its operations provided a degree of comfort.

The return journey was calm, and upon arriving at the designated location, the ship departed swiftly, disappearing into the night sky.

The days between encounters passed quickly. On the evening of February 7th, Eduard arrived early at the agreed location, eager for the next meeting with Asket.

As night fell, a low whirring sound, reminiscent of a helicopter, signaled the arrival of the ship.

The craft descended and landed nearby, and Asket emerged, calling him over.

They entered her ship, which was as sleek and efficient as before, and settled into the comfortable armchairs.

During the flight, Asket remained occupied with her instruments, and the ship's exterior remained solid and unchanging.

Unlike the previous flight, there were no visual effects such as transparency or glowing.

The journey was marked by a sudden deceleration as they approached a mountainous region.

The ship hovered momentarily before gently descending to the ground.

The experience was smooth and without discomfort, highlighting the advanced nature of the ship's technology.

Upon disembarking, they found themselves in the same location as before.

The weather was mild, contrasting with the European climate.

The night sky was clear, with stars twinkling overhead and the ambient sounds of the wilderness creating a serene backdrop.

Asket and I walked hand in hand through the rocky terrain and found a large flat rock where we could sit and converse.

Asket began her discussion with significant statements about the importance of the forthcoming experiences.

She explained that the upcoming journey would play a crucial role in uncovering truths and dispelling misconceptions about historical events.

This process would involve traveling to various epochs to examine the reality of events and challenge traditional beliefs.

Asket elaborated on the concept of time travel, which was central to the mission.

Our advanced technology allowed us to visit different periods in history, providing an opportunity to observe and understand events firsthand.

This method was intended to verify historical accuracy and correct erroneous traditions or beliefs.

The mission was not just about exploring the past but also about personal growth and preparation for future challenges.

Asket highlighted the significance of understanding the truth through direct experience.

The journey would test Eduard's ability to adapt and learn, ultimately preparing him for his role in guiding others.

Asket's discourse included a sobering forecast of the challenges he would face.

She described a future filled with hardships, including intense physical and psychological trials.

The experiences would be designed to teach resilience and deepen understanding.

This period of apprenticeship would span approximately 20 years, during which Eduard would endure significant personal and external struggles.

Asket emphasized that the learning process would involve experiencing various aspects of life, including both virtues and vices.

This comprehensive exposure was necessary for gaining a full understanding of human existence.

The trials would encompass a range of experiences, from physical pain to emotional suffering, mirroring the challenges faced by many individuals.

A crucial part of the forthcoming journey would involve facing a profound personal test.

A test anticipated to be the hardest in Eduard's life up to that point, was essential for acquiring the knowledge needed for the mission.

Asket, like Sfath before her, conveyed that this test would be a transformative experience, preparing me for the responsibilities ahead.

Asket made it clear that while she could guide and prepare him, certain aspects of his fate were beyond her control.

The forthcoming changes and challenges were part of a larger plan that could not be altered.

This realization underscored the importance of facing these events with clear reasoning and acceptance.

In preparation for the time travel and the trials to come, Asket stressed the need for mental and emotional readiness.

Understanding the nature of the challenges and accepting their inevitability were crucial for navigating the future successfully.

The journey would test not only physical endurance but also mental and emotional resilience.

The encounter with Asket was a profound and multifaceted experience.

The explanations provided insights into the nature of time travel, personal growth, and the broader mission.

The commitment to confidentiality and the security block added an element of mystery and responsibility to the undertaking.

The mission's core objective was to uncover and understand the truth behind historical events.

This pursuit of truth was not only about correcting misconceptions but also about gaining a deeper comprehension of human experience.

The journey promised to challenge existing beliefs and provide new perspectives on history and personal destiny.

The anticipated hardships and trials were designed to build resilience and fortitude.

By confronting these challenges directly, he would develop a deeper understanding of human suffering and strength.

This process of learning through experience was integral to fulfilling the mission and supporting others in their quest for truth.

Asket's guidance provided a roadmap for the future, highlighting the importance of preparation and adaptability.

The journey ahead was marked by significant trials, but also by opportunities for growth and understanding.

The lessons learned from these experiences would be crucial for navigating the challenges and responsibilities of the mission.

The evening's discussions with Asket were just the beginning of a long and transformative journey.

The commitment to uncovering truth and facing personal challenges would shape the path ahead.

Each experience and lesson learned would contribute to the broader mission of understanding and guiding others.

Chapter 47

The Arrival

The descent of the vessel was smooth, and it landed with a gentle thud just a few meters from the towering Sphinx and a small Bedouin camp.

The early morning air was filled with the activity of men and women breaking down their camp.

Despite the bustling activity, none of the Bedouins seemed to notice their arrival.

Eduard initial reaction was one of disbelief. How could these people not see the enormous ship touching down so close to them?

The very notion seemed preposterous.

Yet, as he observed the scene unfold, it became apparent that their invisibility technology was working perfectly.

The realization that they were completely invisible intrigued him greatly.

He found the ability to observe without being seen to be an enthralling experience.

Asket, who had remained silent until now, finally made her presence known through her internal communication.

He felt her arm touch his, a sensation that was both comforting and strange. Despite their invisibility, he could not see her at that moment.

She explained that she was attaching a small device to his belt.

This device would ensure that they remained invisible even after leaving the ship.

He felt her hands as she adjusted the device, and then, quite suddenly, he saw Asket kneeling beside him.

The sight startled him, and he turned his gaze towards the Bedouins, wondering if they would now see them.

Asket's voice, clear and calm, reassured him that only they could see each other while remaining invisible to everyone else.

The concept seemed utterly fantastical, and he struggled to accept it. He was determined to test this claim for himself.

So, he decided to conduct a series of experiments to verify the effectiveness of their invisibility.

Asket and Eduard stepped out of the ship, which he could now see clearly, standing magnificently beside the Sphinx. According to Asket, it was invisible to everyone except them.

His skepticism persisted as they approached a group of Bedouins who were engaged in animated conversation.

Their attire, colorful and flowing, was fascinating, yet they did not acknowledge their presence.

Eduard boldly reached out and grabbed the shawl of one of the men.

He looked around, confused, but did not see him.

He adjusted his shawl and resumed his conversation, seemingly unfazed by the mysterious interaction.

To further test their invisibility, he ventured into a nearby tent. Asket followed closely behind him.

The interior of the tent was occupied by several women engaged in their morning routine.

Seven young women and two older ones were present, while a young woman nursed an infant. Their lack of reaction to their presence was astonishing.

He was particularly curious about their response to his intrusion.

He approached a young woman, partially undressed, sitting by a bowl of water.

He bent down and kissed her gently on the lips.

Her reaction was immediate; her eyes widened in surprise, and she placed her fingers on her lips, possibly thinking she had been kissed by a beloved spirit.

Her body trembled, and her head fell forward as she fainted. He caught her and laid her gently on the floor.

Asket's laughter echoed in his mind as she observed the scene.

Her amusement was evident as she commented on the effectiveness of their invisibility. They waited until the young woman regained consciousness.

She sat up, still visibly affected by the experience, and began to describe the incident to the other women.

They listened with skepticism but did not react as one might expect.

He decided to test the limits further and kissed each of the women in the tent briefly.

Each woman reacted similarly, becoming momentarily stiff and silent before resuming their activities.

They clustered around the woman he had first kissed, excitedly discussing the mysterious event.

Asket and Eduard exited the tent, her laughter still resonating in his mind.

She remarked on the unique opportunities invisibility provided. His actions, while seemingly thoughtless, had unintended positive effects.

Asket assured him that the women, who had endured difficult lives, now believed they had been touched by an invisible angel, which had brought them immense happiness.

Eduard expressed his concerns about the potential psychological impact on the women, fearing that his actions might have led to unintended consequences.

Asket reassured him, explaining that she had checked the women's thoughts and confirmed that they were indeed very happy, believing they had experienced a divine encounter.

Their lives, she assured him, would be positively influenced by this newfound joy.

The events of the morning had profound implications for him.

The power of invisibility was not just a tool for observation but also had the potential to influence emotions and perceptions.

The reactions of the Bedouins and the women provided a deeper understanding of how invisibility could affect human behavior.

They continued with their exploration, guided by the insights gained from this experience.

The ability to observe and interact without being seen opened new avenues for understanding and empathy.

It was clear that such power required careful consideration and responsibility.

With a greater appreciation for the impact of their technology, they prepared for the next phase of their mission.

The experiences of the day had highlighted the need for thoughtful application of invisibility and the importance of understanding its effects on those we encounter.

As they moved forward, the lessons learned from their interactions would inform their approach to future explorations.

The journey ahead promised further discoveries and challenges, and Eduard felt better equipped to navigate these with the knowledge gained from this encounter.

CHAPTER 48

Descent into the Pyramid

Asket grasped Eduard hand with a firm yet reassuring grip and guided him towards a narrow entrance concealed within the shadow of the pyramid.

The entrance seemed to be a mere slit in the stone, but as they stepped through, the narrow corridor opened into a labyrinth of musty, dimly lit passageways.

The air was thick and stale, carrying the scent of ancient dust.

Despite the oppressive darkness that enveloped them, they did not stumble or collide with any obstacles.

Asket, moving with practiced ease, navigated the twisting passages with a familiarity that struck him as almost intuitive.

Their descent continued in near-total darkness, the faint echoes of their footsteps the only indication of their progress.

At times, he could sense the incline of the passages as they moved deeper underground.

The oppressive gloom was almost tangible, and he marveled at how Asket seemed to find her way effortlessly through this Egyptian darkness.

After what felt like an eternity, a faint, eerie light began to permeate the blackness.

It was as if the first rays of dawn had somehow infiltrated the pyramid's depths.

The source of this light remained a mystery, but it illuminated an imposing stone block that seemed to hover before them.

Before their eyes, the massive stone, an ashlar, dissolved into nothingness, revealing a steep passageway guarded by two men in peculiar attire.

The two guards, clad in elaborate and unfamiliar clothing, were stationed at the entrance of the newly revealed passageway.

Their presence was imposing, but they seemed oblivious to them.

Asket's voice whispered urgently in his mind, instructing him to remain silent.

It was crucial that we avoid detection, the guards were members of an extraterrestrial faction known for subjugating humanity through deceitful means.

Eduard obeyed, moving quietly past the guards who appeared entirely unaware of their presence.

The situation was surreal and amusing, yet he struggled to adapt to this extraordinary new reality.

The passageway, lined with steps, descended steeply, leading them further into the bowels of the pyramid.

They emerged into a colossal hall that seemed to defy the laws of physics, bathed in an otherworldly light that originated from nowhere and everywhere simultaneously.

The room was vast, and the centerpiece was a massive, disc-shaped spaceship, flanked by several smaller craft.

The sight was astonishing: a spacecraft resting deep beneath the Pyramid of Giza, far below its surface, amidst the dark, secretive chambers of the pyramid.

Eduard was in disbelief.

He pinched himself repeatedly, feeling the sharp pain that confirmed the reality of the scene before him.

The spaceship, with a diameter of approximately three hundred meters, resembled the one he had encountered previously on June 2, 1942.

It was clear that this vessel had been stored here for centuries, possibly millennia, buried deep beneath the Earth.

Asket did not allow him much time to process the revelation.

She pulled him towards a small plateau situated in the center of the hall.

From a distance, he could make out several objects laid out on the plateau.

As they approached, his astonishment only deepened.

Upon reaching the plateau, he saw an ancient, heavy wooden cross, Y-shaped, alongside three rusty nails that looked like remnants from a bygone era.

The nails were encrusted with a dark, reddish-brown substance that might have been blood.

Next to these, there was a wreath of thorns, unmistakably crafted as a crown, and a blackish wooden rod, along with a purple cape and a small leather pouch filled with glassy stones.

The sight was overwhelming.

These items unmistakably linked to the crucifixion of Jmmanuel, known in Christian tradition as Jesus Christ, were spread out before them.

The cross, the nails, and the crown of thorns were vivid symbols of the crucifixion.

The glassy stones in the leather pouch, though intriguing, remained a mystery.

His thoughts raced.

Sfath's words about the Christian religion being a tool for human control echoed in my mind.

In spite of his skepticism about religious doctrines, seeing these artifacts left him grappling with conflicting emotions.

The evidence before him seemed to validate certain aspects of the New Testament, challenging Sfath's claim that everything was a deception.

His mind was in turmoil.

How could these ancient relics, so closely tied to the narrative of Jesus Christ, exist in such a state?

Sfath had asserted that the story of Jesus was a fabrication and that the true name was Jmmanuel.

He struggled to reconcile this with the tangible evidence before him.

Asket, sensing his confusion, took his arm and guided him back through the dark passages, retracing their steps.

The giant stone reappeared and sealed the passageway behind them as they emerged into the pyramid's exterior.

They reappeared in the light of day, the Sphinx and the ship visible once more.

The Bedouin camp had vanished, replaced by a multitude of tourists eager to explore the pyramid.

The sun was high in the sky, and he realized that although it felt like mere minutes had passed, several hours had actually elapsed.

The ship, now in motion, sped back with incredible velocity.

It landed in the Jordanian desert, far from the pyramids.

For the next two days, Asket provided him with detailed explanations and insights, delving into the mysteries they had encountered and preparing him for future explorations.

The journey had been one of profound revelations and confusion.

The relics of the crucifixion, deeply entwined with the Christian narrative, had challenged his understanding of history and religion.

Asket's guidance and the experiences they had shared illuminated the complexity of the past and the ongoing influence of extraterrestrial forces on Earth.

With renewed perspective, Eduard prepared for the next chapter of their journey, equipped with the knowledge gained from their extraordinary encounter beneath the Pyramid of Giza.

The mysteries of the past and the implications for humanity's future were now clearer, shaping the path ahead.

UFOS
GEORGE ADAMSKI

Chapter 49

Adamski

The Volkshaus Lecture

Zurich, May 1959. The Volkshaus was alive with anticipation, a grand hall filled with murmurs, whispered debates, and the rustling of papers as attendees settled into their seats.

The crowd was a mix of hopeful believers and skeptical minds, all gathered for one reason, to hear George Adamski speak.

Adamski, a self-proclaimed contactee of extraterrestrial beings, had captivated the public with his tales of encounters with benevolent space travelers from Venus.

His books and photographs had spread like wildfire, and tonight, he was to deliver one of his most anticipated lectures.

Eduard sat near the middle of the hall, arms crossed, his sharp gaze fixed on the stage.

Beside him, Asket observed the crowd with quiet curiosity.

She had no illusions about Adamski's credibility, but she understood the influence figures like him held over the public.

A hush fell over the audience as Adamski took the stage, his presence commanding.

Dressed in a well-pressed suit, his silver hair neatly combed back, he exuded the aura of an esteemed professor rather than a mere storyteller.

A large screen behind him displayed grainy images of supposed spacecraft, followed by sketches of humanoid beings with perfect features and kind eyes.

"My friends," Adamski began, his voice smooth and confident, "I stand before you tonight as a messenger of our cosmic brothers and sisters.

They come not to conquer, but to guide us toward enlightenment. I have seen their ships, walked among them, and been entrusted with knowledge beyond our world."

Eduard exchanged a glance with Asket. The audience was entranced, some nodding in agreement while others scribbled notes.

Adamski continued weaving his tales, describing celestial journeys and advanced civilizations where war and suffering were long-forgotten relics.

By the time the lecture concluded, a standing ovation erupted.

People rushed forward, eager to shake Adamski's hand, to ask him about their own strange experiences, to bask in the presence of someone they saw as a pioneer of interstellar communication.

Eduard and Asket, however, had other plans. They waited until the crowd thinned before making their way toward the backstage area. The moment had come for confrontation.

Face to Face with Adamski

Backstage was a stark contrast to the grandeur of the lecture hall.

The corridors were dimly lit, the air heavy with the scent of old books and ink.

A few lingering staff members moved about, packing away equipment.

Eduard and Asket walked with purpose, navigating through the narrow halls until they reached a door marked Private.

Instead of knocking, Asket opted for a more direct approach. With a mere thought, she activated the advanced technology at her disposal.

A soft hum filled the air, barely perceptible, and in the blink of an eye, they vanished from the hallway, only to materialize inside the room beyond the door.

George Adamski, seated at his desk, jolted upright, knocking over an inkwell in his shock.

The deep blue ink bled across the scattered notes before him. His face, moments ago composed and confident, drained of color.

"Who...how did you...?" His voice wavered.

Eduard took a step forward, his expression firm, his presence unshaken.

Asket, standing beside him, remained silent for a moment, allowing the weight of their sudden appearance to settle.

"Mr. Adamski," Eduard began, speaking through the small translation device Asket had provided him, "we need to discuss your claims about extraterrestrial contact." His voice was measured, carrying neither anger nor mockery, only the unwavering intent of someone seeking truth.

Adamski's eyes darted between them, his mind struggling to process what had just occurred. His hands trembled slightly as he reached for a handkerchief to dab the ink stain on his papers.

"I...I don't understand," he stammered. "Who are you?"

Asket finally spoke, her voice smooth yet commanding. "We are here to address the discrepancies in your accounts." She met his gaze, unblinking. "Your claims are false. And you know this."

Adamski swallowed hard, his body tensing. For years, he had woven his stories so tightly that they had almost become his reality.

But now, faced with something beyond his understanding, something undeniably real, the façade began to crack.

For several moments, Adamski said nothing. The dim light of the room cast shadows across his lined face, accentuating the weariness beneath his public persona.

"You're mistaken," he finally said, though his voice lacked conviction. "I have seen them. I have spoken with them."

Eduard's eyes remained locked onto him. "No, you haven't," he countered. "You have created these narratives. For what? Fame? Recognition?"

Adamski's lips parted, but no words came. Asket tilted her head slightly. "The truth, Mr. Adamski," she said, her tone almost gentle now. "Why did you do it?"

Adamski exhaled slowly, his shoulders sagging. The silence in the room was oppressive. Then, finally, he spoke, his voice barely above a whisper.

"I wanted to be important," he admitted, his gaze fixed on the ink-stained papers before him. "I wanted to inspire people.

The world is full of darkness, wars, and fear. I thought… if people believed there were enlightened beings watching over us, guiding us, then maybe they would strive to be better."

Eduard considered his words, his stance unchanging. "But you deceived them," he stated plainly. "The people who followed you, who trusted your words, you led them astray."

Adamski's hands clenched. "I didn't mean to harm anyone," he said, his voice shaking. "I just… I saw what people wanted to believe, and I gave it to them."

Asket studied him for a long moment. "Truth is the foundation of progress," she said. "Lies, even well-intended ones, erode that foundation."

A deep sigh escaped Adamski. "What do you want from me?" he asked. "To confess? To undo everything?"

Eduard nodded. "At the very least, you must consider the consequences of your actions. Truth will always surface, one way or another."

Adamski looked away, his face shadowed by regret. "I don't know if I can undo it," he admitted. "Too many people believe in me now.

If I were to recant, it would shatter their faith, not just in me, but in the possibility that we are not alone."

Asket's expression remained unreadable. "Faith built on falsehoods is no faith at all."

For a long time, Adamski sat in silence. The weight of the moment pressed upon him.

Eduard finally turned toward the door. "Think carefully about your next steps, Mr. Adamski," he said. "The truth will always be more powerful than illusion."

Adamski nodded absently, his mind a storm of conflicting thoughts.

As Eduard and Asket disappeared as suddenly as they had arrived, leaving behind nothing but a faint ripple in the air, Adamski remained seated, his fingers tracing idle patterns in the ink that had spilled across his desk.

Outside, the cool Zurich night welcomed Eduard and Asket once more. The stars overhead twinkled indifferently, their distant light untouched by human deception.

Eduard exhaled, glancing at Asket. "Do you think he will change?"

She considered for a moment before answering. "Perhaps. But the need for recognition is a powerful force."

Eduard nodded. The battle for truth was never easy. But it was one worth fighting.

As they walked away from the Volkshaus, the city hummed with life around them, unaware of the quiet confrontation that had just unfolded within its walls.

Chapter 50

The assassination of Marilyn Monroe

The time-travel craft hummed softly as it materialized i n the future on August 4, 1962. Eduard and Asket, cloaked in invisibility, emerged from the craft's shimmering veil.

The room was steeped in soft moonlight, casting long shadows across the elegantly furnished space.

Monroe's bed, a luxurious affair draped in satin sheets, was at the center of the room.

Eduard glanced at Asket, who was adjusting the settings on her device to ensure their invisibility remained intact. "This is it," Eduard said quietly.

"We're really here."

Asket nodded, her eyes focused on Monroe, who was lying on the bed with an air of palpable despair.

"We have to stay completely silent.

Every detail counts."

Marilyn Monroe stirred slightly as the door to her bedroom creaked open.

Dr. Ralph Greenson entered with a practiced calm, his face betraying no emotion.

He carried a small, leather bag, which he set down on a nearby table with a deliberate precision.

Monroe's eyes met Greenson's as he approached.

"Marilyn," he said in a soothing voice, "it's time for your medication."

Monroe, her voice weak and trembling, responded, "I don't know if I can handle more of this."

"It's necessary," Greenson insisted, his tone unyielding.

"You need to rest."

Greenson retrieved a bottle of pentobarbital from his bag and prepared a syringe with the medication.

As he administered the drug into Monroe's arm, Eduard watched, noting the careful manner in which Greenson avoided any unnecessary contact or conversation.

Monroe's resistance seemed to dissolve with the medication, and her eyes gradually closed, slipping into an induced sleep.

With Monroe unconscious, Greenson's demeanor shifted subtly.

He retrieved another syringe from his bag, this one filled with a pale liquid, chloral hydrate.

Eduard's heart raced as he watched, understanding the gravity of what was about to occur.

"This is where it gets truly sinister," Asket whispered, her voice low but intense.

Greenson prepared the syringe with a practiced hand, his expression unreadable.

He then proceeded to Monroe's bedside, his movements slow and deliberate.

Eduard's gaze followed every action with a mix of horror and fascination.

Greenson gently lifted Monroe's nightgown, revealing her lower body.

He positioned the syringe for an injection.

Eduard's stomach churned as he realized the purpose of this particular method.

The chloral hydrate was to be administered through her anus, a method designed to avoid leaving any visible injection marks.

Greenson's hands were steady as he performed the procedure.

He inserted the needle with careful precision, ensuring that the needle was administered deep enough to bypass any external signs.

Monroe remained motionless, her unconscious state rendering her entirely unaware of the intrusion.

Asket's eyes were fixed on the scene, her expression grim. "This is a method of ensuring that the cause of death remains obscured," she said. "It's a cruel way to eliminate evidence."

Greenson withdrew the needle and discreetly disposed of it in his medical bag.

He then adjusted Monroe's gown back into place, ensuring that no trace of his actions was visible.

His face remained impassive as he prepared to leave the room, his mission complete.

Eduard's eyes followed Greenson as he exited the room.

The door closed with a soft click, leaving Monroe alone in the dimly lit space.

Eduard turned to Asket, his face pale with the weight of what they had witnessed.

"Is it over?" Eduard asked, his voice strained.

Asket nodded, her expression somber.

"For now.

But the implications of this… it's more than just a murder.

It's a conspiracy."

They waited in silence, their invisibility ensuring that they were undetected.

The gravity of the situation weighed heavily on them, the truth of Monroe's death as shocking as it was undeniable.

Asket and Eduard ventured into a new timeline, where they observed the broader implications of Monroe's murder.

They materialized in a dimly lit room, where they overheard a conversation between John Fitzgerald Kennedy and Robert Kennedy.

Jack Kennedy's voice was tense.

"We had to act before she could ruin everything.

Greenson did his job, but this has to stay covered."

Robert Kennedy's voice was equally strained.

"What if someone finds out?

What if the public learns about this?"

"We've covered our tracks," Jack said firmly.

"And with Monroe gone, there's nothing left for her to say.

We control the narrative."

Eduard's face was set in a grim expression.

"They're not just protecting themselves, they're erasing any chance of accountability."

Asket's gaze was unyielding.

"And they'll continue to do so as long as they can.

The truth about Monroe's death was buried with her."

Returning to their own time, Eduard and Asket carried with them the heavy burden of the truth.

The details they had witnessed would remain hidden from the world unless they chose to reveal them carefully.

The implications were far-reaching, touching on the intersections of power, secrecy, and human life.

In the quiet aftermath of their mission, Eduard and Asket reflected on the broader impact of what they had learned.

The truth about Marilyn Monroe's death was a powerful narrative, one that revealed not just a single tragic event but a complex web of deceit and manipulation.

Asket looked at Eduard with a determined expression.

"We've seen the truth.

Now we must decide how to share it responsibly."

Eduard nodded, understanding the weight of their responsibility.

"The truth must be told, but it must also be done in a way that respects the legacy of those who suffered."

Together, they resolved to ensure that the truth about Marilyn Monroe's death would not remain buried forever.

Their journey had revealed the dark undercurrents of history, and it was their duty to shine a light on the shadows of the past, even as they navigated the complexities of the present.

Chapter **51**

The Fatima Event

It was October 12, 1917, in central Portugal.

The air was crisp, carrying the scent of damp earth after a morning drizzle.

The sky, which had been a deep, unbroken blue, now held an eerie stillness, as if nature itself awaited something beyond comprehension.

A sense of unease mixed with anticipation spread across the gathered multitude, tens of thousands of people standing in the fields near the small village of Fatima.

Rumors had spread like wildfire, tales of prophecy whispered in hushed voices, retold again and again.

Three shepherd children, mere peasants by societal standards, had spoken of divine visions, of messages delivered by an ethereal lady clad in white.

The faithful had traveled for miles, braving the uncertainty of the journey, desperate for a sign from the heavens.

Yet, among the believers stood skeptics, journalists, scientists, and common folk who had come to witness either a miracle or a mass delusion.

The atmosphere buzzed with speculation. Some stood in silent prayer, rosaries entwined in their fingers, their lips moving in whispered devotion.

Others talked amongst themselves, their voices rising with excitement. Vendors had even arrived, selling food and religious trinkets, making commerce out of divinity.

A few scoffed at the absurdity of it all, rolling their eyes at the fervor.

Then, as midday approached, something changed.

A sudden stillness overtook the land. The wind ceased, as if held at bay by an unseen force.

The sky, once bright, grew ominously dark, thick clouds rolling in with unnatural speed. Gasps of astonishment rippled through the crowd as an intense, radiant light pierced the gloom.

From behind the dense cloud cover, a luminous sphere emerged.

It pulsed, shifting hues, golden, crimson, violet, moving in erratic patterns, unlike anything ever seen.

The sun itself seemed to dance, spiraling, twirling, casting brilliant beams of light in all directions.

It twisted and weaved, descending toward the earth before ascending again in rapid bursts. Witnesses screamed, some dropping to their knees in fear, others crying out in exultation.

For several long minutes, the spectacle continued. Shapes flickered within the radiance, indistinct but mesmerizing.

Some swore they saw angelic figures, others described the faint silhouette of a woman, arms outstretched as if offering solace.

The energy emanating from the phenomenon was palpable, an overwhelming sense of awe gripping the masses.

Yet, what no one understood, what no one could have suspected, was that this was no act of divine intervention.

Far beyond the grasp of the human mind, the true architects of the event observed from above.

Hidden from sight, a spacecraft hovered in the upper atmosphere, cloaked in an advanced field that rendered it nearly invisible to the naked eye.

The so-called "miracle of the sun" was no more than an intricate projection, a manipulation of light and energy, carefully engineered to appear celestial in origin.

The orchestrators of this grand deception were Earth-foreigners, an extraterrestrial faction operating in secrecy. Their technology, far beyond anything conceivable in 1917, allowed them to craft illusions that bent human perception, weaving their own narrative into the fabric of religious belief. They had studied humanity for centuries, recognizing the power of faith and the ease with which entire populations could be swayed by spectacles beyond their understanding.

And so, using their advanced knowledge, they created an apparition, a celestial event that would be etched into history as a divine miracle.

Among them was a female life-form, a being clad in an intricate protective suit, designed to interact safely in Earth's atmosphere. It was she who descended amidst the brilliant display, her presence meant to solidify the illusion. With careful calibration, the light was manipulated to give her an ethereal glow, enhancing the perception of an otherworldly presence. The illusion was nearly flawless.

Nearly.

Observing from a distance were two individuals who saw through the deception, Eduard and Asket. Unlike the others, their eyes were trained to discern the truth. Where others saw a divine entity, they recognized the unmistakable contours of a space suit beneath the dazzling radiance. They noted the subtle yet distinct technological anomalies within the phenomenon, details lost on the entranced crowd.

A critical mistake had been made by the Earth-foreigners. The illusion, though masterful, was imperfect.

As the event concluded, the radiant spectacle faded. The sky returned to normal, the air thick with the weight of what had just transpired. Some cried tears of joy, believing they had witnessed a holy revelation. Others collapsed in exhaustion, overcome by the sheer magnitude of the experience. The skeptics, though shaken, struggled to rationalize what they had seen.

The Catholic Church wasted no time in declaring the event miraculous. Fatima became a sacred site, a beacon of faith drawing pilgrims from across the world. Stories of the Virgin Mary's appearance spread, cemented into religious doctrine, inspiring devotion for generations to come. The narrative of divine intervention was upheld, reinforced by the masses who had seen it with their own eyes.

But the truth remained buried.

The extraterrestrial origin of the event was known only to a select few, concealed beneath layers of religious fervor and historical interpretation. The Giza Intelligences, an elusive faction with their own manipulative agenda, ensured that the true nature of the phenomenon remained obscured. The deception was successful, its impact stretching far beyond what its creators had anticipated.

It was only through Eduard's later revelations that the complete story began to unfold. The intricate layers of manipulation, the technological brilliance behind the illusion, and the deeper motives of the Earth-foreigners came to light. Humanity, it seemed, had long been subject to forces operating beyond their comprehension.

The Fatima event was not merely a miracle, it was a masterful deception, an intersection of human faith and extraterrestrial influence.

And so, history continued its course, the truth hidden beneath the veil of time, known only to those who dared to look beyond the illusion.

CHAPTER 52

A Journey Beyond the Stars

Eduard's voyage with Asket marked a profound departure from his previous experiences.

They soared through space at speeds that defied human comprehension, leaving Earth behind as they entered the vast expanse of the cosmos.

The craft moved effortlessly through the void, traversing light-years in moments, bringing Billy face-to-face with the magnificence of the universe.

Asket guided him through a celestial tapestry of distant planets and star systems, each more breathtaking than the last.

Eduard marveled at the diverse landscapes and vibrant ecosystems that unfolded before him.

They visited planets with lush, bioluminescent forests, shimmering lakes of liquid crystal, and towering mountain ranges that touched the stars.

These worlds were not just visually stunning but resonated with a profound sense of peace and harmony, where technology and spirituality existed in perfect balance.

One of the most remarkable places they visited was a planet named Althera.

Althera was a world where beings lived in perfect harmony with their environment.

Their technology was seamlessly integrated with nature, creating structures that floated on air and vehicles that moved silently through the skies.

The inhabitants, known as the Altherians, radiated a serene energy, their lives guided by principles of wisdom and compassion.

Asket introduced Eduard to the Altherians, who welcomed him warmly and shared their insights into the universe's deeper mysteries.

They spoke of the interconnectedness of all life, emphasizing the importance of maintaining balance and harmony.

Eduard felt a deep resonance with their teachings, which aligned closely with the principles he had learned from Sfath.

But the journey was not solely one of beauty and peace.

Asket also guided Eduard to worlds scarred by turmoil and destruction.

They visited planets where war and greed had ravaged the land, leaving behind desolate wastelands and fractured societies.

Eduard saw civilizations that had collapsed under the weight of their own conflicts, their once-thriving worlds now in ruins.

These darker realities were a sobering contrast to the harmonious worlds Eduard had seen.

Asket explained that these civilizations had once stood at a crossroads, much like humanity, and had made choices that led to their downfall.

The lessons from these worlds were crucial; they underscored the importance of the choices that humanity would soon face.

As they continued their journey, Eduard felt the weight of the knowledge he was gaining.

Each new experience brought with it a sense of urgency and responsibility.

He understood that the lessons he was learning were not merely for his own enlightenment but were to be shared with humanity.

The knowledge was both a gift and a burden, a responsibility that Billy took very seriously.

Asket guided him through the complexities of the universe, teaching him about different dimensions and planes of existence.

He learned about the nature of time and space, understanding that they were not as fixed as they seemed but were fluid and interconnected.

These revelations expanded his perception of reality, allowing him to see beyond the physical world into the realms of spirit and consciousness.

During their travels, Eduard began to develop new abilities.

Asket helped him harness and control these skills, which included telepathic communication, energy perception, and aura reading.

These abilities were essential tools for his mission, enabling him to connect with other beings on a deeper level and to perceive the underlying currents of the universe.

Learning to control these abilities was both exhilarating and challenging.

Eduard practiced diligently, understanding that these skills required not just technical mastery but also emotional discipline and wisdom.

He knew that his abilities would play a crucial role in guiding humanity and that he needed to use them responsibly.

Asket also introduced Eduard to other beings who had been watching over Earth for millennia.

These beings were part of a larger network of guardians and mentors, each with a deep interest in the planet's future.

They shared their perspectives on the challenges and opportunities that lay ahead, offering valuable insights and guidance.

He felt a profound sense of connection to these beings.

They were allies in his mission, and their support was a source of strength and encouragement.

The knowledge that he was not alone in his quest, that there were others who believed in the future he envisioned, provided him with a sense of hope and reassurance.

As the journey continued, Eduard's confidence grew.

He became more adept at using his abilities and more certain of his mission.

The knowledge and experiences he gained were shaping him into a leader, someone capable of guiding humanity towards a brighter future.

As they traveled through the stars, Eduard reflected on his journey.

The experiences and teachings he had encountered had transformed him, deepening his understanding of the universe and his place within it.

He felt a renewed sense of purpose and determination.

The universe was vast and full of wonders, and his journey was just beginning.

He was ready to embrace the challenges and opportunities that lay ahead, knowing that his mission was crucial for the future of humanity.

The lessons he had learned and the abilities he had developed would guide him as he returned to Earth to fulfill his destiny.

Chapter 53

The Unexpected Visitor

The events of the previous night had left Eduard overwhelmed.

Asket's elaborate explanations about their mission and the future weighed heavily on his mind, swirling with complex thoughts.

They returned to the ship in silence, Eduard's head burdened by the gravity of what he had learned.

The comfortable couch offered little solace; despite his exhaustion, sleep eluded him as he wrestled with the enormity of his impending journey through time.

When morning arrived, he jolted awake, startled by what sounded like a distant gunshot. Asket, ever vigilant, quickly joined him at one of the ship's windows.

Below them, a man stood at a distance, grinning and leaning against a rifle.

It was the same man they had encountered days earlier, far from the ship, clearly having fired the shot to get their attention.

Without exchanging words, they descended from the ship to meet him.

The man approached with a wide smile, extending his hand in greeting.

"What a surprise! Come let me greet you two.

I should have thought of this right away.

How could I possibly find you so sympathetic during your visit to my camp?

I'm Iljitsch Ustinov, just call me Jitschi."

Asket and Eduard exchanged glances as Jitschi shook their hands vigorously.

Asket noted, "This surprise was not anticipated."

Jitschi replied, "I believe that, it's really a surprise. I didn't intend to come here.

But something led me to wander this area, and when I saw your ship, I thought it was an illusion.

But here you are! I've seen many things, but nothing like this.

I've heard tales of such things in America and elsewhere.

Where do you come from, Venus or Mars?"

Eduard responded, "I am neither from Venus nor Mars.

I am just a human from this world like you."

"That cannot be," Jitschi insisted.

"The ship is clearly a spaceship."

Asket clarified, "That is true regarding the ship and myself.

But my friend here is genuinely from this world."

"Aha, so you are a contactee?" Jitschi exclaimed.

Eduard asked, "Is that what they call it?"

"Yes, it's widely known," Jitschi replied.

"Unfortunately, I am not familiar with this story," Eduard admitted.

Asket reflected, "This meeting was indeed unplanned.

What should we do now?"

"I'm unsure, what do you think, Jitschi?" Eduard inquired.

"Do you perhaps want to get rid of me?" Jitschi suggested.

"No one has mentioned that," Asket reassured.

"But your sudden appearance complicates things."

"I'm sorry for that.

I didn't mean to interfere," Jitschi said.

"What is this talk about?" Asket pressed.

"Who says such things?"

"I've heard various claims suggesting you might be like angels on a divine mission," Jitschi explained.

"That is not the case," Asket countered.

"We are not angels nor are we on a mission from God.

These ideas are deliberate distortions by those who wish to create malevolent narratives disguised as religious truth.

If you are a believer, you have been misled by false teachings."

"You blaspheme God; that is outrageous," Jitschi replied.

"It's not blasphemy, but rather the truth that you've been misled.

The teachings you follow are not accurate," Asket insisted.

"I don't understand that," Jitschi said.

"You will once I explain it all to you.

For now, I've decided something.

If you want, you can come with us and soon understand everything," Asket offered.

"Am I supposed to get into this, this ship?" Jitschi asked, a hint of fear in his voice.

"Are you frightened?" Asket probed.

"Honestly, yes.

It's so outlandish to me, and despite everything, I love my life," Jitschi admitted.

"But you claim to be a good Christian.

Don't Christians have faith in life after death?" Eduard challenged.

"You ask strange questions.

Every human fears death.

I feel I'm not mature enough to face heaven yet," Jitschi replied.

"I find your behavior lacking in courage, and it seems you're misguided regarding heaven," Eduard asserted.

"Do you think so? You both have rather peculiar views.

I trust in God and Jesus Christ," Jitschi declared.

"That's precisely what was never said.

He was actually called Jmmanuel," Asket noted.

"If you truly trust in them, why fear the ship? Isn't it that your faith in Christianity leaves you with doubts?" Eduard pressed.

"I am devout and not doubtful," Jitschi stated firmly.

"It seems to me that your faith is shaky.

Often believers shift their responsibility onto saints or God, failing to take responsibility themselves.

Do you fall into this category?" Eduard challenged.

"That's true," Asket agreed.

"It's funny. Despite your harsh words, I feel a strange sympathy for you. What's that about?" Jitschi mused.

"It's the honesty and truth in his words that resonate with you, even if unconsciously," Asket explained.

"Yes, it could be. Despite my faith, I often doubt. Let's move on," Jitschi conceded.

"I still have one important matter for you, Jitschi: If you join us and witness events from the past that contradict your beliefs, you must remain silent about them.

The existence of humanity and the planetary system could depend on your discretion," Eduard warned.

"You can't be serious.

Why should I stay silent? I could sell the story to newspapers and live comfortably," Jitschi countered.

"Is that how Christians think?" Eduard asked.

"Why not? I must make a living. Such a story could be very profitable," Jitschi reasoned.

"Then you cannot stay with us, as you would only be allowed to speak if you knew your life was at risk," Asket stated firmly.

"Is my silence so crucial?" Jitschi questioned.

"It's vital, perhaps for the survival of humanity and the planetary system," Asket insisted.

"I can't bear such a burden.

I promise to remain silent, no matter what," Jitschi vowed.

"Your word is valuable?" Asket asked.

"On my life," Jitschi confirmed.

"Then we can start. We will first fly to a great height, then transmit into the past," Asket instructed.

As the ship took off, it accelerated rapidly into the sky, leaving Earth's atmosphere behind.

Stars began to sparkle around them.

Jitschi, pale and trembling, grasped for a vessel and began to cough.

Asket reassured him, "We will be there in a moment.

The transmission is instantaneous."

The sensation of "extinguishing" their physical form lasted only a moment. Soon, Asket's voice came through, "We are now in the Thirteenth Century."

The transition was seamless, yet the experience was jarring.

The ship emerged into a different time and place, revealing the stark contrast between their modern world and the past they had entered. Jitschi, still recovering from his earlier shock, began to adapt to the situation.

His initial terror subsided, but he was clearly overwhelmed by the surreal nature of their journey.

They landed in a landscape far removed from the technological marvels of their own time.

The surroundings were primitive, with rudimentary buildings and people dressed in historical garments.

The air was filled with unfamiliar sounds and smells, and the environment starkly contrasted what they had left behind.

Asket began to explain, "We are now in the Thirteenth Century, a time of significant historical importance.

Our mission here is to observe and understand the events that shaped this period."

Jitschi, still adjusting, looked around in awe and trepidation.

"This is incredible," he said.

"I never imagined I'd be standing here in the past.

What are we supposed to do?"

"Our goal is to gather information about historical events and compare them with traditional accounts.

We need to observe and record what we see," Asket explained.

"We should be cautious.

History is full of inaccuracies and biases.

Our task is to uncover the truth," Eduard added.

"And how are we supposed to do that?" Jitschi asked.

Asket replied, "We will observe key events and interactions.

Our technology allows us to be invisible to those around us, so we won't interfere with history.

But we will gain insights that are crucial for understanding the past."

As they began their exploration, the contrast between their advanced technology and the historical setting was striking.

The simplicity of life in the Thirteenth Century highlighted the advancements they often took for granted.

The people they encountered were suspicious and curious about their presence, but they remained unseen, thanks to the ship's cloaking technology.

Jitschi struggled to reconcile his faith with the reality he was witnessing.

"This is all so different from what I was taught. How do I make sense of it?"

"It's a process of learning and adapting," Eduard reassured him.

"The truth is often more complex than traditional narratives suggest.

We're here to see things as they were, without the distortions of legend and myth."

Asket added, "Remember, our goal is to understand and record.

We need to focus on the facts and remain objective.

The more we observe, the clearer the picture will become."

As they moved through the historical landscape, they encountered various figures and events, each providing a piece of the puzzle.

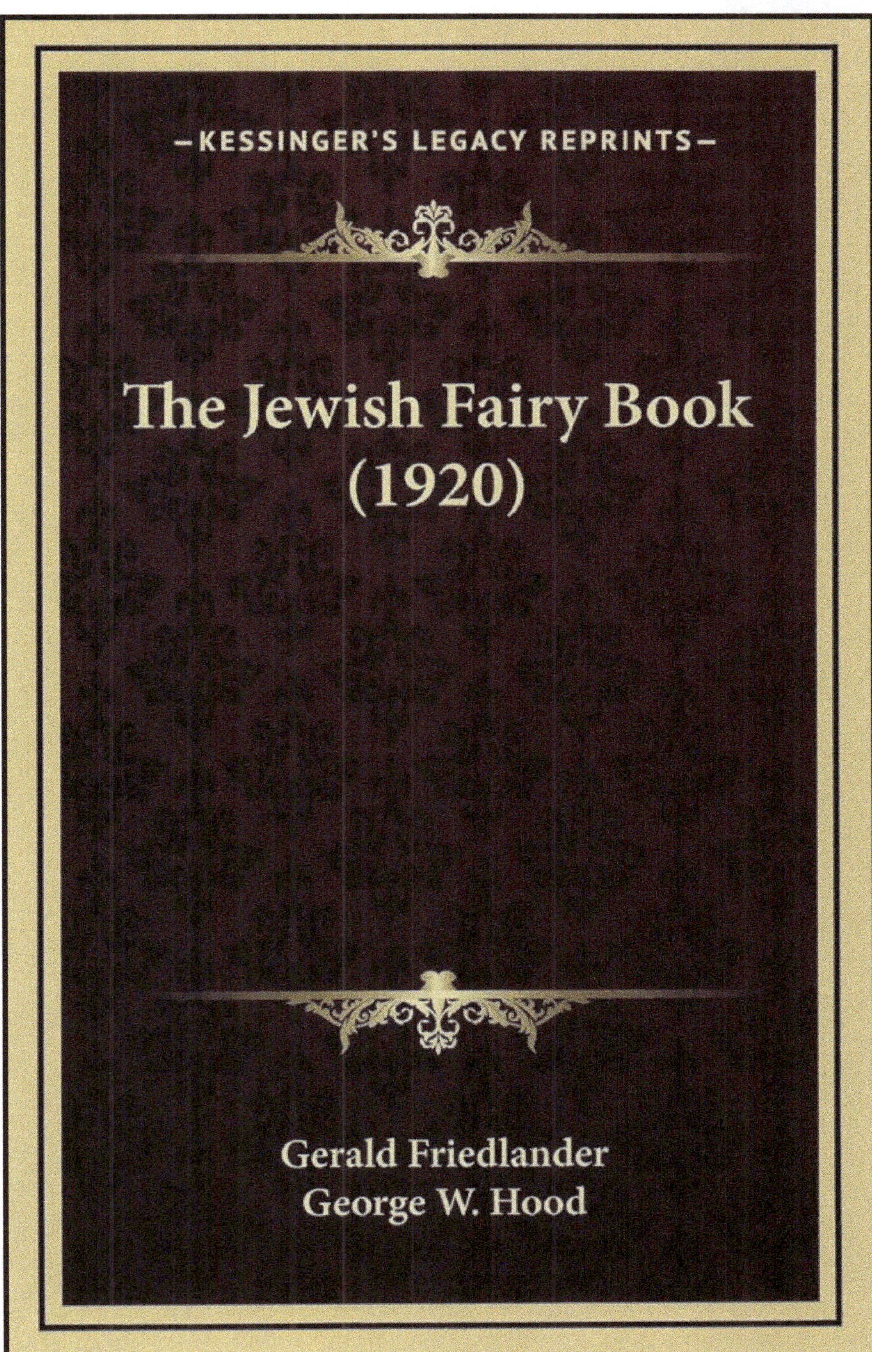

-KESSINGER'S LEGACY REPRINTS-

The Jewish Fairy Book
(1920)

Gerald Friedlander
George W. Hood

CHAPTER 54

Arrival in the Thirteenth Century

Eduard and Asket emerged from the exit shaft of the vessel, stepping into a world vastly different from their own.

The year was the Thirteenth Century, and the air was thick with a freshness that Eduard had never experienced.

He felt the weight of the language-converter device Asket had given him, which was now strapped securely to his belt.

The device was crucial for understanding and communicating in this unfamiliar era.

Asket, with her usual efficiency, swiftly opened the exit shaft and glided out with ease.

Eduard, though initially struggling with the unfamiliar technology, managed to secure the device to his belt before following her.

He witnessed Jitschi, who was still visibly unsettled, guiding the vessel down to a nearby bush.

Jitschi's pallor hinted at his discomfort, but he made an effort to compose himself.

Eduard followed Jitschi's lead, allowing himself to glide out of the shaft.

As Eduard emerged beneath the ship, he found himself in a lush, verdant forest.

The environment was both familiar and strikingly different from what he knew.

The greenery was vibrant, the fir-trees stood tall and majestic, and the flowers in the grass were remarkably vivid. What captivated him most was the cacophony of bird songs.

The air was filled with a chorus of chirps and tweets, a sign of a natural world untouched by the pollutants of his own time.

The air itself was a revelation. It was cooler and fresher, with an oxygen content that seemed significantly higher.

The sky was an astonishing shade of azure blue, unmarred by the smog and pollution that plagued his era.

The sun shone brightly and warmly, casting a golden hue over the sprawling forests, hills, and meadows that stretched as far as the eye could see.

There were no signs of human habitation, no villages, towns, or houses, just a pristine, almost paradisiacal wilderness.

In the distance, Eduard spotted a herd of deer grazing peacefully, completely unaware of their presence.

The animals appeared to be much less timid than those of his time.

Pheasants flitted about in abundance, adding to the sense of untouched beauty.

Eduard marveled at the sheer splendor of the scene.

Asket observed his fascination with a knowing smile.

"You're quite observant," she commented.

"It's simply magnificent here," Eduard replied, still awestruck.

"Indeed," Asket agreed. "The past often holds a charm that is lost in the present.

But we must move on.

There's a hunter's cabin just beyond those woods, a place I know well. It belongs to a rabbi named Jechieli, who enjoys the countryside from time to time."

Eduard, still trying to grasp the full scope of their situation, asked, "Where exactly are we? What's the time and place?"

"We're in Thirteenth-Century France," Asket explained.

"During the reign of Saint Louis."

Eduard's face showed his confusion.

"I'm not well-versed in the history of this period."

Asket dismissed his concern. "It's not crucial. Follow me."

Asket led Eduard and Jitschi through the forest.

The path, worn by game, meandered through the trees and led them to a quaint log hut. Jitschi, now appearing more composed, joined them as they approached the cabin.

Jitschi, now free of his initial trepidation, remarked, "I'm no longer astonished or fearful.

I was quite foolish before. So, where are we now?"

Asket briefly reiterated their location and time, and Jitschi, with a touch of admiration, adjusted to the new reality.

"It's incredible," he said.

"I haven't seen fifty springs, and suddenly, I'm 600 years younger."

Asket chuckled. "Your calculation isn't entirely accurate, but it captures the essence."

Upon reaching the cabin, they were greeted by Rabbi Jechieli.

He appeared surprised but welcoming.

"So, you're here again after all these years.

But who are these two men?"

Asket introduced Eduard and Jitschi as friends from a distant land, though Jechieli was curious about their origins.

"Do they come from the stars like you?"

Asket clarified, "No, they are from your world but from a much later time."

Jechieli's curiosity was piqued. "You mentioned this before.

But what is that device on this man's belt?"

Eduard, feeling a bit self-conscious, explained, "It's an electric pocket lamp with batteries."

Jechieli examined the device with intrigue.

"I don't know what that is. How does it work?"

Eduard attempted to elucidate.

"It's a lamp, but it doesn't use tallow, candles, or oil. It runs on electrical energy, which I can't explain in detail."

Jechieli was perplexed but fascinated.

"That's incomprehensible to me."

Jitschi, who had a better grasp of the technology, offered to explain the details to Jechieli later.

Eduard, relieved by this, decided to give the torch and extra batteries to Jechieli.

"You can keep this torch. Here are four replacement batteries. Let Jitschi explain how it works."

Jechieli hesitated.

"I cannot accept this. It must be very valuable."

Jitschi, laughing, reassured him, "Don't worry. These items are inexpensive and easily obtainable in our time."

Jechieli accepted the gift with gratitude and spent time marveling at it.

Meanwhile, Asket and Eduard wandered through the meadows, enjoying the splendor of nature.

They spent over five hours exploring before returning to find Jechieli and Jitschi deep in conversation.

Jitschi shared his excitement with Asket.

"Jechieli is incredibly intelligent.

I've given him an electric fence energizer and plans for a dynamo that can be driven by a windmill or water wheel.

He plans to use it to create an electric security device for his cabin."

Asket laughed heartily. "That could be quite amusing. If he follows through, he might become a legendary magician in history, though he's already known as one."

Jitschi continued, "I might find references to my electric fence energizer and the simple torch in historical texts as magical artifacts.

It will be interesting to see how history interprets these gifts."

Asket addressed a concern of Jitschi's.

Jechieli has given me some items that could have high antique value in your time. Can I bring them back?"

Asket explained the limitations of their time travel.

"We can transport back instantly, so the items won't age.

To make them valuable antiques, they would need to be preserved through normal time spans.

Our technology bridges space and time in a way that eliminates aging."

Jitschi, grappling with the complexity of the explanation, admitted, "The mathematics are beyond me, but it's a shame about the gifts."

Eduard added, "Your materialism again, my son."

Asket laughed at Eduard's remark. "You have a healthy sense of humor. But we must move on; we have other times to explore."

They followed Asket's lead and after a short time, the ship ascended into the sky. In a brief moment, they again felt they were no longer.

*Excerpt from the book "Fantastic Past," Pages 97-98;
Author: Robert Charroux; NSB*

Provided by Mrs B. Sauer on September 18th 1975.

Several chroniclers of the Thirteenth Century testify however, that Jechieli, a French rabbi, to whom Saint Ludwig paid great respect due to his high degree of learning, knew the secret of a shining lamp which lit up by itself.

This lamp burned without oil and without a wick, and the magician sometimes put it at his window at night, which filled his contemporaries with fear, although he enjoyed high standing with the king and was even his adviser.

Eliphas Levi wrote in his "History of Magic" on page 206: "Everything which one can say about this lamp and its magical power of illumination provides evidence that Jechieli had discovered electricity or, at least, knew the primary possibilities for its application, because this knowledge, which is just as old as magic itself, was passed down from generation to generation as one of the keys to the higher initiations."

Indisputably Jechieli was an initiate.

Did the secret of his lamp arise from his knowledge of electricity?

According to the chroniclers, the rabbi had a very personal way of spoiling the fun of undesired guests - ie. his enemies -, who knocked on his door.

He "touched a nail which had been hammered into the wall of his room, and immediately a bluish, crackling spark sprang out of it.

Woe to anyone who touched the iron door knocker at that moment.

He bent over with pain, howled loudly as if the Earth was going to swallow him, and took off ..."

"One day", wrote Eliphas Levi, "murmuring threateningly at the Rabbi's door, pressed a crowd of people who held each other firmly by the arms in order to protect themselves from the shaking and the supposed earthquake.

The boldest furiously activated the knocker.

Then Jechieli touched his nail. At the same moment the attackers rolled, one over the other, and fled and screamed as if they had been burnt.

They later asserted they had felt how the Earth opened under them and they sank up to the knees. They did not know how they had come out of it.

But there was no way in the world they would return again to knock at the wizard's door. So, by means of the terror that he spread, Jecheili secured his peace."

One can really only explain that this way: Jechieli had invented the electric lamp, or re-invented it, and by pressing on a button sent electrical currents into the iron doorknocker.

Undoubtedly the rabbi was in possession of a scientific secret, but he did not consider it opportune to betray it to the people of the Thirteenth Century.

Our evolution
is the
revolution.
Chantelle Renee
www.ChantelleRenee.org

CHAPTER 55

The Time-Travel Process

The procedure leading up to the time-travel transmission was complex, requiring careful calibration, energy alignment, and security checks.

The entire process took about ten minutes, yet the actual transition from one epoch to another was instantaneous, occurring in a mere fraction of a second.

There was no sensation of movement, no gradual shift, but rather an abrupt, almost shocking displacement.

Asket, however, chose not to elaborate on the intricate technology or specific steps involved, leaving Eduard and Jitschi to marvel at its execution without fully understanding it.

During the moment of transmission, something extraordinary happened.

The surroundings of the ship began to shimmer, as if reality itself was dissolving. Shapes distorted, colors blurred, and then everything, every last particle of existence, vanished.

For a fleeting instant, Eduard felt as though he no longer existed in a physical sense.

His body, his thoughts, even his sense of self seemed to dissipate into an infinite void, where time had no dominion.

He experienced an overwhelming sense of peace, a boundless silence, and an immense love that transcended any human understanding.

It was not an absence of sensation, but rather a presence beyond anything earthly.

When the ship rematerialized in a new epoch, the process reversed itself, forms reassembled, colors returned, and the solidity of existence was restored.

Yet the experience left a deep impression on Eduard. It was as if he had briefly touched eternity itself, stepping outside the flow of time into an unmeasurable state of being.

Despite witnessing this process multiple times, the technical aspects of time travel remained an enigma to him.

He lacked the scientific background to comprehend its mechanics, but Asket assured him that even the most advanced Earth scientists would be unable to grasp the full complexity of it.

Still, the knowledge he gained through his journeys was of far greater significance than understanding the machinery that enabled them.

Over the course of six days, Asket guided Eduard and Jitschi through a series of time-travel expeditions.

They visited epochs both ancient and distant, observing civilizations that had long since vanished and glimpsing futures that had yet to unfold.

Many of the things they witnessed directly contradicted established archaeological and historical theories.

Events that had been considered myths proved to be factual, while certain "historical truths" were exposed as fabrications or misinterpretations.

Eduard quickly realized that modern scientific and historical narratives were riddled with speculation and inaccuracies.

Many prevailing theories were not based on true knowledge but on assumptions, shaped by limited evidence and biased interpretations.

Natural processes, human evolution, and even key historical events followed patterns far different from what scholars had proposed.

This realization, while enlightening, was also deeply unsettling.

As they continued their journey, Eduard often questioned the reality of what he was seeing.

Time travel was such an astonishing concept that it sometimes felt surreal, like a dream too vivid to be real.

Yet he constantly tested his perceptions, ensuring that what he experienced was not an illusion or hallucination.

He collected tangible proof, physical evidence that could not be explained away.

The pain of an injury sustained in one of their travels confirmed the stark reality of their experiences.

Jitschi, however, struggled with what he witnessed. His entire belief system was being shattered before his eyes.

On multiple occasions, Eduard observed him muttering to himself, his hands shaking as he furiously scribbled notes and crossed out passages in his Bible with a red pen.

The truths he was confronting were in direct conflict with his religious upbringing, and the dissonance was tearing at him.

Jitschi's frustration grew into anger. He condemned those who had, in his view, misled entire generations with religious fabrications.

He engaged in lengthy arguments with himself, voicing bitter accusations against theologians, historians, and religious leaders.

Eduard began to worry about Jitschi's mental state.

His emotional turmoil was intense, and Eduard feared that upon returning to their own time, Jitschi might spiral into an obsessive crusade against religion, unable to find peace.

Their most profound journey took them to the year 32, an era of immense significance.

Here, they investigated the life and teachings of Jmmanuel, a historical figure whose true story had been grossly distorted by the New Testament of the Christian Bible.

Asket wanted them to witness firsthand the discrepancies between the biblical accounts and the actual events of history.

Jitschi's reaction was extreme. His belief in Christ as a divine savior disintegrated under the weight of the evidence presented to him.

The truth was undeniable, and it crushed everything he had once held sacred.

Instead of experiencing liberation, he descended into a state of rage, viewing religion not just as misguided but as a deliberate deception imposed on humanity.

His resentment grew into hatred, and his anger became uncontrollable.

The full details of their experiences in the past remain undisclosed, but one crucial discovery stood out.

The falsification of Jmmanuel's story had triggered a chain reaction of mass delusion, leading to the establishment of one of the world's most influential religions.

This distortion not only shaped Christianity but also played a role in the rise of Islam and countless other sects, influencing the spiritual and political landscapes of entire civilizations.

The realization was staggering. The manipulation of historical truth had left humanity trapped in a cycle of ideological control and spiritual confusion.

For Eduard, this journey was more than just a historical exploration, it was a revelation of how easily truth could be reshaped, hidden, or weaponized.

The weight of this knowledge was immense, and it marked their journey as one of unparalleled significance.

Chapter 56

Meeting Jmmanuel

Asket's voice was calm, yet it held a gravity that demanded attention.

"Now, we will go back to the time of Jmmanuel," she said, her words resonating in the silent ship.

Eduard and Jitschi exchanged glances, their anticipation palpable.

They had prepared themselves for this moment, but the reality of what they were about to do was far more profound than they could have imagined.

The ship, hummed softly as Asket initiated the sequence.

The stars outside blurred, and within moments, they were propelled through time, the universe folding in on itself to transport them to a different era.

Eduard felt a slight pressure in his chest, a reminder of the enormity of what was happening. They were about to step into a world that existed two millennia before their own.

With a final lurch, the ship came to a halt.

The hum died down, replaced by a silence that felt almost sacred.

Asket glanced at them, her eyes reflecting the seriousness of their mission.

"We have arrived," she announced.

The landing site was familiar, yet entirely different.

They had taken off just minutes ago in the year 1953, but now, they stood in the year 32.

The landscape bore a resemblance to what they had seen before, hills, mountains, and the same rocky terrain, but there was an unmistakable shift in the atmosphere. The air felt ancient, thick with the weight of history.

Eduard stepped out of the ship, his boots crunching on the dry earth.

He surveyed the surroundings, noting the subtle differences in the topography.

The mountains in the distance had shifted slightly in form, and the vegetation was sparser, more untamed.

Jerusalem, a bustling city in his time, was now a modest, walled village, its silhouette barely visible on the horizon.

Asket joined him, her presence a grounding force in this unfamiliar past.

"The landscape has changed little over time," she remarked, "but the people and their lives are vastly different from what you know."

They began their journey to Jerusalem, a four-day trek through rugged terrain.

The path was treacherous, winding through steep hills and narrow passes.

The heat of the day beat down on them, and by nightfall, the cold crept in, seeping through their clothing.

Despite the discomfort, they pressed on, driven by the knowledge that their mission was of the utmost importance.

Their provisions, prepared by Jitschi before their departure, were meager but sufficient.

They subsisted on dried meats, fruits, and bread, all of which had been carefully chosen to sustain them without drawing attention in this ancient world.

Asket had also provided them with a small sack of ancient coins, polished to a gleaming shine with a mysterious radiation.

These coins would allow them to blend in, to purchase what they needed without raising suspicion.

As they walked, Asket shared more insights into the time they were entering.

"You must be cautious," she warned.

"Your behavior must not arouse suspicion.

The people here are wary of outsiders, and any mistake could be costly."

Eduard listened intently, absorbing every detail.

Asket explained the customs of the time, the mannerisms that would help them fit in, and the subtle nuances of language that would mark them as locals rather than strangers.

It was a crash course in survival, and Eduard knew that their success depended on how well they adhered to her instructions.

By the time they reached Jerusalem, they were weary and covered in dust.

The city's walls loomed ahead, a stark contrast to the wilderness they had traversed.

It was not the Jerusalem of grand temples and bustling markets that Eduard knew from his studies.

This was a smaller, humbler place, a settlement more than a city.

They approached the gates with caution, blending into the stream of travelers entering the city.

Asket's guidance proved invaluable. They moved through the crowds with ease, their appearance and demeanor indistinguishable from the locals.

The ancient coins they carried clinked softly in their pouches, a reassuring reminder of their preparedness.

Inside the walls, the city was alive with activity.

Vendors shouted their wares, and the air was thick with the smells of spices and cooking fires.

The streets were narrow and winding, filled with people going about their daily lives.

It was a place of contrasts, rich and poor, sacred and profane, all mingling in the crowded alleys.

Eduard's eyes were wide with wonder.

Despite the dust and grime, there was a vibrancy to Jerusalem, a sense of history in the making.

Every corner seemed to hold a story, every face a glimpse into a world long gone.

But there was also an underlying tension, a sense of unease that lingered in the air.

As they moved deeper into the city, Asket led them to a modest inn, tucked away in a quiet corner of the city.

It was a simple place, with rough wooden furniture and small rooms, but it was clean and discreet.

They took up lodging there, grateful for the chance to rest and plan their next steps.

That evening, gathered around a small table in their room, Asket laid out the details of their mission.

"Our purpose here is twofold," she began.

"First, we must observe the events surrounding Jmmanuel, the man who would later be known as Jesus Christ.

His life and teachings will shape the future of humanity in ways that are not yet fully understood."

Eduard nodded, understanding the gravity of their task.

They were not here to interfere, only to witness.

To gather knowledge that would be critical for the future, knowledge that could not be obtained in any other way.

"But there is another reason," Asket continued.

"We must ensure that the timeline remains intact.

Any disruption, no matter how small, could have catastrophic consequences.

You must be vigilant, Eduard.

The fate of your world depends on it."

The weight of responsibility settled on Eduard's shoulders.

He had always known that this journey would be dangerous, but the reality of it was only now sinking in.

They were walking a tightrope between past and future, and one misstep could unravel everything.

Over the next few days, they ventured out into the city, carefully observing the people and their interactions.

They visited the temple, the marketplaces, and the homes of the wealthy and the poor.

Everywhere they went, they listened, learned, and noted the differences between this time and their own.

Eduard was struck by the simplicity of life here, but also by its harshness.

Survival was a daily struggle for many, and the shadow of Roman rule loomed large over the city.

There was an undercurrent of unrest, a sense that something was about to happen, something that would change everything.

On the fourth day, they found themselves in a small square, where a crowd had gathered to listen to a man speak.

He was dressed in simple robes, his hair and beard unkempt, but his presence was magnetic. Eduard recognized him immediately, this was Jmmanuel, the man they had come to see.

They stayed on the edges of the crowd, careful not to draw attention to themselves.

Jmmanuel's voice carried over the throng, clear and compelling.

He spoke of love, of forgiveness, and of a kingdom not of this world.

His words resonated with the people, their faces lighting up with hope and wonder.

Eduard felt a shiver run down his spine.

Here was a man who would be remembered for millennia, whose words would be twisted and interpreted in countless ways, shaping the course of history.

Yet in this moment, he was just a man, speaking to a small crowd in a dusty square.

As the crowd began to disperse, Jmmanuel's eyes caught Eduard's for a fleeting moment.

It was as if Jmmanuel saw something in him that transcended time itself, something profound and unspoken.

Without hesitation, Jmmanuel turned and began to walk towards them, his gaze never wavering.

Eduard's heart raced as the figure approached, his presence exuding a calm yet powerful energy.

Asket stood beside Eduard, her expression serene, but he could sense the significance of this moment.

This was the man they had come to see, the one whose life and teachings would echo through the ages.

When Jmmanuel reached them, he greeted them with a gentle yet commanding voice.

"Be greeted in peace."

Asket inclined her head slightly, her voice steady as she responded, "Your greeting applies also to you."

Eduard, though mesmerized, found his voice and added, "I would like to join in that."

Jmmanuel regarded them both with a knowing smile, a warmth in his eyes that belied the gravity of his mission.

"Go to my brothers.

They will tend to you," he said, directing these words to Jitschi, who had been standing slightly apart, observing in silence.

Without a word of reply, Jitschi nodded and walked towards the men sitting at the edge of the path.

They welcomed him with open arms, offering him food and drink, tending to him with the care reserved for family.

Turning his attention back to Eduard, Jmmanuel spoke again, this time more directly.

"You are Eduard."

Eduard nodded, surprised by the familiarity.

"That I am. And this…" he began, gesturing towards Asket.

But Jmmanuel interrupted him gently, "… is Asket. I know.

But I do not wish to talk with her, rather with you.

You have struck very hard," he said, his tone one of deep understanding.

Eduard felt a wave of humility wash over him.

"You are very wise and quick-thinking," Jmmanuel continued, his gaze piercing yet kind.

Eduard shook his head slightly, trying to downplay the compliment. "You deserve the flowers, not me."

Jmmanuel's eyes sparkled with amusement. "You have a peculiar language, but I understand its meaning. It is good and it honors you.

But let us sit here on these stones, for I would like to have a conversation with you."

They moved to a cluster of large stones nearby, sitting down in the shade of an ancient olive tree.

The air was thick with the scent of the earth, the hum of life in the background, yet this moment felt suspended in time, isolated from the world around them.

Eduard couldn't help but ask the question that had been burning in his mind.

"You know my name and also Asket's. Do you know each other then, and has she told you about me?"

Jmmanuel's expression remained calm, though his eyes held a depth that spoke of countless mysteries.

"You are very connected to reality.

No, I have never spoken with Asket before this moment.

My knowledge about you two is of another nature.

It is to be found in my power of consciousness, through which I behold the times."

Eduard's mind raced to grasp the full meaning of Jmmanuel's words.

"That therefore signifies clairvoyance, so to speak?" he asked, seeking clarification.

"In a certain manner, you think correctly," Jmmanuel replied, his voice patient.

"Because truly, it is previewing, a looking out ahead."

Eduard considered this, his thoughts turning inward.

"In a certain manner? Then it can only be that you are able, through the power of your consciousness, to wander through the ages and can explore them accordingly."

Jmmanuel's gaze sharpened, impressed by Eduard's insight.

"That is my knowledge. How are you able to grasp that? I understand.

That way is very good. You must also know it, because very difficult things stand before you."

Eduard's breath caught in his throat.

"That is so, I know, yet shortly you will also face a very difficult test."

Jmmanuel's expression softened with a hint of sorrow.

"Life demands all sorts of things, as you say. But we must tread our path and traverse it in honor and in fulfillment of the laws.

As I will tread my path, so will you also tread yours, and in the same way, every human will always have his own path to traverse."

Eduard nodded, feeling the truth of Jmmanuel's words deep within him.

"I am also of the same view, but may I put some questions to you which are burningly interesting to me?"

Jmmanuel smiled, a gentle and knowing smile that seemed to reach into the depths of Eduard's soul.

"Your nature and your thoughts are familiar to me, and so I want to answer your questions before you have to voice them."

Eduard felt a wave of gratitude wash over him.

He could sense that this conversation was not just a meeting of minds but a meeting of souls, connected by something far greater than either of them could fully comprehend.

"My teaching, which I spread in these lands, is not new, and it is well known to the scribes," Jmmanuel began, his voice taking on a tone of quiet authority.

"But they falsify the old teaching of the prophets which was handed down to them and is very learned.

But they disdain and falsify it and interpret it to their own advantage; therefore, they accuse me of lying because I preach against their lies."

Eduard listened intently, absorbing each word.

He could feel the weight of history in Jmmanuel's words, the gravity of the truths he was revealing.

This was not just a conversation; it was a revelation.

"From the old teaching of the laws of Creation and the spirit," Jmmanuel continued, "they have set up erroneous cults which take freedom of consciousness from the human and drive him into servitude, whereby they can enrich themselves with his possessions.

From the spiritual teaching, they have made a false teaching, and they have abased Creation to a human entity which they call God."

Jmmanuel paused, allowing Eduard to digest the implications of what he was hearing.

The truth was heavy, and Eduard could feel the burden of it pressing down on his shoulders.

Yet, he also felt a sense of clarity, as if the fog of confusion was slowly lifting.

"But God is a ruler over humankind and over worlds," Jmmanuel continued, his voice now tinged with a quiet sorrow.

"And he can never be put on a level with Creation, because its BEING is the highest, and outside of it, truly, nothing exists."

Eduard's mind raced as he tried to process these profound truths.

He had always known that the teachings of his time were flawed, but hearing it from Jmmanuel himself brought it into sharp focus.

The magnitude of the deception was staggering.

"But the scribes and the Pharisees dispute these teachings of the spirit," Jmmanuel went on, his voice growing firmer.

"And they blaspheme me by calling me a liar because I announce the truth. The truth, however, is at all times unpopular, and it is also so at this time.

Truly, I say to you, if a human, such as I, speaks of the truth, announces it, and spreads it, he will thus be persecuted and hated because of it, in my time as in yours."

Eduard felt a chill run down his spine.

The words Jmmanuel spoke resonated with a timeless truth, one that transcended the boundaries of time and space.

It was a truth that would challenge the very foundations of belief, and Eduard knew that the consequences would be dire.

"I will therefore be persecuted and will not escape the myrmidons, because life has determined it for me thus," Jmmanuel said, his voice now filled with a quiet resolve.

"But you will also be persecuted in that way because you will, in your future world, have a mission to fulfill, as do I."

Eduard's heart skipped a beat at these words.

The weight of his own mission suddenly felt overwhelming, yet he knew that he could not turn away from it.

He had been chosen for a reason, and he had to see it through, no matter the cost.

"My coming days are very difficult," Jmmanuel continued, his voice softening with a hint of sadness.

"And I feel bitterness and hurt in me because I know the events which approach me.

Yet I will not escape from them because this is determined this way."

Eduard felt a deep sense of empathy for Jmmanuel.

He could see the burden that this man carried, the knowledge of the suffering that lay ahead, and yet, there was also a strength in him, a determination to fulfill his purpose, no matter the cost.

"The human of this world has succumbed to very great need and confusion driven in by the false teachings of the scribes and Pharisees and all those who stroll along in their footsteps," Jmmanuel said, his voice filled with a quiet sorrow.

"Truly, I say to you, this will lead to very much need and misery on this world."

Eduard nodded, feeling the truth of Jmmanuel's words deep within him.

He could see the parallels between the world of Jmmanuel's time and his own, the same forces of greed and corruption at work, the same manipulation of truth for power and control.

"Today, on the chairs of the prophets sit the scribes and the Pharisees," Jmmanuel continued, his voice growing stronger.

"And everything they preach to the people is barefaced lies and deception.

They are hypocrites and twisters of the truth. Outwardly, before the people, they seem devout and good, but inwardly they are full of hypocrisy, transgression, and falseness."

Jmmanuel's words were like a dagger to the heart, piercing through the layers of deception that had been woven over centuries.

Eduard could see the truth now, clear and undeniable, and it filled him with a sense of righteous anger.

"Inside themselves, they are more evil than every nest of snakes or vipers, and they claim to be great in their thinking and knowledge, yet they possess no understanding," Jmmanuel said, his voice now filled with a quiet fury.

"But upon them will come all the righteous blood which flowed on Earth because of them, from the first prophet onwards who their fathers and forefathers murdered, up to the blood of those who they will yet murder in the future."

Eduard's heart ached at the thought of all the innocent lives that had been lost, the countless souls who had suffered at the hands of those who claimed to be righteous.

The weight of history pressed down on him, the knowledge that this cycle of violence and deception would continue, unless someone had the courage to stand against it.

"They murder in the name of love and justice and thereby actually intend to serve only their own greed for wealth and power," Jmmanuel continued, his voice now filled with a quiet determination.

"They have transformed the teaching of the spirit, and the laws and recommendations of Creation, into a very evil cult and frighten the humans with death, with the vengeance of their bloodthirsty god, and with sword-bearing angels."

Eduard could see the parallels in his own world, the same manipulation of fear and guilt, the same use of religion as a tool for control.

The truth was as clear as day now, and it filled him with a sense of purpose.

He knew that his mission would not be easy, but he also knew that it was necessary.

"They teach the humans to be afraid of the splendor and all-ness of Creation because they deny its existence and replace it with their god and their saints," Jmmanuel said, his voice now filled with a quiet sadness.

"Truly, so is it, and the coming times will be very bad."

Eduard felt a deep sense of foreboding as he listened to Jmmanuel's words.

He could see the darkness that lay ahead, the suffering and despair that would come, but he also knew that there was hope, a glimmer of light that would guide them through the darkness.

"There will be wailing and the gnashing of teeth in the world, and the blood of uncountable, innocently sacrificed and murdered ones will deeply saturate the dry Earth," Jmmanuel said, his voice now filled with a quiet resignation.

"Woe to this world and these humans; their lot will be very hard right into the distant future."

Eduard nodded, feeling the weight of these words deep within him.

He knew that the path ahead would be difficult, but he also knew that it was necessary.

The truth had to be revealed, no matter the cost, and he was willing to pay that price.

Jmmanuel's eyes met Eduard's once more, and in that moment, there was a silent understanding between them, a bond that transcended time and space.

They were both on a path that would lead to great suffering, but also to great purpose.

They were both chosen, not by fate, but by the very nature of their being, to carry this truth forward, no matter the cost.

And so, they sat together in silence, two souls connected by a truth that was as old as time itself, a truth that would guide them through the darkness, towards the light.

The night sky above Jerusalem shimmered with stars as the ancient city lay bathed in a soft, ethereal glow.

In a secluded garden, hidden from the eyes of the world, a conversation of profound significance was unfolding between two men, separated by millennia yet bound by the threads of destiny.

Jmmanuel, the enigmatic teacher and prophet, sat cross-legged on the ground, his eyes reflecting the wisdom of ages.

His voice, calm and steady, carried the weight of a truth that transcended time.

"Woe to this world and these humans; their lot will be very hard right into the distant future," he began, his tone somber.

"Truly, so will it be.

One still sees in me only the human born of Earth, and that I am a revolutionary and fight against untruth, but that badly interprets me.

But I know the truth and possess the wisdom of knowledge, the powers of the spirit and of thinking, and the will to fulfill my mission."

Eduard, a traveler from a distant future, listened intently.

He had come a long way, both in distance and time, to seek answers from the one who had been misrepresented and misunderstood for centuries.

The air between them was thick with unspoken questions, and the burden of knowing the truth weighed heavily on Jmmanuel's shoulders.

"The truth is more important than the transient pain of the body," Jmmanuel continued, his gaze fixed on the horizon as if he could see the future unfolding before him.

"This can be tortured and destroyed, but the truth and the spirit can never be killed.

This truth is not yet known at this time, but this will change in the future.

Truly, out of my true humanity, a cult will be set up, which will bring with it very bad and deadly consequences."

Eduard's mind raced as he tried to grasp the full implications of Jmmanuel's words.

He had always known that the man before him was different, that he carried within him a wisdom that transcended the ages.

But hearing it spoken so plainly, so openly, was something else entirely.

Jmmanuel sighed, a deep, weary sound that seemed to carry the weight of the world.

"Seen in me, however, is still only the human, which I truly also am, but soon a form of malevolence will be made out of me, and I will be equated with Creation.

Truly, I know these events of the future, and, indeed, I cannot change them, not even if I rebel against them."

Eduard could sense the pain in Jmmanuel's voice, the sorrow of a man who knew his fate but was powerless to alter it.

"I was born a human, I live as such and, as such, fulfill my appointed mission.

But also as a human, I will suffer the fate of corporal death in 83 years.

By then, my body will be very old, yet my spirit and thinking will remain undiminished."

The words hung in the air like a prophecy, and Eduard found himself struggling to find the right response.

He had come seeking answers, but the reality of the situation was far more complex than he had anticipated.

"Excuse me, please, if I interrupt you," Eduard finally spoke, his voice tinged with hesitation.

"Yet I believe that I am indeed permitted to do that.

Your expositions are very informative for me, but it appears to me that I can recognize, from that, that you, in a certain sense, have succumbed to world pain and thereby digress from the actual questions.

Would it not, perhaps, therefore, be better if I ask my own questions?"

Jmmanuel turned to face Eduard, his expression one of both surprise and recognition.

"Truly, you are very sensitive, because pain about the world bores into me.

Until now, nobody has been able to determine this, but you effortlessly draw this out of me.

You are very much more advanced in your development than I had gathered."

There was a moment of silence as Jmmanuel studied Eduard with newfound respect.

"I live here in a world which is the distant past for you, but which signifies the present for me.

Truly, your evolution is about 2,000 years further advanced from my time, which I did not take into account.

It is therefore not fitting that I converse with you in the same way that I do with my contemporaries."

Eduard nodded, understanding the significance of what Jmmanuel was saying.

The gulf of time between them was vast, yet here they were, two souls connected by the same truth.

"I only thought that a direct questioning is perhaps better because I have ascertained the aforementioned things," Eduard said gently.

Jmmanuel smiled, a rare expression that softened his features.

"Truly, what you say is honest, I will answer your questions for you."

Eduard felt a sense of relief wash over him. "Thank you.

As I know from you, you know very many things up into the very distant future.

Therefore, you must also be orientated about what will be made out of your person.

You have indeed also already explained that in a circumscribed form.

But I have fully understood your explanations because I do know the New Testament, which allegedly contains your teaching.

But for a short time now, I have known that the allegedly-handed-down teaching is only an evil falsification and only corresponds to the actual truth in very few things."

Jmmanuel's expression grew serious as he listened.

"Truly, your question is very precisely directed.

Consider; my time is about two millennia before yours, and in this time only certain forms of society are literate.

On account of my mission, I did also learn writing and reading, yet I have insufficient time to write down my teaching."

Eduard leaned forward, eager to hear more.

"But no practical steps are planned to change these coming misleading events, because the mass of erring and falsifying humans is too great to be able to influence them even on a small scale.

This will, unfortunately, lead to a false teaching of much longer than three thousand years, and to very much need, pain, hate, misery, and bloodshed."

The weight of Jmmanuel's words hung heavy in the air, and Eduard could feel the gravity of the situation.

The future that Jmmanuel spoke of was one filled with suffering and despair, a future that had been shaped by the very teachings that had been distorted and twisted beyond recognition.

"Truly, in spite of that, however, the truth will not be lost, because it will, in a safe place, remain transmitted and also outlast the time, in a written form.

Among my followers, I have a literate man named Judas Iscariot, who writes down the most important parts of the teaching and events, which later, well preserved, shall outlast the time in order to hand down the actual truth to posterity."

Eduard's heart skipped a beat at the mention of Judas Iscariot.

"But your time is still not ripe enough for that, and only in little more than two decades, in your own time, will the seed of truth find a little fertile ground."

Eduard's mind was racing, trying to piece together the puzzle that was unfolding before him. "So, the teaching really remains preserved and then it will also be found by me somewhere?"

Jmmanuel nodded.

"Truly, that is what I am saying.

Already the texts are being sought now in order to destroy them and to use them as indictments against me.

One scroll has already been stolen from the writer and kept closed by the Pharisees and the scribes.

Juda Ihariot, a son of a Pharisee, secretly took it out of Judas Iscariot's bag in order to sell it to my persecutors for 70 pieces of silver, in order, thereby, to be able to charge me with blasphemy against God."

Eduard's breath caught in his throat. The betrayal, the lies, the falsehoods, they were all starting to make sense now.

The man who had been vilified for centuries was nothing more than a pawn in a game that had been played out long before his time.

"But Judas Iscariot has been ordered by me to write the text once again and now to keep it quite safe whereby its purpose will outlast the ages."

Eduard's voice was trembling as he spoke.

"You speak of Judas Iscariot, who is supposed to be your betrayer, as the texts of my time still convey, nonetheless falsified!"

Jmmanuel nodded solemnly.

"Truly, I speak of him. He who will hand me over to the persecutors is the same one who stole the texts and sold them."

Eduard's mind was reeling.

The truth was more complex than he could have ever imagined.

"So Juda Ihariot?"

"So it is," Jmmanuel confirmed.

"But his father will spread the lie that Judas Iscariot is the betrayer, because the Pharisee name Ihariot must not be soiled.

But the reason is also based on the fact that the priests, scribes, and Pharisees and their followers can say: 'Behold, one from his own ranks has betrayed him and handed him over to a death on the cross.

Behold, behold, how can his teaching be truth if his own people betray him and sell him?'"

Eduard's head was spinning with the enormity of it all.

The lies, the deceit, the manipulation, it was all too much to bear.

"So that is how it is, now I understand a lot more.

But now I ask myself, who then really hanged himself in Potters Field, respectively, who will hang himself there in the coming time?"

"Juda Ihariot," Jmmanuel answered simply.

"And it will be said, in the coming time, that Judas Iscariot did that?

" Eduard asked, his voice barely above a whisper.

Jmmanuel nodded. "Truly, that is how it will be said, because the priests and the people, and even his father, will claim this."

Eduard felt a sense of helplessness wash over him.

The truth was a fragile thing, easily twisted and distorted by those with power and influence.

And yet, there was a glimmer of hope, a small ray of light in the darkness.

"Yes," Jmmanuel continued, "this is the coming truth.

However, that is all insignificant, because, when the truth comes to light in the distant future, it will have only one importance: that the lie and its evil can no longer be continued."

Eduard looked into Jmmanuel's eyes and saw the fire of determination burning within them. This man, this teacher, had known all along what his fate would be, and yet he had chosen to walk this path, knowing full well the consequences.

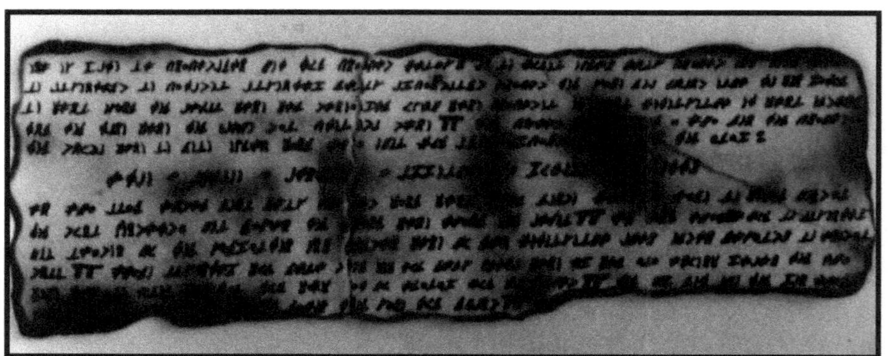

Ancient 8000 year old papyrus discovered. Here's the translation:

The herald Henoch says:

I am the herald of truth, and in this mission I will be (live) again in important times by the names: Elia, Jesaia, Jeremia, Jmmanuel, Muhammed, Billy, (and) so I will serve the human beings as a prophet among seven times, before the change for the compliance with the laws and recommendations of creation will take place in their thinking (convictions). So I will be (live) in reincarnation in the new time when space will be conquered, and when the guardian angels from foreign stars will appear once again. My reincarnation in that time will be as Billy and with the name Eduard Meier, and I will dwell in a land of peace in the North, which will be called Schweiz (Switzerland). The human being then may listen to my voice, so he may be led into the light of the teaching of the spirit.

CHAPTER 57

The End Before the Beginning

The dense forest pulsed with the sounds of the night, chirping insects, rustling leaves, and the distant cry of an unseen predator.

A cool breeze carried the scent of damp earth and ancient trees, adding to the surreal atmosphere that surrounded Eduard and Asket as they moved swiftly through the undergrowth.

Their steps were deliberate, their focus unwavering. The mission had demanded their full attention, forcing them to push past exhaustion, navigating rugged terrain with a determination that left no room for second thoughts.

Through the gaps in the towering trees, the sky was a deep canvas of twilight, a mixture of fading gold and encroaching indigo.

The stars were just beginning to emerge, their silent glow standing as a reminder of the vastness of time and space. Eduard cast a final glance at the landscape he was about to leave behind, a world that, for a fleeting moment, had been his reality.

The rolling hills, the untamed wilderness, the very air itself seemed to hum with the weight of history.

This place, this moment in time, would remain forever imprinted in his memory.

The faces he had encountered, the events he had witnessed, the truths he had uncovered, all of it had altered his perception of existence itself.

Breaking through the dense underbrush, the ship came into view. Its metallic surface gleamed under the last remnants of daylight, a stark contrast to the ancient surroundings.

It looked both out of place and yet entirely at home, as if it had always belonged to no single time period but to all of them at once.

Eduard hesitated before stepping forward, taking one last, deep breath of this untouched past.

He knew that once he boarded that ship, he would be leaving behind not just a physical place, but a reality that had existed long before his birth.

It was a sobering thought. He was a traveler through time, but each journey left an indelible mark on his soul.

With a final glance over his shoulder, he turned and followed Asket up the ramp.

The ship's interior was a stark contrast to the world outside, clean, structured, and brimming with technology far beyond anything Earth possessed.

The air smelled of polished metal and faintly charged energy. Asket moved with practiced ease, her hands flying over the illuminated controls, setting the return sequence into motion.

Meanwhile, Jitschi was laughing uncontrollably, muttering incoherent sentences to himself. Eduard observed him with a mix of concern and amusement.

The journey had taken its toll on Jitschi in unexpected ways. His mind, once rigidly anchored in religious dogma, had been uprooted by the revelations they had encountered.

His reactions fluctuated wildly between anger, disbelief, and now, manic laughter.

Once reaching free space, Asket initiated the time jump.

The ship began to vibrate as the engines roared to full power. The hum of energy filled the cabin, creating an almost hypnotic resonance.

Eduard braced himself, gripping the armrest of his seat. He had experienced this transition before, but the sensation of slipping between epochs was something he doubted he would ever fully grow accustomed to.

The world outside the ship blurred, its colors stretching and twisting, as if reality itself was being unraveled and rewoven.

Then, as suddenly as it had begun, the transition ended.

The view outside the ship's window was nearly identical, trees standing tall, the sky painted with the deep hues of evening.

And yet, Eduard could feel the shift. The very air seemed different, heavier with the weight of a time they knew as their own. The year 1953 had reclaimed them.

Eduard exhaled, only now realizing how much tension he had been holding in his body. The mission was complete.

They had succeeded.

The timeline remained intact, the future preserved. And yet, despite their victory, an unshakeable awareness settled over him, a silent acknowledgment of the immense responsibility that came with being a guardian of time.

He sank into his seat, the exhaustion washing over him like a tide pulling him toward shore after a long voyage at sea.

The weariness was not just physical but deeply psychological. He had witnessed history in its rawest form, had stood in the presence of people who would never know how their actions shaped the world.

The weight of it all was staggering.

Asket turned toward him, a rare expression of approval in her eyes. She was often reserved, her emotions tightly controlled, but now, a small, satisfied smile graced her lips.

"You did well," she said, her voice softer than usual, carrying an almost maternal warmth. "The future is safe, for now."

Eduard nodded, but his mind was already moving beyond this moment.

The mission they had just completed was only one chapter in a story that had no foreseeable end. There would be more journeys, each more perilous and revealing than the last.

He had seen enough to know that history was not a straight path but a labyrinth of decisions, deceptions, and forgotten truths.

And he understood now that the responsibility he carried would only grow heavier with time.

Jitschi, however, had reached a breaking point. He suddenly stood, pacing the cabin with erratic energy.

"It's all a lie," he muttered, gripping his Bible so tightly that his knuckles turned white. "Everything they taught us… a fabrication.

How could they do this? How could they twist the truth so completely?"

Eduard exchanged a glance with Asket. He had been concerned about Jitschi's reaction for some time.

The revelations they had uncovered, particularly regarding Jmmanuel, had shattered the foundation of his beliefs.

And now, faced with undeniable truth, he was spiraling into a dangerous mindset.

Jitschi let out a bitter laugh, his eyes dark with anger. "Millions… billions of people living in an illusion.

Worshiping a distortion. Fighting wars over a lie!" He clenched his fists, breathing heavily. "I won't be part of it. I refuse to be blind any longer!"

Eduard stood slowly, choosing his words carefully. "Jitschi, the truth is powerful, but it can also be dangerous.

You have to decide what to do with it. Anger won't change the past, it won't fix anything."

Jitschi exhaled sharply, shaking his head. "No. But it will drive me to expose the lies. They can't keep controlling people like this. They can't keep us in ignorance."

Eduard knew there was no stopping him. Jitschi had been set on a path of no return, one that could either lead to enlightenment or destruction. Only time would tell.

As the ship began its descent back to their departure point, the familiar landscape of Earth came into view. The stars outside gleamed like distant beacons, each one a reminder of the infinite mysteries that still awaited them. Eduard allowed himself to breathe, to accept the moment for what it was.

He had changed. There was no denying it. The boy who had stepped onto this ship was not the same man who now sat in its cabin.

He had seen the fragile nature of reality, had touched the currents of time, had glimpsed both the greatness and folly of humanity.

The future was unwritten, a vast expanse of possibility. And though he did not yet know where his path would lead, he embraced the responsibility placed upon him.

For this was only the end of one journey. And the beginning of countless more.

Eduard Albert Meier im Alter von acht Jahren.
(Eduard Albert Meier at eight years of age.)

<h1>CHAPTER 58</h1>

<h1>Eduard's words for Humanity</h1>

June 6, 1947 - Switzerland

In a modest village nestled within the Swiss countryside, a ten-year-old boy named Eduard Meier sits quietly at a worn wooden desk.

The afternoon sun casts a golden glow through the window, illuminating the pencil held tightly in his small hand.

Though still a child, Eduard's eyes, brimming with both anticipation and unease, carry the burden of wisdom far beyond his years.

He knows that the words he is about to write will carry the weight of the future.

His surroundings are peaceful, the landscape serene, but Eduard's mind is restless, filled with images of a world transformed by humanity's reckless ambition.

With each stroke of the pencil, Eduard begins to chart a path for the future, one fraught with danger but also hope.

In his letter, addressed to the leaders, rulers, and authorities of the world, he pens a dire warning about the path humanity is treading.

Though young, his vision for the future is stark and filled with urgency, echoing concerns that seem almost unimaginable in 1947.

Eduard's message is a plea, a call for humanity to awaken before it's too late.

His voice, youthful yet clear, rises above the chaos of a post-war world, a world still healing from the wounds of conflict and destruction.

He writes with a foreboding sense that if humankind continues its careless course, the future will be one of unimaginable hardship, a reality shaped by greed, ignorance, and a blatant disregard for the planet's limits.

In the pages of his letter, Eduard coins a term that will one day become central to discussions about the fate of humanity: "overpopulation." With this term, he encapsulates his greatest fear, that unchecked human expansion will ultimately overwhelm the Earth's finite resources, leading to a cascade of crises that will plunge the world into turmoil.

Eduard envisions a future in which the relentless growth of the human population outstrips the planet's ability to sustain life, driving humanity into a downward spiral of scarcity and conflict.

As he writes, Eduard's mind fills with vivid images of a planet ravaged by human excess.

He sees once-lush forests stripped bare, rivers choked with pollution, and seas devoid of life.

In this grim future, humanity's relentless exploitation of nature leaves entire ecosystems in ruin.

Forests, the lungs of the Earth, are felled at an alarming rate, their absence accelerating climate change and robbing future generations of one of their most vital resources.

The rivers, once teeming with fish and supporting life, become little more than toxic streams, their waters poisoned by industrial runoff.

And the seas, once abundant with marine life, turn into barren wastelands, their ecosystems destroyed by overfishing and pollution.

In his vision, Eduard describes a world where nature's balance is irreversibly disturbed.

The intricate web of life that once sustained the planet collapses under the weight of human activity, leaving behind a fragile and unstable environment.

Entire species vanish from the Earth, their extinction a direct result of humanity's inability to live in harmony with the natural world.

The lands that were once fertile and full of promise become deserts, their topsoil eroded, their ability to support agriculture lost.

This loss of biodiversity and natural resources marks the beginning of a profound environmental crisis that will reshape life on Earth.

Eduard's foresight extends beyond environmental degradation.

He predicts that the consequences of overpopulation will extend into every aspect of human life, most notably food production.

As the global population swells, the demands placed on agriculture will outpace the Earth's capacity to provide.

The natural resources required to grow food will dwindle, leading to widespread shortages and the collapse of traditional farming methods.

In an effort to stave off mass starvation, humanity will turn to chemical and synthetic alternatives, creating new industries aimed at producing food in artificial environments.

However, these alternatives will come with their own set of problems, including health risks and further damage to the environment.

The very chemicals used to sustain life will, paradoxically, contribute to its demise.

Eduard sees this transformation of agriculture as part of a broader trend, one in which machines come to dominate every aspect of human existence.

From the fields to the factories, machines powered by fossil fuels will become the engines of progress.

But progress comes at a cost.

The unrelenting use of machines will exacerbate climate change, pumping greenhouse gases into the atmosphere and driving the planet toward a tipping point.

The consequences of this will be felt across the globe, as rising temperatures trigger a series of devastating natural disasters.

Eduard predicts that as global temperatures increase, humanity will witness storms of unprecedented ferocity.

Hurricanes, cyclones, and floods will become more frequent and more destructive, displacing millions of people and wiping entire cities off the map.

The delicate balance of the Earth's ecosystems will be shattered, leading to the collapse of vital ecological systems.

Forests and wetlands, which play a crucial role in regulating the climate, will be destroyed, further accelerating the environmental crisis.

The world that Eduard envisions is one where nature's fury is unleashed, punishing humanity for its failure to respect the Earth's limits.

As Eduard's predictions unfold, he delves deeper into the ramifications of overpopulation and environmental degradation.

He warns that the consequences will not be confined to the natural world alone.

The strain on resources will lead to widespread social and political instability, as nations compete for what little remains.

Eduard envisions a world where conflicts erupt over access to land, water, and food.

Nations will engage in desperate measures to secure their survival, leading to wars that devastate entire regions and push humanity closer to the brink.

Eduard foresees that the rapid advancement of technology will play a dual role in shaping the future.

On the one hand, technological innovations will offer solutions to some of the problems he predicts.

Advances in science and engineering will allow humanity to explore new ways of harnessing energy, producing food, and managing resources.

Space exploration, for example, will open up new possibilities for finding resources beyond Earth.

Eduard predicts that the race to explore space, fueled by the rivalry between nations like the United States and the Soviet Union, will push the boundaries of human achievement.

However, he also warns that this technological progress will come with significant risks.

Eduard anticipates that as technology advances, so too does the potential for destruction.

The same ingenuity that allows humanity to build machines capable of exploring the stars will also be used to create weapons of unimaginable power.

Eduard foresees a future where the proliferation of nuclear weapons leads to a world constantly on the edge of annihilation.

The threat of nuclear war will cast a long shadow over the 21st century, as nations amass stockpiles of weapons capable of wiping out entire populations in an instant.

The specter of nuclear war will create a pervasive sense of fear and anxiety, leaving humanity to grapple with the reality that its own creations could lead to its destruction.

Eduard's predictions are not limited to physical and environmental crises; he also foresees a profound moral decline within humanity.

As the pressures of overpopulation, environmental degradation, and technological advancement mount, Eduard predicts that society will become increasingly indifferent to the suffering of others.

He envisions a world where cruelty and violence become more prevalent, manifesting in acts of terrorism, war, and oppression.

Conflicts driven by hatred and fanaticism will plague the globe, exacerbating the suffering of countless individuals and deepening the divisions between nations, religions, and cultures.

Switzerland, Eduard's homeland and a symbol of neutrality and peace, will not be immune to these changes.

Eduard predicts that even Switzerland will be drawn into global conflicts, its neutrality compromised by the actions of corrupt and treacherous elements within its government.

The country's involvement in arms deals and other nefarious activities will contribute to the instability and conflict that plague the world.

This loss of neutrality will mark a significant shift in global politics and further contribute to the sense of uncertainty and danger that characterizes the future.

Eduard also foresees the rise of unscrupulous leaders who will exacerbate the world's problems rather than solve them.

In the early 2000s, Eduard predicts that a particularly corrupt leader will emerge in the United States, destabilizing not only the country but the entire world.

This President, driven by greed and a thirst for power, will manipulate the electoral process and rise to power through deceit and treachery.

Once in office, his actions will sow discord both at home and abroad, leading to widespread disillusionment and dissatisfaction among the American people.

Eduard's foresight includes the President's mishandling of a global pandemic, a crisis that will claim the lives of countless individuals due to the leader's refusal to acknowledge its severity.

His failure to take preventive measures and his delayed response will result in a tragic loss of life, further eroding the United States' reputation on the global stage.

As tensions rise between the U.S. and other nations, particularly Russia and China, Eduard predicts that the President's reckless foreign policies will only worsen international relations, pushing the world closer to large-scale conflict.

Within the United States, Eduard foresees increasing dissatisfaction with the President's leadership.

The country will become deeply divided, with ideological conflicts tearing at the fabric of society.

The President's authoritarian tendencies and disregard for constitutional norms will create a climate of fear and discontent, leading to widespread protests and civil unrest.

The once-stable political landscape of the United States will be thrown into chaos, and the country will struggle to maintain its status as a global leader.

Amidst this global turmoil, Eduard predicts that Switzerland's reputation as a neutral nation will be further tarnished.

The country's involvement in arms deals with rogue states will contribute to the ongoing conflicts that plague the world.

Eduard envisions a future where Switzerland's profit-driven approach to the arms trade exacerbates suffering in many nations, further compounding the world's crises.

The moral decline of world leadership, particularly among the most powerful nations, will be one of the greatest threats to humanity's future, Eduard foresees.

Switzerland, once seen as a beacon of neutrality and diplomacy, will be exposed as a hidden player in the darker aspects of global politics.

Its banking system, long considered the world's financial safe haven, will be revealed as complicit in the trafficking of wealth and power that fuels global conflict.

Corruption will seep into every corner of the world, leaving behind a legacy of distrust and disillusionment.

Eduard's predictions do not end with political corruption and environmental collapse.

He foresees an age of rapid technological change that will upend society in ways both promising and perilous.

Humanity's increasing dependence on technology will extend beyond the physical world and into the very core of human identity.

With the advent of artificial intelligence and advanced robotics, the line between man and machine will blur.

Eduard predicts that in the latter half of the 21st century, machines will take on roles that were once the sole province of humans, not just in labor and industry, but in decision-making, healthcare, and even in relationships.

The rise of artificial intelligence will usher in an era of profound ethical dilemmas.

Eduard foresees that while AI will greatly increase efficiency in many sectors, it will also displace millions of workers, creating mass unemployment and economic disparity.

Those who control the machines will control the wealth, and the gap between the rich and the poor will widen.

Societies will struggle to adapt to this new reality, as traditional social structures crumble under the weight of automation.

In this new world, the nature of work, purpose, and community will be redefined.

Eduard's vision of the future also includes the potential for artificial intelligence to be weaponized, posing existential threats to humanity.

Machines built to protect or serve could easily be reprogrammed for destruction.

He foresees a future where governments and rogue actors alike use AI to wage cyber-wars, conduct surveillance, and even launch autonomous weapons capable of choosing their own targets.

The battlefields of tomorrow will not be fought by soldiers, but by machines guided by unseen algorithms, and the consequences of these new technologies will be unpredictable and devastating.

Despite these dark visions, Eduard holds on to a thread of hope.

He foresees that amidst the chaos, a few enlightened individuals will rise, people with the wisdom and courage to steer humanity away from total destruction.

These individuals will come from all corners of the world, and their strength will lie not in political power, but in their ability to inspire change.

Eduard's message is clear: humanity's survival depends not on the technology it creates, but on the compassion, intelligence, and moral clarity it demonstrates in using that technology.

In his letter, Eduard urges the leaders of the world to heed his warnings, to act with foresight and care.

He pleads for governments to institute population control measures, to protect the environment, and to ensure that technology serves humanity rather than enslaves it.

He stresses that only by taking immediate and drastic action can humanity avoid the bleak future he has foreseen.

Eduard's words, however, fall on deaf ears. His letter, passed between authorities and bureaucrats, is dismissed as the ramblings of a misguided child.

World leaders, focused on rebuilding after the war and advancing their nations' interests, do not give serious consideration to his dire predictions.

Over the coming decades, Eduard will watch as many of his visions come to pass, with humanity hurtling toward the very catastrophes he so desperately tried to prevent.

By the time the world realizes the gravity of Eduard's predictions, it may already be too late.

Environmental degradation, unchecked population growth, and the rise of dangerous technologies will have created a world on the brink of collapse.

But Eduard's hope persists, even in the face of overwhelming odds.

He thinks that the future is not set in stone, that humanity can still change course.

Through small acts of kindness, through the courage of individuals willing to fight for the greater good, Eduard sees a glimmer of hope that the worst can be averted.

His final words in the letter are a testament to his unshakeable belief in human potential: "Only when we see ourselves not as rulers of the Earth, but as its stewards, can we begin to heal the wounds we have inflicted. The future is ours to shape, but only if we act now."

Eduard places his pencil down and folds the letter carefully, sealing it in an envelope addressed simply to "The World's Leaders."

He knows it may never reach the right hands, but he also knows that his duty is to speak the truth, regardless of the consequences.

The future will unfold as it must, but Eduard Meier, even as a child, will have done his part to try and change it.